Queenship and Power

Series Editors
Charles E. Beem
University of North Carolina
Pembroke, NC, USA

Carole Levin
University of Nebraska
Lincoln, NE, USA

This series focuses on works specializing in gender analysis, women's studies, literary interpretation, and cultural, political, constitutional, and diplomatic history. It aims to broaden our understanding of the strategies that queens—both consorts and regnants, as well as female regents—pursued in order to wield political power within the structures of male-dominant societies. The works describe queenship in Europe as well as many other parts of the world, including East Asia, Sub-Saharan Africa, and Islamic civilization.

More information about this series at
http://www.palgrave.com/gp/series/14523

Zita Eva Rohr • Lisa Benz
Editors

Queenship and the Women of Westeros

Female Agency and Advice in *Game of Thrones*
and *A Song of Ice and Fire*

Editors
Zita Eva Rohr
Macquarie University
Sydney, NSW, Australia

Lisa Benz
Salem, MA, USA

Queenship and Power
ISBN 978-3-030-25040-9   ISBN 978-3-030-25041-6   (eBook)
https://doi.org/10.1007/978-3-030-25041-6

This Palgrave Macmillan imprint is published by the registered company Springer Nature Switzerland AG.
The registered company address is: Gewerbestrasse 11, 6330 Cham, Switzerland

For our families and friends

FOREWORD

"Knowledge is power," smirks Petyr Baelish, signalling to Cersei that he is aware that the semi-secret of her incestuous liaison with her brother and the paternity of her children is now out in the open. Cersei motions to her men to seize Baelish and a sword is held to his throat. "Power is power," retorts the queen, and Baelish's grin vanishes.[1] Both antagonists are correct in different ways; in the imagined world of *A Song of Ice and Fire* and *Game of Thrones*, knowledge confers enormous advantage in the "game," while power, in its myriad forms, enables the exercise of agency and choice.

This book investigates the interactions between queenship and other forms of female leadership, patriarchy, and sources of power. It thinks about queenship in the medieval and early modern periods, and how women made use of the structures available to them to work to achieve their own particular goals; most often, these goals overlapped with the interests of family, kin-group, social community, or even with those of the kingdom. Women harnessed whatever tools came to hand in pursuit of these goals, both working within and at times subverting the traditional norms to which they were nominally subject.

Medieval and early modern monarchs and other women who fulfilled similar leadership roles were enabled to do so by their possession of varying attributes: power, authority, influence, and charisma. As defined by the sociologist Max Weber, "power [*Macht*] is the probability that one actor within a social relationship will be in a position to carry out his own will despite resistance, regardless of the basis on which this probability rests."[2] Power then is an overarching attribute: the capacity to get things done, even if others do not wish those things to be achieved. Authority (Weber's

Herrschaft) has a problematic relationship with legitimacy, for unanimous social agreement about legitimacy is not always present.[3] Nevertheless, authority certainly adheres in certain offices and social roles, even if some sectors of the population or interest groups might refuse to recognize it. Women are very often also able to exercise influence: "to bring about a decision on another's part to act in a certain way because it is felt to be good for the other person … and for positive reasons, not for sanctions that might be imposed."[4] Influence is an unofficial, often covertly exercised social practice that women could perform through their intimate connections to kings and emperors. Advisors, bishops, and courtiers were frequently anxious about what the queen might be saying to the king in the privacy of the bedchamber, or privately to her son in cases of minority.[5] Such influence was hard to pre-empt or to mitigate because of its unseen nature, though ideological moves to discount and devalue female advice, for example, were undertaken at different times precisely to combat this kind of input into royal decision-making processes. And finally, there is the concept of charisma. "Based on irrational personal attraction to and deification of a leader, it stands in radical contrast to rationality and tradition. In its primary aspect, charisma is revolutionary, but to survive it must be institutionalized, which eventually undermines its radical character and emotional power," notes Charles Lindholm.[6] These models of different bases for female agency are highly valuable for considering how medieval and early modern women gained and exercised power, and how those ideas about female power transfer across into the Secondary World(s) created in George R. R. Martin's *A Song of Ice and Fire* and the HBO TV series *Game of Thrones*.

The chapters in the collection consider questions precisely about women and agency across historical eras, proposing comparisons and making contrasts with the women of *Game of Thrones*. Whether or not George R. R. Martin drew upon particular individual historical women as inspiration for his literary characters, he has a social historian's keen sense for the parameters of female power, and the ways in which patriarchal cultures variously constrain women's agency in different eras. Anglo-Saxon women were long thought to be better able to wield power, in the sense of holding and bequeathing property, than their later sisters in any period until the mid-nineteenth century when the Married Woman's Property Act was passed.[7] More recent work has suggested that this view needs nuancing; nevertheless, as Pauline Stafford notes, in the late tenth century, the female relatives of the dowager Empress Adelaide, and the Empress herself, ruled over "much of north-west Europe .... as regents for underage males."[8] Stafford qualifies their agency as individuals: "To call them powerful, however, raises problems," for their effectiveness and influence derive entirely from their relationships to men.[9] If those relationships changed, their roles could vanish overnight. Nevertheless, "[this] should not obscure the fact that these women's activities show their ability to participate in events, with the opportunities to influence those events and to have a strategy of their own towards them – all of which amounts to power," Stafford suggests.[10]

In Old English literary texts, queens are depicted as advice-givers and arbiters of social hierarchy. They recognize, and make public, relative status within the mead-hall by choosing carefully the order in which the ceremonial mead-cup circulates in feasting contexts.[11] So one Old English wisdom poem, known as *Maxims I*, tells us, the king's wife

> must prosper, dear to her people, light in spirit, she must keep counsel, have a generous heart with horses and treasure; on mead-drinking occasions she must always greet the prince first among his kinsmen, pass the first cup to the prince's hand, and know what advice to give him, he and she together, holding the fortress.[12]

This may seem to be an idealized portrait of shared decision-making, but it is borne out both by descriptions of the king and queen, seated enthroned together in the writings of Bede (c. 730) and by the depictions of two Scandinavian queens who feature in the Old English poem *Beowulf*, Wealhtheow and Hygd.[13] Wealhtheow intervenes in the mead-hall in front of the assembled retinue to advise her royal husband, King Hrothgar, not to adopt the hero Beowulf as his son and heir, but rather to leave the kingdom to her sons by him.[14] Wealhtheow indirectly solicits the support of the boys' cousin, should her elderly husband die in the near future—support which a well-informed Anglo-Saxon audience would know was not in the event forthcoming. Hygd, widow of King Hygelac of the Geats, has the authority after her husband's death, on a raiding expedition, to offer the throne to his nephew, Beowulf. Beowulf refuses, determining to act rather as guardian to the young heir Heardred, though he does take the throne when Heardred too is killed.[15] Stephanie Hollis has argued that the secular authority shared between king and queen in early Anglo-Saxon kingdoms was disrupted by the arrival of Christianity; the bishop now becomes a powerful political actor within the court hierarchy, displacing the queen as primary among the king's circle of advice-givers and operating to restrict her functions within the court, in line with Christian ideology.[16]

The society of Westeros's North, centred on Winterfell, has strong affiliations with Anglo-Saxon social organization, as I have argued elsewhere.[17] The relationship between Ned Stark and his bannermen is an affective one, maintained by oaths sworn in the past and renewed by successive lords, not by the regular payment of wages in order to maintain a standing army, the tactic of the Lannisters.[18] Democratic consultation is a hallmark of the politics of the North; on several occasions we see Robb, Jon, and Sansa host the bannermen in the Great Hall of Winterfell, seeking a consensus in support of their authority and their immediate strategies. That Sansa should assume the title of Lady of Winterfell is uncontested, even when Bran returns, just as the very young Lady Lyanna Mormont is able to lead the people of Bear Island. Like Æthelflæd, Lady of the Mercians, daughter of King Alfred, who was highly instrumental in restoring English rule over parts of the Danelaw, these women are credited with authority, strategic insight, and the capacity to rule by the men who serve them.

Catelyn Stark too gives wise counsel to her husband both in the bedchamber and in the weirwood—counsel not to go south, which Ned disregards, but which nevertheless turns out to be sage. Catelyn has been long enough in the North to be confident in her authority: when she orders the seizure of Tyrion at the Inn at the Crossroads and the release of Jaime Lannister, she expects to be—and is—obeyed by the bannermen and the soldiers present on each occasion. Catelyn loves and values her daughters as she does her sons, and is horrified to discover that Robb's *realpolitik* should regard his sisters, held by the Lannisters in King's Landing, as expendable. Catelyn's move causes Robb to exclude her from his decision-making for a while; had he listened more carefully to his mother's advice, he might have forestalled the catastrophe of the Red Wedding.

Early medieval queens likewise wielded a considerable degree of authority, just as Catelyn does, and indeed as Cersei proves when she demonstrates that she could, if she wished, bring about the summary execution of the former Master of Coin without fear of retribution. Merovingian queens, for example, had charge of the royal household, a responsibility that extended to holding the keys to the treasury. Within the Merovingian palace, this role sometimes brought conflict with the mayor, the highest-ranking male official in the household.[19] Ceding economic authority to the queen in this way freed the king to concentrate on his military campaigns, knowing that his wife was taking care of his domestic interests, if we interpret "domestic" in the broadest possible sense. Queen Eleanor of Aquitaine (d. 1204) inherited more than a quarter of what is now

France and kept direct control over it during her two marriages to the French king Louis VII and the English Henry II, going to considerable lengths to make sure that one of her younger sons should inherit the Duchy of Aquitaine, rather than seeing it simply amalgamated with the Crown possessions across the Channel. Again, like Cersei, she endeavoured to control and direct her sons, working in their interests—at times against those of their father—and she outlived her eldest son, Richard I the Lionheart.

Power, along with influence, in varying proportions, is a benefit that could accrue to noble women who were exchanged in marriage with other dynasties. So, like many other women in the series, Catelyn is exchanged in marriage to achieve an alliance that is regarded as politically advantageous to the Tullys of the Riverlands.[20] Her consent is taken for granted; she is to marry the heir to Winterfell, whomever he might be: first, Brandon, and subsequently Eddard Stark. So too Daenerys is given by her brother to Khal Drogo in a deal brokered by Illyrio Mopatis in exchange for Dothraki support for Viserys's bid to regain the Iron Throne. Notably, Robb Stark resists being party to such an exchange, to cooperate in the kind of political sacrifice routinely expected from women. Robb's proposed strategic marriage, intended to seal the alliance with the Freys, requires him to subordinate his own ideas of himself as subject. Women generally cannot reject this role as Robb does. In the show, Robb weds Talisa because he loves her and he clings to the notion that he can privilege desire over political expediency—a thoroughly modern view of the pre-eminence of romantic love. In the books, Robb is trapped by his sense of personal honour when he is seduced by the daughter of a minor nobleman.[21] Either way, just as Robb undervalues his sisters' rights to be rescued from the Lannister clutches, so too he overvalues his own right to self-determination in the face of the political manoeuvring that his status as King in the North demands.

Such alliance-building through marriage is typical of medieval societies, of course, and a fundamental element in Martin's world. What we do not see in the present of the books and show, I would argue, and perhaps against Kris Swank's chapter in this volume, is any true reflection of the Anglo-Saxon archetype of the peace-weaver, a woman married into a social group with whom her own people have been in conflict. Although there are strong political rivalries in the Seven Kingdoms, at the start of the series, all the Kingdoms are united under the Baratheon dynasty. Again, to take examples from *Beowulf*, neither of the two Danish princesses who are married off, one into the Frisian royal house, or, in the "now" of the poem, in order to end a feud between the Danes and the Heathobards, are ultimately successful in making the peace between the peoples hold. Trouble flares already at Freawaru's wedding feast, and soon her husband is attacking her father once again, burning down his great hall, Heorot. Although Hildeburh, queen of Finn of the Frisians, has a son who is old enough to fight in battle, her husband's family nevertheless treacherously ambush her brother and his men when they come on a friendly visit to Frisia; her brother and son are burned on the same funeral pyre.[22]

Intimate relationships, those between husband and wife, man and mistress, mother and son, gave women an unofficial influence that could make the men who surrounded the king or lord uneasy. Alice Perrers, the long-standing mistress of King Edward III, is depicted in William Langland's fourteenth-century allegorical poem *Piers Plowman* in the figure of Lady Meed. She is a beautiful, well-dressed woman who gives gifts and offers bribes, disrupting the established systems of power approved by the allegorical figure of Reason through her covert moves to advance her own and her family's interests. So too visible proofs of fertility, witnessing the king's potency, might be deployed to effect political change. The fourteenth-century chronicler Jean Froissart recounts a story in which the same Edward III is induced by his highly pregnant wife, Queen Philippa, to grant mercy to six hostages selected from among the citizens of Calais who have been defying the king.[23] Although, as Paul Strohm has shown, the circumstances which Froissart relates are highly improbable—a pregnant queen is extremely unlikely to have sailed across the Channel with her husband—for the chronicler's purposes, her visible pregnancy explains and enhances the influence that she brings to bear on her husband. The queen's intercession, her performance of pleading for mercy, allows the king both to demonstrate his just and royal anger with the mutinous citizens and to modulate his vengeance into mercy in a fashion that turns out to be politically advantageous. So too, motherhood, whether actual or projected, grants women in the world of the series special opportunities to achieve what they want. Daenerys's confident performance in devouring the horse's heart confirms the prophecy that the child she bears is the "Stallion Who Mounts the World" and Drogo's pride in her fertile body leads him to swear—at last—that he will lead the Dothraki *khalasar* across the salt water to attack Westeros. Here his promise is not a fulfilment of the exchange that brought him Daenerys as a bride—an exchange in effect annulled by the death of Viserys, but rather it foregrounds the influence that his wife has on him, an influence grounded in her beauty and fertility, and one which will very shortly be instrumental in bringing about Drogo's death. Cersei's last pregnancy by her brother has a powerful effect on Jaime; it postpones his final break with her until he realizes the full extent of her duplicity and disregard for oath-keeping, and it is one element that brings him back to her side for the final *Liebestod* ("love death").

Finally, we come to charisma—that extraordinary power that inheres only in certain women. The medieval period saw charisma wielded in religious figures, such as Abbess Hild of Whitby, whose double abbey is credited with nurturing the birth of religious poetry composed in the Old English vernacular.[24] Hildegard of Bingen, given to a monastery at the age of seven, rose to become the confidante of popes and emperors; a prophet and a healer, she was a powerful cultural mover whose gloriously lyrical poetic compositions are performed to this day.[25] Joan of Arc, a young peasant girl from Domrémy in Lorraine, persuaded the Dauphin, the heir to the French throne, to throw his lot in with hers against the English and brought him victory.[26] These women sometimes operated within existing power structures—the newly re-established Christian church in seventh-century Northumbria, the Benedictine monastic movement. Or, in Joan's case, she was able to harness current political movements, well-established belief systems, combined with unexpectedly transgressive behaviour to achieve her ends. Joan died refusing to renounce her identity, signified by her adoption of masculine clothing. Other religious women such as Marguerite Porete, who was burned as a relapsed heretic in 1310, or the Holy Maid of Kent, Elizabeth Barton, who spoke out against Henry VIII's divorce from Catherine of Aragon, attracted large numbers of followers, who were convinced of their holiness and rightness.[27] Both were executed in part for their beliefs and to nullify the challenges that they and their followers posed to the status quo.

Melisandre, the Red Woman, has charisma; an irresistibly magnetic quality that is partly granted by her beauty, but which is also buttressed by the authority—often brought into question—with which she claims to mediate the will of the Red God. When we first see her in the series, she has induced Stannis and Selyse to abandon their ancestral gods for the newcomer to the distress of Maester Cressen, who tries in vain to prevent the burning and finally to eliminate the newcomer. Melisandre's faith in her visions and her prophetic insight is unwavering almost to the end in the show. It is damaged only by the death of Stannis—by which time she has begun to focus her attention on Jon Snow as perhaps embodying "The

Prince that was Promised," once he has returned from the other side. Melisandre's hold over Stannis is compounded of his fanatical belief and his sexual desire; although she has powders and other devices in her pockets to enhance her effects, nevertheless, she has the capacity both to call Jon Snow back from the dead and to give birth to the monstrous Shadow-baby, and in the show at least, she knows where she will die: in Westeros. The prophecy is fulfilled after the Battle of Winterfell, in which her channelling of the power of the Red God is decisive in the battle for humanity's survival. She prophesies a similar fate for Varys—who stands against everything she represents—and she is not wrong: the Master of Whisperers perishes in dragon-fire, undone by his wish to save the realm.[28]

It is only Daenerys who shares the charismatic aura that has taken Melisandre from slave-born outcast in the alleys of Asshai to become the power behind Stannis's bid for the Iron Throne, and the facilitator of Arya's miraculous action against the Night King. Daenerys's charisma draws men such as Jorah Mormont and Ser Barristan Selmy to her side—the good and bad angels who wrangle for her ear when it comes to strategy, and between whom she must steer a careful path. In part, it is the Targaryen legacy that makes Daenerys so irresistible: her silver hair and violet eyes. Her charismatic power, accrued through her motherhood, is externalized in her children. Unlike Cersei though, who struggles with her role as Queen Mother in relation both to Joffrey and Tommen, once he has fallen prey to Margaery's sexual wiles, Daenerys's is a queer maternity. She gives birth to Rhaego (the prophesied "The Stallion Who Mounts the World") whose brief life fuels the blood-magic that preserves his father's existence: that birthing is juxtaposed with the fiery hatching of her dragon progeny. Although Daenerys's control over her growing "children" is sometimes brought into question—when Drogon burns up a child instead of the goats that he normally consumes, or when she must direct all three dragons at once in battle over Meereen—their existence forms the basis of her power in Essos, and then in Westeros.

Medieval and early modern women could thus occupy social positions which endowed them with power and authority. Lineage, social rank, religious conviction, but also physical presence—beauty, fertility, intelligence, determinations, and that elusive but ineluctable quality, charisma—all these made possible their effective interventions and actions in the cultures in which they lived. Sometimes they fulfilled and exploited the gendered roles that their societies assigned to them in order to achieve their aims; at other times, they transgressed, challenged, or ignored gender, blurring distinctions and questioning convention. Accepted truths are put aside, exceptionality claimed, rules are broken, challenges faced and overcome. "All men must die"—*Valar Morghulis*—is the fatalistic refrain of the series, and indeed of Christian medieval European culture, counterposing the next world with the exile from God that humanity endures in this one. All men must indeed die, as Missandei reminds Daenerys as they walk the battlements of Meereen together. But, so retorts the Mother of Dragons: "we are not men." Whatever that phrase might be in High Valyrian, it serves to embolden alike the former slave, interpreter, and confidante, and Daenerys Targaryen, the First of Her Name. So too, this book aims to embolden and encourage its readers, as it foregrounds and unpacks the many extraordinary ways in which the powerful women who inhabit the world of *A Song of Ice and Fire* and who lived in medieval and early modern cultures might intersect.

St John's College   Carolyne Larrington
The University of Oxford
Oxford, UK

NOTES

1. Season 2, episode 1, 'The North Remembers'.
2. Max Weber, *The Theory of Social and Economic Organization*, transl. A. M. Henderson and Talcott Parsons (New York: Oxford University Press, 1947), 152.
3. Norman Uphoff, 'Distinguishing Power, Authority and Legitimacy: Taking Max Weber at his Word by Using Resources- Exchange Analysis', *Polity* 22 (1989): 295–322. Here 300.
4. Louise Lamphere, "Women in Domestic Groups," in *Woman, Culture and Society*, ed. Michelle Zimbalist Rosaldo and Louise Lamphere (Stanford CA: Stanford University Press, 1974), 99–100.
5. Peggy McCracken, *The Romance of Adultery: Queenship and Sexual Transgression in Old French Literature* (Philadelphia: University of Pennsylvania Press, 1998), Chap. 5.
6. Charles Lindholm, "Charisma," in *The International Encyclopedia of Anthropology* (Wiley Online Library), 2018, https://doi.org/10.1002/9781118924396.wbiea1286
7. See Christine Fell with Cecily Clark, *Women in Anglo-Saxon England* (London: British Museum Press, 1984), 13–14, citing Doris Stenton, "Women were then more nearly the equal companions of their husbands and brothers than at any other period before the modern age." This view

has now been called into question by the work of Stacy Klein, *Ruling Women: Queenship and Gender in Anglo-Saxon Literature* (Notre Dame IN: Notre Dame University Press, 2006), and Pauline Stafford's *Queen Emma and Queen Edith: Queenship and Women's Power in Eleventh-Century England* (Oxford: Blackwell, 1997).

8. Pauline Stafford, "Powerful Women in the Early Middle Ages: Queens and Abbesses," in *The Medieval World*, ed. Peter Linehan, Janet L. Nelson and Marios Costambeys (Abingdon and New York: Routledge, 2001), 378–415 at 398.

9. Stafford, "Powerful Women," 398.

10. Stafford, "Powerful Women," 399.

11. Michael J. Enright, *Lady with a Mead Cup: Ritual, Prophecy and Lordship in the European Warband from La Tène to the Viking Age* (Dublin: Four Courts Press, 1996).

12. My translation of *Maxims* IB, ll. 15–22, in T. A. Shippey, *Poems of Wisdom and Learning in Old English* (Woodbridge and Totowa, NJ: D. S. Brewer, Rowman and Littlefield, 1976), 68.

13. See Stephanie Hollis, *Anglo-Saxon Women and the Church* (Woodbridge: Boydell, 1992), 152.

14. *Beowulf*, ll. 1168–87.

15. *Beowulf*, ll. 2369–79.

16. Hollis, *Anglo-Saxon Women*, 150–78.

17. Carolyne Larrington, *Winter is Coming: The Medieval World of 'Game of Thrones'* (London: I. B. Tauris, 2015), 56–8.

18. See Mikal Gilmore, "George R. R. Martin, The *Rolling Stone* Interview," in *Rolling Stone*, (23 April 2014), https://www.rollingstone.com/culture/culture-news/george-r-r-martin-the-rolling-stone-interview-242487/

19. Pauline Stafford, *Queens, Dowagers and Concubines: The King's Wife in the Early Middle Ages* (London: Batsford, 1983), 99.

20. For a foundational anthropological discussion of this custom see Gayle Rubin, "The Traffic in Women: Notes on the 'Political Economy' of Sex," in *Toward an Anthropology of Women*, ed. Rayna R. Reiter (New York: Monthly Review Press, 1975), 157–210.

21. Carolyne Larrington, "Mediating Medieval(ized) Emotion in Game of Thrones," *Studies in Medievalism* 27 (2018): 35–42.

22. See, however, against my strict definition of the role of the peace-weaver, the looser understanding of Carol Parrish Jamison, *Chivalry in Westeros: The Knightly Code of 'A Song of Ice and Fire'* (Jefferson NC: McFarland, 2018), 160–72.

23. See Paul Strohm, *Hochon's Arrow: The Social Imagination of Fourteenth-Century Texts* (Princeton NJ: Princeton University Press, 1992), 99–105.

24. Hollis, *Anglo-Saxon Women*, 243–70.

25. Fiona Maddocks, *Hildegard of Bingen: The Woman of her Age* (London: Faber, 2013).
26. Marina Warner, *Joan of Arc: The Image of Female Heroism* (London: Penguin, 1983).
27. Sean L. Field, *The Beguine, the Angel and the Inquisitor: The Trials of Marguerite Porete and Guiard of Cressonessart* (Notre Dame: University of Notre Dame Press, 2012); Alan Neame, *The Holy Maid of Kent: Elizabeth Barton 1506–1534* (London: Hodder and Stoughton, 1971).
28. Larrington, *Winter is Coming*, 184–5.

BIBLIOGRAPHY

Beowulf, trans. Heaney, Seamus, London: Faber, 1999. Old English text at http://legacy.fordham.edu/halsall/basis/beowulf-oe.asp

Enright, Michael J., *Lady with a Mead Cup: Ritual, Prophecy and Lordship in the European Warband from La Tène to the Viking Age*, Dublin: Four Courts Press, 1996.

Fell, Christine with Clark, Cecily, *Women in Anglo-Saxon England*, London: British Museum Press, 1984.

Field, Sean L., *The Beguine, the Angel and the Inquisitor: The Trials of Marguerite Porete and Guiard of Cressonessart*, Notre Dame: University of Notre Dame Press, 2012.

Gilmore, Mikal, "George R. R. Martin, The *Rolling Stone* Interview," in *Rolling Stone*, (23 April 2014), https://www.rollingstone.com/culture/culture-news/george-r-r-martin-the-rolling-stone-interview-242487/

Hollis, Stephanie, *Anglo-Saxon Women and the Church*, Woodbridge: Boydell, 1992.

Jamison, Carol Parrish, *Chivalry in Westeros: The Knightly Code of 'A Song of Ice and Fire'*, Jefferson NC: McFarland, 2018.

Klein, Stacy S., *Ruling Women: Queenship and Gender in Anglo-Saxon Literature*, Notre Dame IN: Notre Dame University Press, 2006.

Lamphere, Louise, "Women in Domestic Groups", in *Woman, Culture and Society*, ed. Rosaldo, Michelle Zimbalist and Lamphere, Louise, Stanford CA: Stanford University Press, 1974, 97–112.

Larrington, Carolyne, *Winter is Coming: The Medieval World of 'Game of Thrones'*, London: I. B. Tauris, 2015.

Idem, "Mediating Medieval(ized) Emotion in *Game of Thrones*", *Studies in Medievalism* 27 (2018): 35–42.

Lindholm, Charles, "Charisma", in *The International Encyclopedia of Anthropology* (Wiley Online Library), 2018, https://doi.org/10.1002/9781118924396.wbiea1286

Maddocks, Fiona, *Hildegard of Bingen: The Woman of Her Age*, London: Faber, 2013.

McCracken, Peggy, *The Romance of Adultery: Queenship and Sexual Transgression in Old French Literature*, Philadelphia: University of Pennsylvania Press, 1998.

Neame, Alan, *The Holy Maid of Kent: Elizabeth Barton 1506–1534*, London: Hodder and Stoughton, 1971.

Rubin, Gayle, "The Traffic in Women: Notes on the 'Political Economy' of Sex", in *Toward an Anthropology of Women*, ed. Reiter, Rayna R., New York: Monthly Review Press, 1975, pp. 157–210.

Shippey, T. A., *Poems of Wisdom and Learning in Old English*, Woodbridge and Totowa, NJ: D. S. Brewer, Rowman and Littlefield, 1976.

Stafford, Pauline, *Queens, Dowagers and Concubines: The King's Wife in the Early Middle Ages*, London: Batsford, 1983.

Idem, *Queen Emma and Queen Edith: Queenship and Women's Power in Eleventh-Century England*, Oxford: Blackwell, 1997.

Idem, 'Powerful Women in the Early Middle Ages: Queens and Abbesses', in *The Medieval World*, ed. Linehan, Peter, Janet L. Nelson and Marios Costambeys, Abingdon and New York: Routledge, 2001, pp. 378–415.

Strohm, Paul, *Hochon's Arrow: The Social Imagination of Fourteenth-Century Texts*, Princeton NJ: Princeton University Press, 1992.

Uphoff, Norman "Distinguishing Power, Authority and Legitimacy: Taking Max Weber at his Word by Using Resources- Exchange Analysis", *Polity* 22 (1989): 295–322.

Warner, Marina, *Joan of Arc: The Image of Female Heroism*, London: Penguin, 1983.

Weber, Max, *The Theory of Social and Economic Organization*, transl. Henderson, A. M. and Parsons, Talcott, New York: Oxford University Press, 1947.

Acknowledgements

This volume of collected chapters is the result of the incredible popular interest in many things premodern aroused by George R. R. Martin's *A Song of Ice and Fire* and HBO's eight-season spin-off television series *Game of Thrones*. Harangued by her four sons that she really needed to watch the series and read the novels because "it is all about what you do," Zita thought it might be worth a look after all. Season 6 of the HBO series hooked her, and she pitched her idea for this collection to Lisa Benz, her brilliant co-editor, who generously agreed to reprise their editorial partnership one more time. Zita acknowledges and thanks her sons for opening up this fresh possibility to consider. Serendipitously, and simultaneously, people had been quizzing Lisa about the phenomenon, forcing her to read the series, while her friends, Kaitlyn Foley, Erin Foley, and Geoffrey Morgan, organized *Game of Thrones* viewing parties, inspiring her to take on this project. We express our gratitude for the unwavering support and encouragement of the Queenship and Power series editors, Carole Levin and Charles E. Beem. Megan Laddusaw (History Editor at Palgrave Macmillan) has been likewise enthusiastic, kind, and constructive from the moment we first proposed our project to her as well as throughout the process of bringing this collection to press. The thoroughly engaged Christine Pardue (Editorial Assistant at Palgrave Macmillan) has been of invaluable and caring assistance. We wish to express our gratitude for the hard work and scholarly dedication of our twelve wonderful contributors—whom, to a woman and a man—graciously accepted our sometimes exacting editorship in good humour, wholeheartedly and generously, embracing our vision for this collection. We thank and express our appreciation for the valuable additional collaboration agreed to by our distinguished contributors Professor Carolyne Larrington (St John's College, Oxford) and Dr. Elena Woodacre (The University of Winchester)—cherished friend, scrupulous sounding board, and long-time, dedicated partner-in-crime in matters monarchy. The very kind words, enduring friendship, and constructive feedback extended to us by Professor Tracy Adams (The University of Auckland) deserve recognition and our grateful thanks. We owe a debt of gratitude to our three anonymous external readers, who have enriched our thinking in no small measure. We acknowledge the love and support of our families, in particular Zita's husband Mark as well as Lisa's parents for their unwavering love, patience, and support. Zita also recognizes the generosity of her mentors, friends, and colleagues, Theresa Earenfight, Núria Silleras-Fernández, Andrew Fitzmaurice, Susan Broomhall, and Hélène Sirantoine, for their invaluable encouragement, for their advice, and for acting as her oracles in this as in many other things.

CONTENTS

NOTES ON CONTRIBUTORS

Charles E. Beem is Professor of History at the University of North Carolina at Pembroke. His publications include *The Lioness Roared: The Problems of Female Rule in English History* (2006), *The Royal Minorities of Medieval and Early Modern England* (2008), *The Foreign Relations of Elizabeth I* (2011), *The Name of a Queen: William Fleetwood's Itinerarium ad Windsor* (2013), *The Man Behind the Queen: Male Consorts in History* (2014), and *Queenship in Early Modern Europe* (forthcoming in 2019). He is also, with Carole Levin, the editor of the book series Queenship and Power for Palgrave Macmillan.

Lisa Benz holds a PhD in History from the University of York, UK. She had her first monograph published on late English medieval queenship, *Three Medieval Queens: Queenship and the Crown in Fourteenth-Century England*, with Palgrave Macmillan in 2012. She has also had articles published on Isabella of France and Margaret of France in *Fourteenth-Century England VIII* and in *Queenship, Gender and Reputation in the Medieval and Early Modern West, 1060–1600*, a collection which she co-edited with Zita Rohr in 2016. Her interests lie in political culture, royal and legal institutions, and women's and gender history. She has taught at the University of York and Rutgers University, and was the 2011–2012 Medieval Fellow at Fordham University. She is now an independent scholar.

Sylwia Borowska-Szerszun is an assistant professor at the University of Białystok, Poland, where she teaches courses in English literature and literary theory. She is the author of *Enter the Carnival: Carnivalesque*

Semiotics in Early Tudor Moral Interludes (2016). She co-edited a special issue of *Crossroads. A Journal of English Studies* devoted to Polish speculative fiction and had a number of articles published on both medieval drama and fantasy literature. Her research focuses on medievalism and Gothicism in fantasy literature, particularly on tracing the echoes of medieval cultural and ideological constructs in contemporary discourses related to gender, sexuality, and race.

Shiloh Carroll has a lifelong interest in the portrayal of the Middle Ages in modern fantasy literature accidentally turned into an expertise on George R.R. Martin and *A Song of Ice and Fire*. Her book on the topic, *Medievalism in A Song of Ice and Fire and Game of Thrones*, was published in 2018. When not waiting patiently for the next instalment from Martin, she serves on the editorial boards of *Slayage* and *The Public Medievalist*.

Kavita Mudan Finn is an independent scholar in medieval and early modern literature. She received her PhD from the University of Oxford in 2010 and published her first book, *The Last Plantagenet Consorts: Gender, Genre, and Historiography 1440–1627*, in 2012. Her work has appeared in *Shakespeare, Viator, Critical Survey, Journal of Fandom Studies, Medieval and Renaissance Drama in England*, and *Quarterly Review of Film and Video*, and she has edited several collections, including *Fan Phenomena: Game of Thrones* (2017), *The Palgrave Handbook of Shakespeare's Queens* (2018), and *Becoming: Genre, Queerness, and Transformation in NBC's Hannibal* (Syracuse, forthcoming 2019). Most recently, she taught at Simmons College. Her chapter in this volume is part of a larger project on representations of and fan responses to premodern women in television drama.

James J. Hudson is an historian of modern China. He is an assistant professor in the Department of History at the University of North Carolina at Pembroke. Since completing his PhD from the University of Texas at Austin (2015), he has taught at Knox College (2015–2016), the University of Tennessee-Knoxville (2016–2018), and Pepperdine University (Summer 2016). His research focuses on the modern history of Changsha, the capital of Hunan province, where he served as a visiting Fulbright scholar (2012–2013). His research interests include urban history, popular protest and crowd violence in China, and the history of World War II in East Asia.

Mikayla Hunter is finishing her doctorate at St John's College, University of Oxford, under the supervision of Professor Carolyne Larrington. Her thesis looks at disguise and transformation in Middle English romances and outlaw ballads, and she has recently had her work published on memory, gender, and recognition in *Le Morte Darthur*.

Carolyne Larrington is interested in Old Norse literature, Arthurian literature, the treatment of emotion in medieval European literature, and in the ways in which women are imagined across the literatures of the period. Most recently she has been working in medievalism, the re-mediation of medieval material in the modern period. Her most recent publications have been a monograph on siblings in medieval European literature: *Brothers and Sisters in Medieval European Literature* (2015); an edited collection of essays on emotion in medieval Arthurian literature, co-edited with Frank Brandsma and Corinne Saunders, *Emotions in Medieval Arthurian Literature* (2015); a *Handbook to Eddic Poetry: Myths and Legends of Ancient Scandinavia* (Cambridge University Press, 2016), co-edited with Judy Quinn and Brittany Schorn; and two books in the medievalism field: *Winter Is Coming: The Medieval World of "Game of Thrones"* (2015) and *The Land of the Green Man: A Journey Through the Supernatural Landscapes of the British Isles* (2015). A Folio Society edition of her translation of the *Poetic Edda* has just been published as has an introduction to Norse myths in a series from Thames and Hudson.

Iain A. MacInnes is Senior Lecturer in Scottish History at the UHI Centre for History, University of the Highlands and Islands. His main focus is on medieval warfare and chivalry, and their relation to the period of the fourteenth-century Scottish Wars of Independence. His first monograph was on the theme of *Scotland's Second War of Independence* (2016). Growing out of this speciality, he has increasingly looked to develop these themes as they relate to modern depictions of medieval warfare. This has been done principally through analysis of graphic novel and comic depictions of medieval war and events, such as the Hundred Years' War. He is looking to further this work through examination of medieval and medieval-like conflict as it is represented in comics, film, and television.

Sheilagh Ilona O'Brien has a PhD in Early Modern History from the University of Southern Queensland. Her thesis focused on witch trials in seventeenth-century England. Academic interests include "othering" and oppression, genocide and communal violence, and history as myth: how we tell and retell narratives about the past, and how those narratives reflect current social concerns. Sheilagh has previously written on *Game of Thrones* for *The Conversation*.

Zita Eva Rohr holds a PhD in French History. She is a fellow of the Royal Historical Society and an honorary fellow at Macquarie University, Sydney, Australia, in the Department of Modern History, Politics and International Relations. In 2016, she published a monograph based on her doctoral thesis with Palgrave Macmillan, *Yolande of Aragon, Family and Power 1381–1442: The Reverse of the Tapestry*, and has had, in collaboration with Lisa Benz, an edited collection of scholarly essays, *Queenship, Gender and Reputation in the Medieval and Early Modern West, 1060–1600*, published with Palgrave Macmillan in 2016. She is collaborating currently on an edited collection with Jonathan Spangler, *Aspects of Deviance and Difference in the Premodern World*, and is working on another monograph for Palgrave Macmillan, *Anne of France and Her Family, 1325–1522: A Genealogy of Premodern Female Power and Influence*. In 2004, Zita was admitted to the *Ordre des Palmes Académiques* for her contribution to French education and culture.

Curtis Runstedler recently completed his PhD in Medieval Literature at the University of Durham. His dissertation examined the use of alchemy and exemplary narrative in fourteenth- and fifteenth-century Middle English poetry. He is a teaching and research fellow at the Eberhard Karls University of Tübingen. His research looks at the role of alchemy in Elias Ashmole's compendium *Theatrum chemicum Britannicum* (1652). His other research interests include werewolves, medieval and Renaissance science, and the roles of women in the Middle Ages.

Kris Swank is a library director and Honours instructor at Pima Community College, Tucson, Arizona. She holds a BA, *summa* cum *laude*, in Humanities and English, and three master's degrees, including an MA in Language and Literature from Signum University. Her fantasy literature essays have appeared in *Tolkien Studies* and *Mythlore* journals and in several edited collections. Her essay on adaptations of *Beowulf* appears in *Monsters of Film, Fiction and Fable: The Cultural Links between the Human and Inhuman* (2018), and her essay on celibate societies appears in *Game of Thrones* Versus *History: Written in Blood* (2017). She has also written for *Library Journal, American Libraries,* and other professional publications.

Elena Woodacre is Senior Lecturer in Early Modern European History at the University of Winchester. She is a specialist in queenship and royal studies and has written extensively in this area. Her publications include her monograph *The Queens Regnant of Navarre; Succession, Politics and Partnership* (Palgrave Macmillan, 2013) and edited collections on queenship and monarchy in various contexts and settings. Elena is the organizer of the "Kings & Queens" conference series, founder of the Royal Studies Network (www.royalstudiesnetwork.org), and Editor-in-Chief of the *Royal Studies Journal* (www.rsj.winchester.ac.uk). Elena is also the co-editor of the Queens of England series at Routledge and the Gender and Power in the Premodern World series at ARC Humanities Press.

INTRODUCTION: *CHERCHEZ LES FEMMES:* QUEENSHIP AND THE WOMEN OF WESTEROS

As we write, scholars of the medieval and early modern world across a variety of disciplines are living through a significant twenty-first-century cultural "moment." Many of us are being asked—or told—by non-academic fans and critics how much, and how obviously, Martin's book series, *A Song of Ice and Fire,* and the HBO television series spin-off, *Game of Thrones,* are "medieval"—and that they represent the real (and possibly definitive) Middle Ages. When confronted with such claims and questions, academics tend to launch into discussions about the definitions and theories of "medieval," "historical," "medievalism," "fantasy," and so forth, understandably leading to the rolling and glazing over of eyes of their interlocutors. Undaunted, and with our scholars' antennae aquiver, we stepped up and plunged into Martin's books and the HBO television series because students, family members, and friends kept repeating their claims or asking their questions. The global success and phenomenal uptake of Martin's inspired creation is not an isolated cultural moment; it has happened before with the works of J. R. R. Tolkien, C. S. Lewis, Umberto Eco, and J. K. Rowling to name just four of the better-known medievalist fantasy practitioners of the modern and post-modern eras. Rather than being unique, the times in which we live have provided Martin with the media and social media tools for his cultural phenomenon's rapid transmission and unsurpassed global reach, both in its original literary and in subsequent televisual incarnations.

For feminist scholars, anxieties surrounding the "Unknowable Woman," women such as Daenerys Targaryen, Cersei Lannister, Melisandre, the "Queen of Thorns" Olenna Tyrell, and her granddaughter Margaery

Tyrell in *Game of Thrones* and *A Song of Ice and Fire*, bring into play such analytical lenses as female agency, reputation, self-fashioning, and gender—themes we highlighted in *Queenship, Gender, and Reputation in the Medieval and Early Modern West, 1060–1600*, our first collaboration for Palgrave Macmillan published in 2016. With this second collaboration, we aim to build upon this earlier scaffolding to incorporate the role, place, and efficacy of advice and advisors, significant themes embedded within all eight HBO seasons of *Game of Thrones* and the epic novels of Martin's *A Song of Ice and Fire* series. For scholars of history and literature, this is of considerable relevance to the study of women such as Christine de Pizan and Anne of France, who counselled queens and elite women to look to the strategic achievement of a spotless reputation and an enduring legacy. To exercise independent agency, power, and influence in what was almost exclusively a man's world, Christine and her "daughter" Anne urged the deployment of measured doses of *juste ypocrisie, discrete dissimulacion*, and *prudent cautele* (just hypocrisy, discreet dissimulation, and prudent guile)[1] combined with conscious acts of self-fashioning and self-representation.[2] Not all the female characters in Martin's world adhere to Christine and Anne's premodern golden rule, nor indeed did historical elite women of the medieval and early modern periods.

Moreover, the evolution and transformation of the character of Tyrion Lannister offers a place to explore the idea of good counsel from not just the perspective of women's studies, but also across wider socio-cultural and gendered contexts. Like the most effective and durable royal advisors, and the ideal "princely" advisor/courtier envisioned in Machiavelli's *Il Principe* (of which Martin is clearly a fan) and Castiglione's roughly contemporaneous *Il Libro del Cortegiano*, Tyrion uses his powerful intellect, combined with his facility for reading the character of others "as easily as he does books," to overcome the travails and prejudices with which he is confronted to rise to the position of Hand of the Queen on Daenerys Targaryen's Small Council and, subsequently, Hand of the King on Bran the Broken's Small Council. The Small Council itself, the body advising the King of the Seven Kingdoms, and its shifting membership are worthy of future scholarly attention in light of the functioning of privy councils and secret councils of both male and female monarchs across multiple geographies, geopolitical contexts, and historical periods that witnessed the emergence of successful territorial monarchies—the precursors of the modern state.

With contemporary popular culture stars aligning for scholars of queenship, women's history, political history, and gender studies, this collection of ten chapters, bookended by a foreword and conclusion contributed by distinguished experts in their fields, offers an innovative platform from which to explore the intersection of academic scholarship on queenship and elite women and popular understanding of the premodern period with G. R. R. Martin's inspired fantasy world. Historical and literary diversity combined with scholarly integrity is anchored to the collection by an expanded and enriched exploration of its unifying themes of queenship, female agency, and the role of advice. Added to these is a third unifying theme: the notion of just rule versus unjust rule and the ethics of power, especially as they intersect with gender, the essential weft woven into the complex tapestry of both Martin's *A Song of Ice and Fire* novel series and HBO's *Game of Thrones* television series. The depth and scope of our contributors' chapters demonstrate how the evolution of queenship studies and the popularity of cultural phenomena such as *A Song of Ice and Fire* and *Game of Thrones* can navigate common ground between the scholarly and the popular, breaching artificial barriers between the academy and the greater public. By drawing specifically upon Martin's cultural phenomenon, this collection advances queenship studies by opening up new approaches and methodologies and deploying these to lay bare key questions regarding power, queens, and gender that have arisen from the broader public consuming the book and television series *and* scholars of history and literature—reflecting the vibrancy of the field and its continually evolving and developing nature.

MEDIEVALISM AND MARTIN: ARE *A SONG OF ICE AND FIRE* AND *GAME OF THRONES* ACTUALLY ALL THAT MEDIEVAL? (AND, DOES THIS MATTER?)

Before Martin, there was Umberto Eco—a gifted academic, novelist, and prolific cultural commentator sometimes accused of "intellectual slumming it" because "he could speak of Donatello's David in the same breath as, say, plastic garden furniture."[3] In the mid-1980s, hard on the heels of the runaway success of his 1980 medieval-themed whodunit, *Il nome della rosa*,[4] set in an Italian monastery in 1327, polyhistor, semiotician, and medievalist, Eco observed that "it seems that people like the Middle Ages."[5] Nothing much has changed since then except that, with the arrival of the global popularity of *A Song of Ice and Fire* and *Game of Thrones*, people seem to like the Middle Ages even more. In the 1980s, Eco reminded us of a "continuous return"[6] to the Middle Ages, affirming that "Modern Ages have revisited the Middle Ages from the moment when, according to historical handbooks, they came to an end."[7] While Renaissance humanists might have dismissed the long period from the fifth to the fourteenth centuries as a "dark age,"[8] there has been a regular return to, and a pervasive nostalgia for, the Middle Ages. According to Eco, this is exemplified in Italian Renaissance poetic revisitings of "Knights saga" themes and their variations, the English Renaissance rediscovery of symbols and emblems of Jewish mysticism, the Counter-Reformation's reworking of scholastic philosophy, Jean Mabillon's Baroque rediscovery and reassessment of the beauties of the medieval illuminated manuscript tradition, and Shakespeare's "borrowing and re-shaping a lot from medieval narrative."[9] Standing upon Eco's sturdy shoulders, seeing further and with contemporary relevance, our contributor Shiloh Carroll concedes elsewhere that "recreating the Middle Ages as 'realistic,' 'authentic' or 'accurate' is impossible." Rather, "what is created is one's *idea* of the Middle Ages based on one's exposure to the past a filtered through historians, whether contemporary or from the era, and medievalist intermediaries."[10]

Unable to rebuild it "from scratch,"[11] in our various attempts to re-create "authentic" Middle Ages, Eco judges that the Middle Ages has been patched up and distorted to reflect contemporary concerns and obsessions—whatever the age of its reinvention, giving us a sense that the Middle Ages is a space "in which we still live."[12] It is here—in the space in which we still live—that Martin's Middle Ages seem most at home. Eco continues his exploration as to why this might be so, observing that "*il Medioeva rappresenta il crogiolo dell'Europa e della civiltà*" (the Middle Ages represents the melting pot of Europe and of civilization). Eco fixes upon points of convergence between our contemporary anxieties and obsessions and those of the historic Middle Ages, saying, "The Middle Ages inaugurated and witnessed all the institutions and concerns with which we must still deal—banks; the organization of landed estates; administrative structures and municipal policies; class struggles and poverty; haranguing between State and Church; the judicial process; fanatical terrorism; religious jurisdiction; and even the organization of tourism."[13] Eco maintains that "Our quest for the Middle Ages is a quest for our roots and, since we want to come back to the real roots, we are looking for a 'reliable Middle Ages'."[14] Carroll sums up subsequent scholarly contributions to the debate concerning "real" history and the "real" Middle Ages, asserting that "recreating the Middle Ages (or any other historical period) in a way that could be called 'realistic', 'authentic', or 'accurate' is impossible." She cites Michael Oakshott's claim that "authenticity with regards to the past does not exist" because "there is nothing that may be properly called 'direct' evidence of a past that has not survived,"[15] reminding us that Keith Jenkins points out the evident reality of not being able to reproduce the past in its realistic entirety because it is "inaccessible simply by virtue of no longer existing."[16]

However, if we are to venture back into the Middle Ages—patching it up but never rebuilding it from scratch in its entirety and its authenticity—which one should it be? Where would we start? Eco suggests that "perhaps every post-medieval dream or vision of the Middle Ages (from 1492 to today) does not represent a vision of *the* Middle Ages but rather a vision of *a* Middle Ages. If so, of which vision of the Middle Ages and of what medieval period do we speak?"[17] In response to his own interrogations, Eco presents us with a user-friendly way into thinking about the many manifestations of "medievalism" that have developed since the end of the long and multiform Middle Ages.[18] He suggests a typology of ten general categories of the many Middle Ages that we have known from the late fifteenth century to today: his "Ten Little Middle Ages." To better understand Martin's fictional universe, Eco's self-proclaimed "rough and generic" typology is well worth revisiting because Martin's Middle Ages falls into more than one, and perhaps quite a few, of Eco's "Ten Little Middle Ages."[19] In determining where, and subsequently how, George R. R. Martin's novel series, *A Song of Ice and Fire*, and the HBO television spin-off, *Game of Thrones*, align with Eco's understanding of the Middle Ages and related medievalisms and neo-medievalisms,[20] herewith a selection of his "Ten Little Middle Ages" that tallies with Martin's fantasy universe.[21]

According to Eco' s Middle Ages as a *mode and pretext*, there is no particular interest in a specific historical context. This Middle Ages exists purely as a canvas upon which to cast contemporary characters helping us "to enjoy the fictional characters" and to explore contemporary and/or universal concerns. Clearly, Martin's medieval fantasy epic falls into this category—perhaps peripherally in some respects at the beginning of his literary journey to Westeros in 1996, but now more evidently in its development and in the context of our current global concerns and geopolitical circumstances.

The second of Eco's "Ten Little Middle Ages" chiming with Martin's work is the Middle Ages as a *barbaric age*—of elementary and outlaw feelings—"a shaggy medievalism, and the shaggier its heroes, the more profoundly ideological its superficial naïveté."[22] In speaking about his gritty settings and "realistic" inspiration, Martin judges that "a lot of the fantasy of Tolkien imitators has a quasi-medieval setting, but it's like the Disneyland Middle Ages. You know, they've got tassels and they've got lords and stuff like that, but they don't really seem to grasp what it was like in the Middle Ages. And then you'd read the historical fiction which was much grittier and more realistic and really give you a sense of what it was like to live in castles or to be in a battle with swords and things like that."[23] Shaggy, gritty realist of the Middle Ages or not, Martin provides his readers with a twenty-first-century alternative to the Middle Ages visions of Tolkien, C. S. Lewis, or the Pre-Raphaelites—and it is indeed a dirtier, gutsier, and more violent world.[24] His *is* a less fantastical and romantic dream of the Middle Ages than its earlier practitioners, with Martin asserting that the "battle between good and evil is thought [fought?] largely within the human heart, by the decisions we make.[25] It's not like evil dresses up in black clothing and you know, they're really ugly."[26] Against a backcloth of "medieval" violence, yet nuanced by internalized conflict and complex emotions, Martin's work has been highly influential both on the public perception of medievalism and of the historical medieval world. Fans of the books have combined their preconceived ideas about the Middle Ages, likely assembled from other neo-medievalist[27] and medievalist material such as Tolkien's and C. S. Lewis's durable works with Martin's alternative Middle Ages. Consciously or unconsciously, Martin has become the conduit by which his fans now understand the Middle Ages.[28] Indeed, Martin is keen to point out the thoroughness of his medieval universe when compared to Tolkien's, whom he says he admires but does not seek to imitate.[29] The more general pre-modernism, and aspects of modernism that Martin has folded together in envisaging and expressing his constructed "historical" world, and specific gendered premodernism are reflected in Kavita Mudan Finn's contribution to this collection, "Queen of Sad Mischance: Medievalism, 'Realism,' and the Case of Cersei Lannister," which unravels the perceived realism of Martin's and his very particular brand of medievalism on perceptions of premodern women. Elsewhere, Carol Jamison posits that Martin's work "is distinguished by the comprehensiveness of his medievalism" and that it "is medieval from its opening pages."[30] The debate continues.

Eco's Middle Ages of *romanticism* is the Middle Ages of sixteenth-century Edmund Spenser,[31] and the nineteenth-century conception of the Middle Ages of "stormy castles and their ghosts"; of fair maidens and chivalric ideals; and the Middle Ages aesthetic, if not the decadence, of the

Pre-Raphaelite Brotherhood.[32] Martin categorically rejects this, Eco's fourth "Little Middle Age," the utopian or Romantic view of the past, aiming, he says, to show readers what the "real" Middle Ages looked like—gritty medievalism—which in some ways aligns with the shaggy barbaric medievalism of Eco's third "Little Middle Age" discussed above. Yet, does Martin really? Despite his strident attempts to break with the Middle Ages of *romanticism*, Martin wades relatively unhindered through the traditional waters of romanticized medievalism, admittedly reshaping them to suit his purposes. Princesses, good kings, bad kings, evil queens, good queens, chivalric ideals—unmet in most cases, and largely unsustainable in others, once "reality" bites—knights, and castles, these all find their way into his multiform literary universe.[33] In rejecting the Middle Ages of *romanticism*, does Martin protest too much? Perhaps. While helping himself to them, Martin subverts many romanticist tropes. One striking example of this is the knight-errant motif—the wandering masculine knight in search of chivalric or courtly adventure. Arya Stark certainly goes a-roving, not only bending her gender, but inverting and subverting the romanticized avatar of the traditional knight-errant. For most of her narrative arc, Arya is on a one-woman mission to wreak unchivalric, merciless, and violent personal vengeance to redress the misfortunes of her House. In his chapter for this collection, "'All I ever wanted was to fight for a lord I believed in. But the good lords are dead and the rest are monsters.' Brienne of Tarth, Jaime Lannister, and the Chivalric 'Other'" Iain A. MacInnes deconstructs and undermines the edifice of the medieval chivalric hero. The chivalric virgin knight is Brienne—yet her position as a knight is compromised by her sex. MacInnes sets her against the character of Jaime Lannister, arguing that, in spending so much time together, they actually end up influencing one another. So intimately associated do they become that, on the eve of the battle against the forces of the Night King, Jaime crashes through the gender boundaries of knighthood, formally dubbing her Ser Brienne of Tarth, knight of the Seven Kingdoms—the first woman in the history of Westeros to be accorded such an investiture. They become lovers, but are separated by their respective duties and allegiances—duty triumphing over authentic love.[34] Jaime perishes protecting his sister-queen-lover Cersei in the battle for King's Landing with a heartbroken, yet victorious Brienne left to complete Ser Jaime Lannister's hitherto scant entry in the Book of Brothers (The White Book).

Eco's Middle Ages of *decadentism* brings the Pre-Raphaelite Brotherhood immediately to mind. The sensual decadence of the

Pre-Raphaelites, and the sumptuous art they produced, contradicted the actual circumstances of their models many of whom came from deprived backgrounds and lived in poverty. Both meanings of decadence, the original meaning of "decline," and the more contemporary meanings of "self-indulgence," "self-awareness," "immorality, yet skilfulness in governing" can be applied to Martin's "world." The Lannisters (like the earlier Targaryens) stand out for their incestuous decadence—twincest in their case—Cersei (a courtly Machiavellian,[35] practising a less subtle take on Machiavelli than her youngest brother, Tyrion) and Jaime (her devoted, yet conflicted liege-man-of-life-and-limb and knight-lover) for their sib-cestuous relationship, yet demonstrated ability to conquer and govern effectively—at least for a time.[36] Their hedonistic, intellectual, morally self-aware, and charming younger brother Tyrion is perhaps Martin's finest (and not particularly "medieval") characterization. Tyrion is of primordial importance to Martin's narrative for his alterity, his "early modern" grasp of prudential politics, and for his ability to fashion himself simultaneously into a Machiavellian advisor[37]—as Machiavelli intended—and a Castiglionian courtier[38] *par excellence* with a pinch of Rabelaisian grotesque and humour thrown in for good measure.[39]

The final of Eco's Middle Ages characterizing Martin's world is the Middle Ages of the *expectation of the millennium*—fuel for every apocalyptic sect and the source of many past (and present) geopolitical insanities. House Stark's motto, "Winter is Coming," is threaded throughout Martin's storyline, implying the need for eternal vigilance and perhaps pointing to the denouement of his narrative. In Jon Snow's warning of approaching Winter and the doomsday threat of the existential catastrophe that lies beyond the Wall—the White Walkers and the Night King, supreme and apparently invincible leader of the Army of the Dead—we witness end of time moments and visions of the forthcoming gelid apocalypse should the Seven Kingdoms and their rulers not unite in an offensive against their common icy enemy. Given the well-guarded and fortified defences of the millenia-old Wall, this hitherto largely contained threat materializes in the final scene of the final episode of Season 7 of the HBO series when the Night King slays Daenerys's dragon-child Viserion with his icy spear. Reanimating it, he rides Viserion like a Targaryen to destroy the Wall with its ice-blue fire.[40] Yet, in the end, he too is not invincible—undone by hubris, prophecy, and the hard-won abilities of the diminutive Arya Stark determinedly and skilfully wielding the Valyrian steel blade presciently gifted to her by her brother Bran.

HISTORY VERSUS MARTIN'S CONSTRUCTED "HISTORICAL WORLD": AESTHETICS AND POLITICS

As we elaborate in greater detail in the next section, medieval and early modern queens and powerful elite women were supposed to adhere to the gold standard set by the Virgin Mary. Moreover, queens were expected to act in accordance with the gender expectations of the patriarchal polities wherein they sought to exercise their authority and exert their influence. However, to be recognized as a force with which to be reckoned in medieval, early modern, and indeed "modern" polities, powerful elite women and queens had to synthesize masculine qualities to manifest a heart of a man,[41] while adhering paradoxically to gendered social norms in projecting non-threatening, pious, and devoted external feminine personae.[42] As is the case with their historical sisters, some might conclude mistakenly that the bulk of female characters in *Game of Throne* and *A Song of Ice and Fire* exist and act solely in the service of their male protagonists.[43] Yet, elite women such as Daenerys Targaryen, Cersei Lannister, Olenna and Margaery Tyrell, and Sansa and Arya Stark exhibit independent agency, propelling the storylines of both narrative artefacts. This is most obvious in Season 6 of *Game of Thrones*, about which a commentator concludes: "is suddenly all about powerful women getting their way."[44] While this might well be the case, Season 6 simultaneously taps into long-standing "anxieties about women being something other than they seem."[45]

One striking example of a queen who manages to "weaponize femininity" and achieve the difficult balancing act between her masculine and feminine qualities is Daenerys Targaryen. Cersei Lannister, Margaery Tyrell, and Sansa Stark are significant others.[46] In pre-constitutionally organized monarchies, queens and elite women carved out careers for themselves in politics and diplomacy by emphasizing their blood ties to their ruling dynasties and/or as guardians and queens-regent for their minor children. It was not just masculine ambition and aggression that created obstacles to their agency, however, because a queen's potential for power not infrequently pitted ambitious elite females against one another. In the imaginary world of *Game of Thrones* and *A Song of Ice and Fire*, we witness fierce female competition for political power and influence between Margaery and Cersei, Olenna and Cersei, Sansa and Cersei, Cersei and Arya, and Cersei and Daenerys.[47] Cersei seems to be the determined queen to overcome, and her competitors—male and female—drop like flies, dying rather than winning. However, both her refusal to heed pragmatic counsel and her profound belief in her power and destiny bring about her pitiful demise, the destruction of King's Landing, and the massacre of her subjects. Cersei's confidence in the "rightness" of her rule shares much with Daenerys's belief that in victory she must fulfil her destiny to liberate the world from tyranny. Against the backdrop of a Nuremberg-style rally for her unquestioningly loyal and triumphant forces, resolutely refusing to heed sound counsel and warnings from both Jon and Tyrion, the HBO final episode depicts Daenerys as just the sort of single-minded tyrant she seeks to defeat.

While the aesthetics of Martin's world often reflect popular under-standings and concepts of the medieval period, the politics and geopolitics of his world would seem to take inspiration from the early modern period when the superstructure of the modern state was under construction. There is considerably more to Martin's agenda in creating his fictionalized "real" Middle Ages than at the superficial, aesthetic level. Writing for *Pacific Standard*, Benjamin Breen argues that *"Game of Thrones* isn't medieval. And it's the *non* medieval features of the series that help explain its enormous popularity."[48] Breen, while making some unforced errors in pointing to the medieval versus early modern phenomena contained in Martin's world,[49] observes that "Martin has created a fantasy world that chimes perfectly with the destabilized and increasingly non-western plan-etary order today." As alluded to earlier, Martin's series, and its HBO television spin-off, fall into the first of Eco's "Ten Little Middle Ages"—a Middle Ages that serves as a *"maniera e pretesto"* (*mode and pretext*). For Eco, this is a Middle Ages of melodrama—of opera, or of Torquato Tasso's 1581 epic poem *Gerusalemme liberata* (Jerusalem Delivered).[50] A central source of lyrical passion in *Gerusalemme liberata* is the emotional conun-drum endured by the characters who are frequently torn between their heart and their duty, with love at odds with martial valour or honour. A highly fantasized and mythologized account of the First Crusade, like other works of the sixteenth century portraying conflicts between Christians and Muslims, Tasso's subject matter *had a topical resonance for his readers* at a time when the Ottoman Empire was sweeping through Eastern Europe.[51] Breen agrees that "fantasy worlds are never just fantasy … they refract our own histories and speak to contemporary interests … Martin's fantasy has grown to enormous popularity in part because of its *modernity*, not its 'medievality.'"[52]

In Eco's *mode and pretext* Middle Ages, there is no real commitment to an authentic contextualized Middle Ages. Martin's settings serve instead as a hyper-real scenescape—distant, yet familiar—for the exploration of contemporary characters and concerns. Carroll contends Martin leans more heavily towards the "Barbaric" Middle Ages model, deliberately undercutting Tolkien's "Romantic" Middle Ages.[53] She identifies the ways in which Martin's political motivations have worked to shape his hyper-real Middle Ages, the devices he has chosen to achieve his vision of the Middle Ages, and what his reconstructed Middle Ages might teach us. She argues that Martin "examines contemporary concerns or anxieties while placing them in a far-distant past, allowing the reader to consider them at a distance"[54]—safely, somewhat disinterestedly, and hypothetically. Rainer Emig maintains that, in spite of its pseudo-medieval reality, *A Song of Ice and Fire*, a highly politicized fantasy, "responds to the political situation of the world at the start of the twenty-first century, where Cold War powers are a thing of the past and new imperial ones are only gradually making their impact felt."[55] There are no white and black hats in Martin's dream or vision of a hyper-real medieval world, liberating his narrative's medieval setting to operate as a pretext for unravelling twenty-first-century political and geopolitical transformations, disruptions, conflicts, and anxieties.[56]

Like the highly successful young people's author J. K. Rowling, Martin harvests selectively from the disciplines of history, philosophy, and literature across diverse times and spaces to create his own fantasy cultural universe for adults, many of whom grew to maturity consuming Rowling's *Harry Potter* novel series, its cinematic (and now theatrical) spin-offs, and its lucrative and pervasive merchandising. Martin rarely names his sources, admitting, however, that he has a preference for "popular" histories and historical fiction rather than scholarly works. When scholars find themselves bombarded with phrases such as "*Game of Thrones* shows how the Middle Ages *really* was," there is a reflexive tendency to dismiss yet another vehicle for misconceptions or skewed beliefs about "what the Middle Ages was like," lamenting the easy way it has blazed its trail into the popular imagination. However, rather than denouncing Martin's fantasy universe as providing the public with yet another inaccurate or filtered perception of the Middle Ages, scholars should seize the opportunity Martin offers us to examine how his "medieval" epic series, which explores our contemporary concerns and realities, might also serve as a lightning rod for themes and connections that are of scholarly value in problematizing, and therefore better understanding our shared and diverse premodern pasts.

Galvanized by Martin's very particular literary characterizations of elite and royal women in his novels and the HBO television series, especially its much discussed Season 6,[57] we felt that the time was right for a collection that takes account of recent developments in the fertile and flourishing field of queenship studies to explore them in relation to the themes of gendered rulership raised by George R. R. Martin's world. Moreover, since we conceived of this project,[58] the serendipitous appearance in late 2018 of his 80,000-word novel *Fire and Blood*[59] contains Archmaester Abelon's chronicle pointing to hundreds of women, especially widows, who ruled after the Dance of the Dragons in the period known as the Winter of Widows. Like many premodern and indeed modern elite and royal women, Martin's "Winter Widows," who lived three centuries before the "current" Martinesque era, ruled in place of their dead or otherwise absent husbands, brothers, fathers—lost or displaced during the Dance of the Dragons war of succession—or their surviving underage sons. In this succession war, Daenerys Targaryen's distinguished foremother, Princess Rhaenyra Targaryen, opponent of her younger stepbrother, Aegon II Targaryen, bears more than a passing resemblance to Empress Mathilda (d. 1167), daughter of Henry I of England and mother of Henry II—her lack of dragon fire-power notwithstanding. Not only are their narratives and motivations very similar but so too are their chronologies; Princess Rhaenyra lived three centuries before her dynastic "daughter", Daenerys Targaryen, just as Empress Maud (as she was also known), countess of Anjou and heiress-presumptive to Henry I's throne of England, lived about three centuries before Margaret of Anjou (d. 1482), queenconsort of Henry VI of England. In his chapter for our collection, "The Royal Minorities of *Game of Thrones*," Charles E. Beem, in examining the relationship between family and power in *Game of Thrones*, argues that Cersei and her sons reflect a pantheon of characters from medieval European history. While in "Wicked Women and the Iron Throne: The Two-Fold Tragedy of Witches as Advisors in *Game of Thrones*," Sheilagh Ilona O'Brien explains how Martin's universe mirrors historical concerns regarding the nature of queenship, how it manifests itself, as well as how media portrays society's concerns over female advice and influence. O'Brien identifies anxieties over female/feminine influence and power, which reflect both historical and contemporary realities.

Having very briefly accounted for the "medieval matter" buttressing Martin's narrative creation,[60] are there aspects of Martin's oeuvre that dovetail with the politics, societies,[61] and conflicts of the early modern period rather than its preceding Middle Ages? From the terrace atop the pyramid of her newly conquered city-state Meereen, Daenerys Targaryen says of her forefather Aegon I Targaryen, the Conqueror (who invaded, conquered, and unified the Seven Kingdoms of Westeros under his rule): "Aegon the Conqueror brought fire and blood to Westeros but afterwards he gave them peace and justice."[62] Her supposedly "medieval" reflection sounds very like something the Italian Renaissance humanist advisor and diplomat Machiavelli recounts in *The Prince*: "Cesare Borgia was accounted cruel; nevertheless, this cruelty of his reformed Romagna, brought it unity, and restored order and obedience."[63] Another of Martin's women, Queen Alyssa Velaryon, who sought to be loved, consort of Aenys I Targaryen, and therefore another of Daenerys's dynastic foremothers, is described with words that echo Machiavelli's instructions on how *not* to govern successfully:

> That Queen Alyssa wished to do the right thing, no man should doubt .... *She desired above all to be loved, admired, and praised,* a yearning she shared with King Aenys, her first husband. *A ruler must sometimes do things that are necessary but unpopular, however, though he knows that opprobrium and censure must surely follow.*[64]

Machiavelli, in responding to the dilemma of whether it is better to be loved or feared, or the reverse, from Dido's words, has Vergil deduce:

> *Res dura, et regni novitas me talia cogunt*
> *Moliri, et late fines custode tueri.* [Harsh necessities and the newness of my kingdom force me to do such things, and to guard my frontiers everywhere.][65]

Machiavelli concluding that, on balance:

> since some men love as they please but fear when the prince pleases, *a wise prince should rely on what he controls, not on what he cannot control.* He must only endeavour ... to escape being hated.[66]

As highlighted by several chapters in this collection, there are numerous "Machiavellian" and early modern moments, characters, and pronouncements in Martin's "brutal political" world, which Elizabeth Beaton agrees elsewhere is "full of assassins, warring families, and shadowy manipulative advisors" not "so far removed from the intrigue-riddled realm of Renaissance Italy."[67] There is even a readily recognizable Girolamo Savonarola-inspired character in the High Sparrow. According to

Machiavelli, who witnessed his sudden rise and precipitous fall in Renaissance Florence, Savonarola (d. 1498) is best understood as an unarmed, mediocre, self-righteous, and ultimately ineffectual contemporary political and spiritual prophet.[68] Jacopo della Quercia asserts that "Savonarola offers an excellent example of how Martin and Machiavelli not only tapped into the same reservoirs of history but wrote about them in comparable ways."[69] Moreover, in the final episode of Season 7, Sansa, Bran, and Arya Stark work together in a very Machiavellian way to "take down" the chirpy, vapid flatterer, and advisor-cum-consort-aspirant, their cunningly counterfeit false-friend, Lord Protector of the Vale, Petyr Baelish (Littlefinger). It is almost as if the Stark siblings had studied three chapters in particular of Machiavelli's *Prince*, "Cruelty and Compassion," "A Prince's Personal Staff," and "How Flatterers Must Be Shunned," absorbing his lessons to great effect.[70]

In 2013, Elizabeth Beaton sat down with Martin when he passed through Melbourne, Australia, raising the question of Machiavelli's apparent influence upon the construction of his political fantasy. Martin responded rather coyly in these terms: "Certainly, I read Machiavelli's work back in college. I'm aware of his ideas and beliefs … as anyone who writes about politics and power is … I don't necessarily agree with his ideas, but they have power. His advice in *The Prince* is one way to approach rule."[71] Beaton casts her gimlet eye over three of Martin's prominent female characters, whom she defines as pragmatic politicians but of three different Machiavellian types: the military Machiavellian (Asha Greyjoy), the court Machiavellian (Cersei Lannister), and the Machiavellian Prince (Daenerys Targaryen) as well as taking a more general look at "Feminism and Female Machiavellian Moments" in Martin's creation.[72] Machiavellian models of power and rule aside, there is also an early modern transformative political moment portrayed vividly in HBO's Season 6 of *Game of Thrones*—the recognition and "institutionalization" of female regency and the rise of female kings.[73] Regarding feminism, Martin has had this to say:

> To me being a feminist is about treating men and women the same, I regard men and women as all human – yes there are differences, but many of those differences are created by the culture that we live in, whether it's the medieval culture of Westeros, or 21st century western culture.[74]

Martin continues, explaining the complexity he tries to build into all of his characters, both male and female, whom he contends he has not rendered in black and white:

Male or female, I believe in painting in shades of grey. All of the characters should be flawed; they should all have good and bad, because that's what I see. Yes, it's fantasy, but the characters still need to be real.[75]

However, not all feminists have embraced Martin's narratives and characters, with Gina Bellafonte starchily denouncing him in *The New York Times* by writing, "*Game of Thrones* is boy fiction patronizingly turned out to reach the populations other half."[76] Others, such as Emily Nussbaum in *The New Yorker*, have defended Martin, pointing out that the strength of the series is "its insight into what it means to be excluded from power: to be a woman, or a bastard, or 'half a man.'"[77] Indeed, if one examines the facts and the contexts carefully, one cannot but conclude that most of the population of the premodern world—male and female—was disenfranchised by the "patriarchy," and that the premodern patriarchy, or ruling class, was made up of both high-ranking and high-wealth males *and* females. Lindy Grant reminds us that "focus on misogyny can lead one to ignore bitter criticism of power and the powerful in general."[78]

A recently published collection of essays poses a legitimate question: "How many exceptional women in positions of authority does it take before powerful elite women become the rule" (in the historiography of our premodern past)? For some three decades, scholars have demonstrated that historical elite women in power were *not* exceptions to the norm, yet many still hold this to be the case.[79] Powerful and politically effective elite and royal women of the premodern period—prior to the industrial revolution—were "expected, accepted, and routine."[80] Martin's universe, and indeed the history of premodern political power, is about family and families. All monarchies and ruling dynasties are essentially about family, "and the ways in which family and familial connections are used to attain sovereignty and buttress power and influence."[81]

FEMALE POWER, AGENCY, AND ADVICE: MEDIEVAL AND EARLY MODERN SCHOLARSHIP

In general, medieval and early modern societies believed that women were subordinate to men. It was assumed that men, as husbands and fathers, should hold authority over their wives and daughters. Aristotle's views of women's biological deficiency provided the foundational justification for the so-called medieval misogyny. According to Aristotle, females were deformed or defective males, who could never reach perfection because of menstruation, and therefore were physiologically inferior.[82] Aristotle's concept was combined with biblical exegesis, which concluded that all women were physically and morally inferior because of Eve's material creation from Adam's body and the corruption of her character by the devil.[83] These two concepts fused to create a society that commonly believed that women were inherently inconstant, foolish, loquacious, insubordinate, and possessed of a perverse inclination towards temptation. These identified feminine traits "proved" that medieval and early modern elite women, both as women and as queens, were unfit to act in areas of masculine authority. The contextualized socio-political reality, however, was very different.

The first modern medieval scholars also gave little critical attention to the study of medieval women. For example, nineteenth-century works on medieval women, and on medieval queens, took the form of individual biographies and personal narratives, were generally divorced from mainstream political history, and mainly focused on prominent aristocratic women—The Great White Women of History. Little analytical attention was given to a woman's place in diverse premodern societies, nor did historians consider that premodern societies might have held different ideas regarding gender roles.[84] Rather than thinking about contextualized premodern understandings of gender, their studies of premodern women relied upon their own particular societal views regarding gender. Twentieth-century feminist movements changed the ways in which academics viewed a woman's place in the world, and therefore the way in which women were studied. Scholars of the premodern world began to consider women through the lenses of gender, power, and status. As part of these new approaches to studying premodern women, researchers concerned with medieval and early modern queens moved away from the early biographical approaches that had focused upon the colourful events and myths surrounding individual queens, and started to think instead about their premodern experiences and what it meant to be a queen in a pre-constitutional monarchy.[85] More recently, scholars have widened their exploration to include premodern understandings of what it meant to be a man.[86]

First-wave feminism's main focus was to bring women out of the private sphere to gain equal opportunities for them in public institutions so that they were no longer denied access to political activity.[87] This concept of the public/private divide was deployed by medievalists giving birth to the study of queenship as an office or an institution.[88] These trail-blazing scholars began to articulate a new vocabulary for discussing the queen's place within the royal spheres of power, authority, and government.[89] Medieval and early modern historians began to argue that applying modern concepts of gender without an awareness of cultural and temporal specificity risked the production of ahistorical and distorted conclusions. Their subsequent analyses of queens explored contextualized understandings of manhood and womanhood, and kingship and queenship.[90] This new framework allowed "medieval misogyny," stemming from Greco-Roman and Judeo-Christian philosophies and theologies, not to be dismissed outright but rather to be deconstructed, interrogated, and rearticulated. This new method of analysis includes, but is by no means limited to, the investigation of the queen's motherhood, her intercession, her patronage, and her household. Within this framework, scholars seek to uncover and communicate the level of agency, power, or authority that was afforded to, and indeed manipulated by, the queen, evaluating how and if these areas contributed to her participation in the governance of the realm. The *unexceptional*—as we now view it—phenomenon of the powerful elite premodern woman problematizes received ideas regarding the blanket misogyny of the "ruling" patriarchy in premodern polities, providing a more nuanced reading of how this might be better understood once reinserted into the diverse contexts and concerns of their times.

It was just as these advances in the study of gender, power, and agency were happening in academia that Martin conceived of his "world," penning his novels from the mid-1990s onwards. Knowingly or not, Martin's world has capitalized and internalized many of the discussions that have preoccupied scholars of premodern women and their subset: queens and elite women. Queens *were* expected to act in accordance with the complementary gender expectations of patriarchal polities wherein they sought to exercise their authority and exert their influence. Across diverse geopolitical spaces, women of the premodern *longue durée* emphasized gendered benchmarks for female action by the conscious and careful display of visible and overt femininity combined with an unassailable devotion to dynasty, state, and religion.[91] This collection focuses primarily upon the institution of queenship and two of its most essential aspects: female agency and the role of advice.

Since queens did not consistently hold positions within government, proffering advice through intercession was one way queens could, and did, make a significant impact upon political undertaking. There were several ways in which queens could act as intercessors: as peacemakers between the king and other people; by securing a privilege, such as a pardon, grant, or appointment from the king at the behest of someone else; by interceding on their own initiative; or by beseeching the king to grant someone a request. Queenly influence was a "means to create and sustain impressions of power."[92] The ideological emphasis on intercession and influence was a consequence of the idea of complementary gender roles. Both men and women could act as intercessors, but it was a duty especially emphasized for women because it was the most effective primary avenue of power available to them.[93] Men could not only intercede with the king, but they also had many more opportunities for active roles in government. Naturally, premodern queens could be, and often were, suspected of improper influence over the king—adultery therefore was one of the first charges brought against a queen when detractors and competitors sought to discredit her.[94] Acting in the role of most intimate advisor to the king—implicit in premodern conceptions of the role of the female consort—queens negotiated the shifting sands of the fine line between legitimate, acceptable power, and dangerous criticism. Moreover, the Virgin Mary was defined generally by her complementary roles of intercessor and mother—the principal duties assigned to a terrestrial queen.[95] As such, associating the terrestrial queen with the celestial Mary was the logical way to disseminate expectations of the queen's duties to the queen herself and her regal authority to her subjects. The queen too therefore had two bodies[96]: Marian intercessor and holy mother, and her corporeal sexual body. Since a terrestrial queen could not be a virgin mother, as the celestial Virgin Mary was held to be there was always a level of anxiety regarding a queen's sexual identity. Unlike a king's, a queen's role and status was uniquely corporeal and, while her intercessory role might allow the conceptualization of the queen's two bodies, her intercessory and reproductive duties could not be completely separated.[97] Kings were seldom, if ever, defined primarily by the fathering of their offspring. Accordingly, queens discussed in chronicles most often fell into general stereotypes of female behaviour: Jezebels, who were over-mighty viragos; adulterous wives; wicked enchantresses; or "Virgin Marys," who were supportive wives and mothers, and modest intercessors and peacemakers.[98]

Premodern queens could act in governing capacities in several ways: they aided the king and chancellor in the chancery, and they acted as mechanisms of authority, administering the kingdom in the king's absence or death. The powers afforded to a queen in these functions varied greatly by geography. For example, there were never any queens-regent or "queens-keeper" in England, but they were largely unexceptional in France, in the Mediterranean, and on the Iberian and Italian peninsulas—regardless of whether or not they carried an official designation.[99] For England's part, in many cases, but not all, when the king was absent from the realm, the *custos,* or keeper, or regent was one of the king's minor sons who held only titular authority. Most often, there was a council administering the realm under the authority of the keeper's name, and the queen usually supported this administrative body along with other important members of the royal administration such as the chancellor. Elsewhere, queens who were fortunate enough to have sons—or even grandsons[100]—in their minorities could aspire to being appointed to the post of regent—either officially or unofficially.[101] Through regency, motherhood gave queens the opportunity to exercise political influence and even ultimate authority in some cases.[102] Their contemporaries expected the queen to act in these roles because she was the safest choice as administrator of the realm during the king's absence, having no blood claims to the throne, unlike a royal uncle, for example, and because the queen was thoroughly and durably incorporated into the premodern concept of the crown.

For premodern women of all estates, the emphasis on motherhood stemmed from the necessity to provide heirs for their husbands' lands or businesses, and to sustain their family lineages.[103] For a queen, however, motherhood not only defined her domestic role, but was an important source of her personal power and political influence.[104] Many historians have pointed out that a queen's position became most secure once she had produced a male heir, and she could use her maternal power to her advantage. Other scholars have established that, once the queen's son began to rule in his own right, whether he immediately succeeded upon the death of his father or when a minority period was brought to an end, she had three options regarding her widowhood: she could retire to her dower lands, she could take the veil, or she could remarry.[105] There has been little study of the agency of queens who retired quietly from courtly life to their dower lands. If a queen wished to remain politically active she could do so through her unique, maternal influence over her son, much in the same way as she had fulfilled her role as queen-consort, and it is this role that has been the focus of most studies on dowager-queens.[106] Moreover, daughters too could be ongoing sources of power—interactions between mothers and daughters perpetuated the roles and powers ascribed to queens-consort. John Carmi Parsons's studies of Plantagenet queens have been especially important in revealing mother/daughter interactions. Through their married daughters, queens were able to perpetuate and expand their power-bases, using the practice of female networking with their own daughters, thereby widening their nominally domestic spheres of agency and increasing their influence in both domestic and foreign affairs.[107]

STRUCTURE OF THE COLLECTION

This volume is divided into three interconnected thematic sections, reflecting the themes and their variations considered by our ten cross-disciplinary contributors, and bookended by an introductory foreword and a concluding afterword. Carolyne Larrington begins our collection, setting up a discussion of Max Weber's distinctions between power, authority, and charisma, connecting these distinctions to the notion of influence. Larrington illustrates her observations by identifying historical paradigms that seem to exemplify the different ways in which women in leadership roles could exercise agency in the premodern period, drawing out comparisons with the women of Martin's fantasy universe.

In Part I, "Queenship," James J. Hudson's chapter, "Game of Thrones and Historical Dowagers: The Case of Cixi, Empress Dowager of China (1835–1908)" strays determinedly from the well-trodden path of medieval comparison with a glimpse into the nineteenth-century political career of empress-dowager Cixi, which he likens to the "brand" of gendered power exemplified by Cersei Lannister. As an anonymous reviewer has pointed out to us recently, assuming that Martin did not know about Cixi, how and why do such parallels work? Is there an even more compelling question about how models of premodern dowager-queenship might be *universal* rejections of the strictures of queen-consortship? This is a very interesting question indeed, one made more enticing by the fact that we might never know. While Cixi reigned during what we understand to be the modern period, Hudson argues that the political and social organization of late Imperial China had far more in common with the emergent states of Western European polities during their late medieval and early modern periods than with "westernized" nineteenth-century empires and kingdoms.

From Imperial China, Kavita Mudan Finn's chapter, "Queen of Sad Mischance: Medievalism, 'Realism,' and the Case of Cersei Lannister," while also focusing upon the ever-mesmerizing Cersei Lannister, diverts our gaze to themes of medievalism and perceived realism to consider the implications of Martin's particular brand of medievalism for our understanding of premodern political women. In the third and final chapter of Part I, "Westerosi Queens: Medievalist Portrayal of Female Power and Authority in *A Song of Ice and Fire*," Sylwia Borowska-Szerszun turns to Martin's novel series to examine Martin's creation of three very different yet powerful queens—Cersei Lannister, Margaery Tyrell, and Daenerys Targaryen—to examine his construction of their characters, evaluating them via the lens of "medieval misogyny" on one hand and, on the other, Alcuin Blamires's premodern "profeminine defences."[108] Borowska-Szerszun's discussion highlights the challenges and opportunities faced by premodern queens, pointing to possible historical inspirations behind the depiction of Martin's fantasy queens, enabling her to examine the influence of power and gender on the perception of power and authority in a contemporary narrative construed as a fantasy of the Middle Ages.

Part II, "Female Agency," is introduced by Iain A. MacInnes's chapter, "'All I ever wanted was to fight for a lord I believed in. But the good lords are dead and the rest are monsters.' Brienne of Tarth, Jaime Lannister, and the Chivalric 'Other.'" MacInnes examines Martin's depiction of these two knightly figures, focusing in particular upon their shared relationship and "chivalric" journey. He considers the place of chivalry as a belief system linking the two, analysing the extent to which these characters represent the medieval chivalric warrior—or something else entirely. Brienne of Tarth, whose position as a knight is initially undermined by her sex, demonstrates her agency not only in fighting for honour, protecting her lord, and those to whom she has sworn her allegiance, but also in the ways in which her contact with Jaime Lannister brings about a gradual, yet durable transformation in him—she does indeed make him a better man. The more time they spend in one another's company, the more they influence each other—albeit in different ways. Kris Swank's chapter, "The Peaceweavers of Winterfell," finds significant points of comparison between the queens in *Beowulf*, the anonymous Anglo-Saxon poem, and Martin's *A Song of Ice and Fire* novel series. Both sets of queens are thrust frequently into that most gendered of premodern female roles—the "peaceweaver," or mediatrix. Does the possibility exist for successful female agency in brokering peace in heroic warrior societies, worlds—real or imagined—that are dominated by conquest and aggression? Can a woman in such an environment do otherwise and win? Swank problematizes and untangles the role of "peaceweaver" by examining the successes and failures of this aspect of premodern female agency in Martin's series via the analytical lens of *Beowulf*, illustrating the ephemeral power of female peaceweavers in societies dominated by men, war, and intrigue. Another aspect of agency, commissioning, is discussed by Curtis Runstedler in the third chapter of this section, "Cersei Lannister, Regal Commissions, and the Alchemists in *Game of Thrones* and *A Song of Ice and Fire*." Runstedler investigates how Martin subversively frames Cersei's commissioning of alchemists to produce wildfire. Rather than a king commissioning alchemists as English history records, it is a strong, powerful queen-regent at the helm of state whom they must satisfy. Runstedler reassesses the connection between alchemical commissions, intention, and royalty in Martin's novel series, setting it against the fifteenth-century English alchemical commissions of Henry V and Henry VI. Runstedler examines Martin's inversion and subversion of the part played by the queen-regent's agency in commissioning this inherently unstable weaponized substance. Martin's portrayal of Cersei's agency balances the masculine and feminine qualities of the queen-regent, yet simultaneously suggests the potential threat of the volatility of both wildfire and Cersei herself. This is visualized to great effect in the penultimate episode of Season 8 of the HBO series where we (and indeed Cersei, momentarily secure in her Red Keep) witness residual caches of stored wildfire explode in King's Landing in response to the fire of Daenerys's pitiless vengeance as she lays waste to Cersei's magnificent capital and its innocent inhabitants. In the final chapter of Part II, "'All Men Must Die, but We Are Not Men': Eastern Faith and Feminine Power in *A Song of Ice and Fire* and HBO's *Game of Thrones*," Mikayla Hunter explores the role of religion as one of the very few sources of power and agency for the women of Essos: Melisandre, Quaithe, and the dosh khaleen. She compares their limited access to power to that of the most powerful Western women, queens who shared a sometimes troubled relationship with faith, finding that often it constricted or undermined more than it empowered. Hunter compares this source of power and agency with the sources of power and agency for heroines of medieval romance and *chansons de geste*, drawing attention to the unusual dearth of conventional love stories in *A Song of Ice and Fire* and *Game of Thrones*. Hunter reshapes the traditional reliance on love and sexual attraction as female sources of power and agency, drawing conclusions about how the series' portrayal of women's relationship with faith interacts with contemporary Western views regarding women in the East.

In Part III, "The Role of Advice," Shiloh Carroll opens with her chapter, "Daenerys the Unready: Advice and Ruling in Meereen," drawing some comparisons with the king of the English, Æthelred II Unræd (the "poorly advised," d. 1016), and examining the various forms of advice, including prophecies, available to Daenerys Targaryen as she attempts to rule her newly conquered city-state of Meereen. Carroll's chapter untangles the threads of advice and intrigue apparent in Daenerys's storyline, demonstrating how Daenerys moves further and further away from the kind of leader she wants to be, and how her dragons symbolize her true self. Carroll draws our attention to the ways in which the adaptation in the HBO television series spin-off radically oversimplifies the politics of Slaver's Bay, losing much of the nuance behind Daenerys's actions and pushing her character towards the "madness" side of Targaryen heritage. Her hitherto dormant hereditary madness is revealed by the HBO writers as their narrative reaches its climactic resolution in Season 8. Such oversimplifications, Carroll argues, work to transform Daenerys into a stereotypical female leader: indecisive, irrational, and governed by her emotions rather than by logic, a characterization that Martin seemed keen to avoid. In his chapter, "The Royal Minorities of *Game of Thrones*," Charles E. Beem reveals how royal minorities are the unavoidable by-products of hereditary systems of succession in medieval Europe and in *Game of Thrones*, making the conduct of royal minority the acid test of a dynasty's strength and power. Queen Cersei Lannister's possession of the Iron Throne has few analogues in medieval western history. However, Cersei's performance as a queen and a mother during the minority reigns of her sons is complicated, mirroring the experiences of many queens-mother in medieval Western Europe. However, Beem argues that, in the final analysis, Cersei, like her elder son Joffrey, slides into caricature, thirsting for power and revenge, becoming the stereotypical "fairy-tale" epitome of the wicked queen. More than any of the male characters in *Game of Thrones*, Cersei epitomizes the savage and remorseless quest for dominance in the "win, or die" game of thrones played by her against the backdrop of her sons' minority reigns. Liberated from the demarcations of regency, Cersei falls victim to her blinkered vision of effective and durable rulership. Both she and Daenerys refuse sound counsel and ignore Machiavelli's advice to avoid being hated, descending instead into bloody tyranny and quite justifiable oblivion. In the final chapter of Part III, "Wicked Women and the Iron Throne: The Problem of Witches and Wise Women as Advisors and Rulers in *Game of Thrones*," Sheilagh Ilona O'Brien reveals how anxieties concerning female and feminine influence and power as portrayed in *A Song of Ice and Fire* and *Game of Thrones* reflect both historical and contemporary realities. For O'Brien, such anxieties reach their zenith in the figure of the witch who embodies the dangerous and/or monstrous feminine, sexually rapacious and desirous of power. O'Brien demonstrates how Martin's universe reflects historical concerns over the nature of queenship, how it occurs, and of "female" or "feminized" advice. By examining how these ideas are discussed in both the novel and spin-off television series, O'Brien lays bare how the media portrays society's concerns regarding "female" advice and power. Whether they seek to rule or merely to advise, women are the frequent targets of criticism in the "game of thrones." Most notable of these gendered motifs is the tragedy and loss that befalls rulers who allow themselves to be influenced by the advice of "witches." The final word on the issues and questions raised by our contributors falls to Elena Woodacre. In her afterword, Woodacre brings our collection full circle, highlighting themes such as female inheritance and succession in response to the ideas advanced by our ten scholarly collaborators.

So, how does Martin's "medieval" fantasy end?[109] Martin is yet to release his literary version, but the HBO *Game of Thrones* storyline's resolution is a nuanced combination of some of the possibilities contained within Eco's "Ten Little Middle Ages." It is certainly grittily *barbaric* and *unromanticized*, with both Cersei and Daenerys denied their claims, dying rather than winning, and Drogon, the surviving dragon, making his opinion very clear regarding the ruthless and apocalyptic quest for an Iron Throne that had cost so many lives and possessions—especially those of his "mother" Daenerys. Jon Snow chooses duty and reason over love, paying heavily for his choice with perpetual exile to the nominally celibate Night's Watch for his crime of regicide. He is denied the possibility of establishing his own Targaryen-Stark dynasty as a compromise to head off rebellion and conflict with Grey Worm and the Unsullied. In the killing of his queen, Jon embodies what Machiavelli refers to as a nobility of the spirit or soul (*grandezza d'animo*) that puts him into considerable danger in his decision to act against Daenerys's nascent tyranny. Yet from this *barbaric* vision surfaces a king-maker, Tyrion Lannister, the last of his line—a handy and able *deus ex machina*, a "swiller of wine, frequenter of brothels, and drinker and knower of things"[110]—"the conscience of Westeros,"[111] who counsels the gathering of sixteen great lords and ladies of the Seven Kingdoms to elect their monarch and cast aside dynastic succession, proposing instead Bran Stark the Broken as their new king. Having apparently long-foreseen his destiny, Bran agrees to his elevation appointing Tyrion his Hand. Fourteen of the gathering approve, apart from Sansa Stark who, with the support of her sister Arya, asserts the North's right to its millennial-long independence, which she will rule henceforth as the Queen in the North. From the ashy apocalypse emerges hope for the Six Kingdoms and the independent Kingdom of the North. Arya, achieving the narrative transformation from knight-vengeant to knight-errant, takes up the challenge of her ancestor, King Bran the Shipwright,[112] sailing west of Westeros to discover what lies beyond the maps. The Small Council is convened by Tyrion Lannister, Hand of the King and enforcer of checks and balances, to rebuild King's Landing and see to the prosperity of the Six Kingdoms.[113] Sansa Stark, Lady of Winterfell, is crowned Queen in the North. Hopes are high for a new world order in Martin's fantasy universe, leaving its architect a free hand to tie off loose threads and expand the conclusion of his inspired "medieval" creation in its literary form.

Barbaric vision of the Middle Ages though it appears to be, in many ways, the denouement of Martin's fantasy narrative is actually a blend of Eco's *mode and pretext* and *expectation of the millennium/apocalyptic* visions. At the approach of the second millennium of the common era, just as Martin was sharpening his quills, an Italian newspaper, *La Correra de la Serra*, invited Eco and the erudite scholar-cardinal, Carlo Maria Martini, to partake in an epistolary exchange of ideas on its pages. It was later published as *In Cosa crede chi non crede? Dialogo epistolare.*[114] The Eco-Martini correspondence would seem to support our conclusion regarding the *mode and pretext* and *expectation of the millennium/apocalyptic* ending of Martin's fantasy narrative. In their first exchange of letters, dated March 1995, "L'ossessione laica della nuovo apocalisse" (The secular obsession with the new apocalypse), they examine key ideas related to end of time notions, history, and hope, with Eco positing:

> I'd be willing to bet that the notion of the end of time is more common today in the secular world than in the Christian ... Only by having a sense of history's trajectory (even if one doesn't believe in Parousia [the second coming]) can one love earthly reality and believe—with charity—that *there is still room for Hope.*[115]

And Martini responding with:

> The dominant theme of apocalyptic stories is usually a flight from the present to a refuge in a future that, upsetting the existing structures of the world, forces upon it *a definitive value system that conforms to the hopes and expectations of the person writing the book* ... In this sense, it must be said that *in every apocalypse there is a heavy utopian freight, a massive reserve of hope,* but *coupled with a woeful resignation in the present.*[116]

The narrative defining apocalypse of *Game of Thrones* did not come from the Seven Kingdoms' common alien enemy, the Night King and his Army of the Dead, but rather from enemies within—the blind ambition and merciless tyranny of two monarchs competing for ascendancy over the Seven Kingdoms and the Iron Throne. They both cast aside sound counsel, unity, and just rule, opting instead for divisive tyranny. Which brings us full circle to Tyrion's address to the ad hoc meeting of the sixteen great and good representatives of Westeros assembled in the Dragonpit of King's Landing to decide his fate (and theirs). He asks rhetorically, "What unites people?" "Armies? Gold? Flags? Stories. There is nothing in the world more powerful than a good story. Nothing can stop it. No enemy can defeat it. And, who has a better story than Bran the Broken? The boy who fell from the high tower and lived." Tyrion's argument would seem to gel with Eco's claim that, in literature as in life, after an apocalyptic moment, "*there is still room for hope*"[117] as well as Martini's contention that *in every apocalypse there is a heavy utopian freight, a massive reserve of hope.*"[118]

Sydney, NSW, Australia   Zita Eva Rohr
Salem, MA, USA   Lisa Benz

Notes

1. Christine de Pizan, Charity Cannon Willard and Eric Hicks, (eds.), *Le Livre des trois vertus*, Paris: Honoré Champion, 1989, 64.
2. Anne de France, *Les Enseignements d'Anne de France, duchesse de Bournonnais et d'Auvergne, à sa fille Suzanne de Bourbon*, Chazaud, A.-M (ed.), Moulins: Desroziers, 1878; idem, *Enseignements à sa fille suivis de l'Histoire du siège de Brest*, Tatiana Clavier and Éliane Viennot, (eds), Saint-Etienne: Publications de l'Université de Saint-Etienne, 2006; Anne of France, Sharon L. Jansen (trans.), *Anne of France: Lessons for my Daughter*, Cambridge: D. S. Brewer, 2004; Pizan, Willard and Hicks (eds), *Le Livre des trois vertus*; Zita Rohr, "Rocking the Cradle and Ruling the World: Queens' Households in Late Medieval and Early Modern Aragon and France," in Theresa Earenfight, *Royal and Elite Households in Medieval and Early Modern Europe: More than Just a Castle*, Leiden and Boston, Brill, 2018, 309–337, 312–313, 314–315; and Tracy Adams, "Appearing Virtuous: Christine de Pizan's *Le Livre des trois vertus* and Anne of France's *Les Enseigenements d'Anne de France*, in Karen Green and Constant J. Mews (eds), *Virtue Ethics for Women 1250–1500*, New York: Springer, 2011, 115–132, 116–131.
3. Ian Thomson, "Umberto Eco Obituary," *The Guardian*, 20 April, 2016 https://www.theguardian.com/books/2016/feb/20/umberto-eco-obituary accessed February 20, 2019.
4. The English translation of his first novel appeared in 1983. Umberto Eco, *Il nome della rosa*, Milan: Bompiani, 1980; Umberto Eco, William Weaver (trans.), *The Name of the Rose*, San Diego, CA: Harcourt, 1983. The film version, *The Name of the Rose*, starred Sean Connery and was directed by

Jean-Jacques Arnnaud. It was released in 1986 around the time Eco started to publish articles such as his lecture "Dieci modi di sognare il medioevo" and his two-article chapter in English, "The Return of the Middle Ages." According to Ian Thomson's obituary for Eco, "In private, Eco judged Annaud's film a travesty of his novel, and found the monks (apart from the one played by Connery) 'too grotesque-looking'. Yet, Eco approved of Annaud's Piranesi-like sets, which he concurred were 'marvellous.'" Ian Thomson, "Umberto Eco Obituary," *The Guardian*, 20 April, 2016 https://www.theguardian.com/books/2016/feb/20/umberto-eco-obituary accessed February 20, 2019.

5. Umberto Eco, "Dreaming of the Middle Ages" in *Travels in Hyper-Reality*, London: Pan Books Ltd, 1987, 61–72, 61.

6. Ibid., 65–67.

7. Ibid., 65. See also Carol Jamison, "Reading Westeros: George R. R. Martin's Multi-Layered Medievalisms," in Karl Fugelso (ed.), *Studies in Medievalism XXVI: Ecomedievalism*, Martlesham, Suffolk and Rochester NY, 2017, 131–142, 131–132; and Riccardo Facchini, "'I watch it for historic reasons'. Representation and Reception of the Middle Ages in *A Song of Ice and Fire* and *Game of Thrones*", *Práticas da História*, n°4 (2017), 43–73, 57–62.

8. See Franco Simone, Chap. 2 "La Luce della Rinascita e le Tenebre Medievali", in *La Coscienza della Rinascita negli umanista francesi*, [Rome: Edizione di Storia E Letteratura, 1949], ACLS Humanities E-Book, 2008, 27–78.

9. Eco, "Dreaming", 66.

10. Shiloh Carroll, *Medievalism in A Song of Ice and Fire and Game of Thrones*, Woodbridge, Suffolk: D. S. Brewer, 2018, 14.

11. Eco, "Dreaming", 67.

12. Ibid., 67–68.

13. "Il Medioevo inventa tutte le cose con cui ancora stiamo facendo i conti, le banche e la cambiale, l'organizzazione del latifondo, la struttura dell'amministrazione e della politica comunale, le lotte di classe e il pauperismo, la diatriba tra Stato e Chiesa, l'università, il terrorismo mistico, il *processo indiziario, l'ospedale e il vescovado, persino l'organizzazione turistica*, [...]." Umberto Eco, "Dieci modi di sognare il medioevo" (Ten ways of Dreaming of the Middle Ages), in *Sugli specchi e altri saggi*, Milan: Bompiani, 1985, 78–89, 82.

14. Eco, "Dreaming", 65.

15. Carroll, *Medievalism*, 14. Veronica Ortenberg, *In Search of the Holy Grail: The Quest for the Middle Ages*, London: Hambledon Continuum, 2006, 192; and Michael Oakshott, *On History and Other Essays*, Totowa, NJ: Barnes and Noble, 1983. 55.

16. Keith Jenkins, *On "What is History": From Carr and Elton to Rorty and White*, New York: Routledge, 1995, 16. Cited by Carroll, *Medievalism*, 14. See also Hilary Jane Locke, "Beyond 'Tits and Dragons': Medievalism, Medieval History, and Perceptions in *Game of Thrones*," in Marina Gerzic and Aidan Norrie (eds), *From Medievalism to Early Modernism: Adapting the English Past*, Abingdon Oxon and New York: Routledge, 2019, 171–187, 172–3, 176–183; and Kavita Mudan Finn, "*Game of Thrones* is Based in History—Outdated History", *The Public Medievalist*, May 16, 2019, https://www.publicmedievalist.com/thrones-outdated-history/ accessed May 25, 2019.

17. Eco, "Dieci modi di sognare il medioevo", 82.

18. See Umberto Eco, *Scritti sul pensiero medievale*, Milan: Bompiani, 2012.

19. His "Little Middle Ages" has been revisited most recently by Carroll, *Medievalism*, 15.

20. For a user-friendly, yet detailed definition of these terms, see Carroll who clarifies: "Medievalism is based on the historically medieval, but is not, itself, medieval ...," while "neo-medieval texts use the trappings of the medieval as filtered through a 'medievalist intermediary.'" Carroll, *Medievalism*, 9–10.

21. Eco, "Dreaming", 68–72.

22. Ibid.

23. James Poniewozik, "George R. R. Martin Interview Part 2: Fantasy and History," *Time*, April 18, 2011 http://entertainment.time.com/2011/04/18/grrm-interview-part-2-fantasy-and-history/ accessed March 5, 2019.

24. Carroll, *Medievalism*, 8–10.

25. This might be read as Martin's acknowledgement of Shakespeare's legacy: his stature as *the* peerless poet of human nature, his durable work observing, exploring, expressing, and exhibiting all aspects of humanity and the "greyness" of human actions and decision-making set against pseudo-historical and historical contexts. See Jessica Walker, "Historical Discourses in Shakespeare and Martin," in Jes Battista and Susan Johnston (eds), *Mastering the Game of Thrones: Essays on George R. R. Martin's A Song of Ice and Fire*, Jefferson, NC: McFarlane Publishing, 2015, 71–91.

26. Poniewozik, "George R. R. Martin Interview Part 2."

27. See Carole L. Robinson and Pamela Clements (eds), *Neomedievalism in the Media: Essays on Film, Television and Electronic Games*, Lewiston, NY, Mellen, 2012.

28. Carroll, *Medievalism*, 16.

29. Mikal Gilmore, "George R. R. Martin: The *Rolling Stone* Interview", *Rolling Stone*, (April 23, 2014), https://www.rollingstone.com/culture/culture-news/george-r-r-martin-the-rolling-stone-interview-242487/ accessed February 19, 2019.

30. Jamison, "Reading Westeros," 134, 135.
31. Edmund Spenser (d. 1599) is best remembered for his unfinished epic poem *The Faerie Queene* (1590–1596), striking for its allegorical fantasy setting that celebrates Elizabeth I and the Tudor Dynasty. Edmund Spenser, Albert Charles Hamilton et al (eds), *The Faerie Queene*, 2nd Ed., Abingdon, Oxon and New York: Routledge, 2013.
32. More on this below. Read on.
33. For a similar appreciation, see Carroll, *Medievalism*, 15.
34. In the final episode of Season 8, "The Iron Throne", written and directed by David Benioff and D. B. Weiss, first aired May 19, 2019, an imprisoned, yet unbroken, Tyrion engages in a pivotal discussion with Jon Snow on the subjects of reason, love, and duty, thereby setting the stage for Jon's quintessential, self-sacrificing redemption arc.
35. Read on. See Elizabeth Beaton, "Female Machiavellians in Westeros," in Gjelsvik and Schubart, *Women of Ice and Fire*, 193–218.
36. Martin deals with this in considerable detail in his latest tome, a chronicle history of the Targaryen kings from Aegon the Conqueror to Aegon III. George R. R. Martin, *Fire and Blood*, New York: Bantam Books, 2018.
37. See Philip J. Kain, "Niccolò Machiavelli: Advisor of Princes", *Canadian Journal of Philosophy*, Vol. 25, N°1, (March 1995), 33–55; Harvey C. Mansfield, *Machiavelli's Virtue*, Chicago and London: University of Chicago Press, 1998; Timothy Fuller (ed.), *Machiavelli's Legacy: The Prince After Five Hundred Years*, Philadelphia: University of Pennsylvania Press, 2016; Patricia Vilches and Gerald Seaman (eds), *Seeking Real Truths: Multidisciplinary Perspectives on Machiavelli*, Leiden and Boston: Brill, 2007; Niccolò Machiavelli and George Bull (trans. and ed.), *The Prince*, London: Penguin Books, 2003; and Niccolò Machiavelli, Julia Conaway Bondanella and Peter E. Bondanella (trans. and eds.) *Discourses on Livy*, Oxford: Oxford University Press, 2008. These two works by Machiavelli should be read together and considered as complementary and highly contextual.
38. See W. R. Albury, *Castiglione's Allegory: Veiled Policy in* The Book of the Courtier *(1528)*, Farnham, Surrey: Ashgate Publishing Ltd., 2014; Baldassare Castiglione, George Bull (trans.), *The Book of the Courtier*, Harmondsworth: Penguin, 1976; idem and A. P. Castiglione (trans.) *Il Cortegiano or The Courtier*, [bilingual edition], London: Bowyer, 1727.
39. While Tyrion is a dwarf rather than a giant, his racy, bawdy, and humorous utterances bear comparison with Rabelais's creations, Pantagruel and Gargantua, as does his earthy and lusty approach to life. See François Rabelais, Donald M. Frame, (trans.), *The Complete Works of François Rabelais*, Berkeley, Los Angeles and London: University of California Press, 1999.

40. *Game of Thrones*, Season 7, Episode 7, "The Dragon and the Wolf," directed by Jeremy Podeswa, written by David Benioff and D. B. Weiss, first aired August 27, 2017.

41. The expression *regina vero sub femineo corpore cor habens virile* (a queen concealing *a heart of a man* beneath a feminine appearance or exterior) first crops up in an eleventh-century text by Bruno Merseburgenis wherein he describes Bertha of Savoy, empress-consort of the Salian Holy Roman Emperor Heinrich IV. Bruno Mersebургensis, Wilhelm Wattenbach (ed.), *De bello Saxonico*, Hannover: impensis bibliopolii Hahniani, 1880, Chap. 7. Available online at: https://www.hs-augsburg.de/~harsch/Chronologia/Lspost11/Bruno/bru_sax0.html accessed, February 27, 2019.

42. See, for example, Christine de Pizan's *Le Livre des trois vertus* and Anne de France's *Enseignements*. See also Ann Katherine Isaacs (ed.), *Political Systems and Definitions of Gender Roles*, Pisa: Edizioni Plus, Università di Pisa, 2001.

43. Tanner et al, "Introduction," *Medieval Elite Women*, 1–2.

44. Catherine LaSota, "'Game of Thrones' Is Suddenly All About Powerful Women Getting Their Way," *Vice*, 16 May, 2016 https://www.vice.com/en_au/article/wdbqqm/game-of-thrones-is-suddenly-all-about-powerful-women-getting-their-way accessed February 26, 2019.

45. Megan Garber, "*Game of Thrones* and the Paradox of Female Beauty," *The Atlantic*, April 25, 2016 https://www.theatlantic.com/entertainment/archive/2016/04/game-of-thones-red-woman-old-age-ism/479760/ accessed February 26, 2019.

46. "But we are not men: Female Warriors and Weaponised Femininity in A Song of Ice and Fire and Game of Thrones," Tower of the Hawk: Scholarly Exploration of the World of George R. R. Martin, April 7, 2015 https://hawkstower.wordpress.com/2015/04/07/but-we-are-not-men-female-warriors-and-weaponized-femininity-in-a-song-of-ice-and-fire-and-game-of-thrones/ accessed February 26, 2019.

47. In the first episode of Season 7, Sansa Stark emphasizes that Cersei is an existential threat to the survival of their House, saying, "If you're her enemy, she'll never stop until she's destroyed you. Everyone who's ever crossed her, she's found a way to murder." Jon appears startled by Sansa's observation. "You almost sound as if you admire her," he says, and Sansa acknowledges that spending time in Cersei's company had its teaching moments. "I learned a great deal from her," she replies. *Game of Thrones*, "Dragon Stone," Season 7, Episode 1, directed by Jeremy Podeswa, written by David Benioff and D. B. Weiss, first aired July 16, 2017.

48. Benjamin Breen, "Why 'Game of Thrones' Isn't Medieval—and Why that Matters," *Pacific Standard*, June 12, 2014 https://psmag.com/social-justice/game-thrones-isnt-medieval-matters-83288 accessed February 24, 2019.

49. Spice guilds like the one in Qarth did exist before the early modern period (for example, the Florentine *Arte dei medici, speziali e merciai* established in the very early fourteenth-century. See Carlo Fiorilli, "I Dipintori a Firenze nelle' Arte Dei Medici Speziali e Merciai", *Archivio Storico Italiano*, Vol. 78, No. 3 (299) (1920), 5–74, 9–11; and Georges Renard, Dorothy Terry (trans.), *Guilds in the Middle Ages*, [London: George Bell and Sons Ltd., 1918], Kitchener, ONT: Batoche Books, 2000, 22. Not just a post-Columbian phenomenon, the slave trade was well established in the early Middle Ages, Dublin hosting the biggest slave market in Europe during the eleventh century. See Charles Verlinden, *L'Esclavage dans l'Europe medieval*, 2 vols, Bruges: De Tempel, 1955 and Ghent: Rijksuniversiteit, 1977; and William D. Phillips Jnr., *Slavery in Medieval and Early Modern Iberia*, Philadelphia: University of Pennsylvania Press, 2014, 10–27. Powerful merchant banks predated the early modern period, inaugurated by Italian grain merchants from 1100–1300; these heralded the beginning of Europe-wide banking. The first big merchant bank was established in Venice in 1157 under state guarantee, harnessing the commercial agency of Venetian traders acting in the interests of Urban II's crusaders. See James William Gilbart, *The History, Principles and Practice of Banking*, London: George Bell and Sons, 1919. And, black-gowned early modern Jesuits were not the only order "to create medicines, study the secrets of the human body," the medieval Dominican order established by Domingo de Guzmán in 1216 predated the Society of Jesus (est. 1534) by a considerable distance as most certainly did the Benedictine order established by Benedict of Nursia in 529. Katarzyna Madra Gackowaka et al., "Medications of Medieval Monastery Medicine", *Journal of Education, Health and Sport*, 8:9, (2018), 1667–1674. While the telescope was not invented until 1608 by Hans Lippershey (and improved upon by Galileo Galilei in 1610), spectacles—arguably the most useful and durable invention of the premodern era— were an early thirteenth-century invention. See Vincent Ilardi, *Renaissance Vision from Spectacles to Telescopes*, Philadelphia: American Philosophical Society, 2007, 2–30. Likewise, during the Middle Ages—particularly the high to late Middle Ages—many aristocrats could read, including women, and both genders patronized authors and accumulated libraries.

50. Eco, *Travels*, 68–9; idem "Dieci modi", 82.

51. Torquato Tasso, Lanfranco Caretti (ed.), *Gerusalemme liberata*, Milan: Arnoldo Mondadori, 1983, lxv and lxix; and see also Emilio Russo, *Guida all lettura della "Gerusalemme liberata" di Tasso*, Bari and Rome: Laterza, 2014, 3–25, 111–139.

52. Eco, *Travels*, 68–9; idem "Dieci modi", 82.

53. Carroll, *Medievalism*, 15.

54. Ibid., 7.
55. Rainer Emig, "Fantasy as Politics: George R. R. Martin's *A Song of Ice and Fire*," in Gerold Sedlmayr and Nicole Waller (eds), *Politics in Fantasy Media: Essays on Ideologies and Gender in Fiction, Film, Television, and Games*, Jefferson, NC: McFarland, 2014, 85–96, 94.
56. Originating in Antiquity, the *visio* or Dream Vision genre is a very medieval allegorical device used in myriad ways by its proponents to explore sometimes dangerous ideas, to make social criticism, and to reveal knowledge not available in the wakened state. Reborn with Romanticism, it is perhaps best imagined as both a creative portal to imagined possibilities beyond rational calculation and the rhetoric of authority. John T. Bickley, "Dreams, Visions, and the Rhetoric of Authority," unpublished doctoral thesis, Florida State University, 2013, 1–6, 54–55, and 149–155; Stephen F. Kruger, *Dreaming in the Middle Ages*, Cambridge: Cambridge University Press, 1992, 150–165; and Bernat Metge, Lola Badia (ed.), *Lo Somni*, Barcelona: Quaderns Crema, 1999; and Bernat Metge, Antonio Cortijo Ocaña and Elisabeth Laresa (trans), '*The Dream*' *of Bernat Metge/ Del Somni d'en Bernat Metge*, Amsterdam and Philadelphia: John Benjamins Publishing Company, 2013, 13–18, 78–103. Book II focuses upon an explanation of the historical circumstances of the death of King Joan I of Aragon (d. 1396)— dangerous territory to explore outside of a dream vision given the political circumstances surrounding its context and actuality. Held to have been from his prison cell, Metge sets out to demonstrate his innocence on a dubious matter involving the death of his employer, Joan I.
57. Which parts company with Martin's unfinished *A Song of Ice and Fire* series, having exhausted his narrative-to-date by the end of Season 5. For various points of view regarding the sixth season of the HBO television series, see, for example, Erica Gonzales, "15 Times the Women of 'Game of Thrones' Ruled Season Six: Girl Power Reigned in the Seven Kingdoms," *Harper's Bazaar*, June 23, 2016: https://www.harpersbazaar.com/culture/film-tv/news/a16251/game-of-thrones-female-characters-season-6/ accessed February 21, 2019; Lenny Ann Low, "*Game of Thrones* Season 6: I Am Woman Hear Me Roar," *The Sydney Morning Herald*, June 22, 2016: https://www.smh.com.au/entertainment/tv-and-radio/game-of-thrones-season-6-i-am-woman-hear-me-roar-20160621-gpo8n1.html accessed February 21, 2019; Joanna Robinson, "*Game of Thrones*: How Women Went From Victims to Conquerors," *Vanity Fair* June 26, 2016: https://www.vanityfair.com/hollywood/2016/06/game-of-thrones-winds-of-winter-recap-finale-women-power accessed February 21, 2019; Alyssa Rosenberg, "The arguments about women and power in 'Game of Thrones' have never

been more unsettling," *The Washington Post*, August 9, 2017: https:// www.washingtonpost.com/news/act-four/wp/2017/08/09/the-arguments-about-women-and-power-in-game-of-thrones-have-never-been-more-unsettling/?noredirect=on&utm_term=.afa033ad0204 accessed February 21, 2019; and Natasha Hodgson, "How *Game of Thrones* reflects historical anxieties about women, motherhood and power," *The Conversation*, July 21, 2017: https://theconversation.com/how-game-of-thrones-reflects-historical-anxieties-about-women-motherhood-and-power-81043 accessed February 21, 2019.

58. Following on from his backstory novella, "The Princess and the Queen, or The Blacks and The Greens" with *The She-Wolves of Winterfell* promised, but yet to be announced. George R. R. Martin and Gardner Dozois (eds), *Dangerous Women*, London: Harper Voyager, [2013] 2015, 703–784. This well-received short story/novella collection "explores the heights that brave women can reach and the depths that depraved ones can plumb." *Publishers Weekly* review article, reviewed July 10, 2013: https://www.publishersweekly.com/978-0-7653-3206-6 accessed February 21, 2019.

59. George R. R. Martin, *Fire and Blood*, New York: Bantam Books, 2018.

60. Carolyne Larrington gives a more detailed exposition of the medieval world of Martin's fantasy universe. See Carolyne Larrington, *Winter is Coming: The Medieval World of Game of Thrones*, London and New York: I. B. Tauris, 2016.

61. See Zita Eva Rohr, "No Job for a Man: Fifteenth-Century France and the 'Institutionalization' of Female Regency," in Tracy Adams and Charles-Louis Morand-Métivier (eds), *The Waxing of the Middle Ages: Revisiting the Late French and Burgundian Middle Ages*, The University of Delaware Press, expected 2020; Aubrée David-Chapy, *Anne de France, Louise de Savoie, inventions d'un pouvoir au féminin*, Paris: Classiques Garnier, 2016; Susan Broomhall (ed.), *Gender and Emotions in Medieval and Early Modern Europe: Destroying Order, Structuring Disorder*, Farnham, Surrey: Ashgate, 2015; and William Monter, *The Rise of Female Kings in Europe, 1300–1800*, New Haven, CT and London: Yale University Press, 2012.

62. George R. R. Martin, *A Storm of Swords*, New York: Bantam Books, 2000, Chap. 71, 'Daenerys, VI' 989–990.

63. Machiavelli, *The Prince*, Chap. XVII "Cruelty and Compassion; and whether it is better to be loved than feared, or the reverse," 53–56, 53.

64. George R. R. Martin, *Fire and Blood*, 150. Our emphasis.

65. Aeneid, i, 563. Bull's translation.

66. Machiavelli, *The Prince*, 54, 56. Our emphasis.

67. Beaton, "Female Machiavellians in Westeros," 193. Interestingly, the architecture and aesthetics of King's Landing call to mind Machiavelli's Florence.

68. "Moses, Cyrus, Theseus, and Romulus would not have been able to have their institutions respected a long time if they had been unarmed, as was the case in our time with Fra Savonarola who came to grief with his new institutions when the crowd started to lose faith in him, and he had no way of holding fast those who had believed or of forcing the incredulous to believe." Machiavelli and Bull, *The Prince*, Chap. VI, "New principalities acquired by one's own arms and prowess", 19–22, 21.
69. Jacopo della Quercia, "A Machiavellian Discourse on *Game of Thrones*," in Brian A. Pavlac (ed.), Game of Thrones *versus History*, 33–46, 34.
70. Machiavelli and Bull, *The Prince*, Chaps. XVII, 53–56, and XXII–XXIII, 74–77.
71. Beaton, "Female Machiavellians," 197.
72. Ibid., 193–196, 199–211.
73. While we immediately think of early modern female kings such as Isabel I of Castile, Mary I of England, and Elizabeth I of England, female kingship was not unknown in medieval Europe and beyond: *mepe* (king) Tamari of Georgia (r. 1184–1213); Raziya Sultan of the Delhi Sultanate (r. 1236–1240); and sister-kings St. Jadwiga (Hedvig, r. 1384–1399) of Poland and Mary of Hungary (r. 1382–1385; 1386–1395), daughters of *Nagy Lajos*, Louis I the Great of Hungary. See Antony Eastmond, "Gender and Orientalism in the Age of Queen Tamar," in Liz James (ed.), *Women, Men, and Eunuchs in Byzantium*, London and New York: Routledge, 1997, 100–118; Fatima Mernissi, *The Forgotten Queens of Islam*, Minneapolis, MN: University of Minnesota Press, 2006, 96–97; Gyula Kristó, *Az Anjou-kor háborúi* [Wars in the Age of the Angevins], Budapest: Zrínyi Kiadó, 1988, 205; Pál Engel, Tamás Pálosfalvi (trans.) and Andrew Ayton (ed.), *The Realm of St. Stephen: A History of Medieval Hungary 895–1526*, London and New York: I. B. Tauris, 2005, 196, 170, 201. See also Monter, *The Rise of Female Kings in Europe*; and Armin Wolf, "Reigning Queens in Medieval Europe: When, Where, and Why,", in John Carmi Parsons (ed.), *Medieval Queenship*, New York: St Martin's Press, 1993, 169–188.
74. Jessica Salter, "*Game of Thrones's* George RR Martin: 'I'm a feminist at heart,'" *The Telegraph*, April 1, 2013: https://www.telegraph.co.uk/women/womens-life/9959063/Game-of-Throness-George-RR-Martin-Im-a-feminist.html accessed February 24, 2019.
75. Ibid.
76. Ibid.
77. Ibid.
78. Lindy Grant, *Blanche of Castile, Queen of France*, New Haven, CT and London: Yale University Press, 2016, 13.
79. Heather J. Tanner, L. L. Gathagan, and L. L. Huneycutt, "Introduction," in Heather J. Tanner (ed.), *Medieval Elite Women and The Exercise of Power*, 1–18, 1–2.

80. Ibid., 2.
81. Zita Eva Rohr, *Yolande of Aragon (1381–1442) Family and Power: The Reverse of the Tapestry:* Basingstoke and London: Palgrave Macmillan, 2016, 4; and idem, "Rocking the Cradle and Ruling the World," 309–310, 323.
82. Alcuin Blamires, *Women Defamed and Defended: An Anthology of Medieval Texts,* Oxford: Clarendon Press, 1992, 2.
83. Ibid., 3–5.
84. For example, Strickland, *Lives of the Queens of England from the Norman conquest; compiled from official records and other authentic documents, private as well as public,* Philadelphia: G. Barrie & son, 1902–1903; Mary Anne Everett Green, *Lives of the Princesses of England, from the Norman Conquest,* 6 vols. London: Longman, Brown, Green, Longman & Roberts, 1857.
85. Charles Beem, *The Lioness Roared: The Problems of Female Rule in English History,* New York: Palgrave Macmillan, 2006, 3–4; Judith Bennett, "Medievalism and Feminism," *Speculum* 68 (1993), 309–331, 312, 315–316, 320–3.
86. Jeffrey Jerome Cohen and Bonnie Wheeler (eds), *Becoming Male in the Middle Ages,* New York: Garland, 1997; Dawn M. Hadley (ed.), *Masculinity in Medieval Europe,* London: Longman, 1999; Jacqueline Murray, (ed.), *Conflicted Identities and Multiple Masculinities: Men in the Medieval West,* New York and London: Garland, 1999; Ruth Mazo Karras, *From Boys to Men: Formations of Masculinity in Late Medieval Europe,* Philadelphia: University of Pennsylvania Press, 2002; Derek G. Neal, *The Masculine Self in Late Medieval England,* Chicago and London: University of Chicago Press, 2008.
87. Betty Friedan, *The Feminine Mystique,* New York: W. W. Norton and Co., 1963, particularly 233–57.
88. Jane Tibbetts Schulenburg, "Female Sanctity: Public and Private Roles, c.500–1100," in Mary Erler and Maryanne Kowaleski (eds), *Women and Power in the Middle Ages,* Athens GA: University of Georgia Press, 1988, 105; Caroline Barron, "The 'Golden Age' of Women in Medieval London," *Reading Medieval Studies* 15 (1990), 35–58, 40. See also, Peter Coss, *The Lady in Medieval England,* Stroud: Sutton Publishing, 2000, 70; Maryanne Kowaleski, "Women's Work in a Market Town: Exeter in the Late Fourteenth Century," in *Women and Work in Preindustrial Europe,* B.A Hanawalt (ed.), Bloomington: Indiana University Press, 1986, 145–166, 146; Joan Kelly, "Did Women Have a Renaissance?" in *Women, History, and Theory: The Essays of Joan* Kelly, Chicago: University of Chicago Press, 1986, 19–50; Judith Bennett, "Medieval Women, Modern Women, Across the Great Divide," in David Aers (ed.), *Culture and History, 1350–1600: Essays on English*

Communities, Identities and Writing, Detroit MI: Wayne State University Press, 1992, 147–75.

89. John Carmi Parsons, "Introduction: Family, Sex, and Power: The Rhythms of Medieval Queenship," in John Carmi Parsons (ed.), *Medieval Queenship,* New York: St. Martin's Press, 1998, 1–2.

90. See Theresa Earenfight, "Medieval Queenship," *History Compass,* (2017) 15: e12372, 1–9; Beem, *The Lioness Roared,* 3–4; Katherine Lewis, *Kingship and Medieval Masculinity in Late Medieval England,* New York: Routledge, 2013, 1–17. See also Bennett, "Medievalism and Feminism," 312, 315–6, 320–3; Hadley, *Masculinity in Medieval Europe;* Murray (ed.), *Conflicted Identities;* Karras, *From Boys to Men;* Neal, *The Masculine Self in Late Medieval England.*

91. See Christine de Pizan, *Le Livre des trois vertus;* and Anne de France, *Les Enseignements/Lessons.*

92. Parsons, "The Queen's Intercession," 149; John Carmi Parsons, *Eleanor of Castile, Queen and Society in Thirteenth-Century England,* New York: Palgrave Macmillan, 1998, 73.

93. See the excellent study by Claire Ponsich, "De la parole d'apaisement au reproche. Un glissement rhétorique di conseil ou l'engagement politique d'une reine d'Aragon?", *Cahiers d'études hispaniques médiévales,* n° 31, (2008), 81–117.

94. Parsons, "The Queen's Intercession," 158; idem, "'Never was a body buried in England with such solemnity and honour': the burials and post-humous commemorations of English queens to 1500," in Anne J. Duggan (ed.), *Queens and Queenship in Medieval Europe,* Woodbridge, Suffolk: Boydell Press, 1997, 317–337, 332–33; Pauline Stafford, *Queens, Concubines and Dowagers: The King's Wife in the Early Middle Ages,* Athens, GA: University of Georgia Press, 1983, 19–24; Janet L. Nelson, "Queens as Jezebels: The Careers of Brunhild and Balthild in Merovingian History," in Derek Baker (ed.), *Medieval Women,* Oxford: Oxford University Press, 1978, 31–77; and idem, "Medieval Queenship," in Linda E. Mitchell (ed.), *Women in Medieval Western European Culture,* New York: Garland Publishing Inc., 1999, 179–208, 181.

95. Elizabeth Danbury, "Images of English Queens in the Later Middle Ages," *Historian* 46 (1995), 3–9, 5.

96. See the classic work first published in 1957 on the arcane mysteries of premodern political theology, unravelling the distinctions between the king's body natural (his physical body) and his body politic (his spiritual and political body): Ernst H. Kantorowicz, *The King's Two Bodies. A Study in Medieval Political Theology,* Princeton NJ: Princeton University Press, 2016.

97. Peggy McCracken, *The Romance of Adultery,* Philadelphia: University of Pennsylvania Press, 1998, 42–43.

98. Janet L. Nelson, "Queens as Jezebels," 59; Geoffrey Le Baker, *Chronicon Galfredi Le Baker De Swynebroke*, E. M. Thompson (ed.), Oxford: Oxford University Press 1889, 21; James Raine, (ed.), *Historiae Dunelmensis Scriptores Tres, Gaufridus Coldingham, Robertus de Graystaynes, et Willielmus de Chambre, Surtees Society 9*, London: J.B. Nichols and Son, 1839, 98.

99. Parsons, "Family, Sex and Power," 7; Andre Poulet, "Capetian Women and the Regency: The Genesis of a Vocation," in *Medieval Queenship*, ed. John Carmi Parsons (New York: St. Martin's Press, 1998), 93–116; Theresa Earenfight, "Absent Kings: Queens as Political Partners in the Medieval Crown of Aragon", in Theresa Earenfight (ed.), *Queenship and Political Power in Medieval and Early Modern Spain*, 33–51; *The King's Other Body: María of Castile and the Crown of Aragon*, Philadelphia: University of Pennsylvania Press, 2010.

100. See the case of Violant de Bar, queen-dowager of Aragon (d. 1431), who campaigned vigorously to have her seven-year-old grandson, Louis III of Anjou, crowned king of Aragon with her, his grandmother, the obvious choice as his regent during his minority. Rohr, *Yolande of Aragon*, 88–90. See also Francisca Vendrell Gallostra, *Violante de Bar y el Compromiso de Caspe*, Barcelona: Real Academia de Buenas Letras, 1992.

101. Nelson, "Medieval Queenship," 197; J. L. Laynesmith, *The Last Medieval Queens: English Queenship 1445–1503*, Oxford: Oxford University Press, 2005, 179.

102. Andre Poulet "Capetian Women and the Regency," in Parsons (ed.), *Medieval Queenship*, New York: St. Martin's Press, 1998, 93–116, 105; Miriam Shadis, "Blanche of Castile and Facinger's 'Medieval Queenship': Reassessing the Argument," in Kathleen Nolan (ed.), *Capetian Women*, Basingstoke UK, Palgrave Macmillan, 2003 137–161, 153; Stafford, *Queens, Concubines and Dowagers*, 191–192, 116; Idem, "Powerful Women in the Early Middle Ages: Queens and Abbesses," in Peter Linehan and Janet L. Nelson (eds), *The Medieval World*, London: Routledge, 2001, 398–415, 398; idem, "Emma: The Powers of the Queen in the Eleventh Century," in Anne J. Duggan (ed.), *Queens and Queenship in Medieval Europe*, Woodbridge: Boydell and Brewer, 1997, 3–23, 6; Nelson, "Queens as Jezebels," 38; and Parsons, "The Queen's Intercession," 149.

103. Jennifer Ward, *Women in England in the Middle Ages*, London and New York: Hambledon Continuum, 2006, 37–58.

104. Laynesmith, *The Last Medieval Queens*, 131, 146, 180; Margaret Howell, *Eleanor of Provence: Queenship in Thirteenth-Century England*, Oxford: Oxford University Press, 1998, 27–9, 99–100, 109; John Carmi Parsons, "Mothers, Daughters, Marriage, Power: Some Plantagenet

Evidence, 1150–1500," in John Carmi Parsons (ed.), *Medieval Queenship*, New York: St. Martin's Press, 1998, 63–78, 75; Nelson, "Medieval Queenship," 194; Parsons, "The Burials and Posthumous Commemorations," 328; idem, "The Pregnant Queen as Counsellor and the Medieval Construction of Motherhood," in idem and Bonnie Wheeler (eds), *Medieval Mothering*, New York: Garland Publishing Inc., 1996, 39–62, 42; Miriam Shadis, "Berenguela of Castile's Political Motherhood: The Management of Sexuality, Marriage, and Succession," in idem, 335–358; Marjorie Chibnall, "The Empress Matilda and Her Sons," in idem, 279–294.

105. Nelson, "Medieval Queens," 190; Laynesmith, *The Last Medieval Queens*, 178.

106. Parsons, "Intercessory Patronage," 149, 153–4; Shadis, "Blanche of Castile and Facinger's 'Medieval Queenship'," 140–146; Nelson, "Medieval Queenship," 194–8; Laynesmith, *The Last Medieval Queens*, 208–215; Rohr, *Yolande of Aragon*, 3, 10, 16, 20, 33, 41, 90, 101, 118, 134, 136, 140–141, 146, 155, 164–165, 180, 183, 198, 264n.151.

107. Shadis, "Blanche of Castile," 141, 144; Nelson, "Medieval Queenship," 182, 194.

108. Blamires, *The Case*, 7–9, 50–69, 171–198.

109. Jen Chaney, "Tyrion Lannister Was the Real Winner of the Game of Thrones Finale", https://www.vulture.com/2019/05/game-of-thrones-finale-tyrion-lannister.html accessed May 20, 2019.

110. Niccolò Machiavelli, Harvey C. Mansfield and Nathan Tarcov (trans.), *Discourses on Livy*, Chicago: Chicago University Press, 1998, I., 2, 12; III., 6, 218–235. See also Paul B. Sturtevat, "Who Won *Game of Thrones?*," *The Public Medievalist*, May 23, 2019, https://www.public-medievalist.com/who-won-game-of-thrones/ accessed May 25, 2019.

111. Ibid.

112. George R. R. Martin, *A Game of Thrones: Book One of A Song of Ice and Fire*, New York: Bantam Books, [1996] 2017, Chap. 66, "Bran VII," 613.

113. Chaney, "Tyrion Lannister Was the Real Winner".

114. Carlo Maria Martini and Umberto Eco, *In cosa crede chi non crede? Dialogo epistolare*, [Rome: Liberal (Atlantide Editoriale), 1996], Milan: Bompiani, 2013.

115. Umberto Eco and Cardinal Carlo Maria Martini, Minna Proctor (trans.), *Belief or Unbelief? A Confrontation*, New York: Arcade Publishing, 2000, 18, 22. Our emphasis.

116. Ibid., 29–30. Our emphasis.

117. Ibid., 22.

118. Ibid., 30.

BIBLIOGRAPHY

PRIMARY SOURCES

Anne de France, *Les Enseignements d'Anne de France, duchesse de Bournonnais et d'Auvergne, à sa fille Suzanne de Bourbon*, Chazaud, A.-M (ed.), Moulins: Desroziers, 1878.

Idem, *Enseignements à sa fille suivis de l'Histoire du siège de Brest*, Clavier, Tatiana and Viennot, Éliane (eds), Saint-Etienne: Publications de l'Université de Saint-Etienne, 2006.

Anne of France, Jansen, Sharon L. (trans.), *Anne of France: Lessons for my Daughter*, Cambridge: D. S. Brewer, 2004.

Castiglione, Baldassare, and Castiglione, A. P., (trans.) *Il Cortegiano or The Courtier*, [bilingual edition], London: Bowyer, 1727.

Idem and Bull, George (trans.), *The Book of the Courtier*, Harmondsworth: Penguin, 1976.

Eco, Umberto, *Il nome della rosa*, Milan: Bompiani, 1980.

Idem, Weaver, William (trans.), *The Name of the Rose*, San Diego, CA: Harcourt, 1983.

Idem, "Dieci modi di sognare il medioevo" (Ten ways of Dreaming of the Middle Ages), in idem *Sugli specchi e altri saggi*, Milan: Bompiani, 1985, 78–89.

Idem, "Dreaming of the Middle Ages" in idem, *Travels in Hyper-Reality*, London: Pan Books Ltd, 1987, 61–72.

Idem, *Scritti sul pensiero medievale*, Milan: Bompiani, 2012.

Idem and Martini, Cardinal Carlo Maria, Proctor, Minna (trans.), *Belief or Unbelief? A Confrontation*, New York: Arcade Publishing, 2000.

Game of Thrones, "Dragon Stone", HBO Season 7, Episode 1, (directed by Jeremy Podeswa, written by David Benioff and D. B. Weiss), first aired July 16, 2017.

Game of Thrones, "The Dragon and the Wolf", HBO Season 7, Episode 7 (directed by Jeremy Podeswa, written by David Benioff and D. B. Weiss), first aired August 27, 2017.

Game of Thrones, "The Iron Throne", HBO Season 8, Episode 6, (directed by David Benioff and D. B. Weiss, written by David Benioff and D. B. Weiss), first aired May 19, 2019.

Historiae Dunelmensis Scriptores Tres, Gaufridus Coldingham, Robertus de Graystaynes, et Willielmus de Chambre, Raine, James (ed.), London: J.B. Nichols and Son, 1839.

Le Baker, Geoffrey, Thompson, E. M. (ed.), *Chronicon Galfredi Le Baker De Swynebroke*, Oxford: Oxford University Press 1889.

Machiavelli, Niccolò and Bull, George (trans. and ed.), *The Prince*, London: Penguin Books, 2003.

Idem, Mansfield, Harvey C., and Tarcov, Nathan (trans.), *Discourses on Livy*, Chicago: Chicago University Press, 1998.

Idem, Bondanella, Julia Conaway, and Bondanella, Peter E. (trans. and eds.), *Discourses on Livy*, Oxford: Oxford University Press, 2008.

Martin, George R. R., *A Game of Thrones: Book One of A Song of Ice and Fire*, New York: Bantam Books, [1996] 2017.

Idem, *Fire and Blood*, New York: Bantam Books, 2018.

Martin, George R. R. and Dozois, Gardner (eds), *Dangerous Women*, London: Harper Voyager, [2013] 2015.

Martini, Carlo Maria, and Eco, Umberto, *In cosa crede chi non crede? Dialogo epistolare*, Milan: Bompiani, 2014.

Merseburgensis, Bruno, Wattenbach, Wilhelm (ed.), *De bello Saxonico*, Hannover: impensis bibliopolii Hahniani, 1880. Available on line at: https://www.hs-augsburg.de/~harsch/Chronologia/Lspost11/Bruno/bru_sax0.html

Metge, Bernat, Badia, Lola (ed.), *Lo Somni*, Barcelona: Quaderns Crema, 1999.

Idem, Cortijo Ocaña, Antonio, and Laresa, Elisabeth (trans.), '*The Dream*' of *Bernat Metge/Del Somni d'en Bernat Metge*, Amsterdam and Philadelphia: John Benjamins Publishing Company, 2013.

Pizan, Christine de, Willard, Charity Cannon and Hicks, Eric (eds), *Le Livre des trois vertus*, Paris: Honoré Champion, 1989.

Rabelais, François, Frame, Donald M. (trans.), *The Complete Works of François Rabelais*, Berkeley, Los Angeles and London: The University of California Press, 1999.

Spenser, Edmund, Hamilton, Albert Charles, et al (eds), *The Faerie Queene*, 2nd Ed., Abingdon, Oxon and New York: Routledge, 2013.

Tasso, Torquato, Caretti, Lanfranco, (ed.), *Gerusalemme liberata*, Milan: Arnoldo Mondadori, 1983.

SECONDARY SOURCES

Adams, Tracy, "Appearing Virtuous: Christine de Pizan's *Le Livre des trois vertus* and Anne of France's *Les Enseigenements d'Anne de France*", in Green, Karen and Mews, Constant J. (eds), *Virtue Ethics for Women 1250–1500*, New York: Springer, 2011, 115–132.

Albury, W. R., *Castiglione's Allegory: Veiled Policy in* The Book of the Courtier *(1528)*, Farnham, Surrey: Ashgate Publishing Ltd., 2014.

Barron, Caroline, "The 'Golden Age' of Women in Medieval London," *Reading Medieval Studies* Vol. 15 (1990), 35–58.

Beaton, Elizabeth, "Female Machiavellians in Westeros", in Gjelsvik, Anne and Schubart, Rikke (eds), Women *of Ice and Fire: Gender,* Game of Thrones *and Multiple Media Engagements*, 193–21.

Beem, Charles E., *The Lioness Roared: The Problems of Female Rule in English History*, New York: Palgrave Macmillan, 2006.

Bennett, Judith, in Aers, David (ed.), *Culture and History, 1350–1600: Essays on English Communities, Identities and Writing*, Detroit MI: Wayne State University Press, 1992, 147–75.

Idem, "Medievalism and Feminism," *Speculum* 68 (1993), 309–331.

Bickley, John T., "Dreams, Visions, and the Rhetoric of Authority", unpublished doctoral thesis, Florida State University, 2013.

Blamires, Alcuin, *The Case for Women in Medieval Culture*, Oxford: Clarendon Press, 2005.

Broomhall, Susan (ed.), *Gender and Emotions in Medieval and Early Modern Europe: Destroying Order, Structuring Disorder*, Farnham, Surrey: Ashgate, 2015.

Carroll, Shiloh, *Medievalism in* A Song of Ice and Fire *and* Game of Thrones, Woodbridge, Suffolk: D. S. Brewer, 2018.

Chibnall, Marjorie, "The Empress Matilda and Her Sons," in Parsons, John Carmi and Wheeler, Bonnie (eds), *Medieval Mothering*, New York: Garland Publishing Inc., 1996, 279–294.

Cohen, Jeffrey Jerome and Wheeler, Bonnie (eds.), *Becoming Male in the Middle Ages*, New York: Garland, 1997.

Coss, Peter, The *Lady in Medieval England*, Stroud: Sutton Publishing, 2000.

Danbury, Elizabeth, "Images of English Queens in the Later Middle Ages," *Historian* 46 (1995), 3–9.

David-Chapy, Aubrée, *Anne de France, Louise de Savoie, inventions d'un pouvoir au féminin*, Paris: Classiques Garnier, 2016.

Earenfight, Theresa, "Absent Kings: Queens as Political Partners in the Medieval Crown of Aragon", in Earenfight, Theresa (ed.), *Queenship and Political Power in Medieval and Early Modern Spain*, Burlington: Ashgate, 2005, 33–51.

Idem, *The King's Other Body: María of Castile and the Crown of Aragon*, Philadelphia: University of Pennsylvania Press, 2010.

Idem, "Medieval Queenship", *History Compass*, (2017) 15: e12372, 1–9.

Eastmond, Antony, "Gender and Orientalism in the Age of Queen Tamar", in James, Liz (ed.), *Women, Men, and Eunuchs in Byzantium*, London and New York: Routledge, 1997, 100–118.

Emig, Rainer, "Fantasy as Politics: George R. R. Martin's *A Song of Ice and Fire*", in Sedlmayr, Gerold and Waller, Nicole (eds), *Politics in Fantasy Media: Essays on Ideologies and Gender in Fiction, Film, Television, and Games*, Jefferson, NC: McFarland, 2014.

Engel, Pál, Pálosfalvi, Tamás (trans.), and Ayton, Andrew (ed.), *The Realm of St. Stephen: A History of Medieval Hungary 895–1526*, London and New York: I. B. Tauris, 2005.

Facchini, Riccardo, "'I watch it for historic reasons'. Representation and Reception of the Middle Ages in A Song of Ice and Fire and Game of Thrones", *Práticas da História*, n°4 (2017), 43–73.

Fiorilli, Carlo, "I Dipintori a Firenze nelle' Arte Dei Medici Speziali e Merciai", *Archivio Storico Italiano*, Vol. 78, No. 3 (299) (1920), 5–74.

Friedan, Betty, *The Feminine Mystique*, New York: W. W. Norton and Co., 1963.

Fuller, Timothy (ed.), *Machiavelli's Legacy:* The Prince *After Five Hundred Years*, Philadelphia: University of Pennsylvania Press, 2016.

Gallostra, Francisca Vendrell, *Violante de Bar y el Compromiso de Caspe*, Barcelona: Real Academia de Buenas Letras, 1992.

Gilbart, James William, *The History, Principles and Practice of Banking*, London: George Bell and Sons, 1919.

Grant, Lindy, *Blanche of Castile, Queen of France*, New Haven, CT and London: Yale University Press, 2016.

Hadley, Dawn M. (ed.), *Masculinity in Medieval Europe*, London: Longman, 1999.

Howell, Margaret, *Eleanor of Provence: Queenship in Thirteenth-Century England*, Oxford: Oxford University Press, 1998.

Ilardi, Vincent, *Renaissance Vision from Spectacles to Telescopes*, Philadelphia: American Philosophical Society, 2007.

Isaacs, Ann Katherine (ed.), *Political Systems and Definitions of Gender Roles*, Pisa: Edizioni Plus, Università di Pisa, 2001.

Jamison, Carol, "Reading Westeros: George R. R. Martin's Multi-Layered Medievalisms", in Fugelso, Karl (ed.), *Studies in Medievalism XXVI: Ecomedievalism*, Martlesham, Suffolk and Rochester NY: 2017, 131–142.

Jenkins, Keith, *On "What is History": From Carr and Elton to Rorty and White*, New York: Routledge, 1995.

Kain, Philip J., "Niccolò Machiavelli: Advisor of Princes", *Canadian Journal of Philosophy*, Vol. 25, N°1, (March 1995), 33–55.

Kantorowicz, Ernst H., *The King's Two Bodies. A Study in Medieval Political Theology*, Princeton NJ: Princeton University Press, 2016.

Karras, Ruth Mazo, *From Boys to Men: Formations of Masculinity in Late Medieval Europe*, Philadelphia: University of Pennsylvania Press, 2002.

Kelly, Joan, "Did Women Have a Renaissance?" in *Women, History, and Theory: The Essays of Joan Kelly* Chicago: University of Chicago Press, 1986, 19–50.

Kowaleski, Maryanne "Women's Work in a Market Town: Exeter in the Late Fourteenth Century," in Hanawalt, B.A (ed.), *Women and Work in Preindustrial Europe*, Bloomington: Indiana University Press, 1986.

Kristó, Gyula, *Az Anjou-kor háborúi* [Wars in the Age of the Angevins], Budapest: Zrínyi Kiadó, 1988.

Kruger, Stephen F., *Dreaming in the Middle Ages*, Cambridge: Cambridge University Press, 1992.

Larrington, Carolyne, *Winter is Coming: The Medieval World of Game of Thrones*, London and New York: I. B. Tauris, 2016.

Laynesmith, J. L. *The Last Medieval Queens: English Queenship 1445–1503*, Oxford: Oxford University Press, 2005.

Lewis, Katherine, *Kingship and Medieval Masculinity in Late Medieval England*, New York: Routledge, 2013.

Locke, Hilary Jane, "Beyond 'Tits and Dragons': Medievalism, Medieval History, and Perceptions in *Game of Thrones*", in Gerzic, Marina and Norrie, Aidan (eds), *From Medievalism to Early Modernism: Adapting the English Past*, Abingdon Oxon and New York: Routledge, 2019, 171–187.

Mansfield, Harvey C., *Machiavelli's Virtue*, Chicago and London: University of Chicago Press, 1998.

McCracken, Peggy, *The Romance of Adultery*, Philadelphia: University of Pennsylvania Press, 1998.

Mernissi, Fatima, *The Forgotten Queens of Islam*, Minneapolis, MN: University of Minnesota Press, 2006.

Monter, William, *The Rise of Female Kings in Europe, 1300–1800*, New Haven, CT and London: Yale University Press, 2012.

Murray, Jacqueline (ed.), *Conflicted Identities and Multiple Masculinities: Men in the Medieval West*, New York and London: Garland, 1999.

Neal, Derek G., *The Masculine Self in Late Medieval England*, Chicago and London: University of Chicago Press, 2008.

Nelson, Janet L., "Queens as Jezebels: The Careers of Brunhild and Balthild in Merovingian History," in Baker, Derek (ed.), *Medieval Women: Dedicated and Presented to Professor Rosalind M.T. Hill on the Occasion of her Seventieth Birthday*, Oxford: Oxford University Press, 1978, 31–77.

Idem, "Medieval Queenship," in Mitchell, Linda E. (ed.), *Women in Medieval Western European Culture*, New York: Garland Publishing Inc., 1999, 179–208.

Oakshott, Michael, *On History and Other Essays*, Totowa, NJ: Barnes and Noble, 1983.

Ortenberg, Veronica, *In Search of the Holy Grail: The Quest for the Middle Ages*, London: Hambledon Continuum, 2006.

Parsons, John Carmi, "The Queen's Intercession in Thirteenth-Century England", in Carpenter, Jennifer and MacLean, Sally-Beth (eds), *Power of the Weak: Studies on Medieval Women*, Urbana and Chicago: University of Illinois Press, 1990, 147–177.

Idem, "The Pregnant Queen as Counsellor and the Medieval Construction of Motherhood," in Parsons, John Carmi and Wheeler, Bonnie (eds), *Medieval Mothering*, New York: Garland Publishing Inc., 1996, 39–62.

Idem, "'Never was a body buried in England with such solemnity and honour': the burials and posthumous commemorations of English queens to 1500", in Duggan, Anne J. (ed.), *Queens and Queenship in Medieval Europe*, Woodbridge, Suffolk: Boydell Press, 1997, 317–337.

Idem, "Introduction: Family, Sex, and Power: The Rhythms of Medieval Queenship," in Parsons, John Carmi (ed.), *Medieval Queenship*, New York: St. Martin's Press, 1998, 1–2.

Idem, "Mothers, Daughters, Marriage, Power: Some Plantagenet Evidence, 1150–1500," in Parsons, John Carmi (ed.), *Medieval Queenship*, New York: St. Martin's Press, 1998, 63–78.

Idem, *Eleanor of Castile, Queen and Society in Thirteenth-Century England*, New York: Palgrave Macmillan, 1998.

Phillips Jnr., William D., *Slavery in Medieval and Early Modern Iberia*, Philadelphia: University of Pennsylvania Press, 2014.

Ponsich, Claire, "De la parole d'apaisement au reproche. Un glissement rhétorique di conseil ou l'engagement politique d'une reine d'Aragon?", *Cahiers d'études hispaniques médiévales*, n° 31, (2008), 81–117.

Poulet, Andre, "Capetian Women and the Regency," in Parsons, John Carmi (ed.), *Medieval Queenship*, New York: St. Martin's Press, 1998, 93–116.

Quercia, Jacopo della, "A Machiavellian Discourse on *Game of Thrones*", in Pavlac, Brian A. (ed.), Game of Thrones *versus History*, 33–46.

Renard, Georges, Terry, Dorothy (trans.), *Guilds in the Middle Ages*, [London: George Bell and Sons Ltd., 1918], Kitchener, ONT: Batoche Books, 2000.

Robinson, Carole L. and Clements, Pamela, (eds), *Neomedievalism in the Media: Essays on Film, Television and Electronic Games*, Lewiston, NY, Mellen, 2012.

Rohr, Zita Eva, *Yolande of Aragon (1381–1442) Family and Power: The Reverse of the Tapestry.* Basingstoke and London: Palgrave Macmillan, 2016.

Idem, "Rocking the Cradle and Ruling the World: Queens' Households in Late Medieval and Early Modern Aragon and France", in Earenfight, Theresa, *Royal and Elite Households in Medieval and Early Modern Europe: More than Just a Castle*, Leiden and Boston, Brill, 2018, 309–337.

Idem, "No Job for a Man: Fifteenth-Century France and the 'Institutionalization' of Female Regency", in Adams, Tracy, and Morand-Métivier, Charles-Louis (eds), *The Waxing of the Middle Ages: Revisiting the Late French and Burgundian Middle Ages*, Newark DE: The University of Delaware Press, expected 2020.

Russo, Emilio, *Guida all lettura della "Gerusalemme liberata" di Tasso*, Bari and Rome: Laterza, 2014.

Schulenburg, Jane Tibbetts, "Female Sanctity: Public and Private Roles, c.500–1100," in Erler, Mary and Kowaleski, Maryanne (eds), *Women and Power in the Middle Ages*, Athens GA: University of Georgia Press, 1988, 102–125.

Shadis, Miriam, "Berenguela of Castile's Political Motherhood: The Management of Sexuality, Marriage, and Succession," in Parsons, John Carmi and Wheeler, Bonnie (eds), *Medieval Mothering*, New York: Garland Publishing Inc., 1996, 335–358.

Idem, "Blanche of Castile and Facinger's 'Medieval Queenship': Reassessing the Argument," in Nolan, Kathleen (ed.), *Capetian Women*, Basingstoke UK, Palgrave Macmillan, 2003, 137–161.

Simone, Franco, Chap. 2 "La Luce della Rinascita e le Tenebre Medievali", in *La Coscienza della Rinascita negli umanista francesi*, [Rome: Edizione di Storia E Letteratura, 1949], ACLS Humanities E-Book, 2008, 27–78.

Stafford, Pauline, *Queens, Concubines and Dowagers: The King's Wife in the Early Middle Ages*, Athens, GA: University of Georgia Press, 1983, 19–24.

Idem, "Powerful Women in the Early Middle Ages: Queens and Abbesses," in Linehan, Peter and Nelson, Janet L. (eds), The *Medieval World*, London: Routledge, 2001, 398–415.

Strickland, Agnes, *Lives of the Queens of England from the Norman conquest; comp. from official records and other authentic documents, private as well as public*, Philadelphia: G. Barrie & Son, 1902–1903.

Tanner, Heather J. (ed.), *Medieval Elite Women and The Exercise of Power, 1100–1400: Moving Beyond the Exceptionalist Debate*, Cham, CH: Palgrave Macmillan, 2019.

Verlinden, Charles, *L'Esclavage dans l'Europe medieval*, 2 vols, Bruges: De Tempel, 1955 and Ghent: Rijksuniversiteit, 1977.

Vilches, Patricia and Seaman, Gerald (eds), *Seeking Real truths: Multidisciplinary Perspectives on Machiavelli*, Leiden and Boston: Brill, 2007.

Walker, Jessica, "Historical Discourses in Shakespeare and Martin", in Battista, Jes and Johnston, Susan (eds), *Mastering the Game of Thrones: Essays on George R. R. Martin's* A Song of Ice and Fire, Jefferson, NC: McFarlane Publishing, 2015, 71–91.

Ward, Jennifer, *Women in England in the Middle Ages*, London and New York: Hambledon Continuum, 2006.

Wolf, Armin, "Reigning Queens in Medieval Europe: When, Where, and Why", in Parsons, John Carmi (ed.), *Medieval Queenship*, New York: St Martin's Press, 1993, 169–188.

Young, Helen, "The Real Middle Ages: Gritty Fantasy", in idem (ed.) *Race and Popular Fantasy Literature: Habits of Whiteness*, Abingdon, UK: Routledge, 2016, 63–87.

ELECTRONIC MISCELLANY

Benjamin Breen, "Why 'Game of Thrones' Isn't Medieval—and Why that Matters", *Pacific Standard*, June 12, 2014 https://psmag.com/social-justice/game-thrones-isnt-medieval-matters-83288

Jen Chaney, "Tyrion Lannister Was the Real Winner of the Game of Thrones Finale", https://www.vulture.com/2019/05/game-of-thrones-finale-tyrion-lannister.html

Kavita Mudan Finn, "*Game of Thrones* is Based in History—Outdated History", *The Public Medievalist*, May 16, 2019, https://www.publicmedievalist.com/thrones-outdated-history/

Megan Garber, "*Game of Thrones* and the Paradox of Female Beauty", *The Atlantic*, April 25, 2016 https://www.theatlantic.com/entertainment/archive/2016/04/game-of-thones-red-woman-old-ageism/479760/

Mikal Gilmore, "George R. R. Martin: The *Rolling Stone* Interview", *Rolling Stone*, (April 23, 2014), https://www.rollingstone.com/culture/culture-news/george-r-r-martin-the-rolling-stone-interview-242487/

Erica Gonzales, "15 Times the Women of 'Game of Thrones' Ruled Season Six: Girl Power Reigned in the Seven Kingdoms", *Harper's Bazaar*, June 23, 2016: https://www.harpersbazaar.com/culture/film-tv/news/a16251/game-of-thrones-female-characters-season-6/

Natasha Hodgson, "How Game of Thrones reflects historical anxieties about women, motherhood and power", *The Conversation*, July 21, 2017: https://theconversation.com/how-game-of-thrones-reflects-historical-anxieties-about-women-motherhood-and-power-81043

Jazzfisher, "But we are not men: Female Warriors and Weaponised Femininity in *A Song of Ice and Fire* and *Game of Thrones*", *Tower of the Hawk: Scholarly Exploration of the World of George R. R. Martin*, April 7, 2015 https://hawkstower.wordpress.com/2015/04/07/but-we-are-not-men-female-warriors-and-weaponized-femininity-in-a-song-of-ice-and-fire-and-game-of-thrones/

Catherine LaSota, "'Game of Thrones' Is Suddenly All About Powerful Women Getting Their Way", *Vice*, 16 May, 2016 https://www.vice.com/en_au/article/wdbqqm/game-of-thrones-is-suddenly-all-about-powerful-women-getting-their-way

Lenny Ann Low, "*Game of Thrones* Season 6: I am Woman Hear Me Roar", *The Sydney Morning Herald*, June 22, 2016: https://www.smh.com.au/entertainment/tv-and-radio/game-of-thrones-season-6-i-am-woman-hear-me-roar-20160621-gpo8n1.html

James Poniewozik, "George R. R. Martin Interview Part 2: Fantasy and History", *Time*, April 18, 2011 http://entertainment.time.com/2011/04/18/grrm-interview-part-2-fantasy-and-history/

Joanna Robinson, "*Game of Thrones*: How Women Went From Victims to Conquerors", Vanity Fair June 26, 2016: https://www.vanityfair.com/hollywood/2016/06/game-of-thrones-winds-of-winter-recap-finale-women-power

Alyssa Rosenberg, "The arguments about women and power in 'Game of Thrones' have never been more unsettling", *The Washington Post*, August 9, 2017: https://www.washingtonpost.com/news/act-four/wp/2017/08/09/the-arguments-about-women-and-power-in-game-of-thrones-have-never-been-more-unsettling/?noredirect=on&utm_term=.afa033ad0204

Jessica Salter, "*Game of Thrones's* George RR Martin: 'I'm a feminist at heart'", *The Telegraph*, April 1, 2013: https://www.telegraph.co.uk/women/womens-life/9959063/Game-of-Throness-George-RR-Martin-Im-a-feminist.html

Paul B. Sturtevat, "Who Won *Game of Thrones?*", *The Public Medievalist*, May 23, 2019, https://www.publicmedievalist.com/who-won-game-of-thrones/

Ian Thomson, "Umberto Eco Obituary", *The Guardian*, 20 April, 2016 https://www.theguardian.com/books/2016/feb/20/umberto-eco-obituary

PART I

Queenship

A *Game of Thrones* in China: The Case of Cixi, Empress Dowager of the Qing Dynasty (1835–1908)

James J. Hudson

For viewers of the HBO television series, one of the most intriguing characters in *Game of Thrones* is Lena Headey's villainous and manipulative Cersei Lannister. From the outset of the series, we come to know Cersei as a scorned woman defined by an abusive marriage, an incestuous love affair with her brother Jaime, and the successive deaths of each of their children. Although her character's experiences are exploited for dramatic effect, they draw thought-provoking parallels with what many historical dowagers confronted during their tenures. In truth, regents and dowagers who counselled boy rulers predate historiography. From *ca.* 1478 BCE to *ca.* 1458 BCE, one of several of Egypt's female pharaohs, Hatshepsut, ruled for some 20 years as regent for the boy pharaoh Thutmose III.[1] Another example from antiquity is the influential Roman woman Cornelia Africana (d. *ca.* 115 BCE), mother of Tiberius Gracchus and Gaius Gracchus, during the height of the Roman Empire. In medieval Europe, Eleanor of Aquitaine (d. 1204) and Margaret of Anjou (d. 1482) wielded considerable

J. J. Hudson (✉)
Department of History, University of North Carolina at Pembroke, Pembroke, NC, USA

© The Author(s) 2020
Z. E. Rohr, L. Benz (eds.), *Queenship and the Women of Westeros*,
Queenship and Power, https://doi.org/10.1007/978-3-030-25041-6_1

power and influence, while Catherine II the Great (d. 1796) ruled over one of the most prosperous and dynamic periods in the history of Imperial Russia. In the interests of both fans and scholars, however, this chapter takes a perhaps unexpected turn in exploring points of convergence between the fictional Cersei Lannister and China's factual Empress Dowager Cixi, who governed China during the final years of the Qing dynasty (1861–1908).[2]

It is striking how events and characters from the fictional world of Westeros in *Game of Thrones*, with its seven diverse kingdoms, are so frequently analogous to historical empires and kingdoms of the past. The most obvious of comparisons and, according to its creator and author George R.R. Martin, the one that served as the initial inspiration for his epic series of books is the Wars of the Roses fought between the ruling houses of York and Lancaster for more than three decades in England during the fifteenth century.[3] It is perhaps in this historical conflict that we find Martin's inspiration for the character of Cersei in partisan accounts of the lives and influence of Margaret of Anjou and Elizabeth Woodville.[4]

In addition to his narrative's exploration of warring political rivals, both in the characters and the ideas they represent, are there any parallels to history outside the experience of premodern Europe? When guiding students, or possibly even fans, to understanding the role Empress Dowager Cixi played in the making of modern China, it is useful to draw comparisons to fictional characters such as Cersei in *Game of Thrones*, so that we might better recognize how dowagers such as Cixi functioned historically. Despite the fact that Martin clearly draws upon European history as the main source of inspiration for his novels, Cixi served as head of state for one of the world's most populous and dominant civilizations, and as such she became one of the most powerful women in the world. This demands an honest exploration of how the questions of queenship and authority raised by the various contributors to this volume could be applicable beyond merely the western tradition.

DOWAGERS OF IMPERIAL CHINA

With a complex history of women who have ruled as regents or dowagers, the theatre of late Imperial China serves as a unique platform for studying gendered power in global history. Empress Cixi wielded influence at court during a time when China was becoming increasingly visible to the western world and, as the last in a long tradition of regents who had advised and governed for young emperors, she represents a unique case-study for powerful female dowagers. Moreover, Cersei Lannister's very particular penchant for cruelty and shrewdness throughout the *Game of Thrones* television series offers us a point of comparison with several notorious dowagers from China's imperial history. Empress Lü Zhi (241–180 BCE) consort of the founder of the Han dynasty, Emperor Gaozu of Han, became one of the most powerful—and brutal regents of her day. The Grand Historian Sima Qian noted that Empress Lü became so jealous of her husband's preference for one of his concubines that she cut off both her hands and feet, gouged out her eyes, had her ears burned off, and gave her poison that rendered her mute. Dead, or dying, she was further humiliated by being thrown into a latrine.[5]

During the Tang dynasty, the reign of Wu Zetian, or Empress Wu as she is more commonly known, began her political career as the wife of Emperor Gaozong, seizing the reins of government for herself upon his death and ruling as China's only empress-regnant from 683 to 705 CE. Although very little is known about her reign, analysis of public and other related internal events suggest that she took significant measures to expand her empire and consolidate her power-base. Among these were her decision to relocate the capital from Chang'an to Luoyang, closer to China's geographical centre of commercial activity and the ways in which she transformed the relationship "between ruler and bureaucracy."[6] Like Cersei Lannister, Empress Wu filled her court with advisors and ministers loyal to her rather than from the ranks of the civil service, and her reign initiated a trend of autocracy that continued to evolve in subsequent centuries.[7]

Throughout China's imperial history, female regents frequently took advantage of a crisis in male leadership, when emperors were either too young or too weak to rule, or both. By the time of the Ming and Qing dynasties, "female power because of male weakness remained the single formula for the empowerment of women."[8] It was one that "predicted not only the protocol and expectations for female rulership, but also the way such rulership was framed and interpreted."[9] Moreover, having already borne children, these women were no longer required to produce offspring and, having attained legal personhood often denied to other women, dowager empresses such as Cixi fulfilled unique gender roles for their time and place. In diverse cultures, many elite mature women were endowed with legal and social privileges that differed from those of younger women, or women whose husbands were still alive, assuming gender roles more frequently applied to men. By studying the ways in which such privileged women conformed to, or transgressed, societal expectations of them we can better understand gender norms and digressions in the societies that produced these women. Likewise, in her ascent to power within the fictional world of Westeros in *Game of Thrones*, Cersei Lannister remains a consistent and dominant presence determined to challenge male rulership. This is apparent in a pivotal moment in the first season of the television series wherein Cersei warns Ned Stark that he should have taken the Iron Throne for himself when he had the chance. Her staged entrance to the scene, presented from Ned's point of view, with the sun in his eyes and Cersei looking down on him, is meant to imply her dominance and command over Ned.[10] In late Imperial China, Cixi similarly exercised political power most often reserved for men.[11]

MODES OF STATECRAFT

In terms of traditions of governance, statecraft in Imperial China can be traced to the teachings of Confucius, the basis of which, by the Han dynasty, came to constitute a kind of "Imperial Confucianism," or even an "amalgam" of Legalist-Confucian Statecraft.[12] China's "Golden Age" of philosophy also produced the Legalist political thinker, Han Fei, "China's Machiavelli,"[13] or the "Big L." Writing during the Axial Age,[14] Han Fei criticized Confucius and his disciples for their naïve doctrines of self-cultivation and benevolent rule, arguing instead for a specific body of laws to govern society with severe penalties for disobedience to be "accomplished by concentrating power in the hands of a single ruler and by adopting governmental institutions that afforded greater centralized control."[15] For the ruler, one central concept of Legalist governance was the concept of *shu*, or "administrative techniques coupled with the ruler's artful deviousness," which have been described as "Machiavellian."[16] Han Fei and his disciples would have admired how Cersei and the Lannisters shrewdly deal with their enemies and eliminate their rivals. Han Fei's distain for Confucianism, and a telling example of his philosophy, is best understood in his analogy of a wayward son constantly scolded by his parents, teachers, or neighbours, but who refuses to change his ways. According to Han Fei, the most effective remedy for such behaviour was not Confucian education, but rather the summoning of the local magistrate or government soldiers to mete out punishment, forcing the wayward son to conform. For Han Fei therefore, "the love of the parents is not enough to make children learn what is right, but must be backed up by the strict penalties of the local officials; for people by nature grow proud on love, but they listen to authority."[17] In the centuries that followed Han Fei's teachings, such thinking exerted an enormous influence on the emerging philosophy of statecraft in Imperial China and, in many respects, complements the Machiavellian-inspired rulership portrayed in *Game of Thrones*.[18]

By the twelfth century, as the primary founder of the Neo-Confucian school during the Song dynasty (960–1279), another Chinese thinker, Zhu Xi, expanded on Confucian statecraft. Historians have noted how this dynasty developed into the period in which China's governance shifted to a distinct form of autocracy that became further entrenched when the Mongols conquered China and the rest of Asia. The founders of the subsequent dynasty, the Ming, have been credited with establishing a precedent that enabled institutions "to preserve [the] power," of the ruler.[19] Consequently, by China's medieval period, imperial rule had become increasingly authoritarian—a trend not lost on intellectuals of the time.

Commenting on this a few centuries later, and in an interesting parallel to Legalist and even Machiavellian thought, the philosopher and political theorist Huang Zongxi (1610–1695), in his "Waiting for the Dawn: A Plan for the Prince," observed that the self-interest of China's rulers had become a serious hindrance to social progress because a ruler's or prince's "self-interest took the place of the common good of all-under-Heaven."[20] Huang also argued that, from the time of China's earliest mythological kings and emperors, laws were meant to serve all subjects under heaven, and had never been "laid down solely for the benefit of the ruler himself."[21] This demonstrates that, even before the time of Cixi's reign, it was obvious to many that the emperors had been abusing their power. For thinkers such as Huang Zongxi, China's entrenched bureaucracy of court ministers and civil servants became gradually displaced by overzealous autocrats fixated on maintaining familial power, which later served as a significant barrier to China's modernization.

Niccolò Machiavelli's *The Prince* brilliantly catalogues and describes the very particular political landscape of Italy during the sixteenth century and it seems to have furnished a key touchstone of inspiration for George R.R. Martin in writing his novel *A Song of Ice and Fire* and for the spin-off *Game of Thrones* HBO series.[22] Cersei's warning to Littlefinger that "power is power," certainly conjures Machiavelli but traces of such thought can also be found in the Chinese Legalist emphasis on strength and its relationship to virtue, where for the sage ruler, "Strength produces force; force produces prestige; prestige produces virtue. Virtue has its origin in strength. The sage ruler alone possesses it, and therefore he is able to transmit humaneness and rightness to all-under-Heaven."[23] As this passage suggests, Han Fei envisioned a decidedly masculine form of rulership and would have bridled were any woman to seize power for herself—real or imaginary. Throughout her reign Cixi also never hesitated to apply Legalist or even Machiavellian modes of statecraft to eliminate her rivals and assert her power.

Part of the aim of this present chapter is to establish thematic continuity with other contributions to this volume. In addition to placing *Game of Thrones* within a discourse centred on Machiavellian conceptions of power, agency and advice, set against a backdrop of medieval aesthetics, some discussions in this collection demonstrate how the *Game of Thrones* universe is actually more reflective of the early modern period, one where "the superstructure of the modern state was under construction."[24] With this in mind, even by the late nineteenth century, China's pace of industrialization trailed considerably behind Europe's or even its Eastern neighbour, Japan. Inserting China's historical place into the developing modern world has been hotly contested, with scholars fuming and at odds over what informed Europe's rise versus China's relative decline after 1800.[25]

Accordingly, although the late Qing were chronologically "modern," in some respects its governing institutions and society remained mired in the conventions of the early modern world. Were one to visit remote parts of China only a century ago, they would have encountered a world not much different from that of centuries before in Western Europe. Of all the major global powers during the industrial age, China remained considerably behind—part of the reason for its turbulent history. In comparing the European early modern period to the settings and narrative arc of *Game of Thrones*, some have argued that, in areas of science, technology, and the globalized nature of a fully commercialized economy, rather than the medieval period, the books and series actually reflect a geopolitical setting modelled on the early modern period of Europe of the seventeenth and eighteenth centuries.[26]

CIXI'S SUCCESSIONS AND THE PROBLEM OF REFORM

In contrast to Cersei in *Game of Thrones* and *A Song of Ice and Fire*, the woman who came to rule China for more than a quarter of a century, Yehonala, or Empress Cixi as she came to be known, was a middle-ranking consort who did not originate from a privileged background or family.[27]

At least from the time of the Ming emperors (1368–1644), it had become common practice for emperors to marry women from lower ranks of society to check the rise of potentially powerful women from elite families. In this way, both the Ming and Qing dynasties "applied lessons about women learned from the past by creating institutional means of preventing and monitoring powerful women."[28]

Upon the death of her husband the Xianfeng Emperor in 1861, Empress Cixi (r. 1861–1908) became regent for their five-year-old son, the Tongzhi Emperor. The Xianfeng Emperor's relatively brief reign (r. 1850–1861) had witnessed one of the most destructive civil wars in human history, the Taiping Rebellion (1850–1864). In the midst of this conflict, having barely attained 30 years of age, Xianfeng and his court fled the imperial capital in Beijing in the face of an invading British army during the Second Opium War (1856–1860).[29] Despite the limitations imposed by her social rank, Cixi had given birth to Xianfeng's only son and heir, advancing her position in the imperial harem. Before his death, Xianfeng had named Cixi's son Zaichun his heir and he succeeded Xianfeng as the Tongzhi Emperor. Xianfeng had stipulated that the child-emperor was to be guided during his minority by a council of eight ministers who witnessed and recorded Xianfeng's deathbed decree. However, just days after the emperor's death, and with the support of her carefully husbanded family members and allies, Cixi conspired against the eight ministers. One was beheaded and the others forced into either suicide or disgrace. Initially Xianfeng's primary consort, Empress Ci'an, served as co-regent with Cixi but was later deposed. Just as during the first season of the television series, Cersei mockingly dismisses her husband King Robert's written deathbed decree granting rulership to Ned Stark by way of "a piece of paper," Cixi also dismissed the regents' claim that, while on his deathbed, Xianfeng had bestowed an imperial seal on each of them certifying their legitimate regency.[30] Like Cersei, Cixi took advantage of her allies and her newly minted authority to circumvent her late husband's wishes and blaze her own trail to regency.

Ruling first as co-regent with Empress Dowager Ci'an, in the decades that followed, Cixi sidelined Ci'an and manoeuvred herself further into power by maintaining a close and strategic alliance with her late husband's brother, Prince Gong. The Xinyou Coup of 1861 became controversial because, on the surface at least, it appeared that the actions of Cixi and the other conspirators had defied the late emperor's wishes. Subsequently, interpretations of this event have evolved with some historians arguing that the groundwork for a potential coup had been laid in the years prior to Xianfeng's death, mainly because some of the policies of his appointed ministers were not popular with Cixi's camp.[31] By the time Cixi's son, the Tongzhi Emperor, came of age he had contracted syphilis and died in January 1875, leaving behind a wife, the Jiashun Empress, allegedly pregnant at the time. Since Cixi refused to designate her daughter-in-law Empress Dowager—thereby denying Tongzhi's posthumous offspring the position of heir-apparent—another succession crisis inevitably resulted. In a very *Cerseiesque* political manoeuvre, Cixi nominated the next ruler of China, her son's cousin, Zaitian, who ruled as the Guangxu Emperor until 1908.

Cixi's persona of a fawning mother driven by jealousy for her son's affections towards her daughter-in-law, Empress Jiashun, might be compared to Cersei's jealousy of her younger surviving son Tommen's relationship and marriage with the politically self-aware Lady Margaery Tyrell. Driven by her mother-in-law's disdain and cruelty towards her, Jiashun is said to have committed suicide just three months after the death of her husband. She was 20 years old and there is no record of any child, born or unborn, resulting from their union. This second succession crisis further solidified Cixi's regency.[32]

The first season of *Game of Thrones* depicts a similar crisis of succession, wherein Cersei's actions prove pivotal in securing the Lannisters' ascent to power. When Ned Stark uncovers Cersei and Jaimie Lannisters' incestuous relationship, he threatens Cersei that he will reveal the truth to her husband, King Robert. Invoking the name of Martin's first novel in the *A Song of Ice and Fire* series, *A Game of Thrones*, and the HBO series, Cersei cautions Ned against doing so, stating that "when you play the game of thrones you win or you die, there is no middle ground."[33] Cersei's threat serves as a defining statement for the trajectory of her character for the entire series, showcasing her ruthless political acumen. Just as Machiavelli counsels in *The Prince*, Cersei knows that she must at all times remain two steps ahead of her opponents and oftentimes play "dirty" to win. As we have seen, in the wake of the 1861 Xinyou Coup, and in order to secure an influential position over her son, the five-year-old Tongzhi Emperor, Cixi and her allies resorted to similar strategies of violence to achieve their ambitions.

By the end of the first *Game of Thrones* season, and largely owing to Cersei's influence, Ned has been outmanoeuvred at every turn. After King Robert is mortally wounded in hunting accident—orchestrated by Cersei—and Ned is named regent for Prince Joffrey, the Lannisters conspire to overturn Robert's wishes. In the penultimate episode of Season One, Ned is sentenced to death for treason by Joffrey before a passionate crowd—having ignored both Cersei's direction that he spare Ned and his fiancée Sansa Stark's pleas for mercy on behalf of her father.[34] How Ned meets his fate in the fictionalized world of *Game of Thrones* is but one example of many of shrewd and strategic ruthlessness succeeding in the face of nobility and idealism. Ned's removal enables the Lannisters, and ultimately Cersei, to assume control of the Iron Throne.

As portrayed in the television series, the death of a ruler, from natural causes or by other means, opens significant opportunities for a dowager to rise from the status of a mere concubine or wife, sometimes with little to no pre-existing influence, to a position of power. Just as Cersei takes advantage of King Robert's death to place her son Joffrey on the throne in *Game of Thrones*, during the late Qing dynasty Cixi used her husband-emperor's death to achieve a similar result. Cersei's political move against Ned Stark echoes the initial strategies by which Cixi eliminated most of Xianfeng's appointed regents.[35] First in 1861, and then again in 1875, when her son and his wife died within months of one another, Cixi's nomination of the Guangxu Emperor also broke from established precedent. When her son, the Tongzhi Emperor, died without heirs, the new emperor should have been chosen from the next generation of princely candidates. Instead of maintaining tradition and nominating one of her brother-in-law Prince Gong's sons as the next emperor, Cixi forced the appointment of her nephew, Zaitian (who was of the same generation as her late son), the Guangxu Emperor (whose name, and official title of office, is translated as "Glorious Succession").[36]

Familial tensions between the Starks and the Lannisters illustrate how characters such as Cersei and Ned represent divergent political philosophies. Ned fits the classic trope of a noble warrior and loyal officer, committed to moral ideals of justice, honesty, and mercy. Though cast as the series' villains, and unfailingly ruthless, Cersei and her family typify a more pragmatic, and ultimately Machiavellian, form of leadership. At this and other moments in the television series, viewers must try to grapple with how the ideals of Ned and the Stark family, ones that we usually associate with heroes and heroines, are no match for the brutal realities of political intrigue and governance, while the Lannisters show themselves to be masters in the application of Machiavellian realpolitik and possessors of political *virtù*.[37]

Ned's embrace of the classic narrative tropes of heroism, idealism, and justice are the very things that lead to his undoing. When Cersei warns Ned that to play the game of thrones, one must "play to win," she is evoking the classic, yet much misunderstood, Machiavellian dictum of "when to do wrong the right way."[38] A similar fate befalls Jon Snow at the end of Season Five, when his comrades in the Night's Watch betray him. He is subsequently murdered for trying to broker peace with their sworn enemies, the Wildlings, who live north of the wall, and with whom the Night's Watch have been fighting for centuries. Although he is later magically resurrected, Jon is another example of a character in the series undone by his own ideals and virtues.

We similarly find examples of the defeat of idealism late in Cixi's regency. By the summer of 1898, the young Emperor Guangxu, by then of age, initiated the Hundred Days of Reform. Largely inspired by the influence of reform-minded intellectuals courted by Guangxu, these were a series of sweeping measures meant to modernize Chinese society and secure its membership of the global community of industrialized nineteenth-century nation states. However, Cixi famously put an end to the movement by placing Guangxu under house arrest and into exile, and ordering six of the most prominent reformers executed.[39] Both at the time and in the decades that followed, historical accounts in China and the West pointed to this episode as one instance among many of the corrupt and despotic nature of imperial rule. Empress Dowager Cixi, they reasoned, had used her authority to rule China from "behind the curtain," side-lining the young emperor by staging a palace coup. Nevertheless, reassessments of this period have pointed out that the young emperor was equally to blame for the reform's failures and, that in acting too impulsively, he only "provoked fear, resentment, and resistance among officials, anything but conducive to the joint effort he had hoped for."[40] Seen in this light, Guangxu's inexperience and overzealousness could be viewed as a fusion of the characters of Cersei's offspring, Princes Joffrey and Tommen, in the television series.

Cersei's ability to outmanoeuvre Ned Stark who, in the best of all possible worlds, ought to have become king, represents the same zealous and autocratic spirit by which Cixi defeated the Hundred Days of Reform. Although later raised from the dead, Jon Snow was murdered for his ideals and, in some ways he is analogous to late Qing dynasty reformers such as Tan Sitong (1865–1898), one of the six intellectuals who were publically executed on Cixi's orders. The reforms proposed by the young Emperor Guangxu, and the intellectuals who endorsed them, reflected a certain moral and economic vision for China's future and for its potential development into a modern nation state. Yet, their efforts failed, crushed by Cixi's insistence on maintaining the status quo, aided by her ability to outmanoeuvre the reformist camp.

In 1900, only two years following the defeat of the Hundred Days of Reform, the anti-foreigner Boxer Rebellion swept through northern China, resulting in the deaths of hundreds of missionaries and other westerners. Eager to maintain popular support within the empire, Cixi sided with the Boxers, an indigenous rebel group skilled in martial arts, who believed that through their faith in spirit possession they were literally bulletproof. Although maligned in the West, they enjoyed enthusiastic support in communities throughout North-Eastern China.[41] Understood in this way, Cixi's support of them is quite understandable, and is in some ways comparable to Cersei's support of the Faith Militant in Season Five. The insurgent quality of the Boxers also makes them similar to the rebel group, the Sons of the Harpy, with whom Daenerys must contend in the same season. Cersei's support of the High Sparrow and the Faith Militant ultimately backfires, reflective of how, in supporting the Boxers, Cixi had essentially ignored the advice of all her top ministers, including the young emperor who viewed her judgment in the matter as being "dangerously out of touch with reality."[42] An international, combined European and American force was sent to quell the uprising, and thousands of Chinese were killed in the process. Cixi and the rest of the imperial court fled Beijing in humiliation. In the following decade, during the last years of her life, Cixi eventually supported some of the very initiatives she had opposed just a few years earlier, agreeing to reform the government, as well as efforts to modernize the education system, and strengthen the military. However, these proved essentially futile and came too late to make any lasting impact.

As in life, Cixi's death was not without controversy and her legacy and afterlife remain contentious. Her death on November 15, 1908 followed the sudden death the day before of the 37-year-old Guangxu Emperor. Cixi had appointed Guangxu's infant nephew Puyi (aged two years and ten months) his heir, and he was to be China's last emperor.[43] At the time, rumours circulated that Cixi might have been responsible for the death of Guangxu. In 2008, an examination of his exhumed remains revealed traces of arsenic more than 2000 times greater than normal levels, evidence perhaps that Guangxu had been poisoned, which some scholars have dismissed as mere "conjecture."[44] Commenting on King Joffrey's death by poison at the beginning of season four of *Game of Thrones*, Sandor Clegane, known as "The Hound," remarks that, "poison is a woman's weapon."[45] This is confirmed when we learn later that Lady Olenna Tyrell orchestrated Joffrey's poisoning. Were this the case with Cixi in 1908, any reassessments of her legacy should be informed by the knowledge that she might well have been responsible for Guangxu's death.

In Season Seven of *Game of Thrones*, while gloating over the capture of Ellaria and Tyrene Sand from Dorn, who were responsible for the death of Cersei and Jaime's daughter Myrcella, Cersei tells them, "I lie in bed and I stare at the canopy, and imagine ways of killing my enemies."[46] Cixi might well have been thinking along the same lines while lying on her deathbed. Whatever the case, casting Cixi as a contemptuous figure, responsible for China's decline, remains the dominant interpretation of her legacy, even appearing in textbooks, one of which states that Cixi was "selfish and ignorant," for suppressing the reform movement in 1898, and that she had failed her country at a time when it needed "bold, risk-taking leadership."[47] Her legacy therefore has been and will continue to be debated, perhaps because, in a history as turbulent and controversial as modern China's, there will always be plenty of blame to go around.

In its final years, the Qing dynasty remained mired in entropy grinding inevitably towards collapse, with the court finally abdicating on February 12, 1912. In the months that followed, those who founded China's first republic also failed to establish a stable regime grounded on the principles of constitutionalism and representative government. Their hopes and ideals were vanquished by a motley collection of warlords and would-be presidents, each playing a "game of thrones" to win, exerting an enormous toll on Chinese society from which it took decades to recover.

CHALLENGING RACIAL AND GENDER NORMS

As a leader forged in the crucible of early modern statecraft, thrust into a rapidly changing and globalizing modern world, Cixi challenged both gender and political norms, not only due to her status as secondary consort, but also because her dynasty was the product of a foreign ruling power in China, the Manchus. Originally a conglomeration of steppe-based nomadic ethnic groups, the Manchus came to power in the mid-seventeenth century following the conquests of Nurachi (r. 1616–1626) who became the founding emperor of the dynasty. In contrast to Han women—the dominant ethnic group of China—Manchu women enjoyed considerable freedoms. They did not adhere to the dominant social custom of foot binding, they socialized outside the household, they hunted, and, in some cases, served as military leaders. Such freedoms also extended to the imperial harem. In contrast to the practices of the preceding Ming dynasty, the Qing ended the practice of "serial monogamy," and under the Qing, any one of the emperor's concurrent consorts could produce a legitimate heir. Throughout its reign, the Qing state also experienced a number of periods of regency—all with women serving as regents, empress dowagers, or both, assuming active roles in each.[48] During her adolescence, Cixi had been fortunate enough to have found her way into the imperial harem, which ultimately resulted in her giving birth to and providing the dynasty with its only legitimate direct male heir.

Unlike the Manchus, Han women were expected to abide by and follow traditional Confucian values, which enforced traditional gender roles and confined women to the "inner quarters" of the household. Throughout the course of their life stages they were subject to the "three obediences": to one's father as a child; to one's husband when married; and, to one's eldest son during old age.[49] Hence, throughout the empire, from the time the Manchus conquered the Han, the lack of adherence to these traditional values, but especially due to their status as alien rulers, the Manchus were resented by the subjugated Han.[50] That Cixi became the head of state of a foreign ruling dynasty, one whose customs and practices challenged the gender norms of the majority of China's population, made her a source of derision for many. Further informing such disdain was the fact that most of the reformers she had purged in 1898 were ethnically Han, and that many Manchus had sided with the rebel Boxers in 1900.[51]

Although in some respects progressive in how it portrays strong female characters, *Game of Thrones* has been scrutinized for its graphic depictions of nudity, sex, and violence against women. Focusing on issues such as gender stereotypes, feminism, and graphic depictions of rape, some studies in particular have critically discussed the series' at times controversial and exploitive portrayal of women.[52] More troubling perhaps is the way in which, throughout the series, female characters are frequently portrayed as oversexed or sensual. Moreover, many female characters in *Game of Thrones* are also representative of certain orientalist tropes that portray women in power, vis-à-vis Cersei, conjuring images of the wicked "empress dowager," a stereotype based at least in part on strong female rulers like Cixi and other controversial dowagers throughout history. Cersei is a fascinating character who challenges normative constructs of male-gendered power, but she is also representative of certain kinds of inherently flawed medieval representations of women, ones associated with orientalist othering, the male gaze, and the patriarchy. Cersei is portrayed as ruthless, oversexed, power hungry, and manipulative. In this volume, Kavita Mudan Finn makes the cogent observation that "the problem with Cersei Lannister is not that she conforms to negative medieval stereotypes; it is that Martin—and the HBO producers—insist on incorporating all of those stereotypes at once."[53] Despite such stereotypes, much of the plot lines of the later seasons served to highlight the experiences of its two main female protagonists—Cersei and Daenerys. But this is also the reason why the series finale from the much-anticipated end of Season Eight proved so disappointing; these two characters were never really given a genuine opportunity to confront one another. Both Cersei and Jaime perish following Daenerys's decision to "turn heel" and burn King's Landing to the ground, leaving Cersei's fate, as well as fans' expectations of a satisfying conclusion to a beloved series, beneath the rubble of the Red Keep.[54]

In the years following her death, some popular orientalist literature published in the West by J.O. Bland and Edmund Backhouse, respectively, *China Under the Empress Dowager* (1910) and *Annals and Memoirs of the Court of Peking* (1914), became bestsellers and helped shape Cixi's image as a despot within the western imagination. However, history has not been kind to Backhouse for it has been revealed that at least some of his "facts" were entirely fabricated.[55] More troubling still is that the recent official publication of Backhouse's memoir, written towards the end of his life, provides explicit and highly eroticized details of a concocted and completely fanaticized sexual relationship between him and the empress.[56] The story of Backhouse is one of many outrageous accounts of western imperialism run amok in the colonized world portrayed by fantasist, sexually adventurous men with a perverted vision of life in the "Orient."

Edmund Backhouse's fantasy of a lurid and even pornographic sexual encounter with the empress is also an example of how, at least for some in the West, Cixi became a source for Orientalist "otherings" of both China and the personification of decadent female power. This is especially true when one considers the dominant role of West's presence in China throughout the nineteenth century. In the schema of such colonial encounters, roles of gender and sex have stood at the forefront of exotic or perverse constructions of the "other," whereby within "any cross-cultural encounter, gender roles and sexuality supply a medium for clarifying and symbolizing the essential cultural differences that separate 'us' from 'them'."[57] Such encounters were viewed via the male gaze and the patriarchal desire to dominate and sexualize non-western women.

Although fictional, Cersei's situation resembles the plight of Cixi and other dowagers because all were obliged to work within a political framework constructed and dominated by men. In this regard, "Most of the female characters in *Game of Thrones* find themselves either the only woman or one of few women surrounded by men in male-centric situations."[58] In retrospect, it seems that during Cixi's reign she similarly acted alone and against the interests of powerful men. Originally a concubine of her eventual father-in-law, the Daoguang Emperor, she became empress-regent by virtue of her sexual relationship with his son and heir, the Xianfeng Emperor, producing his only surviving son. Cixi then conspired to eliminate or depose each of the men appointed governing regents by her late husband. By the time her son was old enough and fit enough to rule, Cixi's jealousy for his affections might have driven his young wife to suicide. At this point in her career, Cixi again took advantage of the ensuing political vacuum to advance her own interests. We can also recognize certain aspects of such proactive female agency in the way in which Cersei claims the Iron Throne in the television series. At the end of Season Six, confronted with the death of all three of her children, Cersei has no narrative choice but to scramble to the top of her dynasty's hierarchy—"to win or die" politically. Similarly, Cixi lost her emperor-husband, then her only son, then her daughter-in-law perhaps pregnant with her son's heir, thereafter using every means at her disposal to continue her regency and suppressing the reform movement by executing some of its main proponents.

CONCLUSION

Both within the books and television series, much of the storyline of *Game of Thrones* concerned itself with the ways in which dynasties come to and maintain power during periods of instability. What serves as a key connecting point between the events of actual history and the narrative of a popular television and literary phenomenon is the degree to which reigning dynasties either maintain power or succumb to the pressure of popular resistance. Discussing Cersei Lannister, a character from a popular novel and television series, in the context of the historical Empress Dowager Cixi, offers fans and scholars an opportunity to learn about a prominent non-western female head of state. Especially for scholars, it offers a new lens for those seeking fresher and more innovative world history pedagogies. Cixi's regency contains all the elements of a *Game of Thrones* storyline: palace coups, poison and, most importantly, a woman driven by unchecked political ambition. This chapter draws from the work of some of the most prominent scholars specializing in the history of late Imperial China as well as recent work by scholars from diverse fields who have contributed their own fascinating research on the connection of *Game of Thrones* to history. This study has sought to create a narrative understanding of Cixi's regency, and its discussion of Cersei can easily be weighed against, and compared to, the agency of other historical dowagers in global histories. Many other aspects of both the book and television series await analysis and comparison to an impressive catalogue of historical moments and identities.

Especially as the series neared its conclusion, Cersei's creators situated her within the classic literary trope of the villain who must be undone and conquered by the forces of good, divesting her of any possible sympathy we might have had for her when the series began. Cersei's signature moment of villainy came at the end of Season Six, when she conspired to destroy the Sept of Baelor with explosives. However, the penultimate moment of her cruelty was the decision to behead Missandei in the final season, incurring Daenerys's wrath, hard on the heels of the death of her dragon Rhaegal, which led to the eventual destruction of King's Landing. By ordering the execution of the Tongzhi Emperor's appointed regents in 1861, and members of the reform movement in 1898, Cixi displayed a similar penchant for cruelty. It is possible that her ruthlessness remained with her to the very end of her life, as she may have conspired to have her nephew poisoned in 1908. Even if this were not the case, her agency and ambition transcend anything conceived of in the world of fiction, confronting historians and other scholars with a reality that will continue to invite further explanation and interpretation.

NOTES

1. On the subject of Hatshepsut (and other female pharaohs), see Aidan Norrie's recent overview wherein he advises us to consult Kara Cooney, *The Woman Who Would Be King: Hatshepsut's Rise to Power in Ancient Egypt* (New York: Crown Publishers, 2014); Joyce Tyldesley, *Chronicle of the Queens of Egypt: From Early Dynastic Times to the Death of Cleopatra* (London: Thames and Hudson, 2006); idem, *Hatchepsut: The Female*

Pharaoh (London: Penguin, 1996); Catharine H. Roehrig, (ed.), *Hatshepsut: From Queen to Pharaoh* (New York: The Metropolitan Museum of Art, 2005). Aidan Norrie, "Female Pharaohs in Ancient Egypt," in Elena Woodacre, Lucinda Dean, Chris Jones, Russell Martin, and Zita Rohr (eds), *The Routledge History of Monarchy: New Perspectives on Rulers and Rulership* (Abingdon, UK: Routledge, 2019), 501–517, 514.

2. In this chapter, the usage of the terms "dowager," and "regent," refer to designations applicable to both Cixi during the Qing dynasty, and Cersei Lannister in *Game of Thrones*. Both were dowagers because they were widowed and both were regents because they advised young emperors or kings. In Mandarin, Cixi's name is the pinyin Romanization of the two-character compound "慈禧," which can be pronounced "Tse—Shee."

3. George R.R. Martin, interviewed by Mikal Gilmore, "George R.R. Martin: The Rolling Stone Interview: the novelist goes deep on the future of his books and the TV series they begat," *Rolling Stone*/ https://www.rolling-stone.com/culture/culture-news/george-r-r-martin-the-rolling-stone-interview-242487/, April 23, 2014. For an excellent account and analysis of the Wars of the Roses consult Michael Hicks, *The Wars of the Roses* (New Haven, CT: Yale University Press), 2012.

4. Kavita Mudan Finn, "Queen of Sad Mischance: Medievalism, 'Realism,' and the Case of Cersei Lannister," in Zita Eva Rohr and Lisa Benz (eds), *Queenship and the Women of Westeros: Female Agency and Advice in* Game of Thrones *and* A Song of Ice and Fire (Basingstoke, UK: Palgrave Macmillan, 2019), 29–52.

5. Thomas R. Martin (ed.), "A Woman in Power: Empress Lu," in *Herodotus and Sima Qian, The First Great Historians of Greece and China: A Brief History with Documents* (New York: Bedford/St. Martins, 2010), Chapter 10, "A Woman in Power: Empress Lu," 105–114, 106–107; and, William H. Nienhauser Jnr (ed.), *The Grand Scribe's Records Volume IX: The Memoirs of Han China Part II by Ssu-ma-Ch'ien* (Bloomington, IN: Indiana University Press, 2010), 269.

6. Mark Edward Lewis, *China's Cosmopolitan Empire: The Tang Dynasty* (Cambridge: Harvard University Press, 2009), 38. See also Denis Twitchett, "Kao-tsung (reign 649–83) and the Empress Wu: The Inheritor and the Usurper," in *Cambridge History of China*, Vol. 3, *Sui and T'ang China, Part I*, Denis Twitchett and John K. Fairbank (eds), (Cambridge: Cambridge University Press, 1979).

7. Lewis, *China's Cosmopolitan Empire*, 38.

8. Keith McMahon, "Women Rulers in Imperial China," *Nan Nu* 15-2 (2013), 179–218, 201–202.

9. Ibid.

10. *Game of Thrones*, Season 1, Episode 7, "You Win or You Die," Directed by Daniel Minahan/Written by David Benioff and D.B. Weiss, aired May 29, 2011, on HBO.

11. Cf. Sue Fawn Chung, "The Much Maligned Empress Dowager Tz'u-hsi," *Modern Asian Studies*, 13:2 (1979), 177–196.

12. John King Fairbank and Merle Goldman, *China: A New History* (Cambridge: Belknap Press, 2006), 62.

13. Ryan Mitchell, "Is China's 'Machiavelli' Now Its Most Important Political Philosopher?" *The Diplomat*, January 16, 2015. https://thediplomat.com/2015/01/is-chinas-machiavelli-now-its-most-important-political-philosopher

14. A term coined by the German philosopher Karl Jaspers (d. 1969), the Axial or Axis Age represents a "pivotal age" characterized the period of ancient history from about the eighth to the third century BCE. According to Jaspers's concept, new ways of thinking appeared in Persia, India, China and the Greco-Roman world in religion and philosophy in a striking parallel development, without any obvious direct cultural contact between all of the participating Eurasian cultures. See Karl Jaspers, *Origin and Goal of History* (Abingdon, UK: Routledge Revivals, [1949], 2010), 2–3, 8–21.

15. Han Feizi, Chapter 7, "Legalists and Militarists," in William Theodore de Bary and Irene Bloom et al. (eds.), *Sources of Chinese Tradition, 2nd ed. Vol. I: From Earliest Times to 1600* (New York: Columbia University Press, 1999), 190.

16. Zhao Dingxin, *The Confucian-Legalist State: A New Theory of Chinese History* (Oxford: Oxford University Press, 2015), 186.

17. Han Feizi, "Legalists and Militarists," 201.

18. On the subject of Machiavelli, *Game of Thrones*, and *A Song of Ice and Fire* see Marcus Schulzke, "Playing the Game of Thrones: Some Lessons from Machiavelli," 33–48; and David Hahn, "The Death of Lord Stark: The Perils of Idealism," 75–86, both in Henry Jacoby (ed.), Game of Thrones *and Philosophy: Logic Cuts Deeper Than Swords* (Hoboken, NJ: John Wiley and Sons, 2012); Jacopo della Quercia, "A Machiavellian Discourse on *Game of Thrones*," in Brian A. Pavlac (ed.), Game of Thrones *versus History: Written in Blood* (Hoboken, NJ: Wiley Blackwell, 2017), 33–46; and Elizabeth Beaton, "Female Machiavellians in Westeros," in Anne Gjelsvik and Rikke Schubart (eds), *Women of Ice and Fire: Gender*, Game of Thrones, *and Multiple Media Engagements* (New York-London-Oxford: Bloomsbury, 2016), 193–218.

19. Timothy Brook, *The Troubled Empire: China in the Yuan and Ming Dynasties* (Cambridge: Harvard University Press, 2010), 86–87. See also Edward Farmer, *Zhu Yuanzhang and Early Ming Legislation: The*

Reordering of Chinese Society Following the Era of Mongol Rule (Leiden: Brill, 1995).

20. Huang Zongxi, "Waiting for the Dawn: A Plan for the Prince," compiled by William Theodore de Bary and Richard Lufrano (eds), *Sources of Chinese Tradition, Vol II, 2nd ed., From 1600 Through the Twentieth Century* (New York: Columbia University Press, 2000), 6.

21. Ibid., 10.

22. Quercia, "A Machiavellian Discourse," 38.

23. Han Feizi, 'The Guanzi' "Legalists and Militarists," 197. And, for Cersei's warning to Littlefinger: *Game of Thrones*, Season 2, Episode 1, "The North Remembers," Directed by Alan Taylor/Written by David Benioff and D.B. Weiss, aired April 1, 2012 on HBO.

24. Zita Rohr and Lisa Benz (eds), "Introduction," in *Queenship, and the Women of Westeros*.

25. Scholars, such as Kenneth Pomeranz, have stressed that China lacked the necessary coal reserves that fuelled England's industrial revolution. Others, such as Philip Huang, have argued that China's inability to industrialize was just as much attributable to the involuted nature of its agriculture. See Kenneth Pomeranz, *The Great Divergence: China, Europe, and the Making of the Modern World Economy* (Princeton: Princeton University Press, 2001). For Huang's rebuttal of this book, see Philip C.C. Huang, "Development or Involution in Eighteenth Century Britain and China? A Review of Kenneth Pomeranz's, *The Great Divergence: China, Europe, and the Making of the Modern World Economy*," *The Journal of Asian Studies* Vol. 61, No. 2 (May 2002), 501–538.

26. Benjamin Breen, "Why Game of Thrones Isn't Medieval—And Why That Matters," June 12, 2014, *Pacific Standard* (accessed January 26, 2019 at https://psmag.com/social-justice/game-thrones-isnt-medieval-matters-83288). Also cited in Mat Hardy, "The Eastern Question," in Brian A. Pavlac (ed.), Game of Thrones *versus History: Written in Blood* (Hoboken, NJ: Wiley Blackwell, 2017), 108.

27. Evelyn Rawski, *The Last Emperors: A Social History of Qing Imperial Institutions* (Berkeley: University of California Press, 1998), 133.

28. Keith McMahon, "Women Rulers in Imperial China," *Nan Nu* 15-2 (2013), 179–218, 212.

29. Stephen R. Platt, *Autumn in the Heavenly Kingdom: China, the West, and the Epic Story of the Taiping Civil War* (New York: Alfred A. Knopf, 2012), 216–217.

30. Luke S.K. Kwong, "Imperial Authority in Crisis: An Interpretation of the Coup D'état of 1861," *Modern Asian Studies*, Vol. 17, No. 2 (1983), 222–223.

31. Ibid., 223.

32. Orville Schell and John Delury, "Western Methods, Chinese Core: Empress Dowager Cixi," in *Wealth and Power: China's Long March to the Twenty-first Century* (New York: Random House, 2013), 67.

33. *Game of Thrones*, Episode 7, "You Win or You Die," Directed by Daniel Minahan/Written by David Benioff and D.B. Weiss, aired May 29, 2011 on HBO.

34. *Game of Thrones*, Episode 9, "Baelor," Directed by Alan Taylor/Written by David Benioff and D.B. Weiss, aired June 12, 2011 on HBO.

35. Cersei, however, stopped short of calling for Ned's execution. She and Sansa both plead for mercy on his behalf, which Joffrey, the teenaged political novice, ignored.

36. Li Yuhuang and Harriet T. Zurndorfer, "Rethinking Empress Dowager Cixi through the Production of Art," in *Nan Nu* 14 (2012), 3. See also, Liu Kwang-Ching, "The Ch'ing Restoration," in John K. Fairbank (ed.), *The Cambridge History of China, vol. 10: The Late Ch'ing*, Part 1 (Cambridge: Cambridge University Press, 1978), 409–490.

37. See Beaton, "Female Machiavellians in Westeros," 171–192, esp. the section, "The Court Machiavellian" (Cersei), 199–204. See also reactions to the political career of Catherine de' Medici, R. J. Knecht, *Catherine de' Medici* (Abingdon, UK: Routlege, 2014), 164, 177; and, for a discussion and analysis of Machiavelli and his theoretical concept of political *virtù* see Martyn de Bruyn, "Machiavelli and the Politics of Virtù," unpublished doctoral thesis, Purdue University, West Lafayette IN, USA, 2003.

38. Querica, "A Machiavellian Discourse," 38–41.

39. Jonathan Spence, *The Search for Modern China*, 3rd ed. (New York: W.W. Norton and Company, 2013), 221.

40. Luke S.K. Kwong, "Chinese Politics at the Crossroads: Reflections on the Hundred Days Reform of 1898," *Modern Asian Studies*, Vol. 34, No. 3 (July 2000), 670.

41. Joseph W. Esherick, *The Origins of the Boxer Uprising* (Berkeley: University of California Press, 1987), 289.

42. Pamela Crossley, "In the Hornet's Nest," review of *Empress Dowager Cixi: The Concubine Who Launched Modern China* by Jung Chang, *The London Review of Books*, April 9, 2014. Crossley's review contains a brief and informative scholarly treatment of Cixi.

43. William A. Joseph, *Politics in China: An Introduction* (Oxford: Oxford University Press, 2010), 47–50.

44. Louisa Lim, "Who Murdered China's Emperor a 100 years ago," NPR, https://www.npr.org/templates/story/story.php?storyId=96993694. November 14, 2008. Orville Schell and John Delury seem to dismiss the theory that she was behind the poisoning. See Orville Schell and John Delury, "Western Methods, Chinese Core: Empress Dowager Cixi," in

Wealth and Power: China's Long March to the Twenty-first Century (New York: Random House, 2013), 87. Astonishingly high levels of arsenic and other toxins have been found in exhumed remains once tested by modern technologies (such as the famous case of Agnès Sorel (d. 1450), official favourite of Charles VII of France). See Philippe Charlier, "Qui a tué la Dame de la Beauté? Étude scientifique des restes d'Agnès Sorel (1422–1450),"
*Histoire des Sciences Médicales,*Tome XL, N°3 (2006), 255–263. Charlier's telling phrase of the inconclusiveness of such investigations: "Ainsi l'empoisonnement d'Agnès a été confirmé […] mais nul ne peut dire si celui-ci est volontaire [surdose de mercure] ou non [meurtre par poison]" (Thus the poisoning of Agnès Sorel has been confirmed ... but no one can say if it was unintentional [an overdose of prescribed mercury] or deliberate [murder by poisoning]), 262. http://www.biusante.parisdescartes.fr/sfhm/hsm/HSMx2006x040x003/HSMx2006x040x003x0255.pdf accessed February 10, 2019. Arsenic, lead, and mercury were used routinely in complexion refining and whitening cosmetics as well as in medical therapies such as for the treatment of intestinal parasites like the painful and debilitating condition suffered by Agnès Sorel whose doses of mercury were increased over a number of years to dangerous levels due to acquired immunity and the extreme pain she suffered. She also used dangerous compounds containing arsenic, lead, and mercury to whiten her complexion.

45. *Game of Thrones*, Season 4, Episode 8, "The Mountain and the Viper," Directed by Alex Graves/Written by David Benioff and D.B. Weiss, aired June 1, 2014 on HBO.

46. *Game of Thrones*, Season 7, Episode 3, "The Queen's Justice," Directed by Mark Mylod/Written by David Benioff and D.B. Weiss, aired July 30, 2017 on HBO.

47. Patricia Buckley Ebrey, *The Cambridge Illustrated History of China* (London: Cambridge University Press, 1996), 254. For revisionist accounts of Cixi's life and reign, see also Jung Chang, *Empress Dowager Cixi: The Concubine Who Launched Modern China* (New York: Alfred A. Knopf, 2013), and Sterling Seagrave, *Dragon Lady: The Life and Legend of the Last Empress of China* (New York: Vintage Books, 1993).

48. Evelyn Rawski, *The Last Emperors: A Social History of Qing Imperial Institutions* (Berkeley: University of California Press, 1998), 128–129, 132.

49. Patricia Ebrey, *The Inner Quarters: Marriage and the Lives of Chinese Women in the Sung Period* (Berkeley: University of California Press, 1993), 50.

50. Edward J.M. Rhoads, *Manchus and Han: Ethnic Relations and Political Power in Late Qing and Early Republican China, 1861–1928* (Seattle: University of Washington Press, 2000), 68.

51. Ibid., 71.
52. See Valerie Estelle Frankel, *Women in Game of Thrones: Power, Conformity, Resistance* (Jefferson: McFarland and Company, 2014).
53. Kavita Mudan Finn, "Queen of Sad Mischance: Medievalism, 'Realism,' and the Case of Cersei Lannister," in Rohr and Benz (eds.) *Queenship and the Women of Westeros*, 29–52.
54. *Game of Thrones*, Season 8, Episode 5, "The Bells," Directed by Miguel Sapochnik/Written by David Benioff and D.B. Weiss, aired May 12, 2019 on HBO. On Daenerys' "heel turn," see Randall Colburn, "So did *Game of Thrones* earn that turn or not?," May 13, 2019, *AV Club* (accessed May 27, 2019 at https://news.avclub.com/so-did-game-of-thrones-earn-that-or-not-1834723024).
55. See Hugh Trevor Roper, *The Hermit of Peking: The Hidden Life of Sir Edmond Backhouse* (London: Elan Books, 2011).
56. Edmund Trelawny Backhouse, *Decadence Mandchoue: The China Memoirs of Sir Edmund Trelawny Backhouse*, ed. Derek Sandhaus (Hong Kong: Earnshaw Books, 2011).
57. Susan L. Mann, *Gender and Sexuality in Modern Chinese History* (New York: Cambridge University Press, 2011), 169.
58. Kavita Mudan Finn, "High and Mighty Queens of Westeros," in Brian A. Pavlac (ed.), Game of Thrones *versus History: Written in Blood* (Hoboken, NJ: Wiley Blackwell, 2017), 28.

BIBLIOGRAPHY

Backhouse, Edmund Trelawny. *Decadence Mandchoue: The China Memoirs of Sir Edmund Trelawny Backhouse*, edited by Derek Sandhaus. Hong Kong: Earnshaw Books, 2011.

Bary, William Theodore de, and Bloom, Irene, et al (eds), *Sources of Chinese Tradition, 2nd ed. Vol. 1: From Earliest Times to 1600*. New York: Columbia University Press, 1999.

Beaton, Elizabeth. "Female Machiavellians in Westeros." In *Women of Ice and Fire: Gender, Game of Thrones, and Multiple Media Engagements*, edited by Anne Gjelsvik and Rikke Schubart. New York-London-Oxford: Bloomsbury, 2016.

Breen, Benjamin. "Why Game of Thrones Isn't Medieval—And Why That Matters." *Pacific Standard*, June 12, 2014. Accessed January 26, 2019 at https://psmag.com/social-justice/game-thrones-isnt-medieval-matters-83288.

Brook, Timothy. *The Troubled Empire: China in the Yuan and Ming Dynasties*. Cambridge: Harvard University Press, 2010.

Bruyn, Martyn de, "Machiavelli and the Politics of Virtù." PhD diss., Purdue University, 2003.

Chang, Jung. *Empress Dowager Cixi: The Concubine Who Launched Modern China*. New York: Alfred A. Knopf, 2013.

Charlier, Phillippe. "Qui a tué la Dame de la Beauté? Étude scientifique des restes d'Agnès Sorel (1422–1450)." *Histoire des Sciences Médicales*, Tome XL, N°3, (2006), 255–263.

Chung, Sue Fawn. "The Much Maligned Empress Dowager Tz'u-Hsi." *Modern Asian Studies*, 13:2 (1979), 177–196.

Cooney, Kara. *The Woman Who Would Be King: Hatshepsut's Rise to Power in Ancient Egypt*. New York: Crown Publishers, 2014.

Crossley, Pamela. "In the Hornet's Nest." Review of *Empress Dowager Cixi: The Concubine Who Launched Modern China* by Jung Chang. *The London Review of Books*, April 9, 2014.

Ebrey, Patricia Buckley. *The Cambridge Illustrated History of China*. London: Cambridge University Press, 1996.

Ebrey, Patricia Buckley. *The Inner Quarters: Marriage and the Lives of Chinese Women in the Sung Period*. Berkeley: University of California Press, 1993.

Esherick, Joseph W. *The Origins of the Boxer Uprising*. Berkeley: University of California Press, 1987.

Fairbank, John King, and Merle Goldman. *China: A New History*. Cambridge: Belknap Press, 2006.

Farmer, Edward. *Zhu Yuanzhang and Early Ming Legislation: The Reordering of Chinese Society Following the Era of Mongol Rule*. Leiden: Brill, 1995.

Finn, Kavita Mudan. "Queen of Sad Mischance: Medievalism, 'Realism,' and the Case of Cersei Lannister." In *Queenship and the Women of Westeros: Female Agency and Advice in Game of Thrones and A Song of Ice and Fire*, edited by Zita Eva Rohr and Lisa Benz. Basingstoke, UK: Palgrave Macmillan, 2019.

Finn, Kavita Mudan. "High and Mighty Queens of Westeros." In Game of Thrones *versus History: Written in Blood*, edited by Brian A. Pavlac. Hoboken: Wiley Blackwell, 2017.

Frankel, Valerie Estelle. *Women in* Game of Thrones: *Power, Conformity, Resistance*. Jefferson: McFarland and Company, 2014.

Gjelsvik, Anne and Rikke Schubart, eds. *Women of Ice and Fire: Gender,* Game of Thrones, *and Multiple Media Engagements*. New York-London-Oxford: Bloomsbury, 2016.

Hahn, David. "The Death of Lord Stark: The Perils of Idealism." In Game of Thrones *and Philosophy: Logic Cuts Deeper Than Swords*, edited by Henry Jacoby. Hoboken: John Wiley and Sons, 2012.

Hardy, Matt. "The Eastern Question." In *Game of Thrones versus History: Written in Blood*. Edited by Brian A. Pavlac. Hoboken: Wiley Blackwell, 2017.

Hicks, Michael. *The Wars of the Roses*. New Haven: Yale University Press, 2012.

Huang, Phillip C.C. "Development or Involution in Eighteenth Century Britain and China? A Review of Kenneth Pomeranz's, *The Great Divergence: China,*

Europe, and the Making of the Modern World Economy." *The Journal of Asian Studies*, Vol. 61, No. 2 (May 2002), 501–538.

Jaspers, Karl. *Origin and Goal of History*, Abingdon, UK: Routledge Revivals, [1949], 2010.

Joseph, William A. *Politics in China: An Introduction.* Oxford: Oxford University Press, 2010.

Knecht, R.J. *Catherine de' Medici.* Abingdon, UK: Routledge, 2014.

Kwong, Luke S.K. "Imperial Authority in Crisis: An Interpretation of the Coup D'état of 1861." *Modern Asian Studies*, Vol. 17, No. 2 (1983): 222–223.

Kwong, Luke S.K. "Chinese Politics at the Crossroads: Reflections on the Hundred Days Reform of 1898." *Modern Asian Studies*, Vol. 34, No. 3 (July 2000): 663–695.

Lewis, Mark Edward. *China's Cosmopolitan Empire: The Tang Dynasty.* Cambridge: Harvard University Press, 2009.

Li Yuhuang and Harriet T. Zurndorfer. "Rethinking Empress Dowager Cixi through the Production of Art," in *Nan Nu* 14 (2012): 1–20.

Lim, Louisa. "Who Murdered China's Emperor a 100 years ago," *NPR*, November 14, 2008. https://www.npr.org/templates/story/story.php?storyId=96993694.

Liu, Kwang-Ching. "The Ch'ing Restoration." *The Cambridge History of China*, vol. 10: *The Late Ch'ing*, Part 1, edited by John K. Fairbank. Cambridge: Cambridge University Press, 1978.

Mann, Susan L. *Gender and Sexuality in Modern Chinese History.* New York: Cambridge University Press, 2011.

Martin, George R.R. "George R.R. Martin: The Rolling Stone Interview: the novelist goes deep on the future of his books and the TV series they begat." Interview by Mikal Gilmore. *Rolling Stone*, April 23, 2014. https://www.rollingstone.com/culture/culture-news/george-r-r-martin-the-rolling-stone-interview-242487/.

Martin, Thomas R., ed. "A Woman in Power: Empress Lu." In *Herodotus and Sima Qian, The First Great Historians of Greece and China: A Brief History with Documents.* New York: Bedford/St. Martins, 2010.

McMahon, Keith. "Women Rulers in Imperial China." *Nan Nu* 15-2 (2013), 179–218.

Mitchell, Ryan. "Is China's 'Machiavelli' Now Its Most Important Political Philosopher?" *The Diplomat*, January 16, 2015. https://thediplomat.com/2015/01/is-chinas-machiavelli-now-its-most-important-political-philosopher.

Nienhauser, Jr, William H., ed. *The Grand Scribe's Records Volume IX: The Memoirs of Han China Part II by Ssu-ma-Ch'ien.* Bloomington IN: Indiana University Press, 2010.

Norrie, Aidan. "Female Pharaohs in Ancient Egypt." In *The Routledge History of Monarchy: New Perspectives on Rulers and Rulership*, edited by Elena Woodacre, Lucinda Dean, Chris Jones, Russell Martin, and Zita Rohr. Abingdon, UK: Routledge, 2019, 501–517.

Platt, Stephen R. *Autumn in the Heavenly Kingdom: China, the West, and the Epic Story of the Taiping Civil War.* New York: Alfred A. Knopf, 2012.

Pomeranz, Kenneth. *The Great Divergence: China, Europe, and the Making of the Modern World Economy.* Princeton: Princeton University Press, 2001.

Quercia, Jacopo della, "A Machiavellian Discourse on Game of Thrones." In Game of Thrones *versus History: Written in Blood.* Edited by Brian A. Pavlac. Hoboken: Wiley Blackwell, 2017.

Rawski, Evelyn. *The Last Emperors: A Social History of Qing Imperial Institutions.* Berkeley: University of California Press, 1998.

Rhoads, Edward J.M. *Manchus and Han: Ethnic Relations and Political Power in Late Qing and Early Republican China, 1861–1928.* Seattle: University of Washington Press, 2000.

Roehrig, Catharine H., ed. *Hatshepsut: From Queen to Pharaoh.* New York: The Metropolitan Museum of Art, 2005.

Rohr, Zita Eva and Lisa Benz, eds. *Queenship and the Women of Westeros: Female Agency and Advice in Game of Thrones and A Song of Ice and Fire.* Basingstoke, UK: Palgrave Macmillan, 2019.

Schell, Orville and John Delury. "Western Methods, Chinese Core: Empress Dowager Cixi." In *Wealth and Power: China's Long March to the Twenty-first Century.* New York: Random House, 2013.

Schulzke, Marcus. "Playing the Game of Thrones: Some Lessons from Machiavelli." In *Game of Thrones and Philosophy: Logic Cuts Deeper Than Swords.* Edited by Henry Jacoby. Hoboken: John Wiley and Sons, 2012.

Seagrave, Sterling. *Dragon Lady: The Life and Legend of the Last Empress of China.* New York: Vintage Books, 1993.

Spence, Jonathan. *The Search for Modern China*, 3rd ed. New York: W.W. Norton and Company, 2013.

Trevor-Roper, Hugh. *The Hermit of Peking: The Secret Life of Sir Edmond Backhouse.* London: Eland Books, 2011.

Twitchett, Denis. "Kao-tsung (reign 649–83) and the Empress Wu: The Inheritor and the Usurper." In *The Cambridge History of China*, Vol. 3, *Sui and T'ang China, Part I*, edited by Denis Twitchett and John K. Fairbank. Cambridge: Cambridge University Press, 1979.

Tyldesley, Joyce. *Chronicle of the Queens of Egypt: From Early Dynastic Times to the Death of Cleopatra.* London: Thames and Hudson, 2006.

Tyldesley, Joyce. *Hatchepsut: The Female Pharaoh.* London: Penguin, 1996.

Zhao, Dingxin. *The Confucian-Legalist State: A New Theory of Chinese History.* Oxford: Oxford University Press, 2015.

Queen of Sad Mischance: Medievalism, "Realism," and the Case of Cersei Lannister

Kavita Mudan Finn

George R.R. Martin's epic fantasy series *A Song of Ice and Fire* and the accompanying HBO television series *Game of Thrones* have garnered both praise and censure for their treatment of women. On the one hand, Martin's universe contains many female characters, admirable and otherwise, who take on a variety of roles from the traditional daughters, wives, and mothers of the aristocratic classes to the lady knight Brienne of Tarth, the sorceress Melisandre of Asshai, the assassin Arya Stark, and the pirate Asha (or Yara) Greyjoy. However, Martin and the producers of the HBO series have also been criticized for relying on misogynist tropes that objectify women and trivialize sexual assault in the name of realism. Through the character of Queen Cersei Lannister, this chapter will confront and examine some of that perceived realism, especially the implications of Martin's particular brand of medievalism on perceptions of premodern women, and consider how fans have chosen to reclaim the character. In short, Cersei sometimes seems less a fully formed character than a series of quasi-medieval tropes jumbled together, and much of the depth that can be read into her comes from her fans and from Lena Headey's nuanced and complex performance in the HBO series.

K. M. Finn (✉)
Manchester, NH, USA

© The Author(s) 2020
Z. E. Rohr, L. Benz (eds.), *Queenship and the Women of Westeros*,
Queenship and Power, https://doi.org/10.1007/978-3-030-25041-6_2

Before focusing on Cersei, however, it is important to elucidate what constitutes "realism" in the context of a series explicitly created and marketed as fantasy. This loaded term has come to represent one side of the argument surrounding the treatment of women and other disenfranchised groups in both *A Song of Ice and Fire* and *Game of Thrones*.[1] The "realism" defence asserts that the misogynist, racist, and ableist attitudes of Westeros and Essos merely reflect the culture on which the series are based, namely Western Europe in the medieval and early modern periods. George R.R. Martin has explained in multiple interviews that he, like J.R.R. Tolkien before him, drew on medieval Europe as inspiration for the world of *A Song of Ice and Fire*.[2] He has also fallen back on his medieval inspiration when fans have critiqued his treatment of women and characters of colour such as the Dothraki and the inhabitants of Slaver's Bay. In a 2013 interview with Charlie Jane Anders of *The Observation Deck*, for instance, Martin responded to criticism of alleged whitewashing with the following assertion:

> I am drawing from history, even though it's fantasy. I've read a lot of history, The War of the Roses, The Hundred Years War. The World back then was very diverse. Culturally it was perhaps more diverse then [sic] our world, but travel was very difficult back then. So even though there might have been many different races and ethnicities and peoples, they didn't necessarily mix a great deal. I'm drawing largely on medieval England, medieval Scotland, some extent medieval France. There was an occasional person of colour, but certainly not in any great numbers.[3]

This attitude better reflects the failings of nineteenth- and early twentieth-century medievalism than the actual history, as many contemporary medievalists have discussed at length.[4] As Shiloh Carroll argues, building on the work of Helen Young, "readers are caught in a 'feedback loop' in which Martin's work helps to create a neomedieval idea of the Middle Ages, which then becomes their idea of what the Middle Ages 'really' looked like, which is then used to defend Martin's work as 'realistic' because it matches their idea of the real Middle Ages."[5] This is in sharp contrast to fans of *The Lord of the Rings*, none of whom have attempted to claim that Tolkien was writing anything other than fantasy. While this speaks to the immersiveness and exhaustive detail of Martin's universe, it forms part of a troubling trend in modern popular medievalism that deserves closer interrogation.

What the realism defence fails to take into account are the specific interpretive choices Martin makes—that *A Song of Ice and Fire* and *Game of Thrones* do not reflect premodern Europe, but rather, refract it, providing a distorted, sensationalized impression of the period. Within this context, the women of Westeros prove to be less subversive than on first glance, and their persistent victimization more problematic. Nor has this escaped the notice of many fans who do not identify as male, one of whom remarks that the world of Westeros looks less like medieval Europe and "more like a 21st century person's worst nightmares of the medieval period."[6] Academics have attempted to correct these misconceptions, but in light of remarks by the showrunners and Martin himself, they persist.[7]

Cersei Lannister has always been one of the most reviled characters both within Martin's fantasy universe and in its fandom. In her book-length study *Women in Game of Thrones* (2014), Valerie Frankel says of Cersei, "it's unfortunate that she's almost the only one giving speeches about women's rights and why women should have the right to rule, as her selfishness and cruelty mar her agenda."[8] While this assessment was made following the show's fourth season, it is still, in its broadest sense, accurate—Cersei's arc in the seasons extending beyond the books cements her role as a primary antagonist. In the books, Cersei is the only prominent member of the Lannister family who is never given the benefit of the doubt. Her youngest brother Tyrion is a popular point-of-view character from the first book onwards; Jaime and Cersei join him in the third and fourth books respectively, and Jaime's chapters in particular have made him a fan favourite.[9] Cersei's chapters, on the other hand, do little to reverse our initial impressions of her and indeed show her spiralling into alcoholism and self-destruction before being forced to walk naked through the streets of King's Landing as a public punishment for adultery that, as far as most of the characters and a good portion of the fandom are concerned, is entirely warranted. Those who are fans of Cersei, including Lena Headey, the actress who portrayed her, see past the accretion of stereotypes to a woman fighting tooth and nail against a mercilessly patriarchal society that values her only for her beauty and fertility while simultaneously punishing her for using them to gain some semblance of agency.

Cersei's introduction in *A Game of Thrones* plays out over the course of some 40 pages, from the royal family's tense arrival in Winterfell, the northern seat of House Stark, to the first of countless shocking scenes that have become synonymous with the series. Seven-year-old Bran Stark is climbing across rooftops when he hears voices in a normally empty, disused section of the castle. The book devotes several pages to building up suspense—Bran has no idea the significance of the conversation he overhears between two characters the reader can identify from its context as Jaime and Cersei Lannister, but he quickly realizes "it was not meant for his ears."[10] By this point, various conversations and snippets of backstory have made clear that Cersei Lannister is interested in advancing her family's interests, that her marriage to the king is an unhappy one, and that at least one character believes her guilty of murder.[11] The reader—and Bran—learn shortly afterwards that Cersei is having an affair with her twin brother Jaime, but the narrative leaves little time to process that bombshell before Jaime shoves Bran from the window, presumably to his death, uttering a line that defines him as a character: "The things I do for love."[12] This one-two-punch of shock and horror also defines Cersei by extension, though her role in the scene is largely nonverbal—it is *for her* that Jaime commits this heinous act—and the ramifications of her adultery, and their incest, will reverberate through the rest of the series.

˙ These are not tropes unknown to medieval authors and readers. The thirteenth-century French prose romance known as the Vulgate Cycle turns the tales of King Arthur and his Knights of the Round Table into a sprawling five-part narrative beginning with the history of the Grail and ending with the destruction of Arthur and his kingdom.[13] It draws on a variety of sources, from Latin histories to vernacular romances (Chrétien de Troyes, Marie de France) and Biblical apocrypha, and we can see its popularity in the number of manuscript versions that have survived, although its author(s) remain unknown.[14] Much like *Game of Thrones*, despite its magical trappings, the Vulgate Cycle, and its most famous adaptation, Thomas Malory's *Le Morte Darthur* (1469), focus primarily on the flawed human relationships that first create and ultimately destroy the Round Table and all it stands for. At the heart of both conflicts too is a quintessentially medieval problem: the adulterous queen.

It has long been traditional to blame Queen Guenevere for the fall of her husband Arthur's kingdom as well as his death, even though the Vulgate Cycle and all versions based on it make clear that the seeds of Arthur's destruction were sown well before his marriage when he unwittingly slept with his half-sister Morgause and produced an illegitimate son Mordred. In the relevant section of the *Histoire de Merlin*, the author addresses readers directly before explaining that Arthur and Morgause were unaware of their relationship until after the fact, urging them to "understand how Mordred was sired by him, for many people would find King Arthur less worthy because of it if they did not know the truth."[15] It is the later, more conservative Post-Vulgate Cycle, that explicitly connects Mordred's incestuous parentage to his role in Arthur's downfall, while Thomas Malory's version—derived from both French cycles—dances the fine line between foreshadowing Arthur's destruction and emphasizing his innocence in inadvertently bringing it about.[16]

Guenevere's sin is that she knowingly carries on a love affair with the greatest of Arthur's knights, Lancelot of the Lake, and it is the public acknowledgment of that affair that precipitates a civil war between the knights who support Lancelot and those who claim to support Arthur. The adultery itself is not coded as problematic until much later in the narrative—indeed, in the Vulgate Cycle's version of events, Guenevere's affair with Lancelot is juxtaposed with several instances of Arthur's adultery.[17] While this does not justify Guenevere's actions, it certainly puts them in context. Just as significantly, however, Guenevere is, by all indications, unable to have children, as is the other legendary medieval queen to whom she is often compared, Iseult the Fair. If, as is often the case in medieval romance, an adulterous queen has no children, one can argue, as Peggy McCracken does, that her adultery has no direct impact on the succession.[18] Nor does Arthur seem especially troubled about it, in contrast to many methods medieval and early modern kings used to rid themselves of wives who could not produce the desired heirs, or the emphasis in medieval advice literature on the importance of queenly chastity.[19] Christine de Pizan, for instance, observes that a wise princess should value her honour "more than her life, for she ought to lose it [her life] sooner than her honour," adding that "whoever dies well is saved, but whoever is dishonoured is reproached dead and alive forever for as long as there is any memory of her."[20] A century later, Anne de France—who, unusually, served as regent to her younger brother King Charles VIII—also emphasizes the importance of maintaining the appearance of perfect chastity in her *Enseignements*, as a screen behind which a woman could exercise considerable power.[21] The queen's body was very much the property of the state, and to question a queen's chastity was to invite "implications of failed kingship and collapsing regimes, as well as the more obvious issue of illegitimate succession."[22] The gravity of Guenevere's actions—and Cersei's—therefore, is not to be underestimated.

While Cersei carries on an affair with the greatest knight in the kingdom, there are divergences from Guenevere's situation that make hers markedly worse—even as Robert's adultery is more egregious than Arthur's, with at least eight illegitimate children confirmed when the books begin.[23] First, the knight in question with whom Cersei is having an affair is also her twin brother, thus conflating the crimes of Arthur, who committed inadvertent incest and produced a monstrous son, with those of Guenevere, who knowingly committed adultery without jeopardizing the succession. Secondly, Cersei's decision to pass off all three of her children with Jaime as the heirs to the throne is the definition of queenly treason and a medieval king's worst nightmare; the fact that she then conspires to kill her husband during a boar hunt seems almost beside the point.[24]

In the books, Cersei is also behind the massacre of Robert's many bastard children whose distinctive colouring would put the paternity of her children in question. Although the obvious analogue is King Herod's Massacre of the Innocents, there is an Arthurian variant known as the May Day massacre, where King Arthur himself (not Guenevere) sought to avert a prophecy, that the child born of his incestuous union with Morgause would kill him, by ordering that all male children born on or around May Day (the time at which his son would have been born) be put onto a small boat, rowed out to sea, and abandoned to die. Again, we see Martin conflating Arthur's crimes with Guenevere's in the character of Cersei, even if the HBO series displaces that particular crime onto her monstrous son Joffrey.

As we learn in *A Feast for Crows* and in the opening scene of Season Five of *Game of Thrones*, one of the driving forces behind Cersei's actions is a prophecy not dissimilar to King Arthur's, made when she was a girl, that she would become queen only to lose that title to someone "younger and more beautiful"; that she would have three children, all of whom would die—"gold shall be their crowns and gold their shrouds"; and that she would die at the hands of "the *valonqar*" (a term she eventually translates to "little brother").[25] This provides some insight into Cersei's seemingly relentless hatred for her brother Tyrion—not only does she see him as the murderer of her mother, who died in childbirth; he is also prophesied, she thinks, to kill *her*. She forgets that, by a matter of minutes, Jaime is also her younger brother. Even though she is technically the eldest of Tywin Lannister's children and simultaneously the least powerful, this is to some extent the root of her ambition.[26] Excising the reference to Cersei's own death in the show's version of the prophecy severely undercuts her motivations for hating Tyrion. After all, even King Arthur's decision to send a boat filled with infants to their death was somewhat mitigated within the text—however we might feel about it—by the fear that one of them would not only kill him but also destroy his kingdom.

There are many villainous queens in medieval romance, some of whom also commit adultery. Guenevere is usually not among them, even though her adultery—like Cersei's—becomes the *casus belli* for the civil war that destroys Camelot.[27] It is made clear in Malory's *Morte Darthur* (and implied in earlier versions) that the discovery of Lancelot in Guenevere's chambers is in fact a deep-rooted conspiracy against both Lancelot and Arthur in which Guenevere is, for all intents and purposes, a pawn. Malory opens the final section of *Le Morte Darthur* with the statement that two of Sir Gawayne's brothers, Aggravayne and Mordred, "had ever a prevy hate unto the Quene, Dame Gwenyver, and to Sir Launcelot—and dayly and nyghtly they ever wacched upon Sir Launcelot."[28] As Peggy McCracken argues, in medieval romance, the queen's "adulterous love figures the king's affection for his favourite vassal, and accusations of a transgressive relationship between the queen and her knight are a displaced attack on the relationship between the king and the knight which the barons wish to disrupt."[29] This is not the case in *A Song of Ice and Fire*, where Cersei, for all the opacity of her motives early on, appears to be acting on her own behalf, and her narration in *A Feast for Crows* confirms it. She therefore comes to embody *every* bad trait ascribed to medieval women all at once and, even in the chapters written from her point of view in the fourth and fifth books in the series, she rarely rises beyond those negative stereotypes. Guenevere, at least, is given some redeeming qualities, however questionable—the one exception is the Post-Vulgate Cycle, which excises most of the Lancelot romance in favour of the Grail narrative and punishes the entire kingdom for its sins in what is possibly the most dismal ending to a medieval romance one might ever encounter.[30] Malory acknowledges of Guenevere that "whyle she lyved she was a trew lover, and therefor she had a good ende."[31] Cersei is unlikely to get such a eulogy, having alienated nearly everybody who was on her side for reasons that—if one reads her chapters closely—are not entirely her fault, even if the narrative is manifestly against her.

Although Martin has explained in interviews that he draws general, but not specific, inspiration from medieval history, there are two examples from the fifteenth-century English Wars of the Roses that are illustrative of the issues underlying Cersei Lannister's characterization.[32] Both queens during periods of civil war, Margaret of Anjou (1430–83) and Elizabeth

Woodville (c. 1437–92) were routinely at the mercy of hostile writers—chroniclers, diplomats, poets, even official archivists—who manipulated their reputations for political ends.[33] Superficially, Elizabeth is a clearer parallel, having come from a large and unusually attractive family who she then brought into the royal household and rewarded generously, much to the chagrin of the ruling nobility. After her husband King Edward IV's unexpected death in April 1483, she became embroiled in the struggle between those who supported placing her son on the throne as King Edward V and those who supported Edward IV's brother, who took the throne as King Richard III. Sources hostile to Elizabeth claim that her actions following his death were self-serving; the *Titulus Regius*, setting out Richard III's claim to the crown, goes so far as to accuse her of bewitching Edward into marriage.[34] Add to this, echoes of Edward IV in Robert Baratheon's drinking, binge eating, and womanizing and it does not seem far-fetched that Elizabeth, who, until recently, was portrayed in fiction and biography as a cold, self-centred, and ambitious beauty, might have been an inspiration for Cersei.[35] What is not in evidence are the sources favourable to Edward IV (and thus by extension to Elizabeth) that portray her as "the benevolent queen" who had exhibited "al mannar pacience" during the resurgence of civil war that interrupted Edward IV's reign in 1471.[36]

Early on, one of Cersei's most problematic characteristics is her relationship with her sadistic eldest son Joffrey, and for its inspiration we should turn perhaps to Margaret of Anjou rather than Elizabeth Woodville. Margaret was eight months pregnant when her husband King Henry VI fell into catatonia in August 1453. Although he recovered after several months, the power vacuum created by his illness was enough to divide the nobility into factions and plunge England into civil war. After Edward IV took the throne for the house of York in 1461, Margaret and Prince Edward spent the next ten years shuttling between Burgundy and France, seeking aid from increasingly indifferent rulers. In 1467, the Milanese Ambassador in France wrote to the duke and duchess of Milan that Prince Edward, "though only thirteen years of age, already talks of nothing but of cutting of heads or making war, as if he had everything in his hands or was the god of battle or the peaceful occupant of that throne."[37] There are accounts in several Yorkist-leaning chronicles of seven-year-old Prince Edward presiding over the executions of two men who had guarded his father during the second battle of St. Albans in February 1461. Both of these accounts also emphasise his mother's attention—although it is worth keeping in mind that both appear in sources actively hostile to Margaret and might well be exaggerations or outright fabrications. There are more sympathetic accounts of Margaret that appear in French and Burgundian sources, where she better resembles Catelyn Stark than Cersei Lannister, but she nonetheless offers a useful example of how a queen's reputation could be deliberately tarnished, or polished, for political reasons.[38]

After Joffrey's death, Cersei attempts to mould her second son Tommen into his brother's double—and in the HBO series she thereafter only wears black, visually isolating herself from the rest of King's Landing. Margaret of Anjou had only one son, and Prince Edward died either during or shortly after the battle of Tewkesbury in May 1471, leaving his grieving mother to retreat into exile and become an exemplar for why women should not attempt to rule kingdoms.[39] This attitude persists in modern depictions of Margaret—for instance, the BBC and Starz collaborated on a ten-episode series called *The White Queen* in 2013 that featured a borderline-incestuous relationship between Margaret and her son Edward. Although one might make the assumption that the series' producers were capitalizing on a potential shared audience with *Game of Thrones*, the novels by Philippa Gregory, upon which the series was based, featured dodgy incestuous relationships long before the Lannisters made it fashionable on television.

Hanging over Cersei even more than the prophecy that haunts her is the weight of Westeros's patriarchal society. In a 2016 interview with *Mashable*, Lena Headey said, "I don't play her as a villain. I just play a woman who is a survivor and will do exactly what a man would do."[40] Cersei's defenders within the fandom similarly point to the many instances, within her narration but also in earlier books, where Cersei questions, protests, or otherwise condemns the system that offers her twin brother Jaime everything Cersei has ever wanted while denying it to her for a physical fact over which she has no control:

> Men had been looking at her that way since her breasts began to bud. *Because I was so beautiful, they said, but Jaime was beautiful as well, and they never looked at him that way.* When she was small she would sometimes don her brother's clothing as a lark. She was always startled by how differently men treated her when they thought that she was Jaime.[41]

Cersei Lannister's most devoted fans tend to identify as women, and thus read into her experience a reflection of their own, something that cannot be said of author George R.R. Martin or *Game of Thrones*' executive producers, David Benioff and D.B. Weiss. As such, many fans have pinpointed this passage as endemic of not just the toxicity of Westerosi masculinity, but another in a long string of moments in the books and the HBO series where young girls are sexualized. In Cersei's case, this convinces her that using her beauty and sexuality to manipulate men is her best route to power—and, to some extent, she is correct, although that power is always circumscribed by the men around her, particularly her father.

In *A Storm of Swords*, Tyrion, who has little reason to sympathize with the sister who has been cruel to him since his birth, acknowledges that, when faced with their father's plans for her to remarry, Cersei "will do as Father bid. She had proved that with Robert."[42] Even after Tywin's death, however, Cersei's chapters are filled with instances of men doubting her and refusing to follow her orders. As Headey remarked in a 2017 interview with *TIME Magazine*, "she's a woman surviving in a really shitty world, desperate to be heard, saying something seven times when a man says it once."[43] Cersei's first attempt to assert her authority as Queen Regent, for instance, ends with her flinging a glass of wine in her uncle Kevan's face after he calls her "as unfit a mother as you are a ruler."[44] Jaime observes that Cersei "does not lack for wits, but she has no judgement, and no patience,"[45] while Petyr Baelish and Tyrion both use Cersei as an object lesson in how not to play the game of thrones:

> In the game of thrones, even the humblest pieces can have wills of their own. Sometimes they refuse to make the moves you've planned for them. [...] It's a lesson that Cersei Lannister has yet to learn.[46]

> Cersei is as gentle as King Maegor, as selfless as Aegon the Unworthy, as wise as Mad King Aerys. She never forgets a slight, real or imagined. She takes caution for cowardice and dissent for defiance. And she is greedy. Greedy for power, for honour, for love. Tommen's rule is bolstered by all of the alliances that my lord father built so carefully, but soon enough she will destroy them, every one.[47]

Nor does Cersei's own narration belie Tyrion's assessment of her motives, although there is a layer beneath her rage and greed that he never takes into account, perhaps understandably given his own marginalized position in Westerosi society:

The rule was hers; Cersei did not mean to give it up until Tommen came of age. *I waited, so can he. I waited half my life.* She had played the dutiful daughter, the blushing bride, the pliant wife. She had suffered Robert's drunken groping, Jaime's jealousy, Renly's mockery, Varys with his titters, Stannis endlessly grinding his teeth. She had contended with Jon Arryn, Ned Stark, and her vile, treacherous, murderous dwarf brother, all the while promising herself that one day it would be her turn.[48]

For any other character, a revelation like this might have been the start of what the fandom commonly refers to as a redemption arc. After all, as early as Ned Stark's chapters in *A Game of Thrones*, it is confirmed that Robert and Cersei's marriage is an abusive one. Ned witnesses Robert deal Cersei "a vicious backhand blow to the side of the head," and while he later admits that it was not "kingly," he does not dwell on his actions, focusing instead on how unhappy he is in his marriage and his crown.[49] Cersei recalls more abuses in *A Feast for Crows*, including the detail that afterwards Robert claimed, "It was not me, my lady," sounding "like a child caught stealing apple cakes from the kitchen," and blaming the fact that he'd had too much wine[50]:

> The rest had all been lies, though. He *did* remember what he did to her at night, she was convinced of that. She could see it in his eyes. He only pretended to forget; it was easier to do that than to face his shame. Deep down Robert Baratheon was a coward. In time the assaults did grow less frequent. During the first year he took her at least once a fortnight; by the end it was not even once a year. He never stopped completely, though. Sooner or later there would always come a night when he would drink too much and want to claim his rights. What shamed him in the light of day gave him pleasure in the darkness.[51]

As blogger and podcaster Emmett Booth explains, "the particular way in which Robert implodes, and the way he insulates himself from it, makes me doubt there was ever much there to begin with even before he went to seed."[52] Readers don't see much of Robert before his death, but what we do see is a king who spends most of his time drinking and sleeping around, who has an unpredictable and violent temper, and who is willing to countenance the murder of children. By the time the full extent of his abuse of Cersei is revealed, however, Cersei's own actions have moved so far beyond the pale—including supplying victims to her own pet "mad scientist" Qyburn and torturing witnesses into lying about Margaery Tyrell—that it is difficult to sympathize with her, even as a victim of 15 years of abuse. This is especially evident if one uses the chronological reading order for the fourth and fifth books developed by fan and blogger Sean T. Collins, since that order calls attention to the parallels between the situations of Cersei in King's Landing and Daenerys in Meereen.[53] Both find themselves queens over tottering states, surrounded by men who refuse to take them seriously—but, as Shiloh Carroll explains in Chap. 8 of this collection through her analysis of Daenerys's relationship with her council and advisors, the reader has taken Daenerys's entire journey alongside her and understands what motivates her actions.[54] She may be "*unræd*," but that does not make her unsympathetic … at least not until the very end of her narrative arc in the HBO series.

Cersei does make her own poor choices, as opposed to simply mishandling bad situations not of her making. Within *A Feast for Crows* alone, she wastes almost all of her resources pursuing Margaery Tyrell, even allowing herself to be sexually abused by one of the sellswords in her employ in exchange for his agreement to murder Margaery—a plot that never comes to fruition.[55] Prior to the introduction of her point-of-view chapters, Cersei consistently shows herself to be selfish and short-sighted, but that alone should not be enough to damn her in a series full of similar characters. Considering Jaime's opening gambit is to push a seven-year-old boy out of a tower window, a redemptive arc might seem like a tall order, but Jaime nonetheless has a strong following amongst fans of the books.

The HBO series, however, included a controversial scene in the fourth season where Jaime raped Cersei next to their son's dead body. There was a roughly equivalent scene in *A Storm of Swords*, told from Jaime's perspective, but the show altered enough of the circumstances and character dynamics that many fans were offended by it. Martin weighed in with an explanation that the scene in the books was meant to be viewed as dubiously consensual, but refrained from commenting directly on the showrunners' choices. Most of the censure focused on the impact of the scene on Jaime as a character ("Is Jaime Lannister a rapist?" was a frequent discussion in the blogosphere), except for a general sense from the episode's director and others involved in the production that Cersei had deserved it—indeed, before forcing himself on her, Jaime bitterly remarked, "Why have the gods made me love a hateful woman?" a line that does not appear in the books.[56] In the subsequent seasons, their relationship remained in the background unless the plot required a confrontation or reconciliation, only to have Jaime race to Cersei's side in the penultimate episode so he could die with her, albeit after once again describing both himself and her as "hateful."

In short, the problem with Cersei Lannister is not that she conforms to negative medieval stereotypes; it is that Martin—and the HBO producers—insist on incorporating *all* of those stereotypes at once. We see other women in the series who are more effectively drawn, but those characters are notable for their comparative lack of emphasis on sexuality: Brienne of Tarth and Catelyn Stark are the two that immediately come to mind, the lady knight and the *mater dolorosa*. This latter category of course has a number of medieval precedents including sources sympathetic to Elizabeth Woodville and Margaret of Anjou that call upon the language and symbolism of grieving motherhood to describe them almost as often as their detractors accuse them of scheming for power. Brienne of Tarth, on the other hand, is more often compared to characters like Edmund Spenser's Britomart, a lady knight defined by virginity and chastity; even in Brienne's case, engaging in a brief sexual relationship with Jaime Lannister does not preclude her from becoming Lord Commander of the Kingsguard. As for the Mother of Dragons, almost certainly the "younger and more beautiful queen" destined to topple Cersei in the books, the hagiographic underpinnings of her story arc recontextualize the depiction of her sexuality. While both she and Cersei engage in multiple sexual relationships, it is clear from the narration that Daenerys has some emotional investment and closeness with her partners (Khal Drogo, her handmaid Irri, and the mercenary Daario Naharis) that is lacking in Cersei's case, except for her incestuous relationship with Jaime. Cersei's choice to use her beauty and sexual allure as tools to gain power she is otherwise denied by her gender is one the narrative emphatically does not support, and this is encapsulated in the Walk of Shame—itself an exaggeration and conflation of several medieval punishments—she endures in *A Dance with Dragons* and the Season Five finale of *Game of Thrones*.[57] As Sylwia Borowska-Szerszun observes in Chap. 3 of this collection, the Walk of Shame also undermines Cersei's status by according her the same treatment as lower-class medieval women accused of adultery. Immediately before her penance begins, Cersei recalls her grandfather's "grasping, lowborn mistress" who her father forced to walk naked through the streets of Lannisport, and observes that it is her uncle Kevan who is likely the driving force, rather than the High Septon.[58] In short, the Walk of Shame destroys her credibility as a queen, at least in the traditional sense, and she feels this keenly by the end: "Gowned and crowned, she was a queen. Naked, bloody, limping, she was only a woman."[59]

This is where Cersei's story diverges: in the books, we do not know what lies in store for her, while the show merges her storyline with that of several other characters to make her one of the primary antagonists of the final two seasons. If her punishment operates as an exercise in misogyny that invites the audience to shame Cersei alongside the crowds that jeer at her in King's Landing, her explosive revenge upon the Faith Militant, by blowing up the Sept of Baelor in the Season Six finale, is a spectacular moment of catharsis a full season in the making. That the shock of seeing hundreds of people killed in seconds prompts her remaining child Tommen to commit suicide is, for her, merely the final fulfilment of the prophecy.[60] Lena Headey observes that even as Cersei ascends the Iron Throne late in that episode, "she's aware of all the shit, the pain she's created for everybody."[61] This awareness, however, does not stop Cersei from barrelling further down the path she's created for herself, "trapped in a web of her own making," according to Headey.[62] Once she is crowned queen, she turns all of her attention to destroying the newly arrived Daenerys—to the point of refusing to send the Lannister armies north to fight the arguably greater enemy, the Army of the Dead, on the assumption that she can reap the spoils of what is left after that battle.

There are characters in the medieval Arthurian canon who behave similarly, most notably Morgan le Fay, but Morgan possesses "such powers as confer an extraordinary autonomy upon [her], an untrammelled freedom to act that is denied others," and, in spite of her questionable morality, wields political power in her own right as King Arthur's half-sister.[63] The seasons of *Game of Thrones* that have picked up after the end of the fifth book have lacked the strong internal logic of the prior seasons, to the point that Cersei sometimes seems to have magical powers, at least in terms of her ability to move her military forces from one place to another. However, Morgan also appears at the end of the narrative in a more ambiguous role as the guardian of King Arthur's body. Queen Guenevere, on the other hand, makes the conscious choice to abandon both worldly goods and carnal love by retiring to a convent and refusing to join Lancelot although she has the freedom by then to do so without consequence. Cersei's behaviour falls so far outside the bounds of what is considered acceptable that neither of these endpoints makes sense for her character.

Cersei's arc, furthermore, suffers as a result of the uneven writing in the final two seasons of *Game of Thrones*, as do both of her brothers and her antagonist, Daenerys. All four characters converge in the penultimate episode, "The Bells," and by the end of the episode, both Cersei and Jaime are dead, killed by the collapsing walls of the Red Keep, with Cersei weeping, begging Jaime to "please let me live," and thus *partly* fulfilling the witch's prophecy that she should die "when your tears have drowned you." Jaime does not, in fact, wrap his hands about her throat and choke the life from her, but she does die in his arms, bringing their twisted, co-dependent relationship full circle. Cersei's limited appearances prior to her death, however, left many viewers unsatisfied with this ending; while thematically clean, it, like Daenerys's descent into mass-murderous rage, felt unearned.

If the greatest praise that we can offer to a genre normally derided as escapist nonsense is for its realism, should we not be working to emphasize the more positive aspects of that "realism" as well as its darkness? I do not advocate a return to the gold-lamé wonderland of John Boorman's *Excalibur* (1981) nor the sanitized world of Pre-Raphaelite paintings and Disney cartoons, but surely we can look beyond these tired stereotypes about women that litter our supposedly realistic depictions of both medieval and medievalist worlds to a more expansive idea of female power and potential that is, surprising as it may seem, *more* historically accurate. The *Game of Thrones* fans who defend characters like Cersei Lannister certainly can; it remains to be seen if showrunners and media creators can follow suit.

Notes

1. "Realistic," "gritty," and "brutal" are all descriptions that have been applied to *Game of Thrones*. For example, in his *Guardian* review of 24 March 2013, Tom Holland observes, "there are sequences where the invented world of Westeros can seem more realistic than the evocations of the past to be found in many a historical novel."
2. Any attempt to explain the lack of boundaries between medieval and Renaissance/early modern culture is beyond the scope of this chapter, but suffice it to say that Martin's evocation of "the Middle Ages" can apply to anything from the fall of the Roman Empire to the seventeenth century.
3. Charlie Jane Anders, "George R.R. Martin: The Complete Unedited Interview," *The Observation Deck* (23 July 2013), https://observationdeck. kinja.com/george-r-r-martin-the-complete-unedited-interview-886117845.
4. See Jonathan Hsy and Julie Orlemanski, "Race and medieval studies: A partial bibliography," *postmedieval: A journal of medieval cultural studies* 8 (2017), 500–31.
5. Shiloh Carroll, *Medievalism in A Song of Ice and Fire and Game of Thrones* (Cambridge: D.S. Brewer, 2018), 16–17. Helen Young, "Authenticity and *Game of Thrones*," presented at the 48th Annual International Congress on Medieval Studies, Kalamazoo, MI, 10 May 2013.

6. joannalannister, "I'm curious. It was always told to me," *Joanna Lannister* [Tumblr] (4 August 2015), http://joannalannister.tumblr. com/post/125827358911/im-curious-it-was-always-told-to-me-that-the. For a more detailed discussion of racism and sexism in the series, see bitchfromtheseventhhell and lyannas, "I agree with farty old man GRRM," *the one that leads them is a she-wolf* [Tumblr] (9 June 2016), http://bitchfromtheseventhhell.tumblr.com/post/145690854453/ i-agree-with-farty-old-man-grrm-and-id-like-to.

7. Dave Itzkoff, "George R.R. Martin on 'Game of Thrones' and Sexual Violence," *The New York Times Arts Beat* (2 May 2014), https:// artsbeat.blogs.nytimes.com/2014/05/02/george-r-r-martin-on-game-of-thrones-and-sexual-violence/?_php=true&_type=blogs&_php=true&_type=blogs&_r=1&.

8. Valerie Estelle Frankel, *Women in* Game of Thrones: *Power, Conformity, and Resistance* (Jefferson, NC: McFarland, 2013), 88.

9. The five volumes of *A Song of Ice and Fire* are written in tight third-person perspective, and each chapter follows a different character, sometimes jumping across enormous distances.

10. George R.R. Martin, *A Game of Thrones. Book One of A Song of Ice and Fire* (New York: Bantam Spectra, 1996), 73.

11. Cersei turns out to have been innocent of that particular murder (Lysa Arryn murdered her husband Jon herself and framed Cersei), but this does little to mitigate her other crimes.

12. Martin, *A Game of Thrones*, 75. The HBO series moves the majority of Jaime and Cersei's political dialogue from the tower to a separate, earlier scene, but preserves the incest reveal in its original location, ending the first episode "Winter Is Coming" with Jaime's line and Bran's fall.

13. The most recent English translation of the Vulgate and Post-Vulgate Cycles is Norris J. Lacy's ten-volume edition *Lancelot-Grail* (Cambridge: D.S. Brewer, 2010). There are several French editions available, although these tend to separate the cycle into its constituent parts: *Estoire de Saint Graal* (*History of the Grail*), *Estoire de Merlin* (*The History of Merlin*), *Lancelot, Queste del Saint Graal* (*The Quest for the Grail*), and *Le Mort Le Roi Artu* (*The Death of Arthur*).

14. The origins of the Arthurian legend are a contested topic, but for medieval audiences, the earliest text is a chapter in Geoffrey of Monmouth's *Historia Regum Britanniæ* (*History of the Kings of Britain*, 1136), which was translated first into Anglo-Norman French by Wace (c. 1155) and then into English by Layamon (c. 1210). In the last two decades of the twelfth century, Chrétien de Troyes produced a series of stand-alone poems that featured individual knights of the Round Table. All of these sources were brought together in the prose romances now known as the Vulgate Cycle,

although the order in which these romances were written or which author or authors were responsible remain unknown. For a discussion of early manuscripts of the Cycle, see Elspeth Kennedy, "The Making of the *Lancelot-Grail* Cycle," in *A Companion to the Lancelot-Grail Cycle*, ed. Carol Dover (Cambridge: D.S. Brewer, 2003), 13–22.

15. Anon., *The Story of Merlin*, trans. Rupert T. Pickens, vol. 2 of *Lancelot-Grail: The Old French Arthurian Vulgate and Post-Vulgate in Translation* (Cambridge: D.S. Brewer, 2010), 139.

16. According to Malory, Arthur is captivated by Queen Morgause of Orkney and "desired to ly by her." The two agree, "but all thys tyme, Kynge Arthure knew nat that Kynge Lottis wyf was his sister." In Thomas Malory, *Le Morte Darthur* (New York, 2004), 30.

17. Lancelot and Guenevere consummate their love while Arthur is off with a Saxon enchantress named Gamille; he in fact notifies Guenevere "that she would not have him with her that night" (439). In *Lancelot Parts 1 & 2*, trans. Samuel N. Rosenberg and Carleton W. Carroll, vol. 3 of *Lancelot-Grail* (Cambridge: D.S. Brewer, 2010). More egregiously, Arthur is later deceived by a "false" Guenevere (the real Guenevere's illegitimate half-sister) and sends his true queen into exile. She spends two years living as a guest with Galehaut, a neighbouring ruler, who happens to also be hosting Lancelot. Arthur eventually comes to his senses and realizes his mistake. He takes Guenevere back, and the incident is never mentioned again. The Post-Vulgate cycle cuts most of the Lancelot-centric material except for the sections that directly pertain to the quest for the Holy Grail, so Guenevere's adultery loses its larger context.

18. In the earliest Welsh versions of the legend, Guenevere has three sons. For a detailed discussion of the significance of childless queens in the French romance tradition, see Peggy McCracken, *The Romance of Adultery: Queenship and Sexual Transgression in Old French Literature* (Philadelphia: University of Pennsylvania Press, 1998), 119–43.

19. Also in contrast to King Mark of the equally popular *Tristan* romances, who is best known as Iseult the Fair's cuckolded husband. Mark is frequently presented as a contrast to Arthur, particularly in Malory's telling, the first to explicitly incorporate Tristan.

20. Christine de Pizan, *The* Treasure of the City of Ladies *or the* Book of the Three Virtues, ed. and trans. Sarah Lawson (New York: Penguin, 1985), 56. In her discussion of queenly reputation, Christine may well have drawn on the contemporary situation of Queen Isabeau of France, who served as regent for her incapacitated husband Charles VI and who suffered repeated accusations of infidelity and adultery designed to weaken her politically. See Tracy Adams, *The Life and Afterlife of Isabeau of Bavaria* (Baltimore: Johns Hopkins University Press, 2010), esp. 113–48.

21. *Les Enseignements d'Anne de France, duchesse de Bourbonnois et d'Auvergne à sa fille Susanne de Bourbon*, ed. A.-M. Chazaud (Moulins: C. Desrosiers, 1878). For a discussion of Anne's emphasis on chastity, see ÉlianeViennot, "Rhétorique de la chasteté dans les *Enseignements d'Anne de France à sa fille Suzanne de Bourbon*," in *Souillure et Pureté: le Corps et son environnement culturel et politique*, ed. Jean-Jacques Vincensini (Paris: Maisonneuve& Larose, 2003), 1–6. See also Zita Eva Rohr, *Yolande of Aragon (1381–1442): Family and Power* (New York: Palgrave, 2016), 4–6, for Anne's use of Christine de Pizan's concept of *juste ypocrisie* and her parallels with Machiavelli.

22. Joanna Laynesmith, "Telling Tales of Adulterous Queens in Medieval England: From Olympias of Macedonia to Elizabeth Woodville," in *Every Inch a King: Comparative Studies on Kings and Kingship in the Ancient and Medieval Worlds*, ed. Lynette Mitchell and Charles Melville (Leiden: Brill, 2012), 198.

23. George R.R. Martin, *A Clash of Kings: Book Two of A Song of Ice and Fire* (London: Voyager, 2003), 178.

24. She confesses to Tyrion in *A Clash of Kings*, "he did that himself. All we did was help," and specifies that she and their cousin Lancel (one of Robert's squires) served Robert stronger wine than was his custom, and that prompted him to drunkenly charge a wild boar (45).

25. George R.R. Martin, *A Feast for Crows. Book Four of A Song of Ice and Fire* (New York: Bantam Spectra, 2005), 179.

26. The most popular fan theory names Jaime as the *valonquar* who will eventually kill Cersei, thus fulfilling the prophecy in the books, even if the HBO series chose to kill them both by happenstance.

27. The exception is Marie de France's *Lanval*, where Guenevere accuses the titular knight Lanval of dishonouring her, after he rejects her advances, and nearly gets him executed.

28. Malory, 646. In this, he follows an earlier tradition found in the anonymous *Stanzaic Morte Arthur*, where Guenevere's innocence is emphasized.

29. McCracken, *Romance of Adultery*, 99–100.

30. In the post-Vulgate Cycle, Lancelot and Guenevere do not get their final meeting after Arthur dies and, in a stroke of particularly vicious irony, King Mark of Cornwall charges into Arthur's lands and burns everything to the ground so he can supposedly rebuild it better, except that one of Arthur's former knights kills him before he can rebuild.

31. Malory, 625.

32. Martin acknowledged in a 2002 interview with Roz Kaveney that he has "drawn on the Wars of the Roses" but that he uses "historical sources in a mix and match way." The examples he mentions are that Tywin Lannister

is not Warwick the Kingmaker and Tyrion Lannister is not Richard of Gloucester.

33. For Margaret, see Helen Maurer, *Margaret of Anjou: Queenship and Power in Late Medieval England* (Woodbridge: Boydell, 2003). For Elizabeth, see David Baldwin, *Elizabeth Woodville: Mother of the Princes in the Tower.* (New York: Sutton, 2002). Both are discussed at length in J.L. Laynesmith, *The Last Medieval Queens: English Queenship 1445–1503* (Oxford: Oxford University Press, 2004), and in Kavita Mudan Finn, *The Last Plantagenet Consorts: Gender, Genre, and Historiography, 1440–1627* (New York: Palgrave, 2012).

34. See "January 1484. Titulus Regius," in *The Parliament Rolls of Medieval England 1275–1504,* XV, ed. Rosemary Horrox (London: The Boydell Press, 2005), pp. 15–16. Dominic Mancini, writing in 1483, emphasizes Elizabeth's perceived low birth and accuses her of having "ennobled many of her family" after "easily persuad[ing] the king" to have his brother George of Clarence executed for treason. In *The Usurpation of Richard the Third,* trans. C.A.J. Armstrong (Oxford: Clarendon Press, 1969), 65, 63. Early Henrician histories such as Polydore Vergil's *Anglica Historia* (1534, 1543, 1555) and Edward Hall's *Vnion of the Two Noble & Illustre Houses of Yorke & Lancastre* (1548) follow suit, although Thomas More's unfinished *History of Richard III* (c. 1513) offers an alternate interpretation where Elizabeth is one of very few characters who sees through Richard's schemes, and his is most likely the version used by William Shakespeare in *Richard III* (c. 1595).

35. Philippe de Commynes, an advisor first to the duke of Burgundy and later to King Louis XI of France, observes in his *Mémoires*, that while Edward had once been "among the handsomest princes in the world" in his youth, he gave himself up "to his pleasures, especially ladies, parties and banquets, and hunting," and died suddenly as a result. See Commynes, *Mémoires*, vol. 1, ed. Joël Blanchard (Geneva: Droz, 2007), 505–06, translation mine. From the Victorian period onwards, Elizabeth was portrayed in both scholarship and fiction as a grasping parvenu, with even the acclaimed biography of Edward IV by Charles Ross referring to her "rather cold beauty" and claiming that she lacked "any warmth or generosity of temperament." Ross, *Edward IV* (New Haven: Yale University Press, 1997 [orig. 1974]), 88–89. While recent scholarship (see note 32) has pushed back against this characterization, it was the accepted interpretation at the time at which Martin began writing *A Song of Ice and Fire*.

36. Nicholas Pronay and John Cox, *The Crowland Chronicle Continuations: 1459–1486* (London: Alan Sutton, 1986), 15. *The Historie of the Arrivall of King Edward IV. A.D. 1471,* ed. John Bruce (London: Camden Society, 1838), 17.

37. *Calendar of State Papers and Manuscripts Existing in the Archives and Collections of Milan*, ed. Allen B. Hinds (London: His Majesty's Stationery Office, 1912), pp. 118.

38. See Kavita Mudan Finn, "Tragedy, Transgression, and Women's Voices: The Cases of Eleanor Cobham and Margaret of Anjou," *Viator* 47.2 (2016), 277–303.

39. Once again, Shakespeare is the exception. His Margaret returns from the dead in *Richard III* to haunt the York family and predict the events of the play with the unparalleled accuracy of hindsight.

40. Sam Haysom, "'Game of Thrones' star Lena Headey hints Cersei is headed to an even darker place," *Mashable* (12 December 2016), https://mashable.com/2016/12/12/lena-headey-cersei-season-7/.

41. Martin, *A Feast for Crows*, 243. This praise of Cersei's youthful beauty is echoed in the epilogue to *A Dance with Dragons*, narrated by her uncle Kevan Lannister, who later reflects that he has "pulled [Cersei's] claws" (Martin, *A Dance with Dragons*, 953). If her arc in the show is any indication, this is anything but the case.

42. George R.R. Martin, *A Storm of Swords: Book Three of A Song of Ice and Fire* (New York: Bantam Spectra, 2002), 219.

43. Daniel d'Addario, "Lena Headey on Playing Cersei on *Game of Thrones*: 'I Admire Her'," *TIME Magazine*, 10 July 2017, http://time.com/4773785/lena-headey-cersei-game-of-thrones/.

44. Martin, *A Feast for Crows*, 114.

45. Ibid., 234.

46. Ibid., 335.

47. George R.R. Martin, *A Dance with Dragons. Book Five of A Song of Ice and Fire* (New York: Bantam Spectra, 2011), 281.

48. Martin, *A Feast for Crows*, 345.

49. Martin, *A Game of Thrones*, 377.

50. Martin, *A Feast for Crows*, 481.

51. Ibid., 481.

52. Emmett Booth, "Do you think that under different circumstances Robert might have been a good king?" *Poor Quentyn* [Tumblr] (27 September 2017), http://poorquentyn.tumblr.com/post/165804293848/do-you-think-that-under-different-circumstances. The podcast is NotACastASOIAF and Booth is one of two hosts.

53. Sean T. Collins, "A proposed A Feast for Crows/A Dance with Dragons merged reading order," *All Leather Must Be Boiled* (6 June 2012), http://boiledleather.com/post/24543217702/a-proposed-a-feast-for-crowsa-dance-with-dragons.

54. This is not without its own issues; Daenerys' Meereen arc has come under attack for both implicit and explicit racism that, for better or worse, is largely absent from Cersei's plotline (Taena Merryweather being a notable exception). See Emmett Booth, "So … racism in ASOIAF," *Poor Quentyn* [Tumblr] (27 August 2017), http://poorquentyn.tumblr.com/post/164680125528/soracism-in-asoif-pretty-blatant-no-his.

55. Martin, *A Feast for Crows*, 586.

56. *Game of Thrones*, "Breaker of Chains," Season 4, Episode 3, dir. Alex Graves, written by David Benioff and D.B. Weiss (HBO, 20 April 2014).

57. I discuss this in "High and Mighty Queens of Westeros," Game of Thrones *vs. History: Written in Blood*, ed. Brian A. Pawlac and Elizabeth Lott (Oxford: Wiley, 2017), 26–28.

58. Martin, *A Dance with Dragons*, 853. This incident is first mentioned early in *A Feast for Crows* (50), when Cersei encounters the body of Shae, a sex worker, in her father's bed, and it comes up again in the epilogue, where Kevan confirms his role in choosing Cersei's punishment (953). Nor has it gone unnoticed amongst fans that Tywin Lannister's punishments hinge on sexual degradation, not just in the case of his father's mistress, but also the rape and murder of Princess Elia Martell, and forcing Tyrion to participate in the gang rape of his wife Tysha when the two of them are teenagers.

59. Martin, *A Dance with Dragons*, 858.

60. In the books, only Joffrey has died, murdered at his wedding by Olenna Tyrell. In the HBO series, Myrcella died in the final episode of Season Five after being poisoned by Ellaria Sand in Dorne.

61. Headey, in d'Addario.

62. Headey in James Hibberd, "*Game of Thrones*: Lena Headey reacts to that King's Landing battle ending," *Entertainment Weekly* (12 May 2019), https://ew.com/tv/2019/05/12/game-thrones-cersei-kings-landing-battle-interview/.

63. Geraldine Heng, "Enchanted Ground: The Feminine Subtext in Malory," *Courtly Literature: Culture and Context. Selected Papers from the 5th Triennial Congress of the International Courtly Literature Society, Dalfsen, the Netherlands, 9–16 August, 1986*, vol. 25, ed. Keith Busby and Erik Kooper (Amsterdam: John Benjamins, 1990), 290.

Bibliography

Adams, Tracy. *The Life and Afterlife of Isabeau of Bavaria*. Baltimore: Johns Hopkins University Press, 2010.

Anders, Charlie Jane. "George R.R. Martin: The Complete Unedited Interview." *The Observation Deck* [Kinja]. 23 July 2013. https://observationdeck.kinja.com/george-r-r-martin-the-complete-unedited-interview-886117845.

Anne de France [Anne de Beaujeu]. *Les Enseignements d'Anne de France, duchesse de Bourbonnois et d'Auvergne à sa fille Susanne de Bourbon.* Ed. A.-M. Chazaud. Moulins: C. Desrosiers, 1878.

Baldwin, David. *Elizabeth Woodville: Mother of the Princes in the Tower.* New York: Sutton, 2002.

Benioff, David, and D.B. Weiss. *Game of Thrones.* "Breaker of Chains." Season 4, Episode 3. Directed by Alex Graves. Los Angeles: HBO, 2014.

———. *Game of Thrones.* "The Wars to Come." Season Five, Episode 1. Directed by Michael Slovis. Los Angeles: HBO, 2015.

———. *Game of Thrones.* "The Winds of Winter." Season 6, Episode 10. Directed by Miguel Sapochnik. Los Angeles: HBO, 2016.

———. *Game of Thrones.* "The Bells." Season 8, Episode 5. Directed by Miguel Sapochnik. Los Angeles: HBO, 2019.

bitchfromtheseventhhell and lyannas. "I agree with farty old man GRRM." *the one that leads them is a she-wolf.* Tumblr. 9 June 2016. http://bitchfromtheseventhhell.tumblr.com/post/145690854453/i-agree-with-farty-old-man-grrm-and-id-like-to.

Booth, Emmett. "So … racism in ASOIAF." *PoorQuentyn.* Tumblr. 27 Aug 2017, http://poorquentyn.tumblr.com/post/164680125528/soracism-in-asoif-pretty-blatant-no-his.

———. "Do you think that under different circumstances Robert might have been a good king?" *PoorQuentyn.* Tumblr. 27 Sep 2017. http://poorquentyn.tumblr.com/post/165804293848/do-you-think-that-under-different-circumstances.

Carroll, Shiloh. "Race in A Song of Ice and Fire: Medievalism Posing as Authenticity." *The Public Medievalist: Race, Racism, and the Middle Ages.* 28 November 2017. https://www.publicmedievalist.com/race-in-asoif/.

Collins, Sean T. "A proposed A Feast for Crows/A Dance with Dragons merged reading order." *All Leather Must Be Boiled.* 6 June 2012. http://boiledleather.com/post/24543217702/a-proposed-a-feast-for-crowsa-dance-with-dragons.

Commynes, Philippe de. *Mémoires.* Ed. Joël Blanchard. 2 vol. Geneva: Droz, 2007.

Finn, Kavita Mudan. *The Last Plantagenet Consorts: Gender, Genre, and Historiography, 1440–1627.* New York: Palgrave, 2012.

———. "Tragedy, Transgression, and Women's Voices: The Cases of Eleanor Cobham and Margaret of Anjou." *Viator* 47.2 (2016): 277–303.

———. "High and Mighty Queens of Westeros." Game of Thrones *vs. History: Written in Blood.* Ed. Brian A. Pawlac and Elizabeth Lott. Oxford: Wiley, 2017. 19–31.

Frankel, Valerie Estelle. *Women in Game of Thrones: Power, Conformity, and Resistance.* Jefferson, NC: McFarland, 2013.

Heng, Geraldine. "Enchanted Ground: The Feminine Subtext in Malory." *Courtly Literature: Culture and Context. Selected Papers from the 5th Triennial Congress of the International Courtly Literature Society, Dalfsen, the Netherlands, 9–16 August, 1986.* vol. 25. Ed. Keith Busby and Erik Kooper. Amsterdam: John Benjamins, 1990. 283–300.

Hinds, Allen B. *Calendar of State Papers and Manuscripts Existing in the Archives and Collections of Milan.* London: His Majesty's Stationery Office, 1912.

Holland, Tom. "*Game of Thrones* is more brutally realistic than most historical novels." *The Guardian.* Posted 24 March 2013. Accessed 23 February 2014. <http://www.theguardian.com/tv-and-radio/2013/mar/24/game-of-thrones-realistic-history>

Hsy, Jonathan and Julie Orlemanski. "Race and medieval studies: a partial bibliography." *postmedieval: a journal of medieval cultural studies* 8 (2017): 500–31.

Itzkoff, Dave. "George R.R. Martin on 'Game of Thrones' and Sexual Violence." *The New York Times ArtsBeat.* 2 May 2014. https://artsbeat.blogs.nytimes.com/2014/05/02/george-r-r-martin-on-game-of-thrones-and-sexual-violence/?_php=true&_type=blogs&_php=true&_type=blogs&_r=1&.

joannalannister. "I'm curious. It was always told to me." *JoannaLannister.* Tumblr. 4 August 2015. http://joannalannister.tumblr.com/post/125827358911/im-curious-it-was-always-told-to-me-that-the.

Kaveney, Roz, with George R.R. Martin. "A Storm Coming: Interview with George R.R. Martin." Amazon.co.uk. 2002. https://www.amazon.co.uk/exec/obidos/tg/feature/-/49161/026-1281322-7450821?tag=westeros-21.

Kennedy, Elspeth. "The Making of the *Lancelot-Grail* Cycle." In *A Companion to the Lancelot-Grail Cycle.* Ed. Carol Dover. Cambridge: D.S. Brewer, 2003. 13–22.

Lancelot-Grail: The Old French Arthurian Vulgate and Post-Vulgate In Translation. 10 vol. Ed. Norris J. Lacy. Cambridge: D.S. Brewer, 2010.

Laynesmith, J.L. *The Last Medieval Queens: English Queenship 1445–1503.* Oxford: Oxford UP, 2004.

———. "Telling Tales of Adulterous Queens in Medieval England: From Olympias of Macedonia to Elizabeth Woodville," in *Every Inch a King: Comparative Studies on Kings and Kingship in the Ancient and Medieval Worlds.* Ed. Lynette Mitchell and Charles Melville. Leiden: Brill, 2012. 195–214.

Malory, Sir Thomas. *Le Morte Darthur.* Ed. Stephen H.A. Shepherd. New York: W.W. Norton, 2004.

Mancini, Dominic. *The Usurpation of Richard the Third.* Trans. C.A.J. Armstrong. Oxford: Clarendon Press, 1969.

Martin, George R.R. *A Game of Thrones. Book One of A Song of Ice and Fire.* New York: Bantam Spectra, 1996.

———. *A Clash of Kings. Book Two of A Song of Ice and Fire.* London: Voyager, 2003.

———. *A Storm of Swords. Book Three of A Song of Ice and Fire.* New York: Bantam Spectra, 2002.

————. *A Feast for Crows. Book Four of A Song of Ice and Fire.* New York: Bantam Spectra, 2005.

————. *A Dance with Dragons. Book Five of A Song of Ice and Fire.* New York: Bantam Spectra, 2011.

Maurer, Helen. *Margaret of Anjou: Queenship and Power in Late Medieval England.* Woodbridge: Boydell, 2003.

McCracken, Peggy. *The Romance of Adultery: Queenship and Sexual Transgression in Old French Literature.* Philadelphia: University of Pennsylvania Press, 1998.

Pronay, Nicholas, and John Cox. *The Crowland Chronicle Continuations: 1459–1486.* London: Alan Sutton, 1986.

The Parliament Rolls of Medieval England 1275–1504. London: The Boydell Press, 2005.

The Historie of the Arrivall of King Edward IV. A.D. 1471. Ed. John Bruce. London: Camden Society, 1838.

Pizan, Christine de. *The Treasure of the City of Ladies, or the Book of the Three Virtues.* Ed. and trans. Sarah Lawson. New York: Penguin, 1985.

Ross, Charles. *Edward IV.* Yale English Monarchs Series. New Haven: Yale University Press, 1997. [orig. 1974].

Viennot, Éliane. "Rhétorique de la chasteté dans les *Enseignements d'Anne de France à sa fille Suzanne de Bourbon.*" In *Souillure et Pureté: le Corps et son environnement culturel et politique.* Ed. Jean-Jacques Vincensini. Paris: Maisonneuve & Larose, 2003. 1–6.

CHAPTER 3

Westerosi Queens: Medievalist Portrayal of Female Power and Authority in *A Song of Ice and Fire*

Sylwia Borowska-Szerszun

When asked about female characters, plotlines, and the level of violence against women in *A Song of Ice and Fire*, George R.R. Martin once remarked that "the books reflect a patriarchal society based on the Middle Ages," which "were not a time of sexual egalitarianism" and "had strong ideas about the roles of women."[1] As a result, his narrative, "chiselled out of the historical and imaginary medieval past,"[2] features a brutal world of violence, torture, and sexual abuse, standing in vivid contrast to the more nostalgic Tolkienian vision of the period that has by now become a somewhat clichéd attribute of much fantasy fiction. Martin's narrative cycle and the HBO television series based on his novels have also inspired a heated debate among both fans and critics about the ambiguous portrayal of women, who on the one hand actively participate in "the game of thrones," but on the other hand remain objectified, victimised, and sexually abused. Consequently, as a recent collection of essays edited by Anne Gjelsvik and Rikke Schubart demonstrates, women of the transmedial *Game of Thrones* universe can be interpreted as either feminist or antifeminist, subversive or

S. Borowska-Szerszun (✉)
University of Białystok, Białystok, Poland

© The Author(s) 2020
Z. E. Rohr, L. Benz (eds.), *Queenship and the Women of Westeros*,
Queenship and Power, https://doi.org/10.1007/978-3-030-25041-6_3

subdued, empowered or disenfranchised.[3] This chapter aims to participate in this discussion and examine the issues of female power and authority through the lens of a medievalist, who perceives Martin's construction of the Middle Ages as a contemporary cultural fantasy that selectively appropriates various medieval motifs and topoi and recasts them for the needs of modern readers and viewers. The chapter's analysis of medieval inspirations behind *A Song of Ice and Fire* is, therefore, grounded in the conviction that "the past is the present, for the past never dies but is continually reborn in the present moment of consideration and consumption."[4]

In a recent article, Martin's cycle has been examined by Bartłomiej Błaszkiewicz against theories defining the nature of kingship during the High Middle Ages.[5] His analysis focuses on the depiction of male rulers and leaders (e.g., Aerys Targaryen, Robert Baratheon, Eddar Stark, and Tywin and Tyrion Lannister) and their understanding of power and monarchy, practically excluding from consideration the issue of Westerosi queens. The focus of his discussion, quite unintentionally perhaps, draws attention to an observation made by Robert Bucholz and Carole Levin that in medieval and early modern period queens who ruled by themselves tended to be seen as "anomalous" and "luminal," whereas their reigns were perceived "like festivals or riots, albeit of a more sustained duration—extended moments of suspension in the normal working of political, social, cultural, and gender history."[6] This is not to say that the Middle Ages failed to recognise leadership by women when the need arose, and indeed politically influential queens appeared and governed on their own, or as co-rulers whose authority pertained to a more private, though inseparably political, sphere of the monarchy (marriage, family, patronage). While some of these queens were subordinate to their husbands, fathers, or brothers, others exercised power alongside the kings, which implies that traditional categories of kingship and queenship are unsatisfactory if the complicated structure of power relationships is to be fully explained.

Instead of focusing on kings and queens separately, Theresa Earenfight proposes the category of "rulership," metaphorically depicted as "a flexible sack" that is capacious enough to incorporate both kings and queens and see their power jointly, as complementary rather than exclusive, without privileging the public over the domestic.[7] In her study of Yolande of Aragon, Zita Eva Rohr takes a similar stance, observing:

> Monarchy is a gendered institution but no successful king or queen has ruled in a vacuum—all needed supporting institutions to succeed and prosper. We should consider queenship and kingship therefore as complemen-

tary, sometimes symbiotic, institutions and this demands that we drop the creaky tendency to study powerful and successful kings and queens in isolation. It is better to study kingdoms and dynasties and kings and queens together, examining them in terms of cooperative rulerships (and sometimes uncooperative, antagonistic ones).[8]

However, even when the notion of pre-modern queenship is approached in this way, it is still, as Earenfight further notes, "bounded by a patriarchal political environment that privileged rule by a king that could either permit or prohibit women from the political sphere." Because queens are not "born" but "become," the office of queenship is less fixed, and can, consequently, be seen as a "discursive" and "generative" one, becoming "an incessant project" and "a daily act of reconstruction," dependent to a greater extent (than in the case of kingship) on the individual personality, temperament, and family connections of the queen, who under certain circumstances (especially when the need to continue a dynastic line was stronger than prejudice) could overcome institutional obstacles.[9]

This context seems crucial when examining the figures of Cersei Lannister, Margaery Tyrell, and Daenerys Targaryen—three powerful female characters of Martin's narrative who aspire to gain and exercise royal power in a fictional society that is unused to and distrustful of female leadership. Taking into account Martin's patchwork approach to medieval history, it is obviously possible to draw parallels between these fictional women and historical figures of queens.[10] However, this chapter predominantly focuses on the images and tactics employed by Cersei, Margaery, and Daenerys against the background of medieval misogynistic tradition on the one hand, and pre-modern "profeminine" defences[11] of women on the other. Furthermore, it discusses the ways in which they exercise their power in order to determine to what extent their actions conform to or challenge the stereotypes associated with female leadership.

CERSEI LANNISTER: MISOGYNISTIC STEREOTYPES OF FEMALE RULE

The depiction of Cersei Lannister seems to correspond to a huge extent to the anti-woman rhetoric of the Middle Ages, which can be seen as "a cultural constant"[12] that not only informed theological and scientific tracts, but also seized the popular imagination. The construction of women as inferior to men stemmed from the interpretation of the Biblical story of creation (Genesis 2: 18–22), which framed woman as a "help meet" created in the image of man, not God. This narrative has twofold implications. Firstly, it depicts Adam as fully partaking in God's divinity, and thus hierarchically higher than a woman, who must remain in a position subordinate to him. Secondly, the fact that Eve is created of human flesh makes her further removed from God and, consequently, more prone to sin. Such views were augmented through Aristotelian physiology, which distinguished between the male principle (soul, form) and the female one (body, matter) and construed woman as a "deformed" or "defective" man,[13] and Galenic medicine, which ascribed female "softness" and "weakness" to an imbalance of humours and a tendency towards "coldness" and "humidity" that were responsible for blocking the exteriorisation of her genitals.[14] Becoming, in Tertullian's famous words, "the gateway of the devil,"[15] a woman is often depicted as more lecherous than man by her very nature. In Jehan le Fevre's *The Lamentations of the Matheolus* (c. 1371–2), for instance, women are portrayed as sexual manipulators, who also torment their spouses with nagging and disobedience, which inevitably leads to their husbands' downfall. It is argued that a woman is the reason behind the failure of men, both great and small—"if the greatest men are deceived, then the lesser naturally fall."[16] In satirical and farcical tradition, female sexuality is usually excessive, uncontrollable, and frequently coupled with rebelliousness, which poses a threat not only to individuals who blame women for tempting them into sin, but also to the established hierarchy and social order (e.g., the institution of marriage, the legitimacy of children, succession, inheritance, and clerical celibacy).[17]

Such misogynistic beliefs and fears materialise in Martin's narrative in the figure of Cersei, whose extramarital incestuous relationship with her twin brother and her unquenchable desire for power lead to the murder of the lawful king, usurpation of the succession line, and civil war. Elsewhere in this volume, Kavita Mudan Finn contrasts the figures of Cersei and Guenevere, noticing that the childless love affair of the latter has not really endangered succession. This is probably why the adulterous queen of the Arthurian lore might evoke empathy, while Cersei's actions, epitomising queenly treason, are never redeemed. Paradoxically, Cersei is most dangerous as Queen Consort when Robert Baratheon—not a model ruler himself—is still alive, and immediately after his death when she acts promptly and effectively to secure the throne for her son. Her moves towards the end of the first novel demonstrate a flair for courtly games, considerable political aptitude, and cold pragmatism that overshadow Ned Stark's naïve belief that proving the truth of Robert's son's illegitimacy is enough to win the throne.[18] As Queen Regent, however, reigning on behalf of the underaged Tommen, Cersei commits mistake after mistake, becoming in fact a short-sighted tyrant in skirts, whose fall is inevitable. Having boldly stepped into the realm of men, she grows paranoid, surrounds herself with half-wits, mistakes blandishment for good council, and, consequently, fails as a leader.

Although she gains an unprecedented share of power in patriarchal Westeros, Cersei inspires little, if any, sympathy from Martin's readers. She negates any qualities traditionally associated with femininity, despises other women, labelling them a "flock of frightened hens,"[19] and often repeats that she should have been born a man, emphasising at the same time the uneven distribution of power in the society:

> We were so much alike, I could never understand why they treated us so *differently*. Jaime learned to fight with sword and lance and mace, while I was taught to smile and sing and please. He was heir to Casterly Rock, while I was to be sold to some stranger like a horse, to be ridden whenever my new owner liked, beaten whenever he liked, and cast aside in time for a younger filly. Jaime's lot was to be glory and power, while mine was birth and moon blood.[20]

Thus, Cersei's fury may be partly explained by her justified objections to the limited number of choices for women in the society, which valued its royal women mainly for their child-bearing capabilities. Similarly, her machinations leading to the murder of King Robert and putting an illegitimate successor on the throne might be seen as a conscious act of vengeance for years of living in a loveless and abusive relationship. In fact, Cersei derives considerable satisfaction from the fact she has never given birth to a child conceived with the king: "'Robert got me with child once,' she said, her voice thick with contempt. 'My brother found a woman to cleanse me.'"[21] Unlike HBO's *Game of Thrones*, where she is, as Marta Eidsvåg argues, more motherly and capable of loving any child irrespective of who the father is, the novels break the taboo of abortion and highlight the fact that in truth Cersei wants to secure power for herself, not her children.[22]

The Cersei of the novels is highly sexualised and consciously uses her body to achieve the ends she desires, which conforms with misogynistic beliefs expressed in the Middle Ages and well beyond the period. Later, when she acts as queen, she rejects any virtues archetypically ascribed to women, such as nurturance, caring, compassion, empathy and collaboration, and fashions herself as a self-centred, aggressive, and violent tyrant. Her attempts to "act like a man" seem grotesque even in the chapters focalised from her perspective, in which she increasingly resembles gluttonous, sottish, abusive, and foolish Robert Baratheon. Cersei's female rule is, in fact, depicted in a manner once more reminiscent of medieval tradition, which featured numerous representations of carnivalesque reversals of gender roles, one of the most widespread being the image of a man beaten by a woman. Invading the margins of the manuscripts[23] and the space of the church,[24] such motifs are also present in theatre and highlight the absurdity of female empowerment, which is seen as a transgression against the natural order of things that should be ridiculed and punished. This is, for instance, the case of Mrs. Noah, who refuses to enter the ark, challenges her husband's authority and abuses him verbally, which in the Noah Play from the Towneley Cycle leads to a physical confrontation between the spouses and accounts for much of the comedy in the scene. However, irrespective of her temporal rebelliousness, Noah's wife is finally chastised and forced to enter the ark—a symbol of male-governed space—and saved against her will, the hierarchy thus being restored and reinforced.[25]

Cersei's ritual punishment, her walk of shame towards the end of *A Dance with Dragons*, serves a similar corrective function. Paraded naked through a jeering crowd, she is deprived of any attributes of royal power and devalued in the eyes of her subjects:

> Cersei was soiled goods now, her power at an end. Every baker's boy and beggar in the city had seen her shame and every tart and tanner from Flea Bottom to Pisswater Bend had gazed upon her nakedness, their eager eyes crawling over her breasts and belly and woman's parts. No queen could expect to rule after that again. In gold and silk and emeralds Cersei had been a queen, the next thing to a goddess; naked, she was only human, an aging woman with stretch marks on her belly and teats that had begun to sag.[26]

While her misdeeds are undeniable, the punishment, framed as a spectacle for the masses, is not meant as penance but has the political purpose of destroying her reputation by making a spectacle of her body. Kavita Mudan Finn has pointed out elsewhere certain inspirations behind Martin's walk of atonement, mentioning the cases of Eleanor Cobham, convicted of witchcraft in 1441, and Jane Shore, an infamous mistress of Edward IV, accused of treason in 1483.[27] However, as *Liber Albus*, a fifteenth-century compilation of customary laws for London demonstrates, similar measures were much more often taken to punish individuals of much lower social status—bawds, whores, or simply adulterous women. The punishments ranged from cutting or shaving a woman's hair and her being paraded to the pillory, with a visual emblem of a sexual offence (striped hood, white rod in her hand), to banishment from the town. Such public shame was primarily understood as a deterrent, whose power derived from a consequent loss of personal reputation.[28]

The striking point in Martin's narrative is that although Cersei has indeed made grave mistakes as a political leader, she is disciplined as a harlot, not a monarch. Her reign is clearly depicted as a carnivalesque suspension of the normal workings of the dynasty, which brings nothing but chaos and social unrest. Yet, her punishment relies mainly on degrading the queen by exposing her naked body to public gaze—an unthinkable measure, if the tyrannical ruler was male. Although Cersei's road to power was bumpy, and that following it required Machiavellian skills, steely determination and personal sacrifice, all this is to be forgotten. In her final appearance in the novels, she is presented as a promiscuous woman, whose unrestrained and uncontrollable sexuality is dangerous, as it has led to the decline of the kingdom. A powerful message emerging from Cersei's narrative is that the power she exercised was never her own, but "stolen" from men who rightfully deserved it. Her attempts to act like a man are similarly discredited, which undermines the tactics of adopting a masculine leadership style by women. In her attempts to emulate hyper-masculine behaviour, Cersei has gained nothing but has instead exposed all the vices attributed to women by misogynists—shallowness, lust, irrationality, instability, jealousy, and petty vengefulness. Such a depiction of one of the most prominent female characters in the novels clearly conforms to the most unfortunate stereotypes that perpetuate misogynistic ideas about women's ability to rule.

Margaery Tyrell: Traditionally Feminine Queenship

Cersei Lannister is not the only woman in King's Landing who aspires to gain power and wield political influence. Her younger rival, Margaery Tyrell, takes a completely different approach to fashioning herself as queen. Instead of challenging traditionally feminine behaviours and objecting to her role of a marriageable political asset, she tries to take full advantage of these to establish the image of a co-ruler, rather than an independent monarch. Yet another woman in *A Song of Ice and Fire* who derives her power from adhering to rather than subverting the model of conventional femininity is Catelyn Stark. In her contribution to this volume, Kris Swank interprets the figure of Catelyn as an Anglo-Saxon peace-weaving queen, reminiscent of Wealhtheow from *Beowulf*, whose responsibilities include bringing peace through marriage, providing legitimate heirs, exercising influence on social hierarchies, and offering advice to the king. Such a strategy was obviously much more widespread in later Middle Ages, which did not conceptualise queenship directly and exhaustively in political theory yet established the Virgin Mary, the Queen of Heaven, as a primary role model. Thus, as Lisa Benz St. John observes, the primary responsibilities of an ideal queen, highlighted in the iconic depictions of royal women, included motherhood, seen as a necessary measure to secure succession, and mediation between the king and his people, parallel to the role of the Virgin Mary as an intercessor between heaven and earth.[29]

One more model of intercession can be seen in the Old Testament narrative of Esther, a beautiful yet eloquent queen, risking her life to mediate on behalf of the Israelites with King Ahasuerus, who had issued an edict to kill all Jews. Esther's persuasive appeal pleases the king so much that the law is reversed, and her people are actually allowed to take revenge upon their enemies. The biblical narrative frames the queen's authority as being complementary, though less direct, to the king's—he stands for intelligence and law; she for the heart and mercy. Clearly, under certain circumstance such a division of roles could be successfully applied in politics as "a device to enable a king to change his mind or become reconciled with his subjects"[30] without actually losing face. It was also promoted by Christine de Pizan, the leading pro-feminine defender of her own sex at the beginning of the fifteenth century. In *The Treasure of the City of Ladies*, a manual for noble women, she establishes peace-making as a crucial female task, resulting from their "sweeter disposition":

> [M]en are by nature more courageous and more hot-headed, and the great desire they have to avenge themselves prevents their considering either the perils or the evils that can result from war. But women are by nature more timid and also of a sweeter disposition, and for this reason, if they are wise and if they wish to, they can be the best means of pacifying men.[31]

In her *Book of the City of Ladies*, Christine de Pizan undertakes the challenging task of dismissing misogynistic attacks and establishing Reason, Rectitude and Justice as key female virtues. *City of Ladies* derives its power not so much from the multitude of examples of virtuous and courageous women, but from offering an alternative vision of history, in which female contribution to the development of civilisation is fully acknowledged and celebrated.[32] These examples imply that, despite medieval misogynistic tradition, medieval aristocratic women were provided with models of exemplary behaviour that would allow them to exercise power in a way approved by their patriarchal society.

Margaery appears on the political stage as a girl who is barely 14, "very pretty, with a doe's soft eyes and a mane of curling brown hair that fell about her shoulders in lazy ringlets," whose "smile was shy and sweet."[33] Yet this large-eyed, pale, and lovable teenager is a much more skilful courtier than she initially appears to be, pragmatically using the gendered means available to her in her struggle for power. More cunning than she looks, she quickly adapts to the fast-changing circumstances and seems not to be bothered by the fact that her family would do practically anything to put her on the throne. Although she is absent in *A Game of Thrones*, there is a plan to bring her to the court in the hope that Robert Baratheon would fall in love with her and dismiss Cersei. In *A Clash of Kings*, after Robert's death, she is quickly married off to his younger brother, Renly, who is planning to seize the throne. Their marriage is brief and allegedly unconsummated, which makes it possible for Margaery to remain on the marriage market after his death and be wedded to Joffrey Baratheon in order to consolidate a political and military alliance. Finally, with Joffrey poisoned on their wedding day, she is remarried to the child-king, Tommen Baratheon, who would have been easy for her to manipulate if not for Cersei. Like most medieval queens at their coronations, Margaery fashions herself as a virgin during her wedding:

> The bride was lovely in ivory silk and Myrish lace, her skirts decorated with floral patterns picked out in seed pearls. As Renly's widow, she might have worn the Baratheon colors, gold and black, yet she came to them a Tyrell, in a maiden's cloak made of a hundred cloth-of-gold roses sewn to green velvet.[34]

Although the young queen is adept at projecting the right image, her virginity is questioned throughout the narrative, with Cersei obsessively scheming to uncover her carnal involvement with other men, in which she eventually succeeds in *A Dance with Dragons*. Martin's inspirations behind the depiction of Margaery Tyrell might have included the case of Katherine of Aragon, who maintained to the end of her life that her marriage with the 15-year-old Prince Arthur was never consummated and wore virginal white at her coronation as Henry VIII's newly wed queen.[35] Paradoxically, however, it is also possible to associate Margaery, accused of adultery and treason, with Anne Boleyn, who faced similar charges that included a love affair with a Flemish musician, Mark Smeaton, a couple of other courtiers, and her own brother, George Boleyn.[36]

Still, before her fall, Margaery Tyrell successfully accommodates herself within the category of a "help meet" who does not threaten patriarchal authority yet establishes her own sphere of influence. Not only does she manage to set up her own household consisting of loyal guards, courtiers, servants, and entertainers, but she also grasps the importance of actively building her image through frequent public appearances:

> She seldom let more than three days pass without going off for a ride ... The little queen was fond of going out on boats as well, sailing up and down the Blackwater Rush to no particular purpose. When she was feeling pious she would leave the castle to pray at Baelor's Sept. She gave her custom to a dozen different seamstresses, was well-known amongst the city's goldsmiths, and had even been known to visit the fish market by the Mud Gate for a look at the day's catch. Wherever she went, the smallfolk fawned on her, and Lady Margaery did all she could to fan their ardor. She was forever giving alms to beggars, buying hot pies off bakers' carts, and reining up to speak to common tradesmen.[37]

The passage clearly indicates that her activities not only encompass courtly entertainments appropriate to a noble woman, but also expose traditional feminine values of kindness, piety, patronage, compassion, and charity. Although actions such as visiting seamstresses, goldsmiths, and the fish market belong to the domestic sphere, and seem to have little political impact, they do have a considerable symbolic potential and effectively generate interest in the crown, consequently increasing the popularity of the ruling monarch. It is important to point out here that in the medieval period the court, like any other noble household, was not so much an architectural but a social and political structure. Built around the basic social unit of the family, it was not just a place of residence but an essential centre for business, trade, and political activity.[38] As a combination of the public and the private with no clearly defined border between the two spheres, it also became an arena where every action had a significant performative quality and was potentially laden with symbolic value.

Thus, Margaery's youthful and gay court, standing in vivid contrast to Cersei's environment dominated by terror and fear, is not only a stage upon which the younger queen might play the lead, but also an alternative centre of domestic power gradually gaining in importance and influence. Aware of the significance of decorum, Margaery Tyrell always acts out a role that projects the right image, and is flexible enough to adapt her behaviour to the changing circumstances. This becomes particularly evident in her treatment of two totally different royal spouses—Joffrey and Tommen. During the wedding feast with the first of them, when her newly wed spouse offends Tyrion by spilling wine on him, Margaery is shown as a positive influence on Joffrey, unobtrusively yet effectively placating his violent and aggressive behaviour.[39] With the much younger Tommen, she acts in a more motherly or sisterly manner, exerting a subtle emotional influence on the boy-king and providing him with the cordiality and encouragement he is denied by his mother.

Margaery Tyrell is a useful foil for Cersei, and their rivalry over Tommen occupies much of their narrative. Both women come from mighty and affluent families and have been groomed to become successful queens, yet their paths to power are depicted very differently. While Cersei strives to remain in the spotlight, and rebels against the established hierarchy, Margaery skilfully seizes opportunities available to women who realise that they can gain more by wielding discreet influence over men than by challenging their authority. Unlike Cersei, who openly despises other women, Margaery believes in female solidarity, relying on her ladies-in-waiting and treating them as her chief allies: "Her women are her castle walls. They sleep with her, dress her, pray with her, read with her, sew with her."[40] On the whole, her tactics, though far from naïve and idealistic, have won her considerable sympathy from Martin's readers, perhaps implying that a less aggressive and more subtle leadership style is still considered more appropriate for a woman. However, there is a twist to this apparently more positive portrayal. When compared with Cersei, especially in the novels, Margaery lacks substance, being more of a function of the narrative than a full-fledged character with a developed personality. Her story of rise and fall is narrated only from the perspective of others, and the young Queen Consort never becomes a character-focaliser in *A Song of Ice and Fire*, emphasising her marginality over the course of events. To some extent, this mirrors the position of queens in traditional historical narratives, which recount the events from the perspective of male chroniclers and at best allow a glimpse into queens' outward actions without insight into their private motivations.

Daenerys Targaryen: Exceptional She-king

While Cersei openly challenges patriarchal authority, and Margaery does her best to play by the rules established by men, Daenerys Targaryen, perhaps the most loved female character in Martin's narrative, is construed as a figure who defies conceptualisation in terms of clearly delineated gender categories. Like Cersei and Margaery, she is initially objectified and virtually sold to a Dothraki leader by her brother Viserys in exchange for a promise of military support:

> "We go home with an army, sweet sister. With Khal Drogo's army, that is how we go home. And if you must wed him and bed him for that, you will." He smiled at her. "I'd let his whole *khalasar* fuck you if need be, sweet sister, all forty thousand men, and their horses too if that was what it took to get my army. Be grateful it is only Drogo."[41]

Yet, already in the first novel of the series, a 13-year-old child bride undergoes a gradual transformation, matures, and gains significant influence, which is construed nonetheless in strikingly sexual terms. Initially forced to have sex with her domineering and powerful husband on his terms, Daenerys slowly learns to change his sexual habits and derive her own pleasure, which is reflected in the couple's growing emotional attachment to one another and her increasing social status. In narrative terms, when we look at the structure of a fairy-tale, Daenerys's story starts where fairy tales usually end for female characters—with marriage and loss of freedom. Yet, this turns out to be just the beginning of a long journey for her, which will consist of a few important stages and tests that she needs to pass to achieve psychological and political maturity.[42]

Already in the course of *A Game of Thrones*, Daenerys has emotionally detached herself from her brother Viserys, who tries to manipulate her, and learned that soft-heartedness and compassion sometimes need to give way to cold-hearted justice, which is an important lesson for a future ruler. She has also gained respect as *khal's* wife, adapted to the customs of her new people, and has fallen pregnant, which significantly increases her status. Furthermore, her future son is prophesised to unite the Dothraki into a single *khalasar* and conquer the world, which associates Daenerys with the Virgin Mary as the mother of a future saviour. All these elements make *khaleesi* the epitome of an ideal queen, who fulfils her traditional duties and wields profound, though indirect, influence on the leader's politics.

These idyllic circumstances do not last long, however, and her narrative powerfully highlights the illusoriness of female power if it relies solely upon male authority. When Drogo is seriously wounded, it turns out that his warriors will not accept orders from a woman because it is against Dothraki custom. An attempt to save her husband in a bloody ritual of magic, in which Daenerys unintentionally sacrifices her unborn child, proves useless and leaves Drogo alive yet catatonic.

The most important transformation of the *khaleesi* happens at the end of the first novel, when she euthanises her half-dead spouse and steps into his funeral pyre to be reborn as the Mother of Dragons, determined to become a leader on her own rather than masculine terms. The symbolism of this scene is significant. When Daenerys emerges from the pyre naked, yet unharmed, with her hair—a stereotypical attribute of feminine beauty—burnt off and with the dragons suckling at her lactating breasts, she is presented for the first time as a character who transcends traditionally defined gender categories. Like her dragons, which in Westeros are believed to be "neither male nor female ... but now one and now the other, as changeable as a flame,"[43] Daenerys does not really discard her femininity, but instead fully embraces more masculine aspects of her personality when they are needed, self-fashioning herself in a way that destabilises the oppositional structure of gender difference, in which masculinity is defined as strong, active, public, and outdoor, and femininity as weak, passive, private, and domestic.

Such blurring of masculine and feminine images in the depiction of Daenerys reminds one of the tactics adopted by Elizabeth I, who "constructed a vocabulary of rule that was largely male while her most popular mythological analogues tended to be female divinities."[44] While Elizabeth frequently referred to herself as the King and placed emphasis on the masculine qualities of intellect, eloquence, and courage as prerequisites for the office of monarch, such an image was counterbalanced with references to her beauty and femininity. Employing the imagery related to mythological Astraea and Diana, Edmund Spenser's Belphoebe of *The Faerie Queene*, and the Marian cult, Elizabeth fashioned herself primarily as a virgin, married to no man but her people, transposing her maternal instincts onto them.[45] However, as Marjorie Swann argues in her discussion of the image of the Tudor queen in Stuart writing, Elizabeth's virginity was often regarded as ambiguous. On the one hand, the queen's virginal self-renunciation could serve to highlight her commitment to the greater good of her subjects. On the other hand, because in pre-modern times virginity was construed as a temporary and pre-marital state, a woman who permanently embraced it and refused to produce legitimate successors opposed the social norms that framed begetting children as the point of female sexuality. Finally, as some writers questioned Elizabeth's chastity, her body could be read as "the site of an extramarital, nonprocreative female eroticism,"[46] the queen becoming a disturbingly transgressive woman engaging in sexual activity with men for pleasure, which was clearly not meant to lead to pregnancy.

In Martin's narrative, Daenerys's image is not grounded in virginity, but her sexuality is rendered in similar terms. Firstly, the portrayal of Daenerys is indebted to the motif of the unattainable lady of chivalric romance, exalted above the men who love her, serve her, and pledge their oaths of loyalty to her.[47] This is particularly striking in her relationship with Ser Jorah Mormont, who is attracted to her sexually yet remains in a subservient position with no possibility of satisfying his desire. Secondly, as in the case of the Tudor queen, Daenerys's sexuality is construed as unrelated to reproduction. Although she cannot conceive and bear children, she does not renounce sexual pleasure, choosing freely her male (Daario Naharis) and female (Irri) erotic partners from amongst people who neither advance nor threaten her political position. While such freedom was considered unnatural and threatening in Elizabethan era, Martin reveals it to be a sign of empowerment, powerfully discrediting the negative stereotypes of female rule through sexual manipulation, which were used in the depiction of Cersei. Finally, Elizabeth's symbolic virginity is substituted with the metaphor of exceptional motherhood, which has equal potential for emphasising Daenerys's uniqueness in comparison with ordinary women.

Her exceptionalism is expressed particularly well through her symbolic and affective connection to her dragons: "I am Daenerys Stormborn, daughter of dragons, bride of dragons, mother of dragons."[48] This link can be interpreted as a certain popular fantasy transformation of the medieval perception of a ruler as one bearing a likeness to God and deriving his wisdom and authority from him, expressed for instance by St. Thomas.[49] The dragons do not stand for divinity here, but they do symbolically strengthen Daenerys's claim to the throne as not only inborn but somehow mystical and originating in the mythical times. They also emphasise the extraordinary nature of her motherhood. Apparently henceforth unable to have children of her own, which would undermine her as a queen if the nature of her rule were rendered in traditional terms, she becomes the mother of monsters and slaves. The former element of this construction highlights the violent, masculine aspect of her personality, whereas the latter refers to her more feminine compassionate and merciful side. Furthermore, the metaphor of motherhood makes it possible for Martin to depict Daenerys's maternal instincts of nurturing and caring as inherent to the well-being of her people and embracing all her subjects, especially the weak, the poor, and the powerless.

The concept of mother being central to the depiction of Daenerys, it is also intertwined with the images traditionally associated with masculinity. Throughout the cycle, she is portrayed as a warrior queen in possession of the most destructive weapons (dragons), leading the army of the Unsullied and conquering the lands, yet always trying to avoid unnecessary combat. Shortly after her transformation into the Mother of Dragons, she starts to perceive her long hair not as an attribute of femininity but as "a function of Dothraki masculinity"[50] and an important symbol of her strength and leadership. As Daenerys conquers new territories and frees slaves in the cities of Essos, her portrayal is enriched by the image of "the breaker of chains,"[51] who offers freedom and hope to anyone, irrespective of their position:

> I see the faces of slaves. I free you. Take off your collars. Go if you wish, no one shall harm you. If you stay, it will be as brothers and sisters, husbands and wives ... I see the children, women, the wrinkled faces of the aged ... To each of you I say, give me your hands and your hearts, and there will always be a place for you.[52]

However, as Daenerys progresses with her quest in Slaver's Bay, she eventually learns that it is easier to conquer than to keep power. Her attempts to free the enslaved from the hands of their masters prove utopian as the liberated cities fall into disorder and back to slavery once she moves on with her conquest, which finally motivates her to stay in Meereen and exercise her power there. Her sense of justice and the ethical imperative to free the slaves stand in conflict with her personal and political ambition to reclaim the Iron Throne, which illustrates a typical dilemma in medieval moral theory—a situation when "an agent discovers equally compelling moral reasons to perform and to desist from an action, and these compelling reasons cannot be voided."[53] Trying to find a degree of balance, Daenerys not only learns to sacrifice her personal desires for the greater good (e.g., her decision to marry the powerful merchant, Hizdahr, to secure peace in Meereen), but also realises that her ethical ideals, when confronted with economic reality, might be insufficient to preserve the well-being of her people (e.g., when she learns that the liberated slaves are selling themselves back to their masters as their situation has deteriorated under her rule). As a consequence, she begins to grasp the pragmatic aspects of successful leadership, requiring swift action and harsh decisions, which makes it possible for readers to see her in terms of a Machiavellian prince, stereotypically connected with male leaders.[54]

Throughout her narrative, Daenerys Targaryen constantly develops and learns to hold back her emotions when justice is required. Unlike Cersei, who sees her gender as a major weakness, Daenerys derives her power from it. Unlike Margaery, whose ascent to power is achieved through family connections and a carefully devised public relations campaign, the Mother of Dragons is truly concerned with the welfare of her subjects. Combining archetypal attributes of masculinity (courage, independence, intellect, assertiveness) and femininity (caring, compassion, mercy), she manages to remain free of the negative stereotypes ascribed to both sexes. She does not hesitate when bold steps are needed, yet again, in contrast to Cersei, she understands the worth of good counsel: "A queen must listen to all. … The highborn and the low, the strong and the weak, the noble and the venal. One voice may speak you false, but in many there is always truth to be found."[55] The problem is, however, that Daenerys's advisors frequently have their own agendas, which might, but do not necessarily, meet her own interests. As Shiloh Carroll demonstrates in this volume, the decision whom to trust becomes crucial to successful rule. Even if Daenerys fails sometimes, her errors of judgment in Meereen might serve as further lessons preparing her to become an effective leader. While not flawless, the character of Daenerys could be interpreted not so much as an exemplary queen, who is traditionally defined by her reproductive and intercessory capabilities, but as an exceptional she-king—a leader, who sometimes errs as all humans do, but knows the costs of personal sacrifice and chooses to work for the common good, not her personal interest.

CONCLUSION

The narratives of Cersei, Margaery, and Daenerys allow us to explore different layers of meanings inherent to the category of medieval and early modern queenship, as well as to uncover various attitudes towards female leadership and authority in a more general sense. Although the stories of these three queens are built from similar foundations, and touch upon similar problems (sexualisation, objectification, marriage, adaptation to the patriarchal system), particular elements have been given a varying amount of emphasis, resulting in strikingly different portrayals of women in power. Firstly, the depiction of Cersei Lannister is grounded in negative stereotypes of femininity and exposes the continuity of misogynistic preconceptions in Western cultural memory. Secondly, the construction of Margaery Tyrell relies heavily on traditional understandings of the role of the queen, one who is supposed to demonstrate feminine values and exercise influence from behind the scenes. Yet, unlike the other two queens, Margaery lacks both substance and voice in Martin's tale, which powerfully undermines the effectiveness of her strategies. Finally, Daenerys Targaryen, one of the most prominent and successful characters in the cycle, is construed in a manner that challenges stereotypical perception of gender roles by combining the metaphors of mother, warrior, and saviour in her depiction.

Despite a touch of magic, *A Song of Ice and Fire* is substantially a medievalist narrative structured as a quest for power, which features several female competitors. For women, this quest is also inseparably connected with their sexuality, and the attention given to their varying attitudes to sex finds no equivalent in the depiction of male characters, whose sexual exploits have no particular influence on their success as rulers. The depiction of Cersei's dangerous and transgressive sexuality draws on a long tradition of linking female power with sexual manipulation and expresses misogynistic stereotypes that have not been securely sealed off in the past but lurk beneath the surface of contemporaneity. On the other hand, the apparent celebration of the traditionally feminine values in the portrayal of Margaery ends up in a spectacular disaster, when she faces accusations of infidelity and treason. In both cases, a woman's suitability as a ruler is measured in terms of her sexual reputation, which again makes one wonder whether the double standards, which applaud men for their sex life yet ostracise women for promiscuity, are really the thing of the past. Only Daenerys, significantly operating on the outskirts of civilisation, liberates herself from conventional morality and enjoys her sexuality, which does not, however, influence her political choices, thus finally projecting a more positive vision of female rule.

While the figures of Cersei and Margaery belong to a long tradition of depicting women as either shrews or "help meets," Daenerys is more ambiguous. Although she is objectified at the outset and sexualised throughout the tale, she becomes an "agent of considerable power who strives to be just, moral, and fair to those who pledge her loyalty."[56] It is debatable whether Daenerys's exceptionalism can be seen as a sign of female empowerment or as an "enduring cultural fantasy of the strong woman who rises above a general condition of female disenfranchisement."[57] However, the presence of such a hybrid and troubling female avatar questions the binary oppositions of much fantasy fiction, as well as revisions certain archetypes that have been appropriated by the genre.

NOTES

1. John Hibberd, "George R.R. Martin explains why there's violence against women on 'Game of Thrones,'" *Entertainment Weekly*, 3 June 2015, http://ew.com/article/2015/06/03/george-rr-martin-thrones-violence-women
2. Carolyne Larrington, *Winter Is Coming: The Medieval World of* Game of Thrones (London, New York: I.B. Tauris, 2016), 1.
3. Rikke Schubart and Anne Gjelsvik, "Introduction," in *Women of Ice and Fire: Gender,* Game of Thrones, *and Multiple Media Engagement*, eds. Anne Gjelsvik and Rikke Schubart (New York: Bloomsbury Academic, 2016), 1–10.
4. Tison Pugh and Angela Jane Weisl, *Medievalism: Making the Past in the Present* (New York: Routledge, 2013), 10.
5. Bartłomiej Błaszkiewicz, "On the Theories of Kingship in George R.R. Martin's *A Song of Ice and Fire*," in *Basic Categories of Fantastic Literature Revisited*, eds. Andrzej Wicher, Piotr Spyra, and Joanna Matyjaszczyk (Newcastle upon Tyne: Cambridge Scholars Publishing, 2014), 115–126.
6. Robert Bucholz and Carole Levin, "Introduction," in *Queens & Power in Medieval and Early Modern England*, eds. Carole Levin and Robert Bucholz (Lincoln: University of Nebraska Press, 2009), xiv.
7. Theresa Earenfight, "Without the Persona of the Prince: Kings, Queens and the Idea of Monarchy in Late Medieval Europe," *Gender and History* 19, no.1 (April 2007): 10.
8. Zita Eva Rohr, *Yolande of Aragon (1381–1442) Family and Power: The Reverse of the Tapestry* (New York: Palgrave Macmillan, 2016), 4.
9. Earenfight, "Without the Persona of the Prince," 14.
10. See, for instance, James J. Hudson's contribution to the present volume and Kavita Mudan Finn's "High and Mighty Queens of Westeros," in Game of Thrones *versus History: Written in Blood*, ed. Brian A. Pavlac (Hoboken: Wiley Blackwell, 2017), 19–31.
11. I use Alcuin Blamires's terminology to refer to texts that construe a more positive view of femininity according to the cultural ideology of the Middle

Ages rather than later feminist understanding. See Alcuin Blamires, *The Case for Women in Medieval Culture* (Oxford: Oxford University Press, 1998), 10–13.

12. Howard R. Bloch, "Medieval Misogyny," in *Misogyny, Misandry, and Misanthropy*, eds. Howard R. Bloch and Frances Ferguson (Berkeley: University of California Press, 1989), 1.

13. Alcuin Blamires, ed., *Woman Defamed and Women Defended: An Anthology of Medieval Texts* (Oxford: Oxford University Press, 1992), 2.

14. For the relevant passages of Galen's *De Usu Partium*, see Blamires, *Woman Defamed*, 41–42.

15. Tertullian, *De Cultu Feminarum*, section I.I, part 2, in Blamires, *Woman Defamed*, 51.

16. Jehan le Févre, *The Lamentations of Matheolus*, in Blamires, *Woman Defamed*, 194.

17. Ruth Mazo Karras, *Common Women: Prostitution and Sexuality in Medieval England* (New York: Oxford University Press, 1998), 108.

18. For a discussion of Cersei's machinations at this point of the narrative in the context of Machiavelli's Prince, see Elizabeth Beaton, "Female Machiavellians in Westeros," in *Women of Ice and Fire: Gender*, Game of Thrones, *and Multiple Media Engagements*, eds. Anne Gjelsvik and Rikke Schubart (New York: Bloomsbury Academic, 2016), 199–204.

19. George R.R. Martin, *A Clash of Kings* (New York: Bantam Books, 2011), 846.

20. Martin, *A Clash of Kings*, 849.

21. George R.R. Martin, *A Game of Thrones* (New York: Bantam Books, 2011), 486.

22. Marta Eidsvåg, " 'Maiden, Mother, and Crone': Motherhood in the World of Ice and Fire," in *Women of Ice and Fire: Gender*, Game of Thrones, *and Multiple Media Engagements*, eds. Anne Gjelsvik and Rikke Schubart (New York: Bloomsbury Academic, 2016), 153–155.

23. For a discussion of the *Luttrell Psalter* illumination of a wife beating her husband with a distaff, see Michael Camille, *Mirror in Parchment: The Luttrell Psalter and the Making of Medieval England* (London: Reaktion Books, 1998), 301–303; Sylwia Borowska-Szerszun, *Enter the Carnival: Carnivalesque Semiotics in Early Tudor Moral Interludes* (Białystok: University of Białystok Press, 2016), 27–31.

24. See Betsy L. Chunko, "The Iconography of 'Husband-Beating' on Late Medieval English Misericords," *The Medieval Journal* 3, no. 2 (2013): 39–68.

25. The scenario, in which Noah's wife initially refuses to enter the Ark, is present in York and Chester plays, but the character is particularly rebellious in the Towneley play, where she also wishes for her husband's death. See

"Play 3: Noah," in *The Towneley Plays*, eds. Martin Stevens and A.C. Cawley, Early English Text Society SS13 (Oxford: Oxford University Press, 1994), ll. 487–606. For a more detailed discussion on the representation of domestic violence in the English Plays of the Flood, see Jane Tolmie, "Mrs Noah and Didactic Abuses," *Early Theatre* 5, no. 1 (2002): 11–35.

26. George R.R. Martin, *A Dance with Dragons* (New York: Bantam Books, 2011), 1040.

27. Finn, "High and Mighty," 27.

28. Karras, *Common Women*, 15–17.

29. Lisa Benz St. John, *Three Medieval Queens: Queenship and the Crown in Fourteenth-Century England* (New York: Palgrave Macmillan, 2012), 20–21.

30. J. L. Laynesmith, *The Last Medieval Queens: English Queenship 1445–1503* (Oxford: Oxford University Press, 2004), 7.

31. Christine de Pizan, *The Treasure of the City of Ladies; or, The Book of the Three Virtues*, trans. S. Lawson (Harmondsworth: Penguin Books, 1985), 51.

32. For an exhaustive discussion of Christine de Pizan's tactics of discrediting misogyny, providing a defence of women, and establishing her own authority as a writer in *The Book of the City of Ladies*, see Rosalind Brown-Grant, *Christine de Pizan and the Moral Defence of Women: Reading Beyond Gender* (Cambridge: Cambridge University Press, 1999), 128–174.

33. Martin, *A Clash of Kings*, 341.

34. George R.R. Martin, *A Storm of Swords* (New York: Bantam Books, 2011), 807.

35. Alison Weir, *The Six Wives of Henry VIII* (New York: Groove Press, 1991), 34.

36. Retha M. Warnicke, *The Rise and Fall of Anne Boleyn: Family Politics at the Court of Henry VIII* (Cambridge: Cambridge University Press, 1989), 191–233.

37. George R.R. Martin, *A Feast for Crows* (New York: Bantam Books, 2011), 605.

38. David Starkey, "The Age of the Household: Politics, Society and the Arts c. 1350–c. 1550," in *The Later Middle Ages*, ed. Stephen Medcalf (London: Methuen, 1981), 225–230.

39. Martin, *A Storm of Swords*, 826.

40. Martin, *A Feast for Crows*, 824.

41. Martin, *A Game of Thrones*, 38.

42. For a detailed discussion of these stages in relation to fairy-tale tests and Joseph Campbell's pattern of the hero's journey, see Rikke Shubart, "Woman with Dragons: Daenerys, Pride, and Postfeminist Possibilities," in *Women of Ice and Fire: Gender*, Game of Thrones, *and Multiple Media Engagements*, eds. Anne Gjelsvik and Rikke Schubart (New York: Bloomsbury Academic, 2016), 108–122.

43. Martin, *A Feast for Crows*, 742.

44. Bucholz and Levin, "Introduction," xxx.
45. See, for instance, Peter McClures and Robin Headlam Wells, "Elizabeth I as a Second Virgin Mary," *Renaissance Studies* 4, no. 1 (1990): 38–70.
46. Marjorie Swann, "Sex and the Single Queen: The Erotic Lives of Elizabeth Tudor in Seventeenth-Century England," in *Queens & Power in Medieval and Early Modern England*, eds. Carole Levin and Robert Bucholz (Lincoln: University of Nebraska Press, 2009), 229.
47. It is worth noting, however, that their acceptance of her elevated status is motivated by their recognition of her personal qualities and leadership skills rather than by adherence to abstract ideals of chivalry and *amour courtois*, which, as the fates of Ned and Sansa Stark demonstrate, are continuously and powerfully discredited throughout the narrative.
48. Martin, *A Game of Thrones*, 806.
49. Błaszkiewicz, "Theories of Kingship," 116.
50. Karin Gresham, "Cursed Womb, Bulging Thighs and Bald Scalp: George R.R. Martin's Grotesque Queen," in *Mastering the Game of Thrones: Essays on George R.R. Martin's A Song of Ice and Fire*, eds. Jes Battis and Susan Johnston (Jefferson: McFarland, 2015), 160.
51. Martin, *A Storm of Swords*, 994.
52. Martin, *A Game of Thrones*, 800.
53. M. V. Dougherty, *Moral Dilemmas in Medieval Thought: From Gratias to Aquinas* (Cambridge: Cambridge University Press, 2011), 4.
54. For a discussion of Daenerys's engagement in Machiavellian politics, see Elizabeth Beaton, "Female Machiavellians," 204–208.
55. Martin, *A Storm of Swords*, 112.
56. Yvonne Tasker and Lindsay Steenberg, "Women Warriors from Chivalry to Vengeance," in *Women of Ice and Fire: Gender, Game of Thrones, and Multiple Media Engagements*, eds. Anne Gjelsvik and Rikke Schubart (New York: Bloomsbury Academic, 2016), 188.
57. Jane Tolmie, "Medievalism and the Fantasy Heroine," *Journal of Gender Studies* 15, no. 2 (2006): 1.

Bibliography

Beaton, Elizabeth. "Female Machiavellians in Westeros." In *Women of Ice and Fire: Gender, Game of Thrones, and Multiple Media Engagements*, edited by Anne Gjelsvik and Rikke Schubart, 193–218. New York: Bloomsbury Academic, 2016.

Benz St. John, Lisa. *Three Medieval Queens: Queenship and the Crown in Fourteenth-Century England*. New York: Palgrave Macmillan, 2012.

Blamires, Alcuin, *The Case for Women in Medieval Culture*. Oxford: Oxford University Press, 1998.

————. ed. *Woman Defamed and Women Defended: An Anthology of Medieval Texts*. Oxford: Oxford University Press, 1992.

Borowska-Szerszun, Sylwia. *Enter the Carnival: Carnivalesque Semiotics in Early Tudor Moral Interludes*. Białystok: University of Białystok Press, 2016.

Bloch, Howard R. "Medieval Misogyny." In *Misogyny, Misandry, and Misanthropy*, edited by R. Howard Bloch and Frances Ferguson, 1–24. Berkeley: University of California Press, 1989.

Błaszkiewicz, Bartłomiej. "On the Theories of Kingship in George R.R. Martin's *A Song of Ice and Fire*." In *Basic Categories of Fantastic Literature Revisited*, edited by Andrzej Wicher, Piotr Spyra, and Joanna Matyjaszczyk, 115–126. Newcastle upon Tyne: Cambridge Scholars Publishing, 2014.

Brown-Grant, Rosalind. *Christine de Pizan and the Moral Defence of Women: Reading Beyond Gender*. Cambridge: Cambridge University Press, 1999.

Bucholz, Robert, and Carole Levin. "Introduction." In *Queens & Power in Medieval and Early Modern England*, edited by Carole Levin and Robert Bucholz, xiii–xxxiii. Lincoln: University of Nebraska Press, 2009.

Camille, Michael. *Mirror in Parchment: The Luttrell Psalter and the Making of Medieval England*. London: Reaktion Books, 1998.

Chunko, Betsy L. "The Iconography of 'Husband-Beating' on Late Medieval English Misericords." *The Medieval Journal* 3, no. 2 (2013): 39–68.

Dougherty, M.V. *Moral Dilemmas in Medieval Thought: from Gratias to Aquinas*. Cambridge: Cambridge University Press, 2011.

Earenfight, Theresa. "Without the Persona of the Prince: Kings, Queens and the Idea of Monarchy in Late Medieval Europe." *Gender and History* 19, no. 1 (April 2007): 1–21.

Eidsvåg, Marta. "'Maiden, Mother, and Crone': Motherhood in the World of Ice and Fire." In *Women of Ice and Fire: Gender,* Game of Thrones, *and Multiple Media Engagements*, edited by Anne Gjelsvik and Rikke Schubart, 151–170. New York: Bloomsbury Academic, 2016.

Finn, Kavita Mudan. "High and Mighty Queens of Westeros." In Game of Thrones *versus History: Written in Blood*, edited by Brian A. Pavlac, 19–31. Hoboken: Wiley Blackwell.

Gresham, Karin. "Cursed Womb, Bulging Thighs and Bald Scalp: George R.R. Martin's Grotesque Queen." In *Mastering the Game of Thrones: Essays on George R.R. Martin's* A Song of Ice and Fire, edited by Jes Battis and Susan Johnston, 151–169. Jefferson: McFarland, 2015.

Hibberd, John. "George R.R. Martin explains why there's violence against women on 'Game of Thrones'." *Entertainment Weekly*. 3 June 2015. http://ew.com/article/2015/06/03/george-rr-martin-thrones-violence-women.

Karras, Ruth Mazo. *Common Women: Prostitution and Sexuality in Medieval England*. New York: Oxford University Press, 1998.

Larrington, Carolyne. *Winter Is Coming: The Medieval World of* Game of Thrones. London: New York: I.B. Tauris, 2016.

Laynesmith, J. L. *The Last Medieval Queens: English Queenship 1445–1503.* Oxford: Oxford University Press, 2004.

Martin, George R.R. *A Clash of Kings.* New York: Bantam Books, 2011.

———. *A Dance with Dragons.* New York: Bantam Books, 2011.

———. *A Feast for Crows.* New York: Bantam Books, 2011.

———. *A Game of Thrones.* New York: Bantam Books, 2011.

———. *A Storm of Swords.* New York: Bantam Books, 2011.

McClure, Peter, and Robin Headlam Wells. "Elizabeth I as a Second Virgin Mary." *Renaissance Studies* 4, no. 1 (March 1990): 38–70.

Pisan, Christine de. *The Treasure of the City of Ladies; or, The Book of the Three Virtues.* Translated by Sarah Lawson. Harmondsworth: Penguin Books, 1985.

Pugh, Tison, and Angela Jane Weisl. *Medievalism: Making the Past in the Present.* New York: Routledge, 2013.

Rohr, Zita Eva. *Yolande of Aragon (1381–1442) Family and Power: The Reverse of the Tapestry.* New York: Palgrave Macmillan, 2016.

Shubart, Rikke. "Woman with Dragons: Daenerys, Pride, and Postfeminist Possibilities." In *Women of Ice and Fire: Gender,* Game of Thrones, *and Multiple Media Engagements,* edited by Anne Gjelsvik and Rikke Schubart, 105–130. New York: Bloomsbury Academic, 2016.

Schubart, Rikke and Anne Gjelsvik. "Introduction." In *Women of Ice and Fire: Gender,* Game of Thrones, *and Multiple Media Engagements,* edited by Anne Gjelsvik and Rikke Schubart, 1–16. New York: Bloomsbury Academic, 2016.

Starkey, David. "The Age of the Household: Politics, Society and the Arts c.1350–c.1550." In *The Later Middle Ages,* edited by Stephen Medcalf, 225–290. London: Methuen, 1981.

Stevens, Martin, and A. C. Cawley, eds. *The Towneley Plays.* Early English Text Society SS13. Oxford: Oxford University Press, 1994.

Swann, Marjorie. "Sex and the Single Queen: The Erotic Lives of Elizabeth Tudor in Seventeenth-Century England." In *Queens & Power in Medieval and Early Modern England,* edited by Carole Levin and Robert Bucholz, 224–241. Lincoln: University of Nebraska Press, 2009.

Tasker, Yvonne, and Lindsay Steenberg. "Women Warriors from Chivalry to Vengeance." In *Women of Ice and Fire: Gender,* Game of Thrones, *and Multiple Media Engagements,* edited by Anne Gjelsvik and Rikke Schubart, 171–192. New York: Bloomsbury Academic, 2016.

Tolmie, Jane. "Medievalism and the Fantasy Heroine." *Journal of Gender Studies* 15, no. 2 (2006): 145–158.

———. "Mrs Noah and Didactic Abuses." *Early Theatre* 5, no. 1 (2002): 11–35.

Warnicke, Retha M. *The Rise and Fall of Anne Boleyn: Family Politics at the Court of Henry VIII.* Cambridge: Cambridge University Press, 1989.

Weir, Alison. *The Six Wives of Henry VIII.* New York: Groove Press, 1991.

CHAPTER 4

"All I Ever Wanted Was to Fight for a Lord I Believed in. But the Good Lords Are Dead and the Rest Are Monsters": Brienne of Tarth, Jaime Lannister, and the Chivalric "Other"

Iain A. MacInnes

The character of Brienne of Tarth is one of the most interesting in George R.R. Martin's series *A Song of Ice and Fire* and its subsequent HBO television adaptation, *A Game of Thrones*. Brienne is a woman who occupies a classically male medieval and fantasy position as a warrior knight: armed, mounted, and capable of defeating the elite of the Westerosi chivalric community. As such, she stands apart from many of the other women depicted in the series.[1] Brienne has been a focus for a good deal of academic consideration, but definition of her position and status in the series is difficult.[2] Analyses of the character have focused largely on her physical appearance and on what she represents within a gender or feminist context. She is, for example, "masculine-identified," a "genderqueer knight," an "Amazon … virgin warrior," a "lesbian-like" character, "a lady knight defined by virginity and chastity," and "a freak," as well as "tall, muscular, flat-chested, unattractive, [and] basically mannish."[3] I would argue,

I. A. MacInnes (✉)
UHI Centre for History, University of the Highlands and Islands, Dornoch, UK

© The Author(s) 2020
Z. E. Rohr, L. Benz (eds.), *Queenship and the Women of Westeros*,
Queenship and Power, https://doi.org/10.1007/978-3-030-25041-6_4

however, that Brienne is above all things a knight. She denies this status quite often, brushing off Jaime Lannister's sarcastic barbs when he suggests addressing her as "Ser Brienne."[4] But, it is clearly what she aspires to be. Perhaps, most importantly, it is what she demonstrates herself to be through her own agency, her actions, her beliefs, and her ideals. Indeed, it is arguable that Brienne influences the behaviour and ideals of another of Westeros's knightly fraternity—Jaime Lannister. Although a knight since he was a teenager, Lannister appears the epitome of all things wrong with Westerosi chivalry. He is outwardly a classic fantasy/medieval hero—handsome, well-armoured, skilled with a sword, a seasoned tourneyer—but Jaime is also revealed as an incestuous would-be child-murderer and 'Kingslayer.'[5] Brienne and Jaime are thrown together after his capture at the battle of the Whispering Wood. After a year's captivity, Catelyn Stark illicitly releases Jaime to try and save her two daughters, themselves captives of the Lannisters. The task of escorting the valuable prisoner through a warzone is given to Brienne of Tarth.[6] The events that follow over the course of this long journey are violent and often harrowing, but they are also arguably transformative for both characters and form the main focus of this analysis.

While Martin's work and its television adaptation are set in the fantasy land of Westeros, there is little doubt of their correlation with the historical medieval world. The imagery of the books, with their depiction of knights, heraldry, castles and jousts, is evidently rooted in the medieval past.[7] As a result, chivalry is an important part of Westerosi knightly and popular culture. It was equally important in medieval sources and discourse around warfare in the Middle Ages.[8] This reinforces the link between Martin's fantasy and the medieval reality, and emphasises the importance of chivalry as both a medieval and a modern concern. At first sight it would appear that, rather than privileging the chivalric ideal, Martin deconstructs and ultimately undermines the concept of the medieval chivalric hero in creating what Kavita Mudan Finn describes as a "distorted, sensationalized impression of the [medieval] period."[9] Examples such as Ser Jaime Lannister and Ser Loras Tyrell are considered to be chivalric paragons by those who do not know them intimately, but both men are revealed to act in numerous ways that are opposed to the chivalric ideal. It is possible that Martin deliberately subverts these characters and their behaviour as a reflection of modern cynical reflections on the past, where even the word 'medieval' is used as a pejorative for all things violent and inhumane. But chivalry is not a concept that is easy to define, and the same is as true of chivalry in the Middle Ages as it is for chivalry today. Chivalry was not codified until the later Middle Ages, and practitioners of chivalry did not always agree on what it meant. It was adapted over a prolonged period of time to suit the social and cultural *mores* of the period in which it was relevant.[10] Chivalry today, and our understanding of it, is a world away from what it epitomised in the medieval period. *A Song of Ice and Fire* exists, however, in a medieval-like setting and Martin has stated that he drew on medieval events and tropes in creating this world. Audiences therefore make an obvious association, consciously or otherwise, between this medieval-like fantasy and a medieval reality. As such it is appropriate that analysis of this world should be considered through a medieval lens.[11]

Despite the increasing volume of scholarship on these works, this medieval perspective has not often been attempted. Stacey Goguen, for example, writes of chivalry in Westeros: "there are no true knights because a knight adhering to chivalry is inherently being unjust."[12] This is a not incomprehensible view to take, considering the events described in Martin's texts. It is, however, a view formed by examining the world of Westeros through the lens of modern societal norms and by basing judgements on twenty-first century sensibilities, as well as a present-day conception of what medieval chivalry actually was. Charles Hackney attempts to consider Westerosi chivalry by comparing it to medieval examples. He notes that "chivalry is presented in the novels as a clash between high ideals and grim reality," recognising the inherent contradictions in medieval chivalry as well as in its Westerosi equivalent.[13] In defining the medieval chivalric ideal, Hackney identifies a number of "core chivalric values" with which to assess the behaviour of Westerosi knights. These include: prowess, courage, justice, temperance, wisdom, benevolence, and courtesy, as well as devotion to the Church.[14] Such characteristics are certainly not out of place in the study of medieval chivalry and have formed the behavioural ideals in studies by various historians.[15] Still, such approaches to the code of chivalry are arguably too complex and bound up in the literature of chivalric romance. There is little doubt that medieval romance literature was enjoyed by the knightly class and that the behaviour of those involved in such tales acted as a mirror for that of the audience/reader.[16] As a result, however, these tales deliberately presented polar opposites of behaviour. The best examples were an aspiration; the worst examples were to be avoided. The reality of the contemporary knightly warrior undoubtedly lay somewhere in between.

It is perhaps more relevant therefore to focus on what may be termed "practical chivalry" and the extent to which it manifested itself in the behaviour of contemporary knights.[17] To do this, it is important to gain the perspective of the warrior himself. A notable example is provided by Sir Thomas Gray of Heaton. Author of the *Scalacronica*, Gray was a knightly warrior of the fourteenth-century Anglo-Scottish frontier. He fought in various skirmishes and sieges, and wrote part of his history while in Scottish captivity in Edinburgh Castle.[18] Gray's views on chivalry, and on warfare more generally, are those of a practical warrior. He had little time for the more romanticised elements of chivalry and focused instead on the fundamentals that made for a successful military career. Gray emphasised the behavioural traits of honour, bravery and honesty as key knightly virtues.[19] When he did refer to the ideals of knighthood, he argued that the chivalric order should be "a support for the old, for maidens and for Holy Church."[20] Interestingly, these protected groups align closely to the Westerosi knightly ideal described by Martin. In "The Hedge Knight," Martin describes the ceremonial dubbing of Ser Raymun Fossoway by Ser Lyonel Baratheon. The words accompanying the ritual are as follows:

> In the name of the Warrior I charge you to be brave ...
> In the name of the Father I charge you to be just ...
> In the name of the Mother I charge you to defend the young and innocent ...
> In the name of the Maid I charge you to protect all women.[21]

There is an obvious resonance then, between the ideals of chivalry in the fictional world of *A Song of Ice and Fire* and the medieval equivalent defined by Gray. This ideal provides a simpler view to Hackney, a definition that is more representative of the reality of medieval knighthood, and one that avoids the romanticised expressions of chivalry found in contemporary literature. Using this ideological framework, it is possible to consider the alignment of Brienne of Tarth and Jaime Lannister with the ideals and realities of chivalry as it was practised in the medieval period.

The possession of honour was a key element in the medieval knight's vision of himself, and honour could be won as well as lost. It was not sufficient, however, simply to possess honour. It also had to be recognised by contemporaries. It had to be remembered, committed to posterity through song or chronicle, so that the knight's honour lived on after their death. In order to gain honour, as Matthew Strickland writes, knights had to display a number of qualities: loyalty to one's lord and kin, sagacity of counsel in war and diplomacy, largesse, particularly to one's vassals or companions in arms, *franchise* or a greatness of spirit, piety and, increasingly ... *courtoisie*, the ability to conduct oneself correctly before ladies and in courtly circles. Yet above all, a knight's reputation, honour and pride rested on his *prouesse* – prowess in combat and on the performance of feats of arms.[22]

Honourable behaviour was a complicated business and the judgement of others was key to its recognition. There was, for example, little honour in committing to an act solely for the purpose of its acquisition, and which ultimately produced a negative result. Thomas Gray relates such an example when he describes the story of Sir William Marmion. Sent by his lady to make a name for himself in the most dangerous part of the kingdom, Marmion rode to the Scottish border and to Gray's father's castle at Norham (Northumberland), then under siege by Scottish troops. Determined to gain honour for himself, Marmion ignored the advice of Gray senior who told him that he should fight with the garrison on foot, and instead rode into the throng of Scottish troops alone and on horseback. Unsurprisingly Marmion's horse was killed underneath him and the knight captured, albeit briefly.[23] While Marmion gained no honour from his conduct, honour was won by Thomas Gray senior who marched out from his castle with his troops to defeat the Scots and rescue the captured knight.[24] Of course, the author Thomas Gray was writing about the deeds of his father and so likely presented him in a favourable light. But the example of Marmion as a preposterous hero is paralleled in some of the events depicted in *A Song of Ice and Fire*. Ser Loras Tyrell rushes into the fray at the siege of Dragonstone, and is seriously wounded as a result of impetuous and unnecessary conduct in the pursuit of acclaim and honour.[25] Ned Stark arguably prioritises his personal honour above the needs of the king and the kingdom, and it ultimately costs him his life.[26] Brienne of Tarth's view of honour is opposite to these examples. It is visible in her determination to deliver Jaime Lannister to King's Landing, in spite of all they go through along the way. It is similarly visible in her resolve to carry on with her search for the Stark daughters, even though she is ignorant of their survival. Brienne possesses honour, and is aware of its importance, but she more often seeks to protect that of others and gains worth by honourably keeping the oaths she swears. Hers is not a self-serving form of honour, and it is through her own agency that she accumulates that which she possesses.

Brienne's sense of honour is also conveyed in the television series when she executes Stannis Baratheon for his involvement in the murder of her lord, Renly Baratheon.[27] There is much in this example that may appear self-serving. Seeking revenge for her murdered lord may appear justified, but in medieval Europe such behaviour was often seen as a negative, especially by religious writers.[28] Still, it has also been argued that "anger, wrath, and a thirst for vengeance … actually constituted sturdy pillars upholding structural elements of [medieval] chivalric ideology."[29] The practice of the feud, for example, was a recognised and legitimate framework in which violence was employed as just recompense for violence suffered.[30] Moreover, Brienne's killing of Stannis is the ultimate demonstration of loyalty to her lord, as well as the final act of resolution of a feud that she pursued against those responsible for his death. As such, her actions align with medieval chivalric convention. Continuing with the theme of revenge, Brienne also exacts ultimate vengeance on Vargo Hoat, her captor and tormenter at Harrenhal. When he tries to rape her she bites his ear in self-defence. Although unintended, revenge is ultimately Brienne's as the bite becomes infected and the erstwhile leader of the Brave Companions is left raving and alone when Gregor Clegane recaptures the castle. Hoat's lingering and painful death at the hands of the Mountain appears to the reader as suitable recompense for his treatment of Brienne.[31] Although Brienne does not directly kill him herself, she ultimately sows the seeds of his demise.

Moreover, Brienne's determination to avenge her lord, and the action of defending herself when attacked, clearly demonstrates the bravery that she possesses in impressive quantities. This is an attribute that Brienne repeatedly demonstrates. She disables the ship of Ser Robyn Riger and ensures the escape of both herself and her prisoner when they are in danger of being captured.[32] She fights a huge bear at Harrenhal armed with nothing but a wooden sword with which to defend herself.[33] Bravery is also demonstrated in her reaction to and treatment of her prisoner. Throughout the journey, Jaime Lannister goads Brienne in an attempt to provoke her into fighting with him. He is confident that, even though he is manacled, he can defeat his captor. Brienne thinks otherwise, but does not rise to the challenge, knowing that any such skirmish will provide Lannister the opportunity to escape. When they do inevitably come to blows, ahead of their capture by the Bloody Mummers, Brienne demonstrates her bravery and *prouesse* in fighting and defeating the greatest swordsman in Westeros.[34] While Jaime may be manacled and his fighting ability blunted by captivity, he remains a dangerous opponent. Brienne's bravery in facing him is matched by her demonstrative skills with the sword and ability in real combat, all qualities that reinforce her chivalric reputation.[35]

Brienne's standing as a chivalric warrior is demonstrated further by other behaviour during her journey. Honour, probity, and *franchise* are exhibited when she cuts down the hanged tavern women, killed for sleeping with enemy soldiers, to provide them with a proper burial.[36] Brienne displays sagacity when she accurately deduces that the innkeeper at the Inn of the Kneeling Man is attempting to lure them into a trap through his suggested directions. Even Jaime grudgingly concedes that "it was the same choice he would have made" and that "she may be ugly but she's not entirely stupid."[37] Honesty is also to the fore in Brienne's dealings with Jaime. Despite the deleterious attitude he displays towards her at various points during their journey, Brienne protects her prisoner, as she is honour-bound to do. More than this, she displays probity towards Jaime in the aftermath of his mutilation by the Bloody Mummers. Brienne consoles him and convinces Jaime of his need to go on: "Live," she said, "live, and fight, and take revenge."[38] The return of the revenge refrain is an interesting one, but this example is arguably different to Brienne's previously discussed vengeance. In this instance, Brienne directs revenge at those she considers unchivalric and in doing so she displays her own beliefs regarding honourable behaviour. For example, both Brienne and Jaime are prisoners of the Bloody Mummers. According to chivalric convention they should be treated with at least some modicum of respect, but their mistreatment reveals the dishonour of the Brave Companions. The Bloody Mummers are themselves warrior "others." They are not knights and therefore not bound by the confines of chivalric behaviour. Vengeance against them is therefore legitimate as a result of their status, as well as their behaviour. Roose Bolton is similarly positioned outwith chivalric convention and thus a target for Brienne's revenge. While visibly angered by Vargo Hoat's mistreatment of his prisoners, Bolton also recognises the usefulness of such forces in the war being fought and ultimately condones their behaviour.[39] Although a lord and knight, he plans to betray Robb Stark out of self-interest and plans to use Jaime as a means to negotiate his advancement.[40] Bolton also mistreats Brienne, a woman in his care, abandoning her at Harrenhal to be Vargo Hoat's plaything. Brienne envisaging revenge against Bolton is therefore legitimised as a result of his own lack of honour and probity. The definition of what is and what is not honourable behaviour in these examples is presented from Brienne's perspective. As a result, it is her agency that influences the reader when judging such episodes. Although the misbehaviour of these characters may seem self-evident, it remains that Brienne's reaction to these dishonourable and unchivalric actions has arguably the greatest influence on the audience. And in a world where violent misconduct is often seen as "the norm," such a perspective is important.

As indicated already, Sir Thomas Gray's chivalric outlook was a very practical one. He was an old soldier himself. He experienced war in various forms, tasted victory and defeat and fought in Scotland, England, and France. His view of war, and chivalry's place within it, was based on that experience. Even he, however, saw fit to include the statement that knights should protect "the old ... maidens and ... Holy Church."[41] Although he had likely witnessed behaviour opposite to this model of behaviour, perhaps even committing such acts himself, he still emphasised the ideal of knighthood in relation to non-combatants.[42] Those deemed unable to defend themselves should not be targeted with violence, and indeed should be protected by those who prosecuted war. Of course this rarely happened in reality. And, as the war in Westeros develops, it is clear that the old certainties—the accepted norms of behaviour represented in peacetime in old stories and romances—are largely abandoned. The war being fought deliberately targets those least able to defend themselves, and it is they who invariably suffer as a result. The reasons behind such tactics are complex. In part they are intended to destroy the enemy's means of supply and production. Targeting non-combatants can be a result of "unofficial warfare," the Bloody Mummers providing one example of forager and non-knightly forces who largely do as they please despite being employed by one lord or another. Indirect results of warfare also affect the non-combatant, with the breakdown of law and order allowing the rise of outlaws like those who attack Brienne and Jaime and kill Ser Cleos Frey.[43] The journey taken by Brienne and Jaime transports them through a landscape that exhibits all of these different aspects of war, and its impact on non-combatants in Westeros. Even in this environment, Brienne of Tarth continues to exhibit knightly concern for those whom Thomas Gray recognised as worthy of protection. For while she is not a knight, as she acknowledges herself, she continues through her actions and attitudes to behave as one.

Brienne is the defender and protector of maidens, tasked to ensure the safety and survival of Arya and Sansa Stark. After Catelyn's death, Brienne is determined to fulfil the oath she took to protect the Stark daughters, an oath that continues in the television series even after they have all been united at Winterfell.[44] Protection of the Stark daughters also positions Brienne as defender of children/the innocent, another important non-combatant group.[45] It is difficult, however, to see defence of other non-combatants in Brienne's actions more broadly. Perhaps Brienne's only encounter with the old is when she meets a traveller/farmer on her journey south. Jaime realises that they have been recognised and encourages Brienne to kill the traveller, but she refuses to do so, an action that ultimately leads to their capture by Locke and his men.[46] This self-defeating act reinforces Brienne's values, demonstrating a determination that a non-combatant should not be sacrificed to ensure her own safety. Brienne's interaction with religious figures is similarly limited, although the Church is shown during her journey as another victim of war.[47] Brienne has no opportunity, for example, to save the septon hanging naked from a tree when she and Jaime first meet Vargo Hoat.[48] Brienne's own religious beliefs are elided in the texts, but her religiosity does appear to be foregrounded in her linking of the Church and the swearing of knightly oaths.[49] As already discussed, Brienne takes the oaths she swears incredibly seriously. Her negative attitude towards Jaime stems in part from Brienne's inability to comprehend his actions in rejecting his oath of fealty and murdering his king. Jaime considers, however, Brienne's view of oaths to be hypocritical. He was, after all, forced to swear an oath to release the Stark girls "while dead drunk, chained to a wall, with a sword pressed to [his] chest," and questions the validity of such in the eyes of the Church.[50] Yet Brienne expects him to keep his oath. The circumstances matter less than the fact that he gave his word. Her view is ultimately based on the fact that such oaths possess a religious foundation, having been sworn before the Gods, and as such Brienne expects Jaime to keep his word, just as she keeps her own.

Brienne of Tarth does not apparently consider herself a maiden in need of protection from others. Jaime Lannister acts at times, however, as if she does. While the first phase of their journey is filled with rancour as he plots his escape, Jaime's view of Brienne changes after their capture by the Brave Companions. In spite of his inherent insensitivity in what he says, Jaime attempts to counsel Brienne regarding her expected rape by their captors. He recognises Brienne's bravery, that she "has built a fortress inside herself," and he intercedes to try and protect her from attack.[51] He barters with Urstwick, offering gold from Casterly Rock and mythical sapphires from Tarth as an inducement to prevent Brienne from being raped.[52] He repeats this ploy in a later incident when Zolo, Rorge, and Shagwell threaten to rape Brienne.[53] Such attempts at protecting his erstwhile captor are precursors to his ultimate action when he returns to Harrenhal to rescue Brienne from the bear pit. Finding Brienne unarmoured, armed only with a wooden sword, and facing the bear as best she can, Jaime jumps into the pit beside her. Although unable to defend Brienne physically, due to the loss of his sword hand, Jaime is at least able to use his political and economic value as a means to an end. In endangering his own life, Jaime forces Steelshanks Walton to intervene to save the man Roose Bolton has ordered to be delivered safely to King's Landing.[54] Jaime's behaviour may be construed as chivalric, in attempting to save the maiden from mortal danger.[55] His actions certainly seem to portray his *prouesse* and *franchise*. They can, however, also be read as Jaime demonstrating his largesse towards a companion in arms. Rather than rescuing a maiden, Jaime may instead be saving a fellow warrior. The text's revealing of Jaime's inner thoughts as the journey progresses demonstrates that he recognises Brienne's courage and bravery, her honour, her probity, and her character.[56] Instead of the "wench" Jaime despises at the outset, Brienne increasingly takes the form of a mirror, her actions reflecting how a knight should behave. Through her own agency, Brienne influences Jaime's internal conflict over the kind of knight he is and wishes to be, and she represents to him what is possible. By the end of the Harrenhal episode, Jaime arguably recognises Brienne as a fellow knight, as a "brother-in-arms."[57]

There is an additional factor that ties both characters together. While both exhibit the norms of medieval knightly conduct at times, neither Jaime Lannister nor Brienne of Tarth are "normal" knights. There are various aspects to both characters that "other" them. Brienne of Tarth is a woman. That in itself was not a wholesale barrier to the medieval warrior. Several prominent women succeeded their husbands or sons and led forces in war as a result. Others participated in crusade activity or in the defence of towns or castles during sieges.[58] Perhaps the most famous female warrior of all, Joan of Arc, led the armies of Charles VII of France to victory at Orleans and helped put the dauphin on the French throne.[59] In spite of such examples, however, female warriors remained unusual in the medieval period and as McLaughlin argues, the medieval view increasingly turned towards opposition of women participating in war at all.[60] In Westeros, this perception is also evident. Randyll Tarly condemns Brienne,

stating that "the gods made men to fight, and women to bear children ...
A woman's war is in the birthing bed."[61] While female warriors are visible
throughout *A Song of Ice and Fire*, including Arya Stark, Yara Greyjoy, and
the Wildling Ygritte, these individuals do not "present exceptional women
who triumph over patriarchal violence; rather [they show] the hopeless
and brutal struggles they face to exist within it."[62] As warriors, then, they
are "other" precisely because of the role they play. That Martin places
women in such roles, and that Brienne in particular fills the void left by
unchivalric male knights, has been perceived alternatively as feminist
empowerment and defeminisation of prominent female characters.[63] In
the case of Brienne, it is arguably important to see her as both a woman
and a knight. As indicated, these were not mutually exclusive in the Middle
Ages. While uncommon, such a possibility was not improbable. Nor is it
improbable in Westeros. Female warriors of the past, such as Nymeria and
Visenya Targaryen, are prominent in the chivalric romances of the present.[64] Yet Brienne is constantly mocked for her knightly pretensions and
the television series reflects that women cannot be knights because of "tradition."[65] This is because she challenges Westerosi knightly masculinity. In
particular, Brienne is arguably the most obvious example of female "other-
ness" for the reason that, like Joan of Arc, she wears men's attire. More
than this, she adopts the distinctive features of the masculine knight by
wearing armour. She adopts the outward visage of a knight, challenging
the very notion of what it is to be a chivalric warrior, but in doing so she
only confirms her position as "chivalric other" as a result of her gender.[66]

Jaime is also signified as "other." Despite the glittering armour, the
lethal sword, and the gold cloak of the Kingsguard, Jaime is revealed to
share an incestuous relationship with his twin sister.[67] Even in the world of
Westeros where moral virtue is often at a premium, such behaviour is
anathema.[68] More than this, Jaime is othered by his nickname of
"Kingslayer." In spite of the chivalric façade that he displays to the world,
it is never enough to cover the stain to his reputation and honour that is
permanently attached as a result of his killing of the "Mad King," Aerys
Targaryen. "Kingslayer" is a pejorative used to criticise, belittle, and
denounce him. Brienne herself spends the first part of the pair's journey
south referring to Jaime solely as "Kingslayer," just as he constantly refers
to her as "wench," a term that in similar ways deconstructs the person she
wishes to be in favour of a derogatory female image.[69] As such, they
"other" each other in their early exchanges, while also affirming what the
rest of Westerosi society thinks about them. Already an "othered" figure,

Jaime is further pushed to the margins of society as a result of his mutilation through the loss of his sword hand. The one element that arguably remained of Jaime's knightly worth—his supreme ability with a sword—is taken from him. It is interesting, then, that it is Brienne who consoles him at this point, who urges him to carry on, if for no other reason than to exact vengeance against those who have wronged him.[70] As a consequence of this burgeoning relationship, she is also the person with whom he shares the true story of his ultimate act of shame: the murder of the man he had sworn to protect.[71] The choice of Brienne as the first person to whom he tells his history reflects Jaime's altered opinion of her. Instead of the "wench," she is a fellow knight, and a fellow Kingsguard. This latter position is also, of course, something that unites the pair in failure. Although guardians of two different kings (Aerys Targaryen and Renly Baratheon), both failed the men they were meant to protect. Jaime in particular is further marginalised as a member of the Kingsguard through his lack of recorded deeds in the White Book, the official account of past commanders and their endeavours. In comparison to the famous knights of renown who fill the pages before his own, Jamie's contribution to the Kingsguard is negligible.[72] While the knightly worth of those who form the Kingsguard has deteriorated over the years, Jaime looks back to commanders of the past and sees himself lacking in comparison. The blank pages in the White Book reinforce Jaime's lack of recorded chivalric deeds, an important aspect in a society where the recognition of others is key to the knightly reputation of the individual. Such was the case too in the Middle Ages. Still, both Jaime and Brienne have performed acts of heroism and chivalric worth in defence of each other on their perilous journey to King's Landing. They have saved each other's lives and have formed a bond of knightly "kinship" that recognises the inherent chivalric worth in each other.[73] Though not the same as acceptance from society more broadly, such recognition provides some solace to these two "othered" chivalric warriors.

The ultimate recognition of this knightly bond at this stage is demonstrated in the gift of armour and sword that Jaime provides Brienne ahead of her onward search for the Stark daughters.[74] In furnishing her with armour, Jaime presents Brienne with knightly protection that recognises her status as a chivalric warrior. It gives back to Brienne the accoutrements of knighthood that had been denied to her by the likes of Roose Bolton, Vargo Hoat and even Septa Donyse, who put her in dresses to reinforce her feminine status.[75] As Dressler argues in relation to depictions of medieval knights in funeral effigies, it was their armour that distinguished them from non-fighting men and from women, emphasising their "corporeal visibility" as well as their warrior masculinity.[76] In medieval society too, the giving of armour as a gift was a notable element of chivalric culture used to cement alliances, seal treaties, and reinforce ties of family and kin.[77] Jaime's gift of armour to Brienne reinforces her knightly mantle and further strengthens the ties between them. Perhaps the most symbolic part of Jaime's gift to Brienne is, however, the sword. Named Oathkeeper by Jaime, it is the sword his father gifted to him.[78] Forged from Ned Stark's sword, Ice, its gift to Brienne as she recommences her search for the Stark daughters is a clear attempt by Jaime to reclaim some honour for a weapon last used in the execution of Stark himself. The gift-giving of this weapon is also deeply symbolic for other reasons, echoing one of the most important aspects in the early career of a knight, being dubbed and belted with knighthood.[79] While Brienne was made a member of Renly's Kingsguard, he did not dub her a knight and she lacks the true entry into knighthood that dubbing would provide. As such, she is signified again as chivalric "other." While Jaime does not dub Brienne either at this point, the gift of the sword can be interpreted as an alternative form of dubbing. Early medieval ceremonies, performed before they had developed fully into more complex rituals, allowed for knighthood to be bestowed by the gift of a sword.[80] The sword, therefore, may well represent Brienne's elevation to knighthood, or at least Jaime's recognition of her status as a dubbed knight. This is a status that Brienne has earned through her own agency, through her bravery, honour, and probity displayed repeatedly on the journey to King's Landing.[81]

Ultimately, Brienne of Tarth both metaphorically and literally "earns her spurs" as a result of her enactment of chivalric deeds throughout the events discussed here. Although Renly Baratheon favoured Brienne and elevated her to his Kingsguard, this did not in itself make her a knight. It is rather as a result of her endeavours throughout her attempt to escort Jaime Lannister safely to King's Landing that Brienne's significance as a knight is made manifest. It is an achievement born of Brienne's own agency, both through the actions she carries out, and the impact those actions have on Jaime and on his perception of the female knight who saves him, comforts him, and fights to protect him. It is Jaime who arguably provides that final recognition of Brienne's knightly status, the public appreciation of her role demonstrated through his gift to her of arms and armour. That both the bestower and the recipient in this exchange are knightly "others" emphasises that this is an exchange that takes place outwith patriarchal norms. For although it may appear that Jaime is the male figure gifting knightly status to the female warrior, it is arguable that by this point Jaime has himself stepped outside of conventional patriarchal society. Jamie rejects his father's wish that he return to Casterly Rock to properly take on the mantle of heir to the Lannister domain. Jaime rejects the sword that Tywin gifted to him, and ultimately rejects his father too, reflecting "I no longer have a father."[82] These decisions emphasise Jaime's choice of a different path and complete the "othering" of this character. Instead of the feudal tradition of father passing on his rights to his son, Jaime rejects his family completely. In choosing to honour his oath as a member of the Kingsguard, Jaime begins to construct a new family for himself. Brienne of Tarth arguably takes her place within this new construct, Jaime's apparent dubbing of her acting to incorporate her into this newly forged familial identity.[83] Jaime's recognition of Brienne as a knight is taken further in other acts. In gifting the sword to Brienne, Jaime passes on the warrior mantel, a role which he himself is less able to satisfy fully as a result of his disability. Finally, Jaime commits his recognition of Brienne's chivalric worth to posterity. The ultimate desire of medieval and Westerosi chivalric warriors was for their acts of renown to be remembered after their deaths. Jaime satisfies this element by writing a new entry into the White Book—the Book of Brothers—in the section dedicated to his own life and career:

> Defeated in the Whispering Wood by the Young Wolf Robb Stark during the War of the Five Kings. Held captive at Riverrun and ransomed for a promise unfulfilled. Captured again by the Brave Companions, and maimed at the word of Vargo Hoat their captain, losing his sword hand to the blade of Zollo the Fat. Returned safely to King's Landing by Brienne, the Maid of Tarth.[84]

In Jaime's mind, Brienne's honour, her bravery, and her standing as a knight is worthy of remembrance. Her knightly qualities and chivalry, demonstrated throughout their journey to King's Landing, are worthy of praise and remembrance. As a result, Brienne is praised alongside the paragons of Westerosi chivalric history. Such recognition is a reflection of Brienne's own behaviour and agency. It is a result of the honourable, brave, and selfless acts she performs throughout *A Song of Ice and Fire*, and is a position she ultimately earns for herself.

Notes

1. See Anne Gjelsvik and Rikke Schubart, eds., *Women of Ice and Fire: Gender, Game of Thrones, and Multiple Media Engagements* (New York: Bloomsbury, 2016); Valerie Estelle Frankel, *Women in Game of Thrones: Power, Conformity and Resistance* (Jefferson: McFarland and Company, 2014); Brian A. Pavlac, ed., Game of Thrones *Versus History: Written in Blood* (Hoboken: Wiley Blackwell, 2017); Carolyne Larrington, *Winter is Coming: The Medieval World of* Game of Thrones (London: I.B. Tauris, 2016); Henry Jacoby, ed., Game of Thrones *and Philosophy: Logic Cuts Deeper than Swords* (Hoboken: John Wiley and Sons, 2012); Jes Battis and Susan Johnston, eds., *Mastering the Game of Thrones: Essays on George R.R. Martin's* A Song of Ice and Fire (Jefferson: McFarland and Company, 2015).

2. Frankel, *Women in* Game of Thrones, 47–55; Jessica Walker, ""Just songs in the end": Historical Discourses in Shakespeare and Martin," in *Mastering the Game of Thrones*, 71–91; Yvonne Tasker and Lindsay Steenberg, "Women Warriors from Chivalry to Vengeance," in *Women of Ice and Fire*, 171–192; Charles H. Hackney, ""Silk ribbons tied around a sword": Knighthood and the Chivalric Virtues in Westeros," in *Mastering the Game of Thrones*, 132–150; Susan Johnston, "Grief poignant as joy: Dyscatastrophe and eucatastrophe in *A Song of Ice and Fire*," *Mythlore: A Journal of J.R.R. Tolkien, C.S. Lewis, Charles Williams, and Mythopoeic Literature*, 31, no. 1 (2012): 133–154; Inbar Shaham, "Brienne of Tarth and Jaime Lannister: A romantic comedy within HBO's *Game of Thrones*," *Mythlore: A Journal of J.R.R. Tolkien, C.S. Lewis, Charles Williams, and Mythopoeic Literature*, 33, no. 2 (2015): 51–73; Stacey Goguen, ""There are no true knights": The Injustice of Chivalry," in Game of Thrones *and Philosophy*, 205–219; Nicole M. Mares, "Writing the Rules of Their Own Game: Medieval Female Agency and *Game of Thrones*," in Game of Thrones *Versus History*, 147–160; Jaime Hovey, "Tyrion's gallantry," *Critical Quarterly*, 57, no. 1 (2015): 86–98; Debra Ferreday, "Game of Thrones, Rape Culture and Feminist Fandom," *Australian Feminist Studies*, 30, no. 83 (2015): 21–36.

3. Hovey, "Tyrion's gallantry," 90–92; Frankel, *Women in* Game of Thrones, 38; Mares, "Writing the Rules of Their Own Game," 150–151; Beth Kozinsky, ""A thousand bloodstained hands": The Malleability of Flesh and Identity," in *Mastering the Game of Thrones*, 170–188, at 179–180; Kavita Mudan Finn, "Queen of Sad Mischance: Medievalism, 'Realism,' and the case of Cersei Lannister," in Zita Eva Rohr and Lisa Benz, eds., *Queenship and the Women of Westeros: Female Agency and Advice in Game of Thrones and A Song of Ice and Fire* (Basingstoke: Palgrave Macmillan,

2019), 29–52; Charles Lambert, "A tender spot in my heart: disability in *A Song of Ice and Fire*," *Critical Quarterly*, 57, no. 1 (2015): 20–33, at 31–32.

4. George R.R. Martin, *A Storm of Swords, 1: Steel and Snow* (hereafter *SoS*1) (London: Harper Voyager, 2011), 21.

5. George R.R. Martin, *A Game of Thrones* (hereafter *GoT*) (London: Harper Voyager, 2011), 77–81.

6. George R.R. Martin, *A Clash of Kings* (hereafter *CoK*) (London: Harper Voyager, 2011), 714–722; *SoS*1, 18–20.

7. For possible specific periods relevant to Martin's construct, see in this volume, Charles Beem, "The Royal Minorities of *Game of Thrones*," in Zita Eva Rohr and Lisa Benz, eds., *Queenship and the Women of Westeros: Female Agency and Advice in* Game of Thrones *and* A Song of Ice and Fire (Basingstoke: Palgrave Macmillan, 2019), 189–204; Finn, "Queen of Sad Mischance," 29–52; Mikayla Hunter, "'All Men Must Die, But We Are Not Men': Eastern Faith and Feminine Power in *A Song of Ice and Fire* and HBO's *Game of Thrones*," in Zita Eva Rohr and Lisa Benz, eds., *Queenship and the Women of Westeros: Female Agency and Advice in* Game of Thrones *and* A Song of Ice and Fire (Basingstoke: Palgrave Macmillan, 2019), 145–168.

8. Maurice Keen, *Chivalry* (New Haven: Yale University Press, 1984), 219–237; Matthew Strickland, *War and Chivalry: The Conduct and Perception of War in England and Normandy, 1066–1217* (Cambridge: Cambridge University Press, 1996), 159–182; Richard Barber, *The Knight and Chivalry* (Woodbridge: Boydell Press, 1995), 225–248.

9. Finn, "Queen of Sad Mischance"; Goguen, "The Injustice of Chivalry," 207.

10. Keen, *Chivalry*, 1–17.

11. Gillian Polack, "Setting up Westeros: The Medievalesque World of *Game of Thrones*," in Game of Thrones *Versus History*, 251–260.

12. Goguen, "The injustice of chivalry," 209.

13. Hackney, "Chivalric Virtues in Westeros," 132.

14. Ibid., 136, 133.

15. Keen, *Chivalry*, 1–17; Richard W. Kaeuper, *Medieval Chivalry* (Cambridge: Cambridge University Press, 2016), 1–56.

16. Barber, *The Knight and Chivalry*, 105–131.

17. Carroll Gilmor, "Practical Chivalry: The Training of Horses for Tournaments and Warfare," *Medieval and Renaissance History*, 13 (1992): 7–29.

18. Thomas Gray, *Scalacronica, 1272–1362*, ed. Andy King (Woodbridge: Surtees Society, 2005); Andy King, "Englishmen, Scots and Marchers: National and Local Identities in Thomas Gray's *Scalacronica*," *Northern*

History, 36 (2000): 217–231; Andy King, "A Helm with a Crest of Gold: the Order of Chivalry in Thomas Gray's *Scalacronica*," *Fourteenth Century England*, 1 (2000): 21–35; Andy King, "War and Peace: a Knight's Tale. The ethics of war in Sir Thomas Gray's *Scalacronica*," in Chris Given-Wilson, Ann Kettle and Len Scales, eds., *War, Government and Aristocracy in the British Isles, c.1150–1500: Essays in Honour of Michael Prestwich* (Woodbridge: Boydell Press, 2008), 148–162.

19. Iain A. MacInnes, *Scotland's Second War of Independence, 1332–1357* (Woodbridge: Boydell Press, 2016), 203–204.
20. *Scalacronica* (King), 3.
21. George R.R. Martin, "The Hedge Knight," in Robert Silverberg, ed., *Legends* (London: Voyager, 1998), 518. This same ritual is utilised in the final television series of *Game of Thrones* when Jaime Lannister does in fact knight Brienne of Tarth at Winterfell ahead of the battle with the White Walkers. It removes, however, the pledge to defend "the young" and removes the final line about protecting women altogether (*Game of Thrones*, 8.2, "A Knight of the Seven Kingdoms" (dir. David Nutter, 2019)).
22. Strickland, *War and Chivalry*, 99.
23. *Scalacronica* (King), 115; King, "A Helm with a Crest of Gold," 34–35.
24. Ibid.
25. George R.R. Martin, *A Feast for Crows* (hereafter *FfC*) (London: Harper Voyager, 2011), 597–600.
26. *GoT*, 110, 611; David Hahn, "The Death of Lord Eddard Stark: The Perils of Idealism," in Game of Thrones *and Philosophy*, 75–86.
27. *Game of Thrones*, 5.10, "Mother's Mercy" (dir. David Nutter, 2015).
28. Thomas Roche, "The Way Vengeance Comes: Rancorous Deeds and Words in the World of Orderic Vitalis," in Susanna A. Throop and Paul R. Hyams, eds., *Vengeance in the Middle Ages: Emotion, Religion and Feud* (London: Routledge, 2010), 115–136.
29. Kaeuper, *Medieval Chivalry*, 353–381.
30. Paul R. Hyams, *Rancor and Reconciliation in Medieval England* (Ithaca: Cornell University Press, 2003), 8–9.
31. George R.R. Martin, *A Storm of Swords, 2: Blood and Gold* (hereafter *SoS2*) (London: Harper Voyager, 2011), 280.
32. *SoS1*, 27–32.
33. *SoS1*, 294, 417–419; *SoS2*, 45–49.
34. *SoS1*, 289–292.
35. The television series continues this depiction of Brienne's bravery, including her defeat of Sandor Clegane ("the Hound") in single combat and her performance, and survival, at the battle of Winterfell (*Game of Thrones*, 4.10, "The Children" (dir. Alex Graves, 2014); *Game of Thrones*, 8.3, "The Long Night" (dir. Miguel Sapochnik, 2019)).

36. *SoS1*, 25–27.
37. Ibid., 154.
38. Ibid., 416.
39. Ibid., 421–425, 503–516.
40. Roose Bolton's duplicitous conduct plays out in full across both volumes of *A Storm of Swords*.
41. *Scalacronica* (King), 3.
42. Gray himself wrote that inducing "fear of harm [amongst an enemy populace], or destruction of property during war…brings honour, profit and joy" (King, "War and Peace," 158).
43. *SoS1*, 287–288.
44. *Game of Thrones*, 7.6, "Beyond the Wall" (dir. Alan Taylor, 2017).
45. Catelyn Stark confronts Jaime Lannister in his prison cell about his attack on her son, Bran, with the words "you were a knight, sworn to defend the weak and innocent" (*CoK*, 717).
46. *Game of Thrones*, 3.2, "Dark Wings, Dark Words" (dir. Daniel Minahan, 2013).
47. See, for example, Arya's stay at a sacked sept in Sallydance (*SoS1*, 300).
48. *SoS1*, 296.
49. For discussion of religion in Westeros, see Don Riggs, "Continuity and Transformation in the Religions of Westeros and Western Europe," in *Game of Thrones Versus History*, 173–184; Maureen Attali, "Religious Violence in *Game of Thrones*: An Historical Background from Antiquity to the European Wars of Religion," in Ibid., 185–194; Daniel J. Clasby, "Coexistence and Conflict in the Religions of *Game of Thrones*," in Ibid., 195–208.
50. *SoS1*, 20.
51. Ibid., 417.
52. Ibid., 294–295.
53. Ibid., 418–419.
54. *SoS2*, 45–49.
55. Shaham, "Brienne of Tarth and Jaime Lannister," 70.
56. *SoS1*, 18, 28, 30, 154, 291, 294, 295, 417, 418.
57. For discussion of Daenerys Targaryen and her ability to adopt the positive aspects of both genders, taking on the role of "she-king," see in this volume, Sylwia Borowska-Szerszun, "Westerosi Queens: Medievalist Portrayal of Female Power and Authority in *A Song of Ice and Fire*," in Zita Eva Rohr and Lisa Benz, eds., *Queenship and the Women of Westeros: Female Agency and Advice in* Game of Thrones *and* A Song of Ice and Fire (Basingstoke: Palgrave Macmillan, 2019), 53–75.

58. Larrington, *Winter is Coming*, 32–34; James M. Blythe, "Women in the military: scholastic arguments and medieval images of female warriors," *History of Political Thought*, 22, no. 2 (2001): 242–269; Megan McLaughlin, "The woman warrior: gender, warfare and society in medieval Europe," *Women's Studies*, 17, no. 3/4 (1990): 193–209; Helen Solterer, "Figures of Female Militancy in Medieval France," *Signs: Journal of Women in Culture and Society*, 16, no. 3 (1991): 522–549.

59. Kelly DeVries, *Joan of Arc: A Military Leader* (Stroud: Sutton, 2003).

60. McLaughlin, "The woman warrior," 194–195.

61. *FfC* 238; D. Marcel DeCoste, "Beyond the Pale? Craster and the Pathological Reproduction of Houses in Westeros," in *Mastering the Game of Thrones*, 225–242, at 241, n. 4.

62. Tasker and Steenberg, "Women Warriors from Chivalry to Vengeance," in *Women of Ice and Fire*, 189.

63. Frankel, *Women in* Game of Thrones, 1–3. See also, in this volume, Finn, "Queen of Sad Mischance," 29–52; Borowska-Szerszun, "Westerosi Queens," 53–75; Kris Swank, "The Peaceweavers of Winterfell," in Zita Eva Rohr and Lisa Benz, eds., *Queenship and the Women of Westeros: Female Agency and Advice in Game of Thrones and A Song of Ice and Fire* (Basingstoke: Palgrave Macmillan, 2019), 105–127.

64. Frankel, *Women in* Game of Thrones, 47–49.

65. *Game of Thrones*, 8.2.

66. For other examples of women challenging, and ultimately being defeated by the patriarchal order of Westerosi and medieval society, see Borowska-Szerszun, "Westerosi Queens," 53–75.

67. *GoT*, 48; Ferreday, "Rape Culture," 28.

68. Katherine Tullman, "Dany's Encounter with the Wild: Cultural Relativism in *A Game of Thrones*," in Game of Thrones *and Philosophy*, 194–204; Martin Bleisteiner, "Perils of Generation: Incest, Romance, and the Proliferation of Narrative in Game of Thrones," in Andrew James Johnston, Margitta Rouse and Philipp Hinz, eds., *The Medieval Motion Picture: The New Middle Ages* (New York: Palgrave Macmillan, 2014), 155–169.

69. *SoS1*, 19–21.

70. Ibid., 416–417.

71. Ibid., 505–508.

72. *SoS2*, 338–342.

73. The television series ultimately takes this relationship further when Jaime rides to Winterfell to satisfy the oath he took to protect "the living" and asks that Brienne allow him to serve at her side, under her command, in the battle to follow (*Game of Thrones*, 8.2).

74. The armour is an addition in the television series, but it is an important one that adds to the gift of the sword provided in the books (see *Game of Thrones*, 4.4, "Oathkeeper" (dir. Michelle MacLaren, 2014); *SoS2*, 432–435).
75. *SoS1*, 508–509; *SoS2*, 45–46, 431–432.
76. Rachel Ann Dressler, *Of Armor and Men in Medieval England: The Chivalric Rhetoric of Three English Knights' Effigies* (London: Routledge, 2004), 98–120.
77. Keen, *Chivalry*, 66–71.
78. *SoS2*, 434–435.
79. Keen, *Chivalry*, 64–82.
80. Ibid., 64–71.
81. As already indicated, the final season of *Game of Thrones* does provide a formal dubbing of Brienne, with Jaime Lannister being the one to promote her to the status of knight. There is a notion here of events coming full circle, although it can also be suggested that the act in itself undercuts the agency with which Brienne made herself a knight. That it requires Jaime Lannister to provide confirmation of a status she has arguably already attained potentially reinforces the patriarchal nature of Westerosi (and modern) society (*Game of Thrones*, 8.2). For discussion of the dubbing, see Elizabeth S. Leet, "Brienne of Tarth is a Heroine for our Age," *The Public Medievalist*, 9 May 2019 (https://www.publicmedievalist.com/brienne-of-tarth-is-a-heroine-for-our-age/); Lily Rothman and Joëlle Rollo-Koster, "The Real History of Medieval Knights Makes Brienne's Big *Game of Thrones* Moment Even More Meaningful," *Time*, 25 April 2019 (http://time.com/5575825/game-of-thrones-brienne-knighting-history/).
82. *SoS2*, 433.
83. The final television series subverts this analysis somewhat by including sexual intimacy between Brienne and Jaime, creating a knight-lover relationship that problematises a more chivalric reading of their bond (*Game of Thrones*, 8.4, "The Last of the Starks" (dir. David Nutter, 2019)). This ultimately occurs, however, at the end of a long period in which their relationship has undergone significant change from the events discussed in this chapter and, crucially, after the events of a climactic battle in which Jaime chose to serve under the command and at the side of his knightly comrade, and which they both survived (*Game of Thrones*, 8.3).
84. *SoS2*, 435. In the final episode of the television series, the entry provided by Jaime Lannister is shorter and does not allude to Brienne at all. Instead it is left to Ser Brienne, now Lord Commander of the Kingsguard of King Brandon the Broken, to complete the entry for Ser Jaime, writing: "Captured in the field at the Whispering Wood, set free by Lady Catelyn Stark in return for an oath to find [and protect] her two daughters, lost

[his hand] ... Took Rivverrun from the Tully rebels, without loss of life. Lured the Unsullied into attacking Casterly Rock, sacrificing his childhood home in service to a greater strategy. Outwitted the Targaryen forces to seize Highgarden. Fought at the Battle of the Goldroad bravely, narrowly escaping death by dragonfire. Pledged himself to the forces of men and rode north to join them at Winterfell, alone. Faced the Army of the Dead and defended the castle against impossible odds until the defeat of the Night King. Escaped imprisonment and rode south in an attempt to save the capital from destruction. Died protecting his Queen" (*Game of Thrones*, 8.6, "The Iron Throne" (dir. David Benioff and D.B. Weiss, 2019)); Anjelica Oswald, "Here's everything Brienne wrote inside the Kingsguard book during the *Game of Thrones* finale," *Business Insider*, 19 May 2019 (https://www.businessinsider.com/game-of-thrones-brienne-wrote-in-kingsguard-book-2019-5?r=US&IR=T). Ser Brienne's entry remains to be written, but it is one that she is likely to write herself.

BIBLIOGRAPHY

PRIMARY SOURCES

Game of Thrones, 3.2, "Dark Wings, Dark Words" (dir. Daniel Minahan, 2013).
Game of Thrones, 4.4, "Oathkeeper" (dir. Michelle MacLaren, 2014).
Game of Thrones, 4.10, "The Children" (dir. Alex Graves, 2014).
Game of Thrones, 5.10, "Mother's Mercy" (dir. David Nutter, 2015).
Game of Thrones, 7.6, "Beyond the Wall" (dir. Alan Taylor, 2017).
Game of Thrones, 8.2, "A Knight of the Seven Kingdoms" (dir. David Nutter, 2019).
Game of Thrones, 8.3, "The Long Night" (dir. Miguel Sapochnik, 2019).
Game of Thrones, 8.4, "The Last of the Starks" (dir. David Nutter, 2019).
Game of Thrones, 8.6, "The Iron Throne" (dir. David Benioff and D.B. Weiss, 2019).
Gray, Thomas. *Scalacronica, 1272–1362*, edited by Andy King. Woodbridge: Surtees Society, 2005.
Martin, George R.R. *A Clash of Kings*. London: Harper Voyager, 2011.
Martin, George R.R. *A Feast for Crows*. London: Harper Voyager, 2011.
Martin, George R.R. *A Game of Thrones*. London: Harper Voyager, 2011.
Martin, George R.R. "The Hedge Knight." In *Legends*, edited by Robert Silverberg. London: Voyager, 1998.
Martin, George R.R. *A Storm of Swords, 1: Steel and Snow*. London: Harper Voyager, 2011.
Martin, George R.R. *A Storm of Swords, 2: Blood and Gold*. London: Harper Voyager, 2011.

SECONDARY SOURCES

Attali, Maureen. "Religious Violence in *Game of Thrones*: An Historical Background from Antiquity to the European Wars of Religion." In *Game of Thrones Versus History: Written in Blood*, edited by Brian A. Pavlac, 185–194. Hoboken: Wiley Blackwell, 2017.

Barber, Richard. *The Knight and Chivalry*. Woodbridge: Boydell Press, 1995.

Battis, Jes, and Johnston, Susan, eds. *Mastering the Game of Thrones: Essays on George R. R. Martin's A Song of Ice and Fire*. Jefferson: McFarland and Company, 2015.

Beem, Charles. "The Royal Minorities of *Game of Thrones*." In *Queenship and the Women of Westeros: Female Agency and Advice in* Game of Thrones *and* A Song of Ice and Fire, edited by Zita Eva Rohr and Lisa Benz, 189–204. Basingstoke: Palgrave Macmillan, 2019.

Bleisteiner, Martin. "Perils of Generation: Incest, Romance, and the Proliferation of Narrative in Game of Thrones." In *The Medieval Motion Picture: The New Middle Ages*, edited by Andrew James Johnston, Margitta Rouse and Philipp Hinz, 155–169. New York: Palgrave Macmillan, 2014.

Blythe, James M. "Women in the military: scholastic arguments and medieval images of female warriors." *History of Political Thought*, 22, no. 2 (2001): 242–269.

Borowska-Szerszun, Sylwia. "Westerosi Queens: Medievalist Portrayal of Female Power and Authority in *A Song of Ice and Fire*." In *Queenship and the Women of Westeros: Female Agency and Advice in* Game of Thrones *and* A Song of Ice and Fire, edited by Zita Eva Rohr and Lisa Benz, 53–75. Basingstoke: Palgrave Macmillan, 2019.

Clasby, Daniel J. "Coexistence and Conflict in the Religions of *Game of Thrones*." In Game of Thrones *Versus History: Written in Blood*, edited by Brian A. Pavlac, 195–208. Hoboken: Wiley Blackwell, 2017.

DeCoste, D. Marcel. "Beyond the Pale? Craster and the Pathological Reproduction of Houses in Westeros." In *Mastering the Game of Thrones: Essays on George R. R. Martin's* A Song of Ice and Fire, edited by Jes Battis and Susan Johnston, 225–242. Jefferson: McFarland and Company, 2015.

DeVries, Kelly. *Joan of Arc: A Military Leader*. Stroud: Sutton, 2003.

Dressler, Rachel Ann. *Of Armor and Men in Medieval England: The Chivalric Rhetoric of Three English Knights' Effigies*. London: Routledge, 2004.

Ferreday, Debra. "*Game of Thrones*, Rape Culture and Feminist Fandom." *Australian Feminist Studies*, 30, no. 83 (2015): 21–36.

Finn, Kavita Mudan. "Queen of Sad Mischance: Medievalism, 'Realism,' and the case of Cersei Lannister." In *Queenship and the Women of Westeros: Female Agency and Advice in* Game of Thrones *and* A Song of Ice and Fire, edited by Zita Eva Rohr and Lisa Benz, 29–52. Basingstoke: Palgrave Macmillan, 2019.

Frankel, Valerie Estelle. *Women in* Game of Thrones*: Power, Conformity and Resistance.* Jefferson: McFarland and Company, 2014.

Gilmor, Carroll. "Practical Chivalry: The Training of Horses for Tournaments and Warfare." *Medieval and Renaissance History*, 13 (1992): 7–29.

Gjelsvik, Anne, and Schubart, Rikke, eds. *Women of Ice and Fire: Gender,* Game of Thrones, *and Multiple Media Engagements.* New York: Bloomsbury, 2016.

Goguen, Stacey. ""There are no true knights": The Injustice of Chivalry." In Game of Thrones *and Philosophy: Logic Cuts Deeper than Swords,* edited by Henry Jacoby, 205–219. Hoboken: John Wiley and Sons, 2012.

Hackney, Charles H. ""Silk ribbons tied around a sword": Knighthood and the Chivalric Virtues in Westeros." In *Mastering the Game of Thrones: Essays on George R.R. Martin's* A Song of Ice and Fire, edited by Jes Battis and Susan Johnston, 132–150. Jefferson: McFarland and Company, 2015.

Hahn, David. "The Death of Lord Eddard Stark: The Perils of Idealism." In Game of Thrones *and Philosophy: Logic Cuts Deeper than Swords,* edited by Henry Jacoby, 75–86. Hoboken: John Wiley and Sons, 2012.

Hovey, Jaime. "Tyrion's gallantry." *Critical Quarterly*, 57, no. 1 (2015): 86–98.

Hunter, Mikayla. "'All Men Must Die, But We Are Not Men': Eastern Faith and Feminine Power in *A Song of Ice and Fire* and HBO's *Game of Thrones.*" In *Queenship and the Women of Westeros: Female Agency and Advice in* Game of Thrones *and* A Song of Ice and Fire, edited by Zita Eva Rohr and Lisa Benz, 145–168. Basingstoke: Palgrave Macmillan, 2019.

Hyams, Paul R. *Rancor and Reconciliation in Medieval England.* Ithaca: Cornell University Press, 2003.

Jacoby, Henry, ed. Game of Thrones *and Philosophy: Logic Cuts Deeper than Swords.* Hoboken: John Wiley and Sons, 2012.

Johnston, Susan. "Grief poignant as joy: Dyscatastrophe and eucatastrophe in *A Song of Ice and Fire.*" *Mythlore: A Journal of J.R.R. Tolkien, C.S. Lewis, Charles Williams, and Mythopoeic Literature*, 31, no. 1 (2012): 133–54.

Kaeuper, Richard W. *Medieval Chivalry.* Cambridge: Cambridge University Press, 2016.

Keen, Maurice. *Chivalry.* New Haven: Yale University Press, 1984.

King, Andy. "Englishmen, Scots and Marchers: National and Local Identities in Thomas Gray's *Scalacronica.*" *Northern History*, 36 (2000): 217–31.

King, Andy. "A Helm with a Crest of Gold: the Order of Chivalry in Thomas Gray's *Scalacronica.*" *Fourteenth Century England*, 1 (2000): 21–35.

King, Andy. "War and Peace: a Knight's Tale. The ethics of war in Sir Thomas Gray's *Scalacronica.*" In *War, Government and Aristocracy in the British Isles, c.1150–1500: Essays in Honour of Michael Prestwich,* edited by Chris Given-Wilson, Ann Kettle and Len Scales, 148–162. Woodbridge: Boydell Press, 2008.

Kozinsky, Beth. ""A thousand bloodstained hands": The Malleability of Flesh and Identity." In *Mastering the Game of Thrones: Essays on George R. R. Martin's A Song of Ice and Fire*, edited by Jes Battis and Susan Johnston, 170–188. Jefferson: McFarland and Company, 2015.

Lambert, Charles. "A tender spot in my heart: disability in *A Song of Ice and Fire*." *Critical Quarterly*, 57, no. 1 (2015): 20–33.

Larrington, Carolyne. *Winter is Coming: The Medieval World of* Game of Thrones. London: I.B. Tauris, 2016.

Leet, Elizabeth S. "Brienne of Tarth is a Heroine for our Age," *The Public Medievalist*, 9 May 2019 (https://www.publicmedievalist.com/brienne-of-tarth-is-a-heroine-for-our-age/).

MacInnes, Iain A. *Scotland's Second War of Independence, 1332–1357*. Woodbridge: Boydell Press, 2016.

Mares, Nicole M. "Writing the Rules of Their Own Game: Medieval Female Agency and *Game of Thrones*." In Game of Thrones *Versus History: Written in Blood*, edited by Brian A. Pavlac, 147–160. Hoboken: Wiley Blackwell, 2017.

McLaughlin, Megan. "The woman warrior: gender, warfare and society in medieval Europe." *Women's Studies*, 17, no. 3/4 (1990): 193–209.

Oswald, Anjelica. "Here's everything Brienne wrote inside the Kingsguard book during the *Game of Thrones* finale," *Business Insider*, 19 May 2019 (https://www.businessinsider.com/game-of-thrones-brienne-wrote-in-kingsguard-book-2019-5?r=US&IR=T).

Pavlac, Brian A., ed. Game of Thrones *Versus History: Written in Blood*. Hoboken: Wiley Blackwell, 2017.

Polack, Gillian. "Setting up Westeros: The Medievalesque World of *Game of Thrones*." In Game of Thrones *Versus History: Written in Blood*, edited by Brian A. Pavlac, 251–60. Hoboken: Wiley Blackwell, 2017.

Riggs, Don. "Continuity and Transformation in the Religions of Westeros and Western Europe." In Game of Thrones *Versus History: Written in Blood*, edited by Brian A. Pavlac, 173–184. Hoboken: Wiley Blackwell, 2017.

Roche, Thomas. "The Way Vengeance Comes: Rancorous Deeds and Words in the World of Orderic Vitalis." In *Vengeance in the Middle Ages: Emotion, Religion and Feud*, edited by Susanna A. Throop and Paul R. Hyams, 115–36. London: Routledge, 2010.

Rothman, Lily and Rollo-Koster, Joëlle. "The Real History of Medieval Knights Makes Brienne's Big *Game of Thrones* Moment Even More Meaningful," *Time*, 25 April 2019 (http://time.com/5575825/game-of-thrones-brienne-knighting-history/).

Shaham, Inbar. "Brienne of Tarth and Jaime Lannister: A romantic comedy within HBO's *Game of Thrones*." *Mythlore: A Journal of J.R.R. Tolkien, C.S. Lewis, Charles Williams, and Mythopoeic Literature*, 33, no. 2 (2015): 51–73.

Solterer, Helen. "Figures of Female Militancy in Medieval France." *Signs: Journal of Women in Culture and Society*, 16, no. 3 (1991): 522–549.

Strickland, Matthew. *War and Chivalry: The conduct and perception of war in England and Normandy, 1066–1217.* Cambridge: Cambridge University Press, 1996.

Swank, Kris. "The Peaceweavers of Winterfell." In *Queenship and the Women of Westeros: Female Agency and Advice in Game of Thrones and A Song of Ice and Fire*, edited by Zita Eva Rohr and Lisa Benz, 105–127. Basingstoke: Palgrave Macmillan, 2019.

Tasker, Yvonne, and Steenberg, Lindsay. "Women Warriors from Chivalry to Vengeance." In *Women of Ice and Fire: Gender*, Game of Thrones, *and Multiple Media Engagements*, edited by Anne Gjelsvik and Rikke Schubart, 171–192. New York: Bloomsbury, 2016.

Tullman, Katherine. "Dany's Encounter with the Wild: Cultural Relativism in *A Game of Thrones.*" In Game of Thrones *and Philosophy: Logic Cuts Deeper than Swords*, edited by Henry Jacoby, 194–204. Hoboken: John Wiley and Sons, 2012.

Walker, Jessica. ""Just songs in the end": Historical Discourses in Shakespeare and Martin." In *Mastering the Game of Thrones: Essays on George R.R. Martin's* A Song of Ice and Fire, edited by Jes Battis and Susan Johnston, 71–91. Jefferson: McFarland and Company, 2015.

PART II

Female Agency

CHAPTER 5

The Peaceweavers of Winterfell

Kris Swank

While the Anglo-Saxon epic poem *Beowulf* focuses squarely upon the heroic career of its titular character and his battles with monsters, it also offers multiple queenship strategies. Among these are the peaceweaving of Wealhtheow and Hygd, the submissiveness of Hildeburh and Freawaru, and the "strife-weaving" of Grendel's mother.[1] Each of these strategies enjoys some short-term success, but ultimately leads to a failure of peace and the end of a noble family's line. Yet, there is a sixth significant female character in *Beowulf*, the equal-parts maligned and praised wife of King Offa, "Thryth," who employs both peaceweaving and strife-weaving to forge a lasting peace.[2] Such a hybrid approach can be likened to a "she-wolf" who is by turns submissive, cunning, or violent as the situation warrants. The internecine plotting and violent overthrows detailed in *Beowulf* tread familiar ground for readers of George R.R. Martin's *A Song of Ice and Fire* series, and viewers of its television adaptation, *Game of Thrones*. The North of Westeros, particularly Winterfell, home of the Stark family, bears a striking resemblance to the Anglo-Saxon and Germanic cultures portrayed in *Beowulf*. Likewise, the same models of queenship exhibited in *Beowulf* find expression in the Stark noblewomen: the peaceweaving of Catelyn, the submissiveness of Sansa, and the strife-weaving of Arya and

K. Swank (✉)
Pima Community College, Tucson, AZ, USA

© The Author(s) 2020
Z. E. Rohr, L. Benz (eds.), *Queenship and the Women of Westeros*,
Queenship and Power, https://doi.org/10.1007/978-3-030-25041-6_5

Lady Stoneheart. As the series progresses, however, an analogue of the she-wolf Thryth also emerges.

The female characters of *Game of Thrones* have been the subject of intense scrutiny as products of mythological, historical, and fictional influence. This includes the influence of Norse, Germanic, and Anglo-Saxon myth and legend. Valerie Estelle Frankel, for example, examines Brienne of Tarth and Arya Stark as representatives of the warrior woman mythic archetype, defined as "the powerful, masculinized woman who often disguises as a boy and operates in a man's world."[3] The sisters Catelyn Stark and Lysa Arryn, on the other hand, represent two sides of the same archetype: the nurturing Good Mother and the devouring Terrible Mother.[4] Kristine Larsen builds upon the works of Helen Damico and Leslie Donovan to analyse the women from Martin's books in relation to the northern European "Valkyrie," equal-parts warrior woman and hero's bride, and best represented by the wildling Ygritte and, though not at first an obvious example, Sansa Stark.[5] Carolyne Larrington compares Cersei Lannister to the scheming Eadburh, daughter of the powerful Anglo-Saxon king, Offa of Mercia.[6] In the present volume, Shiloh Carroll examines the rule of Daenerys Targaryen in decadent Mereen as it echoes the complex bureaucracies and rival factions pervading eleventh-century Anglo-Saxon royal courts.[7] Another fruitful avenue of enquiry towards the understanding of Martin's women in light of historical and mythological queens is through *Beowulf*, the narrative poem composed sometime between the late seventh and early eleventh centuries. Although *Beowulf* was composed in Anglo-Saxon England, it describes events set in fifth-century Scandinavia, and, as such, *Beowulf*'s queens have a particular resonance with the steadfast women of Martin's untamed and frozen north, the Starks of Winterfell.

In the poem, Beowulf, a young warrior, travels to Denmark to kill the ogre Grendel, who has been terrorizing King Hrothgar in his great mead-hall of Heorot. Later, Grendel's monstrous mother invades Heorot to avenge her son's death. Beowulf tracks her back to an underwater cavern where he vanquishes her as well. Beowulf then returns home to Geatland, in southern Sweden, where he eventually becomes king. In old age, Beowulf battles a rampaging dragon, and the two foes destroy one another.

Winterfell, the castle-home of the Stark family and seat of the ancient Kings of Winter (also known as the Kings in the North), resembles the northern European settings of *Beowulf*. Visually, Martin's North is cold, "dark, with heavy fabrics and fur."[8] Culturally, the First Men, ancestors of the Starks, echo aspects of the Anglo-Saxons. Both groups utilized runic writing, worshipped a pantheon of ancient gods, entertained guests in a great hall, and conceived of their semi-mythical history as an Age of Heroes. Much like the ancient poem of Beowulf and his battles with monsters, the First Men had ancient ballads which "tell of how one King of Winter drove the giants from the North, while another felled the skin changer Gaven Greywolf and his kin."[9] *Beowulf* contains several tales of raids involving rival clans, like the Frisians and Heathobards, while Martin's North is raided by the Wildlings from beyond the Wall. Denmark has its monster, Grendel; Westeros has the monstrous Others/White Walkers and wights. Carroll notes the Starks' deeply entrenched sense of duty and loyalty to lord and kin, and their obligation to avenge their deaths, which reflect the heroic moral principles illustrated in *Beowulf* and other Old English poetry.[10] Larrington notes that Ned Stark's "dominion over his castle, household and lands is much closer to that of an Anglo-Saxon earl than the later medieval model of kingship which prevails in King's Landing."[11] The Starks are supported by a system of "bannermen" who owe military service to their lord in times of crisis. Similarly, Anglo-Saxon kings had their *thegns* (aristocratic retainers) and *fyrds* (militias of freemen). Even flaying, the method of torture and execution preferred by Ned's bannermen, the Boltons, evokes the fabled Viking "blood eagle." In short, the North of Westeros is strikingly reminiscent of the heroic world portrayed in *Beowulf*. One would expect then, that noblewomen of the North would also echo *Beowulf*'s queens, in both their successes and their failures.

THE PEACEWEAVING QUEEN

By the late twentieth century, the popular interpretation of the queen in Anglo-Saxon literature was that of "peaceweaver" (Old English: *freoðu-webbe*). Writing in 1991, Andrew Welsh described the peaceweaver's role as twofold: "to create by her marriage peaceful bonds between two previously or potentially hostile kin-groups, or tribes, and after her marriage to encourage and support peaceful and harmonious relations among the members of the kin-group, especially the comitatus, that she has joined."[12] Jane Chance noted in 1986 that producing legitimate heirs was of paramount importance as "a specific means of making peace between two tribes by literally mingling their blood."[13] Gillian Overing wrote in 1990 that *Beowulf*'s queens "enact and embody the process of weaving, they weave and are woven by the ties of kinship."[14] In 2013, Peter S. Baker countered that the concept of peaceweaving was invented by Victorian scholars who interpreted *Beowulf*'s queens in light of Queen Victoria, "whom [the English] glorified as both the ideal mother and benevolent ruler of an empire."[15] Whether the concept was embedded in the original *Beowulf* text, or was a later interpretation, by the 1990s, when Martin began writing *A Song of Ice and Fire*, popular culture had embraced "peaceweaving" as a prevalent function of Anglo-Saxon and *Beowulf*'s queens.

Through this interpretation, the poem can be seen to illustrate a range of expected behaviours for an Anglo-Saxon queen. Chance writes, "The role of woman in *Beowulf*, as in Anglo-Saxon society, primarily depends upon peace making, either biologically through her marital ties with foreign kings as a peace pledge or mother of sons, or socially and psychologically as a cup-passing and peace-weaving queen within a hall."[16] She also serves as a wise counsellor to her husband, rewards valiant retainers with treasure, and establishes social hierarchies through the cup-passing ceremony.[17] These roles are affirmed by the Old English *Maxims I*, a collection of wisdom poetry contemporaneous with the writing of *Beowulf*[18]:

> A royal man must buy his bride
> with cups and rings.
> Both must first be generous with gifts.
> A fighting spirit must grow in the man,
> a brave battle spirit, and the woman
> must find favor with her people—
> gracious she must be, a keeper of secrets,
> kind she must be, generous with horses and gifts.
>
> Always, in all festivities, she must greet
> first her lord, among his companions,
> and put the full cup in his hands.
> She must be wise in the ways of her household,
> giving her husband good counsel.[19]

Wealhtheow, wife of the Danish King Hrothgar, epitomizes this Anglo-Saxon ideal. She arrives on the scene bearing a mead-cup to Hrothgar and his retainers, exactly as described in *Maxims I*:

> Wealhtheow went forth,
> Hrothgar's queen, mindful of customs;
> adorned with gold, she greeted the men in the hall,

Then that courteous wife offered the full cup,
first to the guardian of the East-Danes' kingdom,
bid him be merry at his beer-drinking,
beloved by his people; with pleasure he received
the feast and cup, victorious king.
The lady of the Helmings then went about
to young and old, gave each his portion
of the precious cup, until the moment came
when the ring-adorned queen, of excellent heart,
bore the mead-cup to Beowulf.[20]

Porter writes that mead-serving "appears to be a relatively unimportant function until one reads carefully and examines how this duty is carried out."[21] After serving the cup to the king, Hrothgar, Wealhtheow next serves the young and old retainers, and lastly, the stranger Beowulf. But the next night, after Beowulf has killed Grendel, Wealhtheow serves Beowulf immediately following the king, signalling to those in the hall Beowulf's increased status. Queen Hygd and Wealhtheow's daughter, Freawaru, are also depicted in mead-serving ceremonies. A queen can also signal social status by the presentation of gifts, an act which reflexively serves to illustrate her own generosity.[22] For the defeat of Grendel, Wealhtheow gives Beowulf "two armlets, garments and rings, and the greatest neck-collar ever heard of anywhere on earth."[23] These scenes from *Beowulf*, along with the verses from *Maxims I*, illustrate the peace-weaver's considerable agency in establishing and maintaining social order within the mead-hall.

If *Beowulf*'s ideal queen is Wealhtheow, Martin's is Catelyn Stark, especially in her role as chatelaine of Winterfell at the start of the series. Though not nominally a queen, Catelyn is the closest thing to one outside of King's Landing. She is wife to Ned Stark, the Lord of Winterfell and Warden of the North, a formerly independent kingdom. Like Wealhtheow's marriage between the tribes of Danes and Helmings, Catelyn's is the result of an alliance between two Great Houses, the Starks of Winterfell and the Tullys of Riverrun. While readers do not see Catelyn carrying a mead cup around Winterfell's Great Hall, she exercises a similar sort of authority in determining social hierarchies. In *A Game of Thrones*, during King Robert's royal visit, Catelyn seats Ned's (presumed) bastard, Jon Snow, on a bench down among the younger squires, rather than on the raised platform where she and Ned entertain the king and queen. When Ned's brother

Benjen asks, "Don't you usually eat at table with your brothers?" Jon replies, "Most times ... But tonight Lady Stark thought it might give insult to the royal family to seat a bastard among them."[24] In the TV series, Catelyn banishes Jon from the Great Hall entirely.[25]

As consorts of their respective lords, Wealhtheow's and Catelyn's most important function is producing legitimate heirs. *Maxims I* states, "man and woman bring birth to the world."[26] Wealhtheow has two young sons and heirs, Hrethric and Hrothmund, and a daughter, Freawaru, who is betrothed to Ingeld, lord of the rival Heathobards. Catelyn has three sons and two daughters. Similarly, her eldest, Robb, "would someday inherit Winterfell, and would command great armies as the Warden of the North. Bran and Rickon would be Robb's bannermen and rule holdfasts in his name. His sisters Arya and Sansa would marry the heirs of other great houses and go south as mistress of castles of their own."[27]

Both Wealhtheow and Catelyn are valued advisors to their husbands and both exert considerable influence on the lines of succession. When Wealhtheow hears that her husband has offered to make Beowulf his heir as reward for killing Grendel, Wealhtheow implores Hrothgar in front of his *thegns* to give Beowulf treasure, but to leave the kingdom to their sons. Tom Shippey observes that *Beowulf's* queens give "wise advice, and not in private (something queens are often suspected of doing) but in public and with a note of criticism."[28] Hygd, wife of Beowulf's uncle, Hygelac, the king of the Geats, also possesses some authority over the succession. Following her husband's death, she offers Beowulf "hoard and kingdom, rings and royal throne; she did not trust that her son could hold their ancestral seat against foreign hosts, now that Hygelac was dead."[29] Catelyn is similarly influential. When King Robert proposes a marriage alliance between his son, Joffrey, and Ned's and Catelyn's daughter, Sansa, Ned informs Robert that he must talk to Catelyn.[30] When Robert asks Ned to be his Hand of the King, TV-Catelyn urges Ned to refuse Robert's offer, but book-Catelyn is more strategic concerning her family's fortunes—

> If you refuse to serve him, he will wonder why, and sooner or later he will begin to suspect that you oppose him. Can't you see the danger that would put us in? ... Pride is everything to a king, my lord. Robert came all this way to see you, to bring you these great honors, you cannot throw them back in his face ... He offers his own son in marriage to our daughter, what else would you call that? Sansa might someday be queen. Her sons could rule from the Wall to the mountains of Dorne.[31]

Catelyn is not the only woman in Martin's series to exercise political influence within a marriage alliance. Margaery Tyrell, as a prime example, wields some measure of influence in her three marriage alliances with three different Baratheon men—Renly, Joffrey, and Tommen. In her contribution to this volume, Sylwia Borowska-Szerszun observes, "before her fall, Margaery Tyrell successfully accommodates herself within the category of a 'help meet' who does not threaten patriarchal authority yet establishes her own sphere of influence."[32] She argues that Margaery "realizes she can gain more by wielding discreet influence over men than by challenging their authority."[33] Margaery thus helps Renly to evoke a kingly image; she placates Joffrey's violent outbursts; and, she builds public support for the royals during Tommen's reign. All the while, Margaery behaves in a sweet and non-confrontational manner.

Catelyn Stark, on the other hand, employs assertiveness. Ned follows Catelyn's advice to accept Robert's offer of betrothal between their children, as well as his offer to serve as Robert's Hand of the King. Ned names Catelyn his regent and charges her with teaching their son Robb how to rule, "Make him part of your councils. He must be ready when his time comes."[34] In return, Catelyn demands Jon Snow be sent away, "He is your son, not mine. I will not have him."[35] Catelyn is certainly hurt by the presence of a boy she believes her husband fathered on another woman, but Jon's presence could endanger the succession of Catelyn's own sons. Of a similar age, Jon and Robb have been raised as brothers, and Ned has always acknowledged Jon as his son. When Catelyn hears that Jon would join the celibate Night's Watch, she is relieved to think he "would father no sons who might someday contest with Catelyn's own grandchildren for Winterfell."[36] But neither the princes of Denmark nor the Stark children are safe in their inheritance. Both families harbour vipers in their nests. *Beowulf* foreshadows the usurpation of Wealhtheow's two young sons by their cousin, Hrothulf. Catelyn's two young sons, Bran and Rickon, are also betrayed by a member of the household, Theon Greyjoy, who seizes Winterfell in Ned's and Catelyn's absence.

Alaric Hall writes, "Although the [*Beowulf*] poem hints at how [Wealhtheow] lacks power to constrain impending feuding within her children's generation (lines 76–85, 1163–87), there is no suggestion that her own marriage to Hrothgar has been anything but a success."[37] The marriage of Beowulf's uncle and aunt, Hygelac and Hygd, likewise appears successful as long as Hygelac lives. Catelyn, as chatelaine of Winterfell, also enjoys a happy marriage with Ned, one in which "She had come to love her husband with all her heart."[38] Nevertheless, the stability woven by Wealhtheow, Hygd, and Catelyn does not long outlive the deaths of their powerful husbands. In other marriages, peace is even more short-lived.

THE TRAGIC BRIDE

The Anglo-Saxon world, like its Germanic predecessors, was based upon a code of male honour, strength, and vengeance, which made fertile ground for violence. Baker argues, peaceweaving leads to "a vain hope in this warrior society."[39] Anglo-Saxon noblewomen, according to Chance, are thus "usually depicted as doomed or tragic figures, frequently seen as weeping or suffering."[40] Just as the poem illustrates the limited success of peaceweaving by the queens Wealhtheow and Hygd, *Beowulf* also offers multiple examples of broken treaties and the tragic brides whose marriages fail to secure peace. The story of Hildeburh, a Danish princess, is sung by Hrothgar's *scop* (bard) at the feast celebrating Beowulf's defeat of Grendel. The song suggests that her marriage to the Frisian king Finn is a happy one. She has good relations with her brother, has a beloved son, and enjoys "the greatest worldly joys."[41] Nevertheless, hostilities break out between her husband's *thegns* and those of her brother visiting from Denmark. Her son, brother, and later her husband, are all killed. Although, guiltless herself, Hildeburh is powerless to prevent the fighting, the plundering of Finn's hall, or her own repatriation to Denmark. Chance observes that Hildeburh, "all she does, this sad woman … is to mourn her loss with dirges and stoically place her son on the pyre. In fact, she can do nothing, caught in the very wen she has woven as peace pledge."[42]

Hrothgar's and Wealhtheow's daughter, Freawaru, is betrothed to a neighbouring lord, Ingeld, specifically in order to create peace between his people, the Heathobards, and hers, the Danes. Hrothgar believes, "he might settle his share of feud and slaughter with this young woman."[43] However, Beowulf predicts that violence will break out at the wedding feast over simmering resentments from past battles. The poet writes, "seldom anywhere after the death of a prince does the deadly spear rest, for even a brief while, though the bride be good!"[44] This strife will cause Freawaru's marriage to fail: "on both sides the sword oaths of earls will be broken, once bitter violent hate wells up in Ingeld, and his wife-love grows cooler."[45] Welsh remarks, "A Peaceweaver tale seems always to be a tragic tale, the story of a woman ambivalently situated between two peoples, belonging to both and yet completely to neither, and finally unable (in the imagery of the *Beowulf* poet) to stop the fires of old feud from flaring up again and consuming both."[46] Chance calls Hildeburh, Freawaru, and even Wealhtheow, "failed peaceweavers" who "convey dialectically the idea that women cannot ensure peace in the world."[47]

The image of slaughter between rival factions at a wedding feast is certain to resonate with fans of *Game of Thrones*. When Robert is killed and Ned arrested for treason against the new king, Joffrey, the Stark bannermen declare Ned's son Robb as King in the North. In the ensuing war between the Starks and Joffrey's maternal family, the Lannisters, Catelyn negotiates a marriage alliance for Robb with the daughter of Walder Frey, the lord in control of a vital river crossing. The betrothal is broken, though, when Robb unexpectedly marries another. Attempting to salvage the alliance, Catelyn offers in Robb's stead her brother, Edmure Tully, Lord of Riverrun. Though Frey ostensibly accepts, he feels betrayed, and in revenge betrays the Starks at Edmure's wedding feast, the infamous "Red Wedding." Robb, Catelyn, and many of their followers are murdered there, but Edmure, as blameless and helpless as Hildeburh or Freawaru, is seized as a hostage by the Freys. In a gender-bending twist, Edmure becomes a tragic bride, trapped between the feuding Starks and Freys, belonging to both, yet completely to neither, and unable to stop the fires of kin-strife.

Yet it is Sansa Stark who is cast as the archetypal tragic bride as she is exchanged, manipulated, and abused in the various shifting alliances between the rival Houses of Westeros. Like Hildeburh and Freawaru in *Beowulf*, Sansa begins with high hopes of joy in her arranged marriage to the crown prince, Joffrey. According to Carroll, Sansa begins the series "with idealized views of nobility and knighthood, fed by songs and tales of grand adventures and high chivalry."[48] But from early on, Sansa must negotiate between the Starks and Lannisters when she is forced to choose sides between her sister Arya and her betrothed Joffrey on the King's Road. And just as Hildeburh can only stand by her son's funeral pyre and weep, Sansa can only stand by as Joffrey later executes her father Ned for treason. Chance writes, "the peace pledge must accept a passive role precisely because the ties she knots bind *her*—she *is* the knot, the pledge of peace."[49] Sansa is left essentially powerless. She can only appeal to Joffrey for clemency for her family, and urge her family, in a letter, to bend the knee to Joffrey. Her personal survival lies in her ability to passively submit to Joffrey and his family in King's Landing.

Although she is eventually replaced as Joffrey's fiancée by the wealthier Margaery Tyrell, Sansa remains a valuable hostage. Both the Lannisters and Lord Petyr Baelish, "Littlefinger," attempt to gain control of the North through her. First, the Lannisters marry her to Joffrey's Uncle Tyrion. Later, in *A Feast for Crows*, the last book published in which Sansa appears, Littlefinger contracts a marriage for her with Harrold Hardyng, heir to the Vale of Arryn. Littlefinger tells her, "When [the lords of the Vale] come together for his wedding, and you come out with your long auburn hair, clad in a maiden's cloak of white and grey with a direwolf emblazoned on the back ... why, every knight in the Vale will pledge his sword to win you back your birthright."[50] In the TV series, Littlefinger has a similar goal but accomplishes it instead through a marriage alliance with the Boltons, who, in their turn, usurped Winterfell from Theon Greyjoy. Ramsay Bolton's claim as Warden of the North is legitimized by his marriage to a Stark, but he is even more sadistic than Joffrey, and repeatedly beats and rapes Sansa. Sansa is thus repeatedly traded by men for their benefit, not for hers. Frankel observes that Sansa is "only sought for her claim to the North and the heir she can produce ... She will never be allowed to choose for herself, only be traded and fought over."[51] As Overing notes of *Beowulf*, a marriage alliance "is essentially an alliance of men," with women merely "the visible token of male alliance."[52] Through much of her story, Sansa can only passively allow herself to be bargained as a token of northern nobility. As Chance argues, "passivity rather than heroism generally epitomized the ideal Anglo-Saxon woman."[53] Vengeance is routinely left to the men. But not every woman in *Beowulf* or *Game of Thrones* plays by those gender rules.

THE MONSTROUS MOTHER

While some women try to forge peace, others choose to employ the revenge-strategies usually reserved for males in heroic cultures. Although Catelyn Stark at Winterfell was a model of the Anglo-Saxon peace-weaving queen, when she leaves her domestic realm, she becomes a strife-weaver. The Old English *Maxims I* warns women not to leave the safety of their homes:

> A woman is enjoined   to be with embroidery;
> a wandering woman   engenders gossip;
> she is often taunted   with sordid sayings,
> slandered, insulted,   her complexion compromised.[54]

In *Beowulf*, Grendel's unnamed mother is the archetypal strife-weaver. According to Chance, she is "a parodic inversion of the Anglo-Saxon queen and mother."[55] The night following Beowulf's contest with Grendel, Grendel's mother invades Heorot and kills Hrothgar's counsellor in revenge. Beowulf follows her back to her underwater home and kills her. Immediately prior to this incident, the *scop* recites Hildeburh's story. Like Hildeburh, Grendel's mother is unjustly deprived of her son. But where Hildeburh leaves revenge to her brother's surviving *thegns*, Grendel's mother has no male relatives or retainers to exact vengeance for her son's death. She herself "would avenge her boy, her only offspring."[56] Chance observes, "Grendel's mother monstrously inverts the image of the Anglo-Saxon queen because she behaves in a heroic and masculine way."[57] In fact, Grendel's mother is oddly referred to on occasion with masculine pronouns and epithets.[58] She is also called *ides āglǣcwīf*, often translated as "monstrous woman."[59] Chance writes, "feminine heroism was not countenanced by Anglo-Saxon society."[60] When queens attempted to rule alone or to rule over their husbands, they were typically depicted as incontinent and immoral, and "when linked with warlike or masculine behavior, [they] became a metaphor for unnatural and heathen or devilish proclivities."[61]

Catelyn Stark similarly becomes a metaphor for unnatural and devilish practices on her quest for revenge. When Ned goes south to King's Landing, he charges Catelyn to stay in Winterfell and mentor their eldest, Robb. However, she soon abandons her post and travels to King's Landing to bring Ned news. On the way home, she captures Tyrion Lannister, whom she believes attempted to assassinate Bran. Catelyn then joins Robb in open rebellion against the Lannisters when they retaliate by arresting Ned for treason. Although Robb, now her liege lord, wants Catelyn to return to Winterfell to protect young Bran and Rickon, she decides to stay with the army and serve as Robb's advisor. In many cases, Catelyn's advice is experienced and rational: urging Robb to negotiate for Sansa's and Arya's freedom; warning against Theon Greyjoy; proposing an alliance with Renly Baratheon; negotiating a marriage alliance with Walder Frey. Yet, Catelyn achieves nothing positive after she leaves Winterfell. All her rational plans fail. Finally, in frustration with Robb for ignoring her advice, she secretly releases the prisoner, Jaime Lannister, losing Robb's trust in the process.

At the Red Wedding, Robb and Catelyn are killed. Her body is dumped in the Green Fork River where it floats for three days. In the books, Catelyn is resurrected by Thoros of Myr, a red priest of R'hllor. Only now, Catelyn is monstrous:

[Her] flesh had gone pudding soft in the water and turned the color of curdled milk. Half her hair was gone and the rest had turned as white and brittle as a crone's. Beneath her ravaged scalp, her face was shredded skin and black blood where she had raked herself with her nails. But her eyes were the most terrible thing. Her eyes saw [a Frey], and they hated.[62]

Catelyn is now Lady Stoneheart, Mother Merciless, the Hangwoman.[63] Her only remaining desire is for vengeance as she ruthlessly executes anyone she considers a Frey or Lannister collaborator. Catelyn's character, which began in the domestic sphere of Winterfell with a happy marriage, multiple heirs, and peace, takes a fatal downturn with her departure from Winterfell, in violation of her husband's and son's wishes. By then exercising masculine power to seek revenge as Lady Stoneheart, Catelyn transforms from the epitome of Wealhtheow into that of Grendel's mother.

Arya Stark could also be termed a "strife-weaver" as one who employs violence rather than peace. In contrast to the passive femininity of her sister, Sansa, Arya is drawn to the masculine pursuits of archery, sword-fighting and revenge. In Season One of the TV series, Arya asks her father, "Can I be lord of a holdfast?" Ned laughingly answers, "You will marry a high lord and rule his castle, and your sons shall be knights and princes and lords." Arya replies, "No, that's not me."[64] Choosing the active path, Arya escapes from King's Landing when her father is executed, evading Sansa's fate as a tragic bride. She adopts a masculine persona, Arry, and vows vengeance on all those who have betrayed her. She later travels to Braavos and trains as an assassin with the Faceless Men. Years later, according to the TV series, she returns to Winterfell as a monster. She has become an emotionless and ruthless avenger who can poison the entire Frey family without remorse. She carries a bag of flayed human faces to wear as disguises. Arya has become an excellent warrior, but she is not fit to rule as Lady of Winterfell. Like Lady Stoneheart and Grendel's mother, Arya has become obsessed with revenge. But a successful northern queen must employ both peaceweaving and judicious vengeance.

THE SHE-WOLF

Another story-within-the-story of *Beowulf* tells of King Offa's wife and her "terrible crimes."[65] It is said of Thryth that no man among her retainers "dared to approach her, except as her prince, or dared to look into her eyes by day," else he would be garrotted and slain.[66] The narrator notes wryly, "That is no queenly custom for a lady to perform—no matter how lovely—that a peace-weaver should deprive of life a friendly man after a pretend affront."[67] Shippey declares that the queen behaves "cruelly and irrationally," having men executed for no reason."[68] Chance calls her "a type of the female monster."[69] Yet, Thryth is the only woman in *Beowulf* to be explicitly called a "peaceweaver" (*freoðuwebbe*).

Feminist critiques of the poem interrogate claims that Thyrth is an irrational monster. Baker argues that the unwanted gaze of her male retainers contains an implicit menace.[70] Jessica Hope Jordan maintains, "When men stare at a woman in a sexually desiring way, can this not also be considered, a form of sexual harassment?"[71] Overing writes, "Despite her beauty, [Thryth] will not consent to be a feminine spectacle in a masculine arena, refusing to join the ranks of the gold-adorned queens who circulate among the warriors as visible treasure."[72] When Thryth has her harassers executed, Jordan argues that she not only *refuses* the unwanted male gaze, but *challenges* and *revenges* it.[73] She writes, Thryth's is "less a story of a 'wicked' *cwen* [queen] and becomes instead a *revenge narrative*, a narrative that fits with the warrior ethos contained in the poem itself."[74] Although Chance contends that the Old English peaceweaver must be passive, Baker reasons the medieval queen would have used all the tools at her disposal: both treasure-giving as a peaceful way of binding her warriors to her, and violence, for "using and maintaining power could mean shedding blood."[75] Through this lens then, Thryth is not a monster but a powerful woman who punishes sexual harassers when she must.

Once Thryth marries King Offa, she abruptly ceases her executions and thereafter causes "less calamity to the people, less malicious evil."[76] Some scholars attribute this sudden pivot to the power of Offa's love or his ability to control her. Another possibility is that Offa offers her a previously unavailable protection against sexual harassment. Whatever the reason, once she becomes Offa's queen, Thryth becomes "famous for good things" and "high love."[77]

This raises the possibility of an alternate view of Grendel's mother as well. She is described in Old English as *ides āglæcwīf*, which, Christine Alfano demonstrates, is frequently translated as "monster woman," "monstrous ogress," and similar epithets.[78] Alfano argues that *ides āglæcwīf* should rather be translated as "lady warrior-woman."[79] Chance also offers the alternatives, "fierce combatant" and "strong adversary."[80] R.M. Liuzza translates the Old English *brim-wul[f]*, also in reference to Grendel's mother, as "she-wolf of the sea."[81] As a warrior-woman or she-wolf,

Grendel's mother might be viewed therefore more ambivalently as a family member seeking vengeance, according to the customs of a heroic culture, rather than as an irrational monster.

The image of she-wolves is uniquely appropriate for the Stark women, for their family emblem is the direwolf. Tyrion Lannister uses the term to describe Catelyn in *A Game of Thrones*: "All his life Tyrion had prided himself on his cunning, the only gift the gods had seen fit to give him, yet this seven-times-damned *she-wolf* Catelyn Stark had outwitted him at every turn."[82] Martin also declared his intent to use the image in a Dunk and Egg prequel story. He wrote, "The unfinished novella was indeed set in Winterfell, and involved a group of formidable Stark wives, widows, mothers, and grandmothers that I dubbed 'the She-Wolves'" of Winterfell.[83] Arya and Sansa both adopt orphaned direwolf pups in *A Game of Thrones* which serve as their personal symbols. But where Arya develops into an essentially merciless character, Sansa behaves more like a female wolf: tender with her pack, and brutal with prey or a threat.

Chance argues that Anglo-Saxon queens, "who behaved unconventionally—that is, who attempted to rule or take over a kingdom—were usually castigated as lascivious, immoral, and even diabolic."[84] Examples in *Game of Thrones* include Cersei, Lysa, and Margaery. Finn points out, in her contribution to this volume, that such charges are not without merit, as, for instance, "Cersei's deliberate decision to pass all three of her children with Jaime off as the heirs to the throne is the definition of queenly treason."[85] Sansa Stark, on the other hand, is noted for her conventional feminine passivity, which keeps her image chaste and blameless. Even after her brutal rape by Ramsay Bolton (an interpolation of the TV series which does not occur in the books), when she is robbed of her physical virginity, Sansa still maintains a spiritual purity in the eyes of her bannermen, and the audience. But as Sansa gradually breaks away from her passive role, she, too, suffers accusations of immorality and diabolism. When she escapes from King's Landing, Cersei calls her a "murdering whore."[86] When Sansa becomes Littlefinger's protégée, her Aunt Lysa condemns her as a wanton seducer.

In the final seasons of the TV series, Sansa becomes a lot more like *Beowulf*'s Thryth than the tragic peaceweaver bride, that is, a lady capable of giving wise counsel and engaging in "high love," but also of punishing sexual harassers when she must. It is Sansa who raises the idea of retaking Winterfell by weaving together the Wildlings and the Stark bannermen. It is Sansa who brings the Lords of the Vale into the Battle of the Bastards, tipping the scales for a Stark victory. Yet, the northern lords declare Jon Snow as King in the North. Though Jon is thought to be a bastard, he is a man. Even the name, "The Battle of the Bastards," erases Sansa's contribution. But, she accepts their decision. When Sansa publicly argues with Jon over Cersei, as Wealhtheow publicly argues with Hrothgar over Beowulf, Jon silences and reproaches her rather than heeding her advice. She reminds him that she knows Ramsay and Cersei better than he does, "Did it ever once occur to you that I might have some insight?"[87] Jon finally listens. When he leaves Winterfell to ally himself with Daenerys Targaryen, he names Sansa as regent, just as Ned once named Catelyn. As chatelaine, Sansa handily organizes Winterfell's defences and winter stores. When the Northern lords object to Jon's departure, and voice regrets at not proclaiming Sansa their ruler instead, she tells them sweetly, "You are very kind, my lords, but Jon is our king." Arya wants to behead the lords for treason, but Sansa counters, "I'm sure cutting off heads is very satisfying, but that's not the way you get people working together."[88] All of Sansa's experiences have come down to this: how to effectively weave the peace between various factions. However, passivity is no longer her only weapon; she can also employ violence when necessary. Like Thryth, Sansa can *challenge* and even *revenge* the sexually harassing male gaze. She feeds Ramsay to his own dogs, and has Littlefinger executed for fomenting the War of the Five Kings (and thereby destroying her family). It is decidedly not through her rape-marriage to Ramsay that Sansa learns how to be an effective leader, as the male writers of *Game of Thrones* suggest in Season Eight, Episode 4, "The Last of the Starks." Benioff and Weiss have Sansa say, "Without Ramsay and Littlefinger and the rest, I'd have stayed a 'little bird' all my life," intimating that rape was a beneficial catalyst in her journey to good leadership.[89] However, Carroll aptly argued back in 2015 that Sansa had already abandoned her naïve worldview by the time of Joffrey's murder and her flight from King's Landing.[90] It is arguably Sansa's enduring belief in "her own duties and behavior as a noble,"[91] which best prepare her to become the Lady of Winterfell. Thus, Sansa gives advice to Jon as her mother gave advice to her father. Sansa remains the new she-wolf of Winterfell when Jon leaves for Dragonstone, unlike her mother, who abandoned her wolf-cubs, Bran and Rickon, to seek out Ned in King's Landing. And, yes, Sansa revenges the male gaze and male harassment when she must, as Thryth did in her father's court.

Before Catelyn dies and is resurrected as Lady Stoneheart, she tells Brienne of Tarth, "I am no battle commander." Brienne replies, "No, but you have courage. Not battle courage perhaps but … I don't know … a kind of *woman's* courage."[92] Sansa likewise lacks the battle courage of Brienne or her own sister Arya, but she has a kind of woman's courage. Sansa has grown from the overly idealistic peaceweaver to the tragic bride, and finally to the empowered she-wolf in command of all her many gifts: passivity and assertiveness, grace and strength, wisdom, mercy, and justice. These gifts help Sansa negotiate the precarious political situation at the end of the TV series to become the queen *regnant* of a reconstituted independent Northern Kingdom where she maintains a hard-won peace with both the Wildlings and King's Landing. Perhaps Sansa's peace will be short-lived. As Chance writes of *Beowulf*, "peace was not possible continually in this world."[93] *Game of Thrones* matriarch, Olenna Tyrell, states simply, "Peace never lasts, my dear."[94] But the best hope of peace seemingly results not from peaceweaving alone, but rather peace tempered with justice. In *Beowulf*, it is Thryth who weaves peace *and* uses justifiable violence to win the game of thrones. Sansa Stark is likewise "famous for good things" and "high love," but few of her subjects will forget what happened to the last man who abused her. If Catelyn Stark is the model of the Anglo-Saxon peaceweaver at the start of Martin's series, it is her daughter Sansa who surpasses her in that role by the end of the TV series.

NOTES

1. The term "strife-weaving" in relation to the women of *Beowulf* was coined by Dorothy Carr Porter in "The Social Centrality of Women in *Beowulf*: A New Context," *The Heroic Age* 5 (Summer/Autumn 2001): 7, http://www.heroicage.org/issues/5/porter1.html, accessed May 18, 2019.
2. The name of the wife of Offa has been translated as "Thryth," "Modthryth," or "Modthrytho": the medieval *Beowulf* manuscript is unclear.
3. Valerie Estelle Frankel, *Women in* Game of Thrones: *Power, Conformity and Resistance* (Jefferson, NC: McFarland, 2014), 38, 192.
4. Ibid., 38.
5. Kristine Larsen, "Queens, Assassins, and Zombies: The Valkyrie Reflex in George R.R. Martin's *A Song of Ice and Fire*" (paper presented at the 3rd Mythgard Institute Mythmoot, Linthicum, MD, January 10–11, 2015), 6–7, https://signumuniversity.org/library/signum-digital-collections/mythmoot-2015/#klarsen, accessed May 18, 2019; Helen Damico, "The Valkyrie Reflex in Old English Literature," in *New Readings on Women in Old English Literature*, ed. Helen Damico and Alexandra Hennessey Olsen (Bloomington, IN: Indiana University Press, 1990), 176–190; Leslie A. Donovan, "The Valkyrie Reflex in J.R.R. Tolkien's *The Lord of the*

Rings: Galadriel, Shelob, Éowyn, and Arwen," in *Perilous and Fair: Women in the Works and Life of J.R.R. Tolkien*, ed. Janet Brennan Croft and Leslie A. Donovan (Altadena, CA: Mythopoeic Press, 2015), 221–257.

6. Carolyne Larrington, *Winter Is Coming: The Medieval World of* Game of Thrones (London: I.B. Tauris, 2016), 108–109.

7. Shiloh Carroll, "Daenerys the Unready: Advice and Ruling in Meereen," in *Queenship and the Women of Westeros: Female Agency and Advice in* 'Game of Thrones' *and* 'A Song of Ice and Fire,' ed. Zita Rohr and Lisa Benz (Basingstoke: Palgrave Macmillan, 2019), 169–185.

8. Shiloh Carroll, "Barbarian Colonizers and Postcolonialism in Westeros and Britain," in Game of Thrones *Versus History: Written in Blood*, ed. Brian A. Pavlac (New York: Wiley, 2017), 78.

9. George R. R. Martin, Elio García, and Linda Antonsson, *The World of Ice and Fire: The Untold History of Westeros and the Game of Thrones* (Harper Collins UK, 2014), 137.

10. Carroll, "Barbarian," 76–77.

11. Larrington, *Winter Is Coming*, 57.

12. Andrew Welsh, "Branwen, Beowulf, and the Tragic Peaceweaver Tale," *Viator* 22 (1991): 7.

13. Jane Chance, *Woman as Hero in Old English Literature* (Eugene, OR: Wipf & Stock, [1986] 2005), 1.

14. Gillian R. Overing, *Language, Sign, and Gender in Beowulf* (Carbondale: Southern Illinois University Press, 1990), 75.

15. Peter S. Baker, *Honour, Exchange and Violence in Beowulf* (Cambridge: D. S. Brewer, 2013), 116.

16. Chance, *Woman*, 98.

17. Ibid., 3–4.

18. Leonard Neidorf, "On the Dating and Authorship of *Maxims I*," *Neuphilologische Mitteilungen* 117 (December 2016): 150 and 137.

19. Brigit Pegeen Kelly, translator, "Maxims I-B," in *The Word Exchange: Anglo-Saxon Poems in Translation*, ed. Greg Delanty and Michael Matto (New York, NY: Norton, 2011), 177–179.

20. *Beowulf*, 2nd ed., R.M. Liuzza, translator and editor, Peterborough, ON: Broadview, 2013: 612–624.

21. Porter, "Social Centrality," 2.

22. Ibid., 4.

23. *Beowulf*, 1194–1196.

24. George R.R. Martin, *A Game of Thrones: Book One of a Song of Ice and Fire* (New York, NY: Bantam, 1996), 44.

25. *Game of Thrones*, "Winter Is Coming," Season One, Episode 1, directed by Tim Van Patten, written by David Benioff and D.B. Weiss (Burbank, CA: HBO, April 17, 2011).

26. David Curzon, translator, "Maxims I-A," in *The Word Exchange: Anglo-Saxon Poems in Translation*, ed. Greg Delanty and Michael Matto (New York, NY: Norton, 2011), 171.
27. Martin, *A Game of Thrones*, 45.
28. Tom Shippey, "Wicked Queens and Cousin Strategies in *Beowulf* and Elsewhere," *The Heroic Age* 5 (Summer 2001): 4, http://www.heroicage.org/issues/5/Shippey1.html, accessed May 18, 2019.
29. *Beowulf*, 2369–2372; Beowulf initially refuses Hygd's offer and supports his young cousin instead; only after his cousin's death does Beowulf finally accept the throne.
30. Martin, *A Game of Thrones*, 39.
31. Ibid., 50; in the TV series, that argument is given to Maester Luwin, *Game of Thrones*, "Winter Is Coming."
32. Sylwia Borowska-Szerszun, "Westerosi Queens: Medievalist Portrayal of Female Power and Authority in *A Song of Ice and Fire*," in *Queenship and the Women of Westeros: Female Agency and Advice in 'Game of Thrones' and 'A Song of Ice and Fire,'* ed. Zita Rohr and Lisa Benz (Basingstoke: Palgrave Macmillan, 2019), 53–75.
33. Ibid., 53–75.
34. Martin, *A Game of Thrones*, 53–54.
35. Ibid., 55.
36. Ibid., 56.
37. Alaric Hall, "Hygelac's Only Daughter: A Present, a Potentate and a Peaceweaver in *Beowulf*," *Studia Neophilologica* 78, no. 1 (2006): 5, http://www.tandfonline.com/doi/abs/10.1080/00393270600774719, accessed May 22, 2019.
38. Martin, *A Game of Thrones*, 55.
39. Baker, *Honour*, 122.
40. Chance, *Woman*, 10.
41. *Beowulf*, 1080.
42. Chance, *Woman*, 100.
43. *Beowulf*, 2028–2029.
44. Ibid., 2029–2031.
45. Ibid., 2063–2066.
46. Welsh, "Branwen," 8.
47. Chance, *Woman*, 106.
48. Shiloh Carroll, "Rewriting the Fantasy Archetype: George R.R. Martin, Neomedievalist Fantasy, and the Quest for Realism," in *Fantasy and Science-Fiction Medievalism: From Isaac Asimov to 'A Game of Thrones,'* ed. Helen Young, 59-76. (Amherst, NY: Cambria Press, 2015), 62.
49. Chance, *Woman*, 100.
50. George R.R. Martin, *A Feast for Crows: Book Four of a Song of Ice and Fire* (New York, NY: Bantam, 2005), 627, ellipses in the original.

51. Frankel, *Women*, 107.
52. Overing, *Language*, 74.
53. Chance, *Woman*, xiv.
54. Curzon, "Maxims I-A," 175.
55. Chance, *Woman*, 97.
56. *Beowulf*, 1546–1547.
57. Chance, *Woman*, 107 and xvi.
58. Ibid., 95.
59. *Beowulf*, 1259.
60. Chance, *Woman*, xvii.
61. Ibid., 55.
62. George R.R. Martin, *A Storm of Swords: Book Three of a Song of Ice and Fire* (New York, NY: Bantam, 2000), 924.
63. Martin, *A Feast for Crows*, 631.
64. *Game of Thrones*, "Cripples, Bastards, and Broken Things," Season One, Episode 4, directed by Brian Kirk, written by Bryan Cogman (Burbank, CA: HBO, May 8, 2011).
65. *Beowulf*, 1932.
66. Ibid., 1933–1940.
67. Ibid., 1940–1943.
68. Shippey, "Wicked Queens," 1.
69. Chance, *Woman*, 105.
70. Baker, *Honour*, 144–145 and 149–150.
71. Jessica Hope Jordan, "Women Refusing the Gaze: Theorizing Thryth's 'Unqueenly Custom' in *Beowulf* and The Bride's Revenge in Quentin Tarantino's *Kill Bill, Volume I*," *The Heroic Age: A Journal of Early Medieval Northwestern Europe* 9 (October 2006), http://www.heroicage.org/issues/9/forum2.html, accessed May 18, 2019.
72. Overing, *Language*, 104.
73. Jordan, "Women," n.1.
74. Ibid., 5, emphasis in the original.
75. Baker, *Honour*, 155.
76. *Beowulf*, 1946–1947.
77. Ibid., 1953–1954.
78. Ibid., 1259; Christine Alfano, "The Issue of Feminine Monstrosity: A Reevaluation of Grendel's Mother," *Comitatus: A Journal of Medieval and Renaissance Studies* 23, no. 1 (1992): 2. UCLA, 2017, http://escholarship.org/uc/item/39g6c6rm, accessed May 18, 2019.
79. Alfano, "Issue," 2.
80. Chance, *Woman*, 95.
81. *Beowulf*, 1506.
82. Martin, *A Game of Thrones*, 275–276; emphasis added.

83. George R.R. Martin, "Dunk and Egg," *Not a Blog* (April 15, 2014) (3:37pm), http://grrm.livejournal.com/365715.html, accessed May 18, 2019.
84. Chance, *Woman*, 53.
85. Kavita Mundan Finn, "Queen of Sad Mischance: Medievalism, 'Realism,' and the Case of Cersei Lannister," in *Queenship and the Women of Westeros: Female Agency and Advice in* 'Game of Thrones' *and* 'A Song of Ice and Fire,' ed. Zita Rohr and Lisa Benz (Basingstoke: Palgrave Macmillan, 2019), 29–52.
86. *Game of Thrones*, "Stormborn," Season Seven, Episode 2, directed by Mark Mylod, written by Bryan Cogman (Burbank, CA: HBO, July 23, 2017).
87. *Game of Thrones*, "Battle of the Bastards," Season Six, Episode 9, directed by Miguel Sapochnik, written by David Benioff and D.B. Weiss (Burbank, CA: HBO, June 19, 2016).
88. *Game of Thrones*, "Eastwatch," Season Seven, Episode 5, directed by Matt Shakman, written by Dave Hill (Burbank, CA: HBO, August 13, 2017).
89. *Game of Thrones*, "The Last of the Starks," Season Eight, Episode 4, directed by David Nutter, written by David Benioff and D.B. Weiss (Burbank, CA: HBO, May 5, 2019). The episode received a torrent of criticism for its suggestion that Sansa regarded Ramsay's rapes as character-building experiences. For example, Kaitlin Thomas wrote, "a woman's horrific rape is not the driving force behind her later empowerment and to suggest as much is dangerous and wholly irresponsible." Kaitlin Thomas, "Chances for a Satisfying *Game of Thrones* Finale Are Looking Very Bleak," *TV Guide* (May 6, 2019), https://www.tvguide.com/news/game-of-thrones-ending-unsatisfying-jaime-brienne-sansa-jon-daenerys/, accessed May 18, 2019.
90. Carroll, "Rewriting," 68.
91. Ibid., 68.
92. George R.R. Martin, *A Clash of Kings: Book Two of a Song of Ice and Fire* (New York, NY: Bantam, 1999), 422, italics in the original.
93. Chance, *Woman*, 11.
94. *Game of Thrones*, "Stormborn," July 23, 2017.

BIBLIOGRAPHY

Alfano, Christine. "The Issue of Feminine Monstrosity: A Reevaluation of Grendel's Mother." *Comitatus: A Journal of Medieval and Renaissance Studies* 23, no. 1 (1992). UCLA, http://escholarship.org/uc/item/39g6c6rm.
Baker, Peter S. *Honour, Exchange and Violence in Beowulf.* Cambridge: D. S. Brewer, 2013.

Beowulf. 2nd ed. Translated and edited by R. M. Liuzza. Peterborough, Ontario, Canada, ON: Broadview Press, 2013.

Borowska-Szerszun, Sylwia. "Westerosi Queens: Medievalist Portrayal of Female Power and Authority in *A Song of Ice and Fire.*" In *Queenship and the Women of Westeros: Female Agency and Advice in* 'Game of Thrones' *and* 'A Song of Ice and Fire,' edited by Zita Rohr and Lisa Benz, Basingstoke: Palgrave Macmillan, 2019, 53–75.

Carroll, Shiloh. "Barbarian Colonizers and Postcolonialism in Westeros and Britain." In Game of Thrones *Versus History: Written in Blood,* edited by Brian A. Pavlac, 73–84. New York: Wiley, 2017.

Carroll, Shiloh. "Daenerys the Unready: Advice and Ruling in Meereen." In *Queenship and the Women of Westeros: Female Agency and Advice in* 'Game of Thrones' *and* 'A Song of Ice and Fire,' edited by Zita Rohr and Lisa Benz, Basingstoke: Palgrave Macmillan, 2019, 169–185.

Carroll, Shiloh. "Rewriting the Fantasy Archetype: George R.R. Martin, Neomedievalist Fantasy, and the Quest for Realism." In *Fantasy and Science Fiction Medievalisms: From Isaac Asimov to* A Game of Thrones, edited by Helen Young, 59–76. Amherst, NY: Cambria Press, 2015.

Chance, Jane. *Woman as Hero in Old English Literature.* Eugene, OR: Wipf & Stock, [1986] 2005.

Curzon, David, translator. "Maxims I-A." In *The Word Exchange: Anglo-Saxon Poems in Translation,* edited by Greg Delanty and Michael Matto, 171–175. New York, NY: Norton, 2011.

Damico, Helen. "The Valkyrie Reflex in Old English Literature." In *New Readings on Women in Old English Literature,* edited by Helen Damico and Alexandra Hennessey Olsen, 176–190. Bloomington, IN: Indiana University Press, 1990.

Donovan, Leslie A. "The Valkyrie Reflex in J.R.R. Tolkien's *The Lord of the Rings:* Galadriel, Shelob, Éowyn, and Arwen." In *Perilous and Fair: Women in the Works and Life of J.R.R. Tolkien,* edited by Janet Brennan Croft and Leslie A. Donovan, 221–257. Altadena, CA: Mythopoeic Press, 2015.

Finn, Kavita Mundan. "Queen of Sad Mischance: Medievalism, 'Realism,' and the case of Cersei Lannister." In *Basingstoke and the Women of Westeros: Female Agency and Advice in* 'Game of Thrones' *and* 'A Song of Ice and Fire,' edited by Zita Rohr and Lisa Benz, Basingstoke: Palgrave Macmillan, 2019, 29–52.

Frankel, Valerie Estelle. *Women in* Game of Thrones: *Power, Conformity and Resistance.* Jefferson, NC: McFarland, 2014.

Game of Thrones. "Battle of the Bastards." Season Six, Episode 9. Directed by Miguel Sapochnik. Written by David Benioff and D.B. Weiss. HBO, June 19, 2016.

Game of Thrones. "Cripples, Bastards, and Broken Things." Season One, Episode 4. Directed by Brian Kirk. Written by Bryan Cogman. HBO, May 8, 2011.

Game of Thrones. "Eastwatch." Season Seven, Episode 5. Directed by Matt Shakman. Written by Dave Hill. HBO, August 13, 2017.

Game of Thrones. "The Last of the Starks." Season Eight, Episode 4. Directed by David Nutter. Written by David Benioff and D.B. Weiss. HBO, May 5, 2019.

Game of Thrones. "Stormborn." Season Seven, Episode 2. Directed by Mark Mylod. Written by Bryan Cogman. HBO, July 23, 2017.

Game of Thrones. "Winter Is Coming." Season One, Episode 1. Directed by Tim Van Patten. Written by David Benioff & D. B. Weiss. HBO, April 17, 2011.

Hall, Alaric. "Hygelac's Only Daughter: A Present, a Potentate and a Peaceweaver in *Beowulf.*" *Studia Neophilologica* 78, no. 1 (2006): 1–7. http://www.tandfonline.com/doi/abs/10.1080/00393270600774719.

Jordan, Jessica Hope. "Women Refusing the Gaze: Theorizing Thryth's 'Unqueenly Custom' in *Beowulf* and The Bride's Revenge in Quentin Tarantino's *Kill Bill, Volume I,*" *The Heroic Age: A Journal of Early Medieval Northwestern Europe* 9 (October 2006). http://www.heroicage.org/issues/9/forum2.html.

Kelly, Brigit Pegeen, translator. "Maxims I-B." In *The Word Exchange: Anglo-Saxon Poems in Translation*, edited by Greg Delanty and Michael Matto,177–185. New York, NY: Norton, 2011.

Larrington, Carolyne. *Winter Is Coming: The Medieval World of* Game of Thrones. London: I.B. Tauris, 2016.

Larsen, Kristine. "Queens, Assassins, and Zombies: The Valkyrie Reflex in George R.R. Martin's A Song of Ice and Fire." Paper presented at the *3ʳᵈ Mythgard Institute Mythmoot*, Linthicum, MD, January 10–11, 2015. https://signumuniversity.org/library/signum-digital-collections/mythmoot-2015/#klarsen.

Martin, George R.R. *A Clash of Kings: Book Two of a Song of Ice and Fire.* New York, NY: Bantam, 1999.

Martin, George R.R. "Dunk and Egg," *Not a Blog*, April 15, 2014 (3:37pm), http://grrm.livejournal.com/365715.html.

Martin, George R.R. *A Feast for Crows: Book Four of a Song of Ice and Fire.* New York, NY: Bantam, 2005.

Martin, George R.R. *A Game of Thrones: Book One of a Song of Ice and Fire.* New York, NY: Bantam, 1996.

Martin, George R.R. *A Storm of Swords: Book Three of a Song of Ice and Fire.* New York, NY: Bantam, 2000.

Martin, George R.R., Elio M. García, and Linda Antonsson. *The World of Ice and Fire: The Untold History of Westeros and the Game of Thrones.* New York, NY: Bantam, 2014.

Neidorf, Leonard. "On the Dating and Authorship of *Maxims I.*" *Neuphilologische Mitteilungen* 117 (December 2016): 137–153.

Overing, Gillian R. *Language, Sign, and Gender in* Beowulf. Carbondale: Southern Illinois University Press, 1990.

Porter, Dorothy Carr. "The Social Centrality of Women in *Beowulf:* A New Context." *The Heroic Age* 5 (Summer/Autumn 2001): 1–9. http://www.heroicage.org/issues/5/porter1.html.

Shippey, Tom. "Wicked Queens and Cousin Strategies in *Beowulf* and Elsewhere." *The Heroic Age* 5 (Summer 2001): 1–13. http://www.heroicage.org/issues/5/Shippey1.html.

Thomas, Kaitlin. "Chances for a Satisfying *Game of Thrones* Finale Are Looking Very Bleak." *TV Guide* (May 6, 2019). https://www.tvguide.com/news/game-of-thrones-ending-unsatisfying-jaime-brienne-sansa-jon-daenerys/.

Welsh, Andrew. "Branwen, Beowulf, and the Tragic Peaceweaver Tale." *Viator* 22 (1991): 1–13.

CHAPTER 6

Cersei Lannister, Regal Commissions, and the Alchemists in *Game of Thrones* and *A Song of Ice and Fire*

Curtis Runstedler

In both his *A Song of Fire and Ice* novels and the HBO television series *Game of Thrones*, George R. R. Martin depicts the mysterious experiments and world of the medieval alchemists. His alchemists are depicted as *maesters* in an ancient guild, in which the adepts are known as "wisdoms", and their apprentices help them in their art. The alchemists are known for their skill in making wildfire, which is an uncontrollable and highly flammable substance aided by dragon's fire. Cersei Lannister, acting as queen regent, commissions the alchemists to produce wildfire in the novels and television series. Yet Martin's presentation of Cersei commissioning the alchemists is subversive; rather than the kings commissioning the alchemists as English history has shown, it is instead a strong, powerful queen regent at the helm, suggesting female agency in a predominantly masculine medieval world.

I would like to thank Professor Elizabeth Archibald, Katie Stepek, James Turner, Dr. David Varley, and Robert Pain for their invaluable feedback.

C. Runstedler (✉)
Eberhard Karls University of Tübingen,
Tübingen, Baden-Württemberg, Germany

© The Author(s) 2020
Z. E. Rohr, L. Benz (eds.), *Queenship and the Women of Westeros*,
Queenship and Power, https://doi.org/10.1007/978-3-030-25041-6_6

In this chapter, I argue that in the character of Cersei Lannister, Martin successfully presents a queen figure who has the power to exploit and direct the secrets of alchemy. Moreover, Cersei's commissioning of the alchemists draws from fifteenth-century English commissions to produce the alchemical *elixir vitae*, particularly under Henry VI and Edward IV. Many English alchemists sought patronage and commissions from kings. Edward III abetted alchemy, and two alchemists named William Dalby and John le Rous appear in the *Patent Rolls* for 1329 and are credited under his patronage, although they were not successful.[1]

Yet, alchemical practice in late medieval England was not without its challenges. Henry IV's Statute of 1403–1404 forbade the practise of alchemy in England and greatly affected its legitimacy: "It is ordained and stablished, That none henceforth shall use to multiply Gold or Silver, nor use the Craft of Multiplication: And if any the same do, and be thereof attaint, that he incur the Pain of Felony in this Case".[2] This statute led to a series of responses requesting licences for alchemical practice.[3] In 1414, Henry V passed an act that banned any craft which attempted to multiply gold (i.e. alchemy).[4] Despite this, however, alchemy remained a popular topic of interest, and the fifteenth century in England saw increased literary output on alchemy, suggesting its enduring appeal.

The fifteenth century also saw a growing interest in alchemical licences and commissions from medieval English kings. In 1463, Henry Grey received Edward IV's permission to practise alchemy, but was not successful with his experiments. Edward IV also granted licences to David Beaupree and David Merchaunt, but there is no record of their experiments.[5] D. Geoghegan reveals that a request for a licence to practise alchemy was sent to Henry VI in 1456, but only three of the practitioners were granted the licence (John Fauceby, John Kyrkeby, and John Rayny).[6] In their petition, the writers appeal to the medicinal values of the Philosopher's Stone and alchemy:

[A] medicine whose virtue would be so efficacious and admirable that all curable infirmities would be easily cured by it; human life would be prolonged to its natural term, and man would be marvellously sustained unto the same term in health and natural virility of body and mind, in strength of limb, clearness of memory, and keenness of intellect; moreover, whosoever had curable wounds would be healed without difficulty; and it would also be the best and most perfect medicine against all kinds of poisons. But also many other benefits, most useful to us and the well-being of our kingdom, could result from the same, such as the transmutation of metals into true gold and very fine silver; and we, by much frequent cogitation, have considered how delectable and useful it would be, both for ourselves and the well-being of the kingdom, if precious medicines of this kind were had, with God's grace, by the labours of learned men.[7]

The petitioners hype up the possibilities of alchemy to gain the king's favour, but they also point out the virtuous and medicinal aims of the practice, notably the impact of full-scale transmutation of base metals into gold and its consequences for the economy of the kingdom. There is no record of these alchemists achieving success, however. Coincidentally, the fifteenth-century alchemist Thomas Norton mentions one of the petitioning alchemists, Gilbert Kymer, in his *Ordinal of Alchemy*:

> *Gilbert Kymer* wrote after his devise,
> Of 17 Proportions, but thei maie not suffice
> In this Science, which he coude never finde;
> And yet in Phisick he had a nobil minde.[8]

Anthony Gross points out the advancements of alchemy between 1456 and 1457, which was possibly a response to Henry VI's illness. Alchemical licences were also granted to numerous London and Lancashire knights under his reign between 1444 and 1447, with the Philosopher's Stone functioning as an incentive to eradicate illness and mortal sin.[9] Despite the possibility of acquiring licences to practise alchemy, however, many English alchemists still tried to practise their craft outside the law. Henry VI responded to this in 1452 by appointing three commissioners to arrest anyone who multiplied metals.[10] What is clear, then, is that these late medieval English kings were granting commissions or licences to alchemists with the emphasis on the medicinal aspects of alchemy.

While the alchemists in the English courts pursued alchemy for medicinal and financial purposes, particularly healing the king and generating revenue for his kingdom (or so they say), Cersei instead seeks the alchemists for destructive purposes. Unlike Cersei, her all-knowing, yet despised younger brother Tyrion, acting Hand of the King to her elder son, Joffrey Baratheon, clearly understands the explosive potential of volatile and alchemistic essences when he quotes an old sailor's proverb to Wisdom Hallyne in Season 2 of the HBO television series: "Piss on wildfire and your cock burns off".[11] Discounting such collective wisdom, in *A Clash of*

Kings, Cersei commissions the alchemists to produce significant quantities of wildfire in preparation for the Battle of King's Landing, and in *A Feast for Crows*, she uses wildfire to set alight the Tower of the Hand. In the sixth season of the HBO series, she also summons the alchemists to produce huge amounts of wildfire again, this time in order to vanquish her enemies and blow up the Great Sept of Baelor in King's Landing, and its impact leads to her inadvertently becoming Queen of Westeros. Although the alchemists claim that their alchemy works and their wildfire has proven to work (and the wildfire is clearly shown to be more than successful), there is no evidence of any successful transmutation of the metals. During the War of the Five Kings, the influence of Martin's alchemists upon the Seven Kingdoms is dwindling, and their ability to transmute metals are questioned and viewed with suspicion. Similarly, although there is evidence of successful alchemical commissions being granted under Henry VI, Edward III, and Edward IV, there is no evidence of actual transmutation of the metals or *elixir vitae*, or even records of their actual experiments. Cersei's use of alchemy as well as its parallels in medieval English history reveals the misuse of technology and a regal interest in the occult for their own purposes.

A Brief History of Wildfire

Martin's depiction of wildfire draws from the medieval Byzantine Greek fire, which the Byzantine forces successfully used in the seventh century to lead them to victory and seize Constantinople from the Arabs.[12] Moreover, this victory helped the Byzantines secure prestige in the West and the Balkans during this time.[13] Greek fire was made of petroleum jelly (naptha) mixed with sulphur and resin, which was siphoned and then ignited into flame; upon doing so, it burned everything it touched. It was originally developed in Kallinakos, which was a centre for alchemy in Hellenized Syria.[14] Despite the current knowledge of its chemical basis, the use and employment of Greek fire was not well documented and not much else is known about it.[15]

In Westeros, the "alchemists" are part of an ancient guild that practises magic. Despite their reputation, however, their actions are much more comparable to pyromancy and the production of wildfire. The guild members refer to themselves as "wisdoms", and call their wildfire "the substance". The views of the wisdoms are in stark opposition with the *maesters* of the Citadel, however, who advocate science and oppose magic of any kind (even if it does work), and who have recently supplanted many of the alchemists in Westeros, especially after the fall of the Targaryen dynasty. As Tyrion comments, the old pyromancers "no longer even pretended to transmute metals...but they *could* make wildfire".[16] In the books and TV series, the practitioners devote much of their time to producing wildfire, and it is implied that their efforts to transmute metals were probably fraudulent. Wildfire appears murky green in colour, and is extremely flammable, capable of ignition when under the Sun and burning for hours, and thus requiring great care and attention. Wildfire is stored in numerous jars in the Guildhalls and contained within a booby-trapped room which prevents any accidental fire outbreaks.[17]

Before the events in the *A Song of Fire and Ice* series and *Game of Thrones*, King Aerys "The Mad King" Targaryen notably commissioned the production of wildfire. During his final years, he used wildfire to destroy his enemies and those whom he considered traitorous, including one of his Hands Qarlton Chested, whom he sentenced to death by being burnt alive with wildfire for "bad counsel". After Qarlton's death, Aerys appointed Rossart, who was the Grand Master of the Alchemists' Guild, as his third and final Hand of the King. As Grand Master, Rossart was only too happy to produce more wildfire for the king.[18]

As Aerys becomes increasingly paranoid and delusional, his use of wildfire as a method of execution increases, and this eventually leads to the deaths of Rickard Stark, who was also burnt alive with wildfire, and his son Brandon Stark. In his increasingly erratic state, Aerys orders the alchemists to produce and store wildfire in caches beneath King's Landing; in case the city is breached and he is confronted, he would take King's Landing with him as well as its significant population. He was also convinced that, since he was a Targaryen, he would survive the inferno and rise from the ashes like a dragon.[19] Tywin Lannister does manage to besiege the city during the Sacking of King's Landing, but Ser Jaime Lannister executed the Mad King as well as Rossart before any wildfire plans could come to fruition. These wildfire caches remain beneath King's Landing, however, and as Season 2 and Season 6 of the television series reveal, Cersei uses them to explosive effect.

ALCHEMICAL COMMISSIONS

Unlike alchemy in Westeros, which relies more on pyromancy than traditional alchemy, medieval English alchemy had two aims, including transmuting base metals into gold and creating an *elixir vitae* which prolonged the user's life. Although alchemy had its proponents in medieval England, it was also widely disputed and challenged, with a series of prohibitions and decretals launched against it. Arguably the most infamous decretal against alchemy was Pope John XXII's in 1317, which was primarily aimed at counterfeiters and alchemists: "all who have been found concerned in any capacity in the production of alchemical gold shall incur infamy and shall give to the poor in true gold as much as they have made of the false variety".[20] The opening epigram of Pope John XXII's treatise *De crimine falsi* (*On Counterfeiting*) also criticizes alchemists and counterfeiters for making promises that they cannot keep.[21] Despite the decretal, alchemy continued to be practised, although this may be attributed to the fact that Pope John XXII was not very popular in England.[22] Alchemical practice also faced backlash among the mendicant orders, with impositions notably placed upon friars practising alchemy at Narbonne and Pest in 1272 and 1273 among the Dominicans, and in 1316 in Assisi among the Franciscans.[23]

While alchemical patronages in late medieval England were commissioned by men for men, however, it is worth noting that Queen Elizabeth I (1533–1603) was interested in alchemy and had her own alchemical patron (Dr. John Dee) in Renaissance England.[24] Many alchemists flourished in Elizabeth I's court, and it was rumoured that she may have commissioned alchemists in her own search for the *elixir vitae*. In fact, Cersei and Elizabeth are similar in many ways: they are both strong, powerful women within patriarchal societies and trapped by gender norms and societal expectations, both have dominating and controlling fathers (Henry VIII and Tywin), and they both seek absolute power over their kingdom and often manage to exert it. Elizabeth and Cersei are also quite dangerous, unpredictable, and volatile; even their seemingly closest subjects could face an uncertain fate at any moment, as shown in the devastation of the explosion at King's Landing in Season 6 as well as in Elizabeth's court, where she infamously executed some of her favourites, including Robert Devereux. Both of their kingdoms also live in uncertain times: Elizabeth's Protestant kingdom was religiously closer to her father's proto-Reformation England than her Roman Catholic predecessor Mary, yet her people have lived through Catholic and Protestant religious extremes where the wrong religion at the wrong time could result in death; Martin's story begins shortly before the War of the Five Kings, where a series of kings face their untimely demises, the future of the Iron Throne remain uncertain, and an ill-advised allegiance could result in betrayal and death, as the Red Wedding and the unexpected death of Ned Stark exemplify. Both queens seek alchemy as a means of control, but whereas Elizabeth likely wanted the secrets of eternal life for absolute power, Cersei commissions alchemy as a means of destroying her enemies and gaining absolute control. Yet Martin's use of alchemy in the series and its depiction on the HBO series seems more influenced by its medieval role, and thus Cersei's alchemical commissions subvert the masculine agency of late medieval English alchemical patronage. In fact, Cersei shares her passion for alchemy and wildfire with a specific medieval ruler, but this is one of Martin's own creations: The Mad King.

Not only does Cersei share qualities of the Mad King, including his penchant for using wildfire as well as his increasingly erratic behaviour, but she also shares aspects of wildfire itself, particularly its volatility and instability.[25] This is also comparable to Daenerys Targaryen, who is not only the Mother of (Three) Dragons but shares Cersei and the Mad King's instability and volatility. While Daenerys is initially depicted as quite timid and ineffective, she grows to become a fierce leader who will most certainly not be the ideal queen for Westeros (as the brutality of her actions in the final season reveal). In the first book/season, she allows her husband Khal Drogo to execute her brother Viserys with a "golden crown" which is essentially molten gold poured upon his head ("A Golden Crown"). She also uses her dragons to immolate her enemies, yet her dragons cannot be controlled, and in Season 4 they also kill one of the local children, forcing them into exile ("The Children"). As the dragons continue to grow and become more aggressive, they reflect Daenerys's own growth as a leader yet reveal her lack of control in her inability to effectively control them. More recently, in Season 7 she even torches her prisoners of war (Randall Tarly and his son Dickon) who refuse to surrender ("Eastwatch"), showing her increasingly callous and volatile nature, which I suggest is comparable to Cersei and wildfire. In Season 8, the full destructiveness of Daenerys's powers is revealed when she incinerates most of King's Landing, including innocent and unarmed commonfolk ("The Bells"). Her ruthlessness in this instance is arguably crueller than Cersei and comparable to her father the Mad King, if not worse. Daenerys's title as the Unburnt contrasts Cersei's inner metaphorical wildfire as well. Daenerys has emerged unharmed in numerous instances where fire should have killed her, suggesting her adversarial relationship to Cersei.

While the Mad King's gradual decline in mental health is accountable for his wildfire similarities, I suggest that Cersei's (as well as Daenerys's) similarities are a reaction to a lifetime of patriarchal oppression.[26] Similarly, Edward II's queen Isabella of France (1295–1358) reacted to her patriarchal oppression, having suffered for years due to her husband's lack of interest and homosexual affairs (including his interest in several favourites, notably Piers Gaveston and Hugh Despenser the Younger). Isabella and her paramour Roger Mortimer eventually conspired against Edward II and ultimately executed him and Hugh Despenser the Younger. Henry II's queen Eleanor of Aquitaine (1122–1204) also defied patriarchal oppression and even rebelled against her king, spending time in prison for her role. She later governed England as Queen Mother in the absence of her son Richard the Lionheart, who was fighting for England in the Holy Land. Cersei commissions alchemy as a means of asserting control and authority and breaking free of her patriarchal hegemony, but ironically, she models herself after masculine tactics, particularly those of the male figures in her life such as her father and her husband Robert Baratheon.[27]

CERSEI, WILDFIRE, AND THE BATTLE OF THE BLACKWATER

The reader first encounters wildfire in *A Clash of Kings* and in the television series *Game of Thrones* when Tyrion meets the current Grand Master Hallyne to discuss the production of wildfire for use against Stannis' fleet in the Battle of the Blackwater. However, it is not King Joffrey who orders the commission; Hallyne acts on Queen Mother Cersei's orders, which I suggest subverts the historical alchemical commissioning in late medieval England, which was predominantly enacted by men for men. In this instance, however, the Queen Mother is giving orders. It remains unexplained why Cersei commissions the wildfire rather than King Joffrey, but she appears to act on his behalf while simultaneously fulfilling her desire for power and control. On the other hand, it could also reflect her impulsiveness, hinting at her unthinkable acts with wildfire in Season 6. Like wildfire, Cersei is volatile and unpredictable, yet the use of wildfire in the Battle of the Blackwater is to her advantage, leading to victory against Stannis Baratheon's fleet. Her use of wildfire instead of a tactical strategy against Stannis and his fleet might also suggest that she prefers violence to compromise or negotiation, which becomes more explicit in the sixth season of the HBO series.[28] It is either Cersei's way or wildfire.

Burning Down the House (or the Tower of the Hand)

Wildfire also notably appears in *A Feast for Crows*, when Cersei uses it to burn down the Tower of the Hand in the wake of Tywin Lannister's death at Tyrion's hand and his subsequent escape from King's Landing. Like the Battle of the Blackwater, Cersei commissions the use of wildfire as a means of destruction. Unlike the battle, however, the wildfire is used not as a means of securing victory, but rather as a means of erasing the past, destroying the unpleasant memory of the death of her father which continues to haunt her. Her use of wildfire in this scene is also her attempt to assert her agency; her destruction of the Tower of the Hand is an attempt to destroy her less than ideal past as well as control her increasingly unstable emotions. Cersei also finds a strange comfort in the burning wildfire, comparing the wildfire to her deceased firstborn Joffrey: "No man had ever made her feel as good as she had felt when he took her nipple in his mouth to nurse".[29] Like pyromania, her use of wildfire allows her to reflect upon her most cherished moments, and she finds solace in its chaos. The wildfire also provides her with a sort of catharsis: "The wildfire was cleansing her, burning away all her rage and fear, filling her with resolve".[30] Despite its chaotic nature, Cersei has an affinity to the wildfire because she can control it and its usage empowers her.

"I Choose Violence": Blowing up King's Landing in HBO's *Game of Thrones*

In the HBO series, the season six finale "The Winds of Winter", Cersei orders the destruction of the Great Sept of Baelor using the Mad King's wildfire reserves thereby killing most of the Tyrell family, her own uncle and cousin, the High Sparrow, upon whom she seeks revenge, and countless innocent residents of King's Landing. Paradoxically, this leads to the suicide of her son and her ascension to the throne, since Tommen cannot live with himself after hearing about the deaths of his wife and other family members.[31] The insanity of Cersei's actions shocks her enemies; not even the Queen of Thorns thought she was capable of such volatility ("The

Queen's Justice").[32] Cersei's actions repeatedly mirror those of wildfire. Like it, she is volatile, chaotic, and unpredictable. Not only is the display of wildfire an act of revenge, but it is also a demonstration of Cersei's latent power. Cersei uses wildfire to vanquish her most persistent enemies and those who oppose her (Margaery Tyrell, Kevan Lannister, the Faith Militant, and most importantly the High Sparrow), making an example of them to those who would seek to defy her. Cersei does not compromise or parley but chooses instead violence of such magnitude that not even skeletons remain. Cersei mobilizes wildfire in this instance to gain complete control and to dominate her opponents.

With Tommen dead (not her intention, but an indirect consequence of her actions), there are no longer any patriarchal figures holding her back; her husband, Robert Baratheon, her father, Tywin Lannister, and her eldest son, Joffrey are dead. For most of her life, Cersei has been trapped within the gendered expectations of a patriarchal society, but with the patriarchal figures in her life removed from the game, she is free to do as she pleases.[33] The wildfire reserves provide a means by which she gains her independence and freedom, but her years subordinated within a violent patriarchy have hardened her into a wildly chaotic individual. While Cersei finally achieves her own agency and independence, she has become increasingly unstable with nothing left to lose, making her incredibly dangerous. Indeed, in Season 7, although wildfire is not involved, she continues to assert her authority and control by killing off many of her remaining enemies.

A Song of Wildfire and Chaos?

In both the novels and the HBO series, wildfire is a weapon of chaos which destroys and obliterates everything in its path. Cersei shares an affinity with its instability and unpredictability, and throughout the series and books she uses wildfire to fulfil her desire for power, domination, and control. She commissions the production and use of wildfire, which I have argued subverts the masculine role of king and royal alchemists in medieval England. Martin and the HBO screenwriters present Cersei as a powerful albeit increasingly erratic queen regent who utilizes the secrets of the alchemists (wildfire) for her own personal gain than for the survival of her diminished dynasty, or indeed for the greater good. In *A Clash of Kings*, she commissions the production of wildfire for the Battle of the Blackwater, wherein it is successfully deployed to defeat Stannis Baratheon's naval fleet. In *A Feast for Crows*, she uses wildfire to burn down the Tower of the Hand since it reminds her of her father's death, and she identifies with the wildfire in its burning chaos. In the Season 6 finale of the HBO series ("The Winds of Winter"), Cersei uses wildfire to consolidate her power and vanquish her enemies, blowing up the Great Sept of Baelor in King's Landing and vaporizing most of her major opponents in the process. In all these examples, wildfire links Cersei's agency to her violent display of power.

This chapter reassesses the connection between alchemical commissions, female agency, and royalty in Martin's series and fifteenth-century England. While Martin blends his depiction of the Westeros alchemists with Byzantine alchemy and late medieval Western alchemy, he also draws from fifteenth-century alchemical commissions from kings. Moreover, it reveals the subversive role of the queen regent ascribed by Martin to Cersei Lannister. Rather than the king commissioning alchemical wildfire, is it Cersei who makes the call. While Cersei is comparable to other queens who react against patriarchal expectations and oppression in late medieval England, she emerges in Martin's figure as an exciting subversive figure, one who uses wildfire and alchemy as much as she embodies it in her volatile and unstable nature. This portrayal subverts the gender expectations of the queen regent and suggests the potential danger of the instability and volatility of both wildfire and Cersei herself.

NOTES

1. Ronald Pearsall, *The Alchemists*, London: Weidenfeld and Nicolson, 1976, 65. For more on these medieval alchemists and Edward III's views on alchemy, see F. Sherwood Taylor, *The Alchemists, Founders of Modern Chemistry*, London: W. Heinemann, 1951, 123.
2. See *The Statutes of the Realm*, ed. A. Luders et al., London, 1816, quoted in D. Geoghegan, "A Licence of Henry VI to Practise Alchemy", *Ambix*, 10.1 (1957), 10 n. 1.
3. Geoghegan, "A Licence of Henry VI to Practise Alchemy", 10.
4. Pearsall, *The Alchemists*, 65.
5. Pearsall, *The Alchemists*, 73.
6. Geoghegan, "A Licence of Henry VI to Practise Alchemy", 10, 13. Geoghegan also comments that the petitioners stressed that they were "most learned in natural sciences", which I suggest was likely an attempt to present alchemy as a legitimate and natural study.
7. Geoghegan, "A Licence of Henry VI to Practise Alchemy", 15–16.

8. Thomas Norton, *Thomas Norton's Ordinal of Alchemy*, ed. John Reidy, EETS OS 272, Oxford: Oxford University Press, 1975, V.1559, 50. See also Gilbert Kymer's entry in *Medical Practitioners in Medieval England: A Biographical Register*, ed. C. H. Talbot and E. A. Hammond, London: Wellcome Historical Medical Library, 1965, 60–63.

9. Anthony Gross, *The Dissolution of the Lancastrian Kingship: Sir John Fortescue and the Crisis of Monarchy in Fifteenth-Century England*, Stamford: Paul Watkins, 1996, 6, 19.

10. Taylor, *The Alchemists*, 126.

11. *Game of Thrones*, Season 2, Episode 5, Written by David Benioff and D. B. Weiss, Directed by David Petrarca, first aired 29 April 2012.

12. Andrew Louth, "The Byzantine Empire in the Seventh Century", in *The New Cambridge Medieval History*, ed. Paul Fouracre, 8 vols., Cambridge: Cambridge University Press, 1995–2002, vol. 1, 289–316. See also Steven Runciman, "Byzantine Trade and Industry", in *The Cambridge Economic History of Europe*, ed. Cynthia Postari, Edward Miller, and M. M. Postan, 8 vols., Cambridge: Cambridge University Press, 1966–1989, vol. 2, 132–167. George R. R. Martin acknowledges this influence in Josh Roberts, "*Game of Thrones* Exclusive! George R. R. Martin Talks Season Two, *The Winds of Winter*, and Real-World Influences of *A Song of Ice and Fire*", SmarterTravel, last accessed 14 October 2017, https://www.smarter-travel.com/2012/04/01/game-of-thrones-exclusive-george-r-r-martin-talks-season-two-the-winds-of-winter-and-real-world-influences-for-a-song-of-ice-and-fire, and refers to wildfire as his "magical version of Greek fire".

13. Louth, "The Byzantine Empire in the Seventh Century", 301.

14. Hugh W. Salzberg, *From Caveman to Chemist: Circumstances and Achievements*, Washington, D.C.: American Chemical Society, 1991, 75.

15. Jonathan Shepard, "Approaching Byzantium", in *The Cambridge History of the Byzantine Empire c.500–1492*, ed. Jonathan Shepard, Cambridge: Cambridge University Press, 2008,5 n. 7. While the use or creation of Greek fire is not documented in medieval England, it does appear in English historical fiction. See notably C. J. Sansom, *Dark Fire*, London: Macmillan, 2004, which depicts a plot to steal Greek fire in Renaissance London.

16. Martin, *A Clash of Kings*, London: Voyager, 2003, 280.

17. Martin, *A Clash of Kings*, 280–281.

18. Martin, *The World of Ice and Fire: The Untold History of Westeros and* Game of Thrones, New York: Bantam, 2014, 234.

19. Terri Schwartz, "*Game of Thrones*: Is this Cersei Lannister's Master Plan?," IGN, last accessed 14 October 2017, http://ca.ign.com/articles/2016/06/13/game-of-thrones-is-this-cersei-lannisters-master-plan

20. Lynn Thorndike, *A History of Magic and Experimental Science*, 8 vols., New York: Macmillan, 1923–1958, vol. 3, 32.
21. Despite this, however, Thorndike provides evidence that Pope John XXII may have actually patronized alchemy, relating an incident in 1330 where the Pope gave money to a physician Gufre Isnard, Bishop of Cavaillon, for an alembic to make *aqua ardens* and "a certain secret work", which Thorndike interprets as an attempt to make gold or an *elixir vitae*. See Thorndike, *A History of Magic and Experimental Science*, vol. 3, 34. Thorndike also mentions that several alchemical treatises were attributed to him.
22. Pearsall, *The Alchemists*, 61–63.
23. Angela Montford, *Health, Sickness, Medicine and the Friars in the Thirteenth and Fourteenth Centuries*, Aldershot: Ashgate, 2004, 209–210.
24. Lyndy Abraham, *Marvell and Alchemy*, Aldershot: Scolar Press, 1990, 1–10.
25. Cf. Chanel Vargas, "The Parallels between Cersei and the Mad King Are Eerily Spot-On", *Harper Bazaar*, last accessed 22 March 2018, https://www.harpersbazaar.com/culture/film-tv/a10386491/game-of-thrones-season-seven-cersei-mad-queen
26. See Laura Hudson, "Cersei Lannister: A Defense of the *Game of Thrones* Villain", *Vulture*, last accessed 22 March 2018, http://www.vulture.com/2017/07/cersei-lannister-a-defense-game-of-thrones.html
27. Cf. Kavita Mudan Finn's and Sylwia Borowska-Szerzun's chapters (Chaps. 2 and 3, respectively) in this collection, which also focus on Cersei in this volume. Shiloh Carroll examines elsewhere Cersei's attempts to "rule like a man" in *Medievalism in* A Song of Ice and Fire *and* Game of Thrones, Cambridge: D. S. Brewer, 2018, 65.
28. Cersei's use of wildfire in the sixth season shocks even her most competent enemies. The Queen of Thorns, for example, remarks that Cersei has "done things I was incapable of imagining" ("The Queen's Justice").
29. Martin, *A Feast for Crows*, London: Harper Voyager, 2011, 206.
30. Martin, *A Feast for Crows*, 207.
31. For more on the role of Tommen as king, see Charles E. Beem's chapter (Chap. 9) in this volume.
32. Not only are Cersei's actions dangerous and unprecedented but blowing up the wildfire as she does also runs the risk of blowing up other unexposed caches of wildfire in the city and thus risking the entire city for her cause. Cersei is so driven by her impulses, by her hatred of her enemies and the humiliation that she has faced that she does not consider the consequences. She just wants to see them dead. Her recklessness and impulsive nature contrast her father, who is a more calculating and patient ruler, yet just as cruel if not crueller. Cersei's lack of judgement and forethought in

this regard eventually leads to her downfall. For a reading of how Cersei is an example of how not to play the Game of Thrones, see Finn's chapter (Chap. 2).

33. Caroline Spector, "Power and Feminism in Westeros", in *Beyond the Wall: Exploring George R.R. Martin's* A Song of Ice and Fire, ed. James Lowder, Dallas: BenBella Books, 2012, 133.

BIBLIOGRAPHY

PRIMARY SOURCES

Luders, A., et al (eds.), *The Statutes of the Realm*, London: 1816.
Martin, George R.R., *A Clash of Kings*, London: Voyager, 2003.
———*A Feast for Crows*, London: Harper Voyager, 2011.
———*The World of Ice and Fire: The Untold History of Westeros and Game of Thrones*, New York: Bantam, 2014.
Norton, Thomas, *Thomas Norton's Ordinal of Alchemy*, ed. John Reidy, EETS OS 272, Oxford: Oxford University Press, 1975.

SECONDARY SOURCES

Abraham, Lyndy, *Marvell and Alchemy*, Aldershot: Scolar Press, 1990.
Carroll, Shiloh, *Medievalism in* A Song of Ice and Fire *and* Game of Thrones, Cambridge: D. S. Brewer, 2018.
Fouracre, Paul (ed.), *The New Cambridge Medieval History*, 8 vols., Cambridge: Cambridge University Press, 1995–2002.
Geoghegan, D., "A Licence of Henry VI to Practise Alchemy", *Ambix*, 10. 1 (1957), 10–7.
Gross, Anthony, *The Dissolution of the Lancastrian Kingship: Sir John Fortescue and the Crisis of Monarchy in Fifteenth-Century England*, Stamford: Paul Watkins, 1996.
Hudson, Laura, Vulture. "Cersei Lannister: A Defense of the *Game of Thrones* Villain." Last accessed 22 March 2018. http://www.vulture.com/2017/07/cersei-lannister-a-defense-game-of-thrones.html.
Lowder, James (ed.), *Beyond the Wall: Exploring George R.R. Martin's* A Song of Ice and Fire, Dallas: BenBella Books, 2012.
Montford, Angela, *Health, Sickness, Medicine and the Friars in the Thirteenth and Fourteenth Centuries*, Aldershot: Ashgate, 2004.
Pearsall, Ronald, *The Alchemists*, London: Weidenfeld and Nicolson, 1976.
Postari, Cynthia, Edward Miller, and M.M. Postan (eds.), *The Cambridge Economic History of Europe*, 8 vols., Cambridge: Cambridge University Press, 1966–1989.

Roberts, Josh, Smarter Travel. "*Game of Thrones* Exclusive! George R.R. Martin Talks Season Two, *The Winds of Winter*, and Real-World Influences of *A Song of Ice and Fire.*" Last accessed 22 March 2018. https://www.smartertravel.com/2012/04/01/game-of-thrones-exclusive-george-r-r-martin-talks-season-two-the-winds-of-winter-and-real-world-influences-for-a-song-of-ice-and-fire.

Salzberg, Hugh W., *From Caveman to Chemist: Circumstances and Achievements*, Washington, D.C.: American Chemical Society, 1991.

Sansom, C.J., *Dark Fire*, London: Macmillan, 2004.

Schwartz, Terri, IGN. "*Game of Thrones*: Is this Cersei Lannister's Master Plan?" Last accessed 22 March 2018. http://ca.ign.com/articles/2016/06/13/game-of-thrones-is-this-cersei-lannisters-master-plan.

Shepard, Jonathan (ed.), *The Cambridge History of the Byzantine Empire c. 500–1492*, Cambridge: Cambridge University Press, 2008.

Talbot, C.H., and E.A. Hammond (eds.), *Medical Practitioners in Medieval England: A Biographical Register*, London: Wellcome Historical Medical Library, 1965.

Taylor, F. Sherwood, *The Alchemists, Founders of Modern Chemistry*, London: W. Heinemann, 1951.

Thorndike, Lynn, *A History of Magic and Experimental Science*, 8 vols., New York: Macmillan, 1923–58.

Vargas, Chanel, Harper Bazaar. "The Parallels between Cersei and The Mad Kingare Eerily Spot-On." Last accessed 22 March 2018. https://www.harpersbazaar.com/culture/film-tv/a10386491/game-of-thrones-season-seven-cersei-mad-queen.

CHAPTER 7

'All Men Must Die, but We Are Not Men': Eastern Faith and Feminine Power in *A Song of Ice and Fire* and HBO's *Game of Thrones*

Mikayla Hunter

In George R. R. Martin's *A Song of Ice and Fire* and HBO's *Game of Thrones*, the East is peopled with characters whose lives centre around their faiths. The women of Essos in particular seem to achieve their power and agency through religions. This makes them fundamentally different from many of the high-status women and men in Westeros, who display a loose approach to faith—such as Margaery's calculated displays of piety to gain the favour of her people, or Davos's gestures to the gods only in times of duress—if not outright cynicism and secularism. This is in keeping with a long-standing orientalist view of the West as 'reasonable' in its approach to religious belief and the role religion plays in day-to-day life versus an understanding of Eastern cultures as steeped in a 'backwards' incorporation of religion into all aspects of everyday life, law, and politics.[1] Martin approaches his world of ice and fire from a very Western-centric view, and many of these Westerosi point-of-view characters overlook the value of religion as a source of power, belittling it as the ineffectual, even delusional, refuge of the weak and powerless. And yet it is the religions

M. Hunter (✉)
English Language and Literature, University of Oxford, Oxford, UK

© The Author(s) 2020
Z. E. Rohr, L. Benz (eds.), *Queenship and the Women of Westeros,*
Queenship and Power, https://doi.org/10.1007/978-3-030-25041-6_7

indigenous to, and imported from, Essos which often prove terrifyingly effectual in war and politics.[2] Martin's depiction of the religion of the Lord of Light is more gender-balanced than HBO's depiction, which shifts the membership of the Lord of Light priesthood to be a more feminine institution. By portraying religious worship as the realm of women and old or seemingly weak men, HBO's *Game of Thrones* plays off the concept so many Westerosi characters (and perhaps audience members) seem to hold that religion is soft, nurturing, but relatively ineffectual when compared to other, more Machiavellian methods of affecting political change.[3] This fits within Martin's overarching theme of the repressed and dispossessed inheriting the earth: 'cripples, bastards, and broken things', women and men who rely more on their brains than on their brawn.

Much of Essos is coded as Middle Eastern: as Mat Hardy points out, 'Essos is strikingly similar to Turkey in outline and more akin to Asia in every other way. Its lateral orientation includes sprawling steppes and deserts within which live a host of peoples that correspond to Levantines, Arabs, Turks, and Mongols'.[4] This chapter examines the relationship between religion and Eastern women's access to power in *A Song of Ice and Fire* and *Game of Thrones*, particularly how Essosi women seem largely to achieve political influence and agency through religious institutions, institutions which paradoxically constrain at the same time as they empower. It compares these portrayals of Essosi women to portrayals of Eastern women in Western medieval romances—the precursors to the novel—and to historically powerful Middle Eastern women, looking for medieval bases for this consistent correlation between Essosi (Eastern) women and power gained through religion. Scholars such as Carolyne Larrington, Ayelet Haimson Lushkov, and Brian Pavlac argue that Martin draws on medieval literature, cultures, historical events, and historical figures for inspiration for much of his fantasy epic, and that he is attempting to write *A Song of Ice and Fire* series with a greater eye for medieval realism than other epic fantasy authors such as J.R.R. Tolkien.[5] However, ultimately it seems Martin's portrayal of Eastern women is more grounded in (problematic) modern Western ideas of Eastern women and religion than actual medieval ideas about such figures.

Two major themes of the series are as follows: various approaches to gaining and maintaining power and how women gain agency in patriarchal societies. The soft and hard powers that religion can grant in Martin's world encapsulate both of those themes. However, Martin's decision to portray religion amongst multiple Essosi peoples as one of the only culturally accepted mechanisms of acquiring feminine agency differs noticeably from his depiction of the myriad mechanisms utilised by the women of Westeros: Cersei, Catelyn, Brienne, Ygritte, Margaery, the Sand Snakes, and Lady Lyanna Mormont. Through family connections and/or inheritance, advantageous marriage, personal wealth, sex appeal, physical prowess, or pure cunning, Western women seem to have a much larger variety of options available to them through which to act and influence others.

The Eastern Woman in Medieval Literature

Martin's writing suggests a degree of familiarity with various works of medieval literature, as Larrington and Pavlac have shown, though he habitually refuses to confirm particular influences in interviews. Given Martin's evident familiarity with a variety of medieval cultures and literature, and his portrayal of a number of strong Westerosi women, it is surprising that Martin deviates so far from the forms of feminine power illustrated in medieval romance and *chansons de geste* when portraying Essosi women.

Eastern women appear with fair frequency in Western medieval literature, most often as the stock character of the 'Saracen princess', or what Jacqueline de Weever calls the 'white Saracen'—a woman characterised by her wealth and conformity to white, usually French, standards of beauty, her bold actions, and her loyalty to the European Christian cause—whatever that cause may be in the given romance (e.g., aiding Charlemagne's men who have been imprisoned by her sultan father).[6]

In the romance of *Beves of Hamtoun*, widely popular throughout later medieval England and France, the Saracen heroine Josian earns money through her musical abilities, manipulates and ultimately escapes an emperor and a giant through her wit and ingenuity and, in a reversal of the roles typically found in medieval romance, roams about the countryside seeking her husband while the eponymous hero spends a large part of the text in captivity and confinement.[7] Floripas, heroine of several *chansons de geste*, provides another example of non-religious access to power.[8] Her noble descent from the sultan gives her some command over her father's guards—sufficient enough that she can visit the imprisoned hero and his men nightly and can engineer these knights' escape by luring one of the guards to his death, physically shoving him out of a window. She uses a magic girdle that provides sustenance to make herself indispensable to the imprisoned men and negotiates with them for her escape from her father's tyrannical rule. Her shrewdness and her daring, combined with her wealth, beauty, and willingness to convert to Christianity, win her an advantageous marriage to the hero—thereby securing a powerful position by which to enter Western society.

The HBO television series introduces a 'Saracen princess' figure in the form of Talisa, Robb's love interest and then wife. The character of Talisa replaces that of Jeyne Westerling in the book series, a young woman from the north-western Crag region of Westeros. Talisa comes from a wealthy noble family and Robb meets her when she is acting in capacity of a healer, aiding his men. Healing was another important attribute of noblewomen in Western medieval romance, and not exclusive to the 'Saracen princess' figure. Unfortunately, while her adherence to the conventions associated with this medieval orientalist stock figure—the adoption of a Western value-system—does win Talisa a position of power as the Queen in the North, unlike her medieval literary sisters, her conversion to 'civilised' Westerosi ideology (particularly her abolitionist views) does not save her from a violent death shortly after her on-screen introduction.

In traditional medieval narratives, love and sexual attraction are, like religion, forms of power that equally confine as they enable. The few episodes which include Talisa aside, *A Song of Ice and Fire* and *Game of Thrones* notably lack the kind of high romantic love story that so often gives women power in medieval romances. These narratives happen off-stage, before the events of the narrative, such as the events preceding Lyanna Stark's death, or they manifest as a monstrous form of love, as with Cersei and Jaime. Moreover, there are very few love-based relationships at all amongst the Essosi. The unusual dearth of conventional love stories in Essos reshapes traditional reliance on love and sexual attraction as female sources of power. Without a love story, sexual attractiveness for Essosi women becomes a commodity rather than a weapon, something one trades in or guards rather than wields.

WOMEN IN POWER: MARTIN AND MEDIEVAL HISTORY

In the medieval era, there were several positions of power medieval women could hold. Queenship, one of the highest statuses a woman could obtain, came with many opportunities for exercising power. Queens and empresses could rule in their husbands' absences or as regents, raising levies and armies and administering justice. A number equally raised their own armies against the king, their husband, such as Isabel of France and Eleanor of

Aquitaine. They could and were expected to act as intercessors between the king and his subjects, and a queen 'gained stature and influence in the court through her sexual relationship with the king and through maternity'.[9] While the highest roles within the Church (as within the Jewish and Muslim institutions at the time) were restricted to men, positions of lesser authority were open to women. Abbesses were elected to positions of power, running convents and wielding significant power over the secular communities surrounding their convents. They functioned as landlords and in judicial capacities as well as in undertaking pastoral care. Medieval women could even sometimes lead men into battle. Jeanne d'Arc is, of course, the most famous of these warrior women, but other women such as Caterina Sforza, Jeanne Hachette, and Isabella of Castile assumed roles involving military leadership. Further down the social scale, noblewomen ran estates and would defend them in their husbands' absences. Women could also wield a great deal of 'soft' power—that is, power in unofficial capacities, influencing men behind the scenes. Mistresses of nobles could accomplish much of their own will through persuasion and manipulation.

Beyond the cultural and geographical confines of western Europe, women in various kingdoms and cultures throughout Byzantium, Asia, and northern Africa have also been recorded holding positions as scholars, jurists, stateswomen, and warriors, as well as similar roles to the queens, mistresses, and holy women discussed above. Indeed, no fewer than 'fifteen Muslim women sovereigns ascended the thrones of Muslim states between the thirteenth and seventeenth centuries, holding all of the official insignia of sovereignty'.[10] Sitt al-Mulk ruled as de facto Caliph of the Fatmids from 1021 to 1023 during her son's minority; Asma bint Shihab al-Sulayhiyya and Arwa bint Asma were eleventh- and early-twelfth-century queens of Yemen, and fifteenth-century Yemeni Sharifa Fatima bint al-Hassan proved herself a capable chieftain and military leader.[11] Radiyya al-Din ruled as sultana of Delhi in the mid-thirteenth century, and Shajarat al-Durr ruled as sultana of Egypt about a decade later.[12] The Maldives were ruled by three sultanas in the fourteenth century: Khadija (r. 1347–1380), Dhaain (or Myriam) (r. 1380–1383), and Raadhafathi (or Fatima) (r. 1383–1388).[13]

Equally politically influential were scholars and jurists, such as Zainab bint 'Umar bin al-Kindi in the thirteenth century and Fatima bint Muhammad ibn Ahmad al-Samarqandi in the twelfth.[14] In the sixteenth century, Sayyida al Hurra terrorised the western Mediterranean Sea as queen-turned-pirate.[15] In Byzantium, a culture with which Meereen seems to share common aspects, several women—Irene, Theodora the consort of Justinian I, Zoe and her sister Theodora, Eudokia Makrembolitissa, and Anna Dalassene, for example—ruled in their own right or as consorts and regents.[16] Similarities have also been noted between medieval Mongolian culture and George R. R. Martin's Dothraki culture.[17] Four of Genghis Khan's daughters, Alaqai Beki, Checheyigen, Al-Altun, and Tolai, 'became ruling queens of their own countries and commanded large regiments of soldiers'.[18]

In an interview, George R. R. Martin has said that one of his methods for plot construction and world-building is as follows: 'I take [history], and I file off the serial numbers, and I turn it up to eleven, and I change the colour from red to purple, and I have a great incident for the books'.[19] However, he has not given much specific confirmation of which historical sources he has drawn upon, though he has specifically mentioned the Wars of the Roses, and others (e.g., Hadrian's wall as a source of inspiration for the Wall separating the seven kingdoms from the lands where the wildlings live) seem fairly clear. In another interview, Martin has said: 'I wanted my books to be strongly grounded in history and to show what medieval society was like'.[20] Additionally, Martin has been praised by fans for both his gritty realism in his fantasy novels (referred to as the 'grimdark' subgenre) and his depiction of multiple exceptional women occupying positions of power in *A Song of Ice and Fire*. Cersei, Daenerys, Catelyn Stark, Ygritte, Arya, and Brienne each, at points throughout the novels, maintains substantial levels of power and/or agency, and each in her own unique way.

Carolyne Larrington and Robert Haug have discussed some aspects of Essos that derive from or correlate with Asian history: the similarities between Dothraki and thirteenth-century Mongolian culture and the parallels between the Unsullied and the slave soldiers of the Abbasid caliphate, for instance.[21] And yet, despite Martin's diverse depictions of women attaining power in Westeros, and his evident familiarity with aspects of Asian medieval history, his depictions of Eastern/Essosi women in positions of power seem to draw little on historical medieval Eastern women. Mistresshood, a not uncommon means of indirect power for historical medieval women, seems to provide little power for Essosi women. The *dosh khaleen* and Galazza Galare are not portrayed as sexually desirable or sexually interested in others. The sisterhood of Graces enforces a state of singlehood if not always celibacy; sex is, for the Graces, something which is given to or exchanged with the laity, but it does not empower the Graces themselves. Rather, we are told that '[t]here are little snuggeries in the pleasure gardens [of the temple], and [the red graces] wait there every night until a man chooses them. Those who are not chosen must remain until the sun comes up, feeling lonely and neglected'.[22] The courtesans of Braavos enjoy wealth and celebrity but are not portrayed as holding any political power or influencing any of the world's events. And Shae's angry betrayal of Tyrion is driven precisely by her frustration at having no agency or power as his lover. Indeed, as Daenerys travels throughout Essos, speaking to and negotiating with leaders, magnates, and other powerful and respected individuals, it is striking how few women occupy positions of political influence or power. The members of the Thirteen, Tourmaline Brotherhood, and Ancient Guild of Spicers in Qarth; the Good, Wise, and Great Masters of Astapor, Yunkai, and Meereen, respectively; and the *khals* of the Dothraki—those with the most political power in each of the lands Daenerys visits (and, in some cases, conquers) are predominantly men.[23] Daenerys raises former slave and interpreter Missandei to the position of trusted advisor on her small council—Martin's term for what operates as the equivalent of the medieval privy council—but it is difficult to find women who are or were in positions of power or had demonstrable agency anywhere in Essos prior to Daenerys's overthrow and restructuring of Essosi leadership.

Those few Essosi women who hold positions of power have almost exclusively religious affiliations. This is fundamentally different from both historical record and from many of the high-status women in Westeros, who display an instrumental approach to faith—such as Cersei's miscalculated reinstatement of the Faith Militant without giving sufficient consideration to the longer-term consequences of a fanatical religious revival. Religion is treated as a tool of influence or a means by which to gain power by Cersei and Margaery, but it is only one of many tools at their disposal. Though Cersei uses (or attempts to use) the Faith of the Seven to strengthen her hold on the throne and weaken Margaery's position, she herself is not a religious figure affiliated with the Faith. Moreover, reinstituting the Faith Militant is only one of a variety of means Cersei uses to gain and hold power, and is one she resorts to only when others fail her, for example, her family name, sex, gold or the promise of it, her status as both a Lannister and queen, and the physical strength of soldiers at her command. Margaery uses performative piety to shape her reputation and gain public favour, both before and after the reinstatement of the Faith Militant. However, the foundation of her power and agency is founded on three things: her family's wealth and agricultural assets, which entice the

Lannisters to seek an alliance; her ability to emotionally manipulate her husbands, so that they enact her will while thinking it their own; and her popularity amongst the general populace, which is founded on her generosity as much as, if not more than, on her piety.

POWER THROUGH RELIGION: A DOUBLE-EDGED SWORD

In the detailed examination of each Essosi woman in a position of (religious) power that follows, I have grouped these women by religious affiliation: Mirri Maz Duur, godswife to the Lhazareen who worship the Great Shepherd; Galazza Galare and the Graces of the Ghiscari temple; Melisandre, Kinvara, and Quaithe; and the *dosh khaleen*.

Mirri Maz Duur gains Daenerys's trust specifically because of her position as godswife despite Daenerys's initial misgivings about using the dark sorcery of blood-magic and the urging of the Dothraki not to trust a *maegi*. Her position as godswife of a Lhazareen temple, and her mother's position as godswife before her, provide Mirri with a powerful education, gained from the mages of Asshai, from maesters, *dosh khaleen*, and moonsingers of the Jogos Nhai. It grants her wealth and high social status, evident from her clothing of 'the lightest and finest of woolens, rich with embroidery'.[24] It is also through her religion that Mirri Maz Duur is able to avenge upon the Dothraki the violence wreaked upon herself and her fellow Lhazareen, killing their prophesied 'Stallion Who Mounts the World' with blood-magic and leaving Daenerys and Khal Drogo's people with a living shell of their *khal*.[25]

The political clout held by Galazza Galare (who does not appear in the HBO series) is striking in its rarity. The Ghiscari religion has persisted for millennia, and has adapted to different cultures arriving in Slaver's Bay. As high priestess of the Ghiscari Temple of the Graces in Meereen, Galazza Galare becomes a respected royal counsellor, a position which goes unquestioned either by Daenerys's council or by the traditionally minded nobility of Meereen. She advises Daenerys to marry a Ghiscari nobleman and specifically recommends Hizdahr zo Loraq. By proclaiming (honestly or otherwise, as remains to be seen) to share similar goals as Daenerys (urging the newly conquered Meereenese to act towards Daenerys with 'peace, acceptance, and obedience to lawful authority') while maintaining a position that is, as a religious leader, both widely respected and does not directly compete for Daenerys's throne, Galazza Galare manages to achieve what the threats and violence of the Sons of the Harpy and the demands of many of the Meereenese nobility do not. Her apparent coalition tactics persuade Daenerys to listen to Galazza Galare's advice and respect it out of hand rather than question her requests and look for ulterior motives.[26] Later, when Daenerys has disappeared on her dragon and king-consort Hizdahr rules in her absence, she alone acts as intermediary between the masters and the queen's court. Galazza's religious position even appears to grant her a quasi-judiciary authority, as she proclaims that Hizdahr is innocent of treason simply on the grounds that '[t]he gods of Ghis have told [her]' so.[27] Whether or not this argument for innocence is recognised by Ser Barristan and the other members of the queen's council remains to be seen, as Galazza Galare can advise on matters of Meereenese tradition and spiritual guidance but her permitted influence within the realm of secular politics remains somewhat limited by the same religious institution which lends her authority.

The other Graces of the Ghiscari Temple are equally limited in terms of acceptable roles and behaviour. There are a number of colours of Graces—pink, blue, white, red, green, and others—and each order has only one role: white as vestal virgins, blue as healers, red as sex workers. Women may rise within the strict hierarchy of colours, but each level within that religious hierarchy is narrowly defined, and their movements appear to be dictated to a large degree by the Green Grace's permission.

Kinvara, a character invented for the HBO television series, also enters Daenerys's throne room with authority gained through her position within the red temples.[28] She is introduced as the High Priestess of the Red Temple of Volantis, leader of the faith of R'hllor, a position granted in the books to a man named Benerro. Kinvara's plotline takes the place of Benerro's and his priest Moqorro's plotlines. While it is not made clear in the books whether the High Priest of Volantis is the highest position in the faith of R'hllor, or whether he is one of many high priests, in the television series, the red priesthood is represented as predominantly female. Kinvara leads the religion of the Lord of Light; Melisandre is unarguably one of the most powerful women in Westeros; and those shown preaching support for Daenerys in Meereen and Volantis are also women. Zanrush, the red priest accompanying Kinvara, is shown in a distinctly subordinate position, announcing her to Tyrion and Varys before stepping aside; and the High Priest of Myr who charges Thoros with converting Robert Baratheon remains off-screen, mentioned but not shown.[29] Thoros himself is only presented to readers as a serious threat (or, in the television series, a powerful potential ally for Jon Snow) when he becomes a member of the marginalised Band of Brothers.[30] Prior to that, he is portrayed as a feckless drunkard who jousts with a flaming sword as more of a gimmick than a religious symbol.[31] As a red priest within the Westerosi court and as an outlaw necromancer, the political power he holds due to his religious position is woefully secondary to Melisandre's. At best, he is the John the Baptist to her Christ.

The series' most powerful Essosi woman (notably, one of only two Essosi characters who are given their own point-of-view chapter and who possesses political influence due to her religious affiliation), is Melisandre, red priestess of R'hllor. Melisandre's terrifying abilities as a dedicated servant of the Lord of Light have raised her from childhood slavery to become the right hand and red shadow of King Stannis. Through her role as priestess, she undermines the positions of counsellor originally held by Maester Cressen and then Davos as Hand of the King, soon becoming the king's sole source of advice. When Melisandre is first introduced in *A Storm of Swords*, she has already won the devotion of Selyse and has essentially dislodged Selyse from her role as queen in terms of influence upon and proximity to Stannis. Jon Snow is quick to recognise that Selyse's 'queen's men' are Melisandre's to command in all but name. Her devotion to R'hllor grants her the ability to detect lies, withstand freezing temperatures, create long-lasting glamours, to light wood and weapons on fire (as she does at the Battle of Winterfell in the television series, though she has not yet demonstrated this ability in the books), and to divine the future in flames (though correct interpretation is a more difficult skill). More than this, through her religion, Melisandre gains power over life and death itself. She can survive poisoning, give birth to shadow assassins, and—at least in the television series—raise the dead. Stannis is prepared to kill men and children at her word, and his men stand by and watch as their king and queen burn their own child alive. Melisandre's theatrics, combined with her willingness to bend her morality to her interpretations of her Lord's will, enable her to persuade men to execute, or agree to assist in, extraordinarily horrific acts: fratricide, infanticide, the burning of sacred spaces. This frightening persuasiveness, coupled with her willingness to see violence committed in the name of faith, derives much of its impact from our contemporary fears of religious fanaticism and murder performed on religious grounds.

Melisandre is portrayed in both books and television series as attractive. Stannis's men grumble and speculate that it is her attractiveness which has seduced their king to her red god rather than her prophecies and ability to perform blood-magic. In *A Storm of Swords*, she tries to convince Davos 'to come to [her] chamber one night', offering him 'pleasure such as [he has] never known' in exchange for his 'life-fire' (sperm) to aid her in creating another shadow-assassin. In the HBO series, Melisandre uses glamour and strips naked before Jon Snow when she attempts to seduce him into supporting her. However, both Davos and Jon Snow refuse her sexual enticements, and Stannis seems more interested in the magical powers Melisandre's faith places at his disposal than her body or affection as a prize. Ultimately, it is Melisandre's faith that grants her social position and power, not men's affection or sexual interest in her. Indeed, in the later episodes of the television series, her appearance of beauty and youth (endowed by her magical necklace) seems largely to function not as a means of endearing men to her—as few characters like or trust her—but as a means of keeping her alive until she can fulfil her mission: to be instrumental in saving humanity from the White Walkers. When that mission is fulfilled, she removes the necklace and goes willingly to her rest.

Yet, paradoxically, these religious organisations constrain as they empower. Melisandre's unnatural abilities and fanatical devotion to R'hllor make some men wary and mistrustful of her at the same time that it makes some of them value her, and she repeatedly describes her role as *servant* to the Lord of Light, bound to the rules of her faith and the requirements of blood-magic (such as her need for kings' blood). She is reliant upon her god's will for her pyromantic visions and her ability to perform supernatural acts. The *dosh khaleen* endure harsher constrictions: though greatly respected amongst the Dothraki, they are physically restricted to the confines of the Temple of Vaes Dothrak, and are given no choice over their future. The moment these *khaleesi* are widowed, they face a lifetime within a single, narrowly proscribed role, one which, until Daenerys appears on the scene, seems impossible to escape or even question. One need look no further than the complacent Dothraki refrain, 'It is known', to find evidence of a culturally ingrained belief that new ideas must be sacrificed on the altar of tradition. Curiosity, initiative, and questioning the system are traits that Daenerys brings to Essos. This could be read as a form of white saviourism, and certainly both the novel and television series do frame Daenerys as a white saviour.[32] On the other hand, the people of Westeros too are largely locked in paradigms that restrict and diminish its inhabitants. Arya and Brienne both struggle against the Seven Kingdoms' view that a noble woman should marry a lord and restrict herself to running his holdfast while Melisandre challenges the generally held Westerosi conviction, current amongst those who worship the old gods and the new, that the gods are but distant observers and magic and miracles are the stuff of stories.

Notwithstanding this, Quaithe, the strange prophesying woman Daenerys meets in Qarth, does seem to achieve a sort of shadowy independence. In the books, though not in the television series, Quaithe seems able to appear to whom she will at her own chosen moments, regardless of distance between herself and her contact. Her mask bears the red hue and hexagonal motif used by the red priests of the Lord of Light, but one is left to wonder how she fits in within the community of R'hllor's followers. To whom does she answer, and who is answerable to her? How much freedom does she truly have over her appearances to Daenerys or the prophetic words she imparts? So much about Quaithe's abilities and position within the religious and political structures of the known world remains a mystery, making it difficult to draw many solid conclusions regarding her degree of personal agency.

It is not explicitly clear whether the *dosh khaleen* are viewed by the Dothraki as religious figures, per se. Their roles as prophesiers, if not prophets, and their inhabitation of the Temple of Vaes Dothrak have led the creators of the *Game of Thrones* Wiki website to refer to the widow of Khal Savo as the 'head priestess', though that character is credited in the HBO series as simply 'Dothraki crone' and that term is not used in the books nor in the HBO series to refer to members of the *dosh khaleen*.[33] The *dosh khaleen* are never referred to in the books nor credited in the HBO series as priestesses, godswives, septas, Graces, or similar terms that distinguish women in other Essosi and Westerosi cultures who have devoted themselves to religious institutions. However, there does not seem to be any Dothraki position more closely aligned with interpreting and/or promoting Dothraki religious beliefs, customs, and traditions.

The *dosh khaleen* live as respected wise women, offering counsel and prophesies to *khals*. They approve the marriages of the *khals*, as any new *khaleesi* must be presented to them at Vaes Dothrak, though Martin does not tell his readers what might happen if the *dosh khaleen* were to reject a woman already married to a *khal*. They interpret omens for the Dothraki which can influence the decisions and movements of the *khals* and their *khalasars*. It is the *dosh khaleen* who declare Daenerys's unborn child to be the 'Stallion Who Mounts the World'. Even so, their political authority is limited; the *khals* ultimately decide where each *khalasar* travels and whom they raid. When compared with the freedoms of other members of the Dothraki, the autonomy of the *dosh khaleen* is also severely curtailed: they are confined to the Temple of Vaes Dothrak from the moment they are widowed, and have no option to pursue any other course. Shiloh Carroll, who contributes to this collection, discusses elsewhere the side-lining of the *dosh khaleen* in season six of the television series, pointing out that

> the power structure of the Dothraki clearly is whatever Benioff and Weiss need it to be. The Dosh Khaleen are in charge of Vaes Dothrak until they're not. Joining them is an honor until it's a punishment. [...] There's no internal consistency at all.[34]

Martin openly identifies as a feminist and has stated his interest in 'exploring living in a society that diminishes you'.[35] His portrayal of religions as double-edged swords that confine as much as they promise to empower follows from this interest—particularly those religions practised south of Greywater Watch. More social rules and expectations are incorporated in these (unlike the religion of the North and the free folk, which is distinctly anti-institutional). Institutions operate to erase identity; individuality is lost within the collective body of the faith. The matron in the temple of the *dosh khaleen* is only referred to by her prior position as *khaleesi* to Khal Savo, and later by her role within the *dosh khaleen*; her name—her personal identity—is treated as irrelevant. Her speech to Daenerys conveys the Dothraki view of the singular, lifelong role of the *dosh khaleen* as both inescapable and one of collective anonymity beyond their shared position as widows of *khals*:

> You were the wife of the Great Khal. You thought he would conquer the world with you at his side. He didn't. I was the wife of the Great Khal. Khal Savo. I thought he would conquer the world with me at his side. You're young. We were all young once. But we all understand the way things are. You will learn as well, if you are fortunate enough to stay with us.[36]

WESTEROSI WOMEN IN ESSOS

This erasure of identity is precisely what Arya struggles against most when she seeks to gain power through the Braavosi religion of the Faceless Men. Arya covets the Faceless Men's ability to shape-shift, to take on the faces of the dead, and their powers of assassination. Yet, to claim the refuge of the House of Black and White, to gain the skills and the permission to assassinate with seemingly no legal repercussions, and to learn how to disguise herself beyond possible recognition with the faces of the deceased, the Faceless Men demand that Arya become 'no one'; she must relinquish all thoughts of personal vengeance, morality, and family belonging. Regulation of power is conflated with loss of personal identity. This sort of constriction and erasure that the faith of the Faceless Men demands is treated as an undesirable outcome. In the HBO series, which has moved past the books regarding Arya's narrative, Arya remains a trickster figure and manages to steal the knowledge of face-changing—the mysteries/wonders of the East—without respecting the cultural/institutional limitations that are expected to accompany that knowledge and power. The audience is set to cheer when Arya finds a way to break the constrictions of the faith, to swindle the Faceless Men out of their powerful knowledge of deception and death, without paying the price of regulation of that power. Arya demonstrates a sort of colonialist plundering: she enters a foreign culture and appropriates what she deems the useful, empowering aspects of their knowledge and takes them back to Westeros as tools to benefit her own ends, with no willingness to respect, consider, or honour that same culture's rules and regulations. What is more, the audience is invited to applaud her ingenuity and tenacity in managing to pull off such a cultural heist. Her final scene in the television series implies future colonialist plundering, as Arya sails off to discover what lies west of Westeros: to find new lands, cultures, and marvels for the taking.

It is impossible to speculate how Martin will resolve Arya's struggle to accept the constrictions that come with the power the House of Black and White offers. The most recently published *A Dance with Dragons* leaves readers on a cliff-hanger with Arya blinded as punishment for using the ability to change faces without accepting the limitations the House of Black and White places on that power: using the faces solely for the House's purposes, not one's own ends. Arya's attempt to escape that price, namely, giving up her selfhood ("'Who are you?" "No one." "Another lie," he sighed'), has only resulted in her paying in a different currency: the loss of her eyesight.[37]

In both the Old and New Testaments, blinding is used as a form of divine punishment for religious disobedience and scepticism. It is also associated with disbelief, ignorance, and sin, with a cure possible via conversion to the faith.[38] Martin was raised a Catholic and, as such, one might reasonably expect him to be familiar with such associations between blindness and religious transgression. Equally, in various European cultures throughout the medieval period, blindness was used as, or considered to be, a punishment—legally or otherwise—for infidelity, betrayal, and treason.[39] In refusing to accept the limitations that come with religious power (identity and free will in exchange for power over life and death), Arya essentially commits acts associated with blinding as punishment: religious disobedience, apostasy, and betrayal. It remains to be seen whether Martin will adhere to HBO's colonialist-trickster narrative, with Arya returning to the West no worse for wear with the Faceless Men's 'wonders' in her arsenal of abilities, or remain permanently disabled for her trespasses.

This colonialist appropriation is microcosmic for Arya, in the form of personal vengeance, and macrocosmic for Daenerys in her bid to win the Iron Throne. Daenerys similarly attempts to plunder Essos, to take its cultural ideas and resources (armies, ships) and bring them back to Westeros for the furtherance of her own agenda. Although she spends nearly the entirety of both book and television series in Essos, Daenerys is not an Essosi woman. Though she was raised in Essos, her early education appears to have come primarily from her Westerosi brother. She remains unique precisely because she is neither fully Westerosi nor Essosi, and because she approaches the lands she conquers (or wishes to conquer, as in the case of Westeros) without preconceptions: she is bent on forming new cultures by mixing standing traditions with her own personal morals and worldview. Elizabeth Beaton and Rikke Schubart have discussed the messianic framing of many of Daenerys's scenes in the television show and other aspects of messianic motherhood about her, suggesting Daenerys embodies a break from previous cultural norms in every land she enters.[40] Troublingly, this includes '[l]ingering on shots which surround blonde Daenerys by adoring people who are marked as ethnically other (indeed symbolically Middle Eastern)' as 'one of the central ways the show reinforces her claims to leadership, and [...] reveals a pervasive Orientalism tied to the gendered framework of Daenerys's leadership'.[41]

This messianic framing (but not the motherhood aspect) is more evident in the television series than in the books where Martin depicts Essos as more ethnically diverse than it appears in the show. However, as Shiloh Carroll writes, '[w]hile Martin can be lauded for including people of color in his novels (especially people of color who are not immediately coded evil, as such inclusions are sadly rare in neomedieval fantasy), his characterization of the non-Westerosi peoples yet drifts toward Orientalism and race essentialism'.[42] Daenerys retains the role of the colonial imperialist even as she grows into her role as Essosi *khaleesi*, queen, and essentially empress. Her overarching goal (even when she must temporarily suspend her movements towards it) is always to take what she can from Essos and return to Westeros with the knowledge and resources she gains.

Carroll notes that '[c]ritics often lament the tendency of neomedieval fantasy literature to focus on the European Middle Ages and exclude the Middle East or Asia, so Martin might be credited for including other cultures, but he does not present them in a new or revisionist manner; rather, Martin's non-Western peoples and characterization show remarkable similarities to other colonialist literature'.[43] As a result of the limitation of Essosi women's recourses to power in both books and television show, and the emphasis on Daenerys's self-definition as a mother to her people and her dragons, Daenerys's colonial imperialism is dressed up as, or conflated with, feminist liberation. Essosi women's disenfranchisement, except for within the confines of religious institutions, portrays the East, pan-continentally, as backward and in need of Western influence to liberate women—as if each Essosi society, Dothraki, Astapori, Meereenese, and so forth, is incapable of self-reform without outside influence. As Helen Young argues of Martin's and other fantasy works:

> The medievalist, White Self may not be perfect, but the Eastern Other is invariably marked as comparatively worse because of particular cultural practices which are repellent according to contemporary mores. If Gritty Fantasy challenges dichotomies of good and evil, its worlds and stories still revolve around White characters who live in medievalist worlds.[44]

Young here cites as an example the Dothraki practices of slavery and 'public sex acts and violence at weddings', but the same repellent attitudes can be applied to their erasure of women's identities, as seen with the Dothraki treatment of the *dosh khaleen*, and throughout Essos in various cultures' limitations of women's access to roles of influence and power. Across Essos, the 'Eastern Other' is marked as 'comparatively worse' in its patriarchal societies than the West. Westeros is certainly patriarchal, but even within those social and legal strictures, women find diverse ways to access power. In Essos, as in many other works of fantasy literature,

> [m]edievalist feudal monarchies, made palatable to modern readers by a strong sense of *noblesse obligé* [sic] among high-born protagonists, is conventionally contrasted with an exoticized and often 'Oriental' empire [...] The reader experiences them only through the filter of the White protagonists, even when characters from those realms—often the emperor himself—take a significant role in the story. Each is saved from collapse by the presence and action of White characters [...] These 'White saviour' narratives construct the Othered empires as static, incapable of change without external

intervention, moreover, the change that does come is extremely limited and result [sic] in no political or social development, merely a shoring up of the existing power structure.[45]

This messianic framing and white saviourism is complicated by the final episode of the television series, in which Daenerys is depicted no longer as the white saviour of oppressed and culturally divergent non-white Eastern peoples, but rather as the fascist tyrannical leader of an unthinking mass of soldiers and warriors. In her final public speech, evocative of the Nuremberg Rally, Daenerys speaks almost exclusively in foreign languages while addressing rows of machine-like Unsullied soldiers and a wild, screaming horde of Dothraki warriors, both—all—of whom evidently wholeheart-edly support her massacre of the people of King's Landing. Meanwhile, the Westerosi characters remain the only characters who are depicted questioning Daenerys's choices and sanity, and who voice horror at her massacre of innocents and concern at her unquenched thirst for totali-tarian power.

Returning to the books, the exclusion of Essosi women from political roles and their disenfranchisement except for within the confines of reli-gious institutions ensures that Daenerys stands apart not only as a Targaryen but also as a woman in a man's world. With no woman to chal-lenge Daenerys for rule in Essos, Martin constructs, perhaps uncon-sciously, a narrative of the 'white woman's burden': feminist liberation brought to a tradition- and religion-bound East by a woman who identi-fies with the West.

In summary, though Essos boasts several women in positions of power, all those positions are solely within religious institutions: institutions which constrain these women as they profess to empower them. This lim-ited recourse to power for Essosi women does not reflect medieval histori-cal reality, where Eastern women from a range of cultures used a variety of strategies, religious and secular, to obtain power and agency. They were often holy women, yes, but they were also empresses, regents, consorts, and mistresses; they were jurists and scholars, warriors and pirates. In Martin's world of ice and fire, Essosi religious institutions require varying degrees of erasure of individual identity and suppression or renunciation of personal interests: the collective approach to identity practised by the *dosh khaleen* and the lower and middling levels of Graces, the complete annihilation of the individual by the Faceless Men, and the subordination of Melisandre to the will of R'hllor in order to perform her magic rather than merely exercising her own volition all attest to this. The constrictive nature of these religions is viewed by Arya and Daenerys—women who are Westerosi and who identify closely with Westeros, respectively—as unacceptable. This value judgement on other cultures leads them both to colonialist appropriation on micro- and macrocosmic levels: appropriation which is treated by Martin, Benioff, and Weiss as 'clever' and 'empowering' rather than problematic. Thus, while Martin can be praised for his inclusion of non-Western people and cultures in his book series—diversity which the genre on the whole sadly lacks—his portrayal of the East as uniformly more patriarchal and religiously hidebound than the West is more reflective of modern Western orientalist notions of the East than of the historical realism that Martin is praised for in his renditions of a medieval West.

NOTES

1. Edward Said, *Orientalism*, London: Penguin Books, 1978, 236; Saba Mahmood, 'Preface to the 2012 edition,' *Politics of Piety: The Islamic Revival and the Feminist Subject*, Princeton: Princeton University Press, 2005, xviii.
2. Even so, religion remains the outpost of the marginalised, which certainly was not the situation in the global Middle Ages. Carolyne Larrington believes that in Westeros, this in part may stem from the maesters being the source of education rather than, as it was in medieval Europe, the Church:

   > Why (up until the great renewal of popular religion in the wake of the War of the Five Kings) is the Faith so ineffectual? I suspect it's because the Faith isn't associated with learning, with the vital technologies of reading and writing. The preservation of knowledge and the teaching of future generations are the province of the maesters, who may profess any faith they like and who are expressly apolitical; thus the Faith has lost purchase in the Kingdoms' politics.

   Carolyne Larrington, *Winter is Coming*, London: I. B. Tauris, 2016, 134.
3. This extends beyond the Lord of Light faith. Within the Faith of the Seven, another Essosi import to Westeros, the High Septon, is an old, doddering, lecherous, and thus ridiculous figure; septas focus on teaching soft skills like courtly courtesy and needlework and cannot defend themselves from attack. The High Sparrow similarly is introduced as a mild, grandfatherly figure before revealing his true nature.

4. Mat Hardy, 'The Eastern Question,' Game of Thrones *versus History: Written in Blood*, ed. Brian A. Pavlac, Hoboken, NJ: John Wiley & Sons, Inc., 2017, 97–110, 98. Elizabeth Beaton notes that 'the geography of the world [of Essos and Westeros] replicates the West-East split of much epic fantasy' including 'naming systems that divide the Anglo-Saxon derived peoples (in Westeros) from the Middle Eastern and Asian derived peoples (in Essos)'. Elizabeth Beaton, 'Female Machiavellians in Westeros,' *Women of Ice and Fire*, ed. Rikke Schubart and Anne Gjelsvik, London: Bloomsbury, 2016, 193–218, 210.

5. Excepting deliberate fantasy elements, of course: dragons, wights, and wargs. Larrington, *Winter is Coming*; Ayelet Haimson Lushkov, *You Win or You Die: The Ancient World of* Game of Thrones, London: I. B. Tauris, 2017; Game of Thrones *versus History: Written in Blood*, ed. Brian A. Pavlac, Hoboken, NJ: John Wiley & Sons, Inc., 2017.

6. Jacqueline de Weever, *Sheba's Daughters: Whitening and Demonizing the Saracen Woman in Medieval French Epic*, London: Garland, 1998, xxi, 8–9.

7. *The Romance of Sir Beues of Hamtoun*, ed. Eugen Kölbing and Carl Schmirgel, Early English Text Society, London: K. Paul Trench, Trübner & Co, 1894.

8. See, for example, Floripas's actions throughout 'The Sultan of Babylon,' *Three Middle English Charlemagne Romances*, ed. Alan Lupack, Kalamazoo, MI: Medieval Institute Publications, 1990, 7–103, particularly in the second half of the poem, from l. 1511.

9. Peggy McCracken, *The Romance of Adultery*, Philadelphia: University of Pennsylvania Press, 1998, 7–10.

10. Fatima Mernissi, *The Forgotten Queens of Islam*, trans. Mary Jo Lakeland, Cambridge: Polity, 1993, 107–108.

11. Mernissi, *The Forgotten Queens of Islam*, 14, 19–20, 115–116, 129, 140, 159–178.

12. Mernissi, *The Forgotten Queens of Islam*, 13, 28–29, 88–99.

13. Mernissi, *The Forgotten Queens of Islam*, 107–108.

14. Muhammad Akram Nadwi, *Al-Muhaddithat: The Women Scholars in Islam*, Oxford: Interface Publications, 2007, 118, 144, 202.

15. Mernissi, *The Forgotten Queens of Islam*, 18–19.

16. Lynda Garland, *Byzantine Empresses: Women and Power in Byzantium AD 527–1204*, London: Routledge, 1998, 76–78, 100–104, 144–146, 165–166, 168, 170–171, 186–187.

17. Larrington, *Winter is Coming*, 187–199.

18. Jack Weatherford, *The Secret History of the Mongol Queens*, New York: Random House, 2010, 54, 64–66. Checheyigen ruled the Oirat, Al-Altun the Uighur, Tolai the Karluk Turks in her husband's prolonged absence,

and Alaqai Beki ruled the Onggud. Weatherford notes that 'The confusion over her husbands' identities frustrated generations of scholars, but the vagueness further illustrates the unimportance these men had in her administration. The identity of the Mongol queen mattered; the identity of her consort did not' (54). Tolai's true name is unconfirmed; she was married to Arslan Khan (later Arslan Sartaqtai). (64–65)

19. George R. R. Martin in 'The Real History Behind *Game of Thrones*,' *Game of Thrones: The Complete Fifth Season*, HBO, 2016.
20. George R. R. Martin in James Hibberd, 'George R. R. Martin Explains Why There's Violence Against Women on *Game of Thrones*,' *Entertainment Weekly*, 3 June 2015, http://www.ew.com/article/2015/06/03/george-rr-martin-thrones-violence-women
21. Larrington, *Winter is Coming*, 187–199; Robert Haug, 'Slaves with Swords: Slave-Soldiers in Essos and in the Islamic World,' Game of Thrones *versus History: Written in Blood*, ed. Brian A. Pavlac, Hoboken, NJ: John Wiley & Sons, Inc., 2017, 111–122, 111–113.
22. George R. R. Martin, *A Dance with Dragons: After the Feast*, London: Harper Voyager, 2012, 411.
23. In the HBO series, scenes of the Masters and the Thirteen show solely men; in *ASoIaF* Martin does not specify that the Thirteen, the merchants of Qarth, and the Masters are all men, but no women are mentioned as being amongst their numbers. It appears these widespread male dominated power structures have not always defined Essosi politics, as the widow of the waterfront notes to Tyrion that '[s]ome of the first elephants were women [...] the ones who brought the tigers down and ended the old wars. Trianna was returned four times. That was three hundred years ago, alas. Volantis has had no female triarch since, though some women have the vote. Women of good birth who dwell in ancient palaces behind the Black Walls, not creatures such as me'. George R. R. Martin, *A Dance with Dragons: Dreams and Dust*, London: Harper Voyager, 2011, 428.
24. George R. R. Martin, *A Game of Thrones*, London: Harper Voyager, 1996, 647.
25. In Chap. 10 of this collection, Sheilagh Ilona O'Brien discusses the positions of Mirri Maz Duur and Melisandre as 'witches', and notes the orientalism in the kinds of magical powers eastern religions can grant their practitioners: 'The majority of magic-users perceived to be "evil" in the series are "eastern", "learned", and "diabolic", while those born in Westeros seem to practise "natural" and more ambiguous or even seemingly good or positive magic'.
26. Martin, *A Dance with Dragons: After the Feast*, 41.
27. Martin, *A Dance with Dragons: After the Feast*, 457.

28. Game of Thrones, 'The Door,' 6.5. Directed by Jack Bender. Created by David Benioff and D.B. Weiss. HBO, 23 May 2016.

29. Game of Thrones, 'The Door,' 6.5.

30. Game of Thrones, 'Kissed by Fire,' 3.5. Directed by Alex Graves. Written by Bryan Cogman. HBO, 28 April 2013; Game of Thrones, 'Beyond the Wall,' 7.6. Directed by Alan Taylor. Created by David Benioff and D.B. Weiss. HBO, 21 August 2017.

31. In this, Thoros's character is reminiscent of Bishop Turpin. Turpin, based on the historical Tilpin, the bishop of Reims (c. 748–794), is a warrior-bishop figure in the medieval French epic *The Song of Roland*. Though he begins the epic as one of Charlemagne's advisors, initially he also cuts a somewhat ridiculous figure. When Turpin offers to treat with Spain on behalf of Charlemagne, Charlemagne dismisses him as a parent might dismiss a child, angrily telling Turpin to 'Go and sit down on your white rug, / Do not speak again unless I bid you' ('Li empereres respunt par malta-lant: / 'Alez sedeir desur cel palie blanc; / N'en parlez mais, se je ne l'vos cumant''). Yet Turpin ends his life fighting bravely (though perhaps not in a very priest-like fashion) against the Saracen foe, much like Thoros does while fighting the wight army in the television show. *The Song of Roland*, trans. Jessie Crosland, Cambridge, Ontario: In Parentheses Publications, 1999, 7, verse 19; *La Chanson de Roland*, ed. L. Petit de Julleville, Paris: Alphonse Lemerre, 1878, ll. 271–273. For Thoros fighting with a flaming sword, see George R. R. Martin, *A Storm of Swords*, New York: Bantam, 2000, 254.

32. Rikke Schubart, 'Woman with Dragons: Daenerys, Pride, and Postfeminist Possibilities,' *Women of Ice and Fire*, ed. Anne Gjelsvik and Rikke Schubart, London: Bloomsbury, 2016, 105–129, 120–121; Elizabeth Beaton, 'Female Machiavellians in Westeros,' *Women of Ice and Fire*, 187–189.

33. 'High Priestess of the Dosh Khaleen,' *Game of Thrones Wiki*. http://gameofthrones.wikia.com/wiki/High_Priestess_of_the_Dosh_Khaleen, accessed 20 September 2018. The webpage notes: 'Although this article is based on canonical information, the actual name of this subject is pure conjecture'.

34. Shiloh Carroll, 'Game of Thrones (Re)Watch 6.4: "Book of the Stranger",' Tales after Tolkien Society, 19 June 2017, http://www.talesaftertolkien.blogspot.com/2017/06

35. On Martin identifying as a feminist, see Rikke Schubart and Anne Gjelsvik's introduction to *Women of Ice and Fire*, 2. Quote: Elizabeth Beaton, 'Female Machiavellians in Westeros,' *Women of Ice and Fire*, 209.

36. Game of Thrones, 'Oathbreaker,' 6.3. Directed by Daniel Sackheim. Created by David Benioff and D.B. Weiss. HBO, 9 May 2016.

37. Arya's blinding occurs in *A Feast for Crows* and continues through *A Dance with Dragons*. George R. R. Martin, *A Feast for Crows*, New York: Bantam, 2005, 390, 644.

38. God strikes Saul blind on the road to Damascus, and his sight is restored when he accepts Jesus as his Saviour (Acts 9:1–18). Samson's eyes are gouged out in Judges as a result of his disobedience to God; as punishment for the cutting of his hair (a symbol of the covenant between Samson and God), God rescinds his protection of Samson (Judges 16:17–21). In the book of Jeremiah, Zedekiah is also blinded as a result of his violation of God's will, broken covenant, and profanation of God's name (Jeremiah 34:1–39:7).

39. David Bernstein, 'The Blinding of Harold and the Meaning of the Bayeux Tapestry,' *Anglo-Norman Studies: Proceedings of the Battle Conference 1982*, ed. R. Allen Brown, Woodbridge: Boydell, 1983, 40–64, 56–57; Michael Evans, *The Death of Kings: Royal Deaths in Medieval England*, London: Hambledon and London, 2003, 37, 89; Connie Scarborough, *Viewing Disability in Medieval Spanish Texts*, Croydon, UK: Amsterdam University Press, 2018, 65–87; Edward Wheatley, *Stumbling Blocks before the Blind: Medieval Constructions of a Disability*, Ann Arbor, MI: University of Michigan Press, 2010, 15, 67–69.

40. Schubart, 'Woman with Dragons: Daenerys, Pride, and Postfeminist Possibilities,' *Women of Ice and Fire*, 120–121; Beaton, 'Female Machiavellians in Westeros,' *Women of Ice and Fire*, 187–189.

41. Beaton, 'Female Machiavellians in Westeros,' *Women of Ice and Fire*, 188–189.

42. Shiloh Carroll, *Medievalism in* A Song of Ice and Fire *and* Game of Thrones, Cambridge: Brewer, 2018, 109.

43. Carroll, *Medievalism in* A Song of Ice and Fire *and* Game of Thrones, 119.

44. Helen Young, *Race and Popular Fantasy Literature: Habits of Whiteness*, New York: Routledge, 2016, Chapter 3: Normative whiteness, para. 6. [Calibre E-book viewer EPUB], retrieved from https://bodleian.ldls.org.uk/

45. Helen Young, *Race and Popular Fantasy Literature: Habits of Whiteness*, New York: Routledge, 2016, Chapter 2: Repetitions of race, para. 8.

BIBLIOGRAPHY

PRIMARY SOURCES

The New Oxford Annotated Bible: New Revised Standard Version with the Apocrypha, Coogan, M. D. and others, Oxford: Oxford University Press, 2010.

La Chanson de Roland, ed. Petit de Julleville, L., Paris: Alphonse Lemerre, 1878.

Game of Thrones, 'Beyond the Wall', 7.6. Directed by Alan Taylor. Created by David Benioff and D.B. Weiss. HBO, 21 August 2017.

Game of Thrones, 'The Door', 6.5. Directed by Jack Bender. Created by David Benioff and D.B. Weiss. HBO, 23 May 2016.

Game of Thrones, 'Kissed by Fire', 3.5. Directed by Alex Graves. Written by Bryan Cogman. HBO, 28 April 2013.

Game of Thrones, 'Oathbreaker', 6.3. Directed by Daniel Sackheim. Created by David Benioff and D.B. Weiss. HBO, 9 May 2016.

Martin, George R. R., *A Game of Thrones*, London: Harper Voyager, 1996.

Idem, *A Storm of Swords*, New York: Bantam, 2000.

Idem, *A Feast for Crows*, New York: Bantam, 2005.

Idem, *A Dance with Dragons: Dreams and Dust*, London, Harper Voyager, 2011.

Idem, *A Dance with Dragons: After the Feast*, London: Harper Voyager, 2012.

The Romance of Sir Beues of Hamtoun, ed. Kölbing, Eugen and Schmirgel, Carl, Early English Text Society, London: K. Paul Trench, Trübner & Co, 1894.

The Song of Roland, trans. Crosland, Jessie, Cambridge, Ontario: In Parentheses Publications, 1999.

'The Sultan of Babylon', *Three Middle English Charlemagne Romances*, ed. Lupack, Alan, Kalamazoo, MI: Medieval Institute Publications, 1990, 7–103.

SECONDARY SOURCES

Beaton, Elizabeth, 'Female Machiavellians in Westeros', *Women of Ice and Fire*, ed. Gjelsvik, Anne, and Schubart, Rikke, London: Bloomsbury, 2016, 193–218.

Bernstein, David, 'The Blinding of Harold and the Meaning of the Bayeux Tapestry', *Anglo-Norman Studies: Proceedings of the Battle Conference 1982*, ed. R. Allen Brown, Woodbridge: Boydell, 1983, 40–64.

Carroll, Shiloh, *Medievalism in* A Song of Ice and Fire *and* Game of Thrones, Cambridge: Brewer, 2018.

Idem, 'Game of Thrones (Re)Watch 6.4: "Book of the Stranger"', *Tales after Tolkien Society*, 19 June 2017, http://www.talesaftertolkien.blogspot. com/2017/06.

Evans, Michael, *The Death of Kings: Royal Deaths in Medieval England*, London: Hambledon and London, 2003.

Garland, Lynda, *Byzantine Empresses: Women and Power in Byzantium AD 527–1204*, London: Routledge, 1998.

Hardy, Mat, 'The Eastern Question,' Game of Thrones *versus History: Written in Blood*, ed. Pavlac, Brian A., Hoboken, NJ: John Wiley & Sons, Inc., 2017, 97–110.

Haug, Robert, 'Slaves with Swords: Slave-Soldiers in Essos and in the Islamic World,' Game of Thrones *versus History: Written in Blood*, ed. Pavlac, Brian A., Hoboken, NJ: John Wiley & Sons, Inc., 2017, 111–122.

Hibberd, James, 'George R. R. Martin Explains Why There's Violence Against Women on *Game of Thrones*,' *Entertainment Weekly*, 3 June 2015, http://www.ew.com/article/2015/06/03/george-rr-martin-thrones-violence-women

'High Priestess of the Dosh Khaleen', *Game of Thrones Wiki*. http://gameofthrones.wikia.com/wiki/High_Priestess_of_the_Dosh_Khaleen

Larrington, Carolyne, *Winter is Coming*, London: I. B. Taurus, 2016.

Lushkov, Ayelet Haimson, *You Win or You Die: The Ancient World of* Game of Thrones, London: I. B. Tauris, 2017.

Mahmood, Saba 'Preface to the 2012 edition', *Politics of Piety: The Islamic Revival and the Feminist Subject*, Princeton: Princeton UP, 2005.

Mernissi, Fatima, *The Forgotten Queens of Islam*, trans. Lakeland, Mary Jo, Cambridge: Polity, 1993.

McCracken, Peggy, *The Romance of Adultery*, Philadelphia: University of Pennsylvania Press, 1998.

Nadwi, Muhammad Akram, *Al-Muhaddithat: The Women Scholars in Islam*, Oxford: Interface Publications, 2007.

Pavlac, Brian A., *Game of Thrones versus History: Written in Blood*, Hoboken, NJ: John Wiley & Sons, Inc., 2017.

'The Real History Behind *Game of Thrones*', *Game of Thrones: The Complete Fifth Season* (HBO, 2016).

Said, Edward, Orientalism, London: Penguin Books, 1978.

Scarborough, Connie, *Viewing Disability in Medieval Spanish Texts*, Croydon, UK: Amsterdam University Press, 2018.

Schubart, Rikke, 'Woman with Dragons: Daenerys, Pride, and Postfeminist Possibilities', *Women of Ice and Fire*, ed. Gjelsvik, Anne and Schubart, Rikke, London: Bloomsbury, 2016, 105–129.

Schubart, Rikke and Gjelsvik, Anne 'Introduction', *Women of Ice and Fire*, ed. Gjelsvik, Anne and Schubart, Rikke, London: Bloomsbury, 2016, 1–16.

Weatherford, Jack, *The Secret History of the Mongol Queens*, New York: Random House, 2010.

Weever, Jacqueline de, *Sheba's Daughters: Whitening and Demonizing the Saracen Woman in Medieval French Epic*, London: Garland, 1998.

Wheatley, Edward, *Stumbling Blocks before the Blind: Medieval Constructions of a Disability*, Ann Arbor, MI: University of Michigan Press, 2010.

Young, Helen, *Race and Popular Fantasy Literature: Habits of Whiteness* (New York: Routledge, 2016), [Calibre E-book viewer EPUB], retrieved from https://bodleian.ldls.org.uk/

CHAPTER 8

Daenerys the Unready: Advice and Ruling in Meereen

Shiloh Carroll

In the book series *A Song of Ice and Fire*, George R.R. Martin demonstrates the importance of advice and being able to trust one's advisors to have one's best interests at heart. Failure to listen to advice or failure to recognize the conflicting interests of one's advisors are major factors in the deaths of Robert Baratheon, Ned Stark, Robb Stark, and Viserys Targaryen, and the trials and tribulations of Stannis Baratheon, Cersei Lannister, and Theon Greyjoy. Yet most of those leaders or would-be leaders are adult men, already set in their ways. Halfway around the world, Daenerys Targaryen, a 15-year-old girl, finds herself mired in some of the thickest political intrigue in the novels. Unlike the leaders mentioned above, Daenerys purposefully surrounds herself with diverse advisors and earnestly listens to their council. However, each of her advisors has his or her own agenda, a model of queenship they wish Daenerys to follow, a plan for Meereen that does not necessarily match Daenerys' own. Meereen itself is complicated, with a culture heavily reliant on slavery, which Daenerys unilaterally and immediately outlaws upon conquering the city. Daenerys is pulled in so many conflicting directions by her advisors and

S. Carroll (✉)
Tennessee State University, Nashville, TN, USA

© The Author(s) 2020
Z. E. Rohr, L. Benz (eds.), *Queenship and the Women of Westeros*,
Queenship and Power, https://doi.org/10.1007/978-3-030-25041-6_8

169

the needs and expectations of the people that she nearly loses her own identity and utterly fails to successfully rule Meereen.[1]

A historical English king from the Viking Age, Æthelred II (r. CE 978–1013, 1014–1016), bears many similarities to Daenerys: young, inexperienced, on a throne not meant to be his, surrounded by advisors who have their own agendas. After his reign, he came to be called Æthelred Unræd, which has been modernized to "Æthelred the Unready," though a more accurate translation would be "Æthelred the Ill-Advised."[2] His lack of advisement and his son's dissatisfaction with his leadership led to several years of Danish occupation of the English throne and ruined his legacy and reputation for nearly a thousand years afterwards. While modern scholars generally recognize that political infighting among the English nobility and church and sustained attacks by the Danes after nearly a generation of peace were major contributors to Æthelred's loss of the throne, chroniclers and scholars following his reign placed all the blame on Æthelred himself, coining his nickname.[3]

While argument could be made that every character in authority in *A Song of Ice and Fire* could be labelled "*unræd*," most of their failures come from ignoring the advice of their good advisors or failing to recognize bad ones. For example, as Sylwia Borowska-Szerszun argues elsewhere in this volume, Cersei Lannister is particularly bad at differentiating "advice" from "blandishment." Daenerys, on the other hand, is surrounded by advisors who actively work against her best interests and stated goals. Daenerys' various advisors tend to fall into one of three categories: those whose goals align with hers (the loyalists), those who achieve their own ends by allying themselves with her (the self-serving), and those who work only for their own interests (the disloyal). Added to this tangle are the prophecies of the Undying and Quaithe of the Shadow (discussed in more detail below), the vague nature of which combine to create a constant low-level paranoia in all of Daenerys' inner debates when deciding who can be trusted and who to listen to. Thus, while advice and advising are important in every political storyline in the books, Daenerys is the most "*unræd*" due to the number of advisors who do not share her ideals. Yet Daenerys' own vision of a good leader is one who insists on as many viewpoints as possible to help her make decisions: "A queen must listen to all," she tells Jorah, "[t]he highborn and the low, the strong and the weak, the noble and the venal. One voice may speak you false, but in many there is always truth to be found."[4]

None of this is to suggest that Daenerys is based on Æthelred, or that Martin had Æthelred specifically in mind when writing *A Song of Ice and Fire*. Considering his other influences from English history—the Wars of the Roses, the Hundred Years' War, William of Normandy, and so forth[5]—it is exceedingly likely that Martin is aware of Æthelred, whether or not this knowledge consciously influenced *A Song of Ice and Fire*. Council and advice are major themes in Martin's novels, as is his historical inspiration, and using the idea of "*unræd*" to examine the fictional Daenerys can help illuminate these themes.

"Only Lies Offend Me, Never Honest Counsel": The Loyalists

Two of Daenerys' advisors genuinely want her to succeed, but they have different ideas of what success requires, and they have their own underlying goals that affect the advice they provide. Jorah Mormont travels with Daenerys from the beginning of *A Game of Thrones*, providing her with information on Dothraki customs to help her assimilate into the culture. Jorah wants Daenerys to be a strong queen, a conqueror, to retake Westeros so he can go home—for Jorah was a Westerosi noble, Lord of Bear Island in the North, until he was caught selling slaves and condemned to death by Ned Stark, then fled Westeros rather than submit to beheading.[6] Jorah's values do not entirely align with Daenerys'; he does not condemn slavery, and he sees rape in warfare as inevitable, even allowable as a reward for the warriors' work. His advice always focuses on and pushes Daenerys towards conquest, whatever the cost. He does not understand or agree with Daenerys' desire to be a compassionate and fair leader, arguing against relying on honour in war; when Daenerys disagrees with his suggestion that she buy a slave army on the grounds that her brother, Rhaegar, whom she idolizes, only ever led free men into battle, he replies:

> My queen [...] all you say is true. But Rhaegar lost on the Trident. He lost the battle, he lost the war, he lost the kingdom, and he lost his life. His blood swirled downriver with the rubies from his breastplate, and Robert the Usurper rode over his corpse to steal the Iron Throne. Rhaegar fought valiantly, Rhaegar fought nobly, Rhaegar fought honorably. And Rhaegar *died*.[7]

Jorah's primary goal is to be pardoned of his crime of selling slaves, which he does not see as a true crime, so that he can return home to Westeros. He initially serves as Varys' spy on the Targaryens with the promise that said spying will lead to a pardon and reinstatement of his social status.

Only when Daenerys hatches her dragon eggs, showing the potential to become powerful enough to retake the Iron Throne, and he decides he is in love with her, does he cease acting as a double agent and serve her exclusively. Yet his motivations are still ultimately selfish; he sees that Daenerys' conquest of Westeros would allow him to return, and he also wants Daenerys. His desire for her leads him to advise her not to trust anyone else, and while in many cases this is good advice—Pyatt Pree, Xaro Xhoan Daxos, Daario Naharis, and the masters of Astapor are *not* trustworthy—he primarily seeks to increase her dependence on him and stay in her favour by alienating her from others. Of course, this backfires when he forces Barristan to reveal his identity to Daenerys, as Barristan knows about Jorah's spying.[8] Jorah's generally good advice cannot counteract what Daenerys sees as treason, and she banishes him.[9]

Barristan Selmy serves as a counterpoint to Jorah. He wants Daenerys to retake Westeros as well, but he wants her to be a good leader, not just a conqueror. If his statements are taken entirely at face value, his priority is to see the throne returned to the rightful dynasty.[10] However, since this priority did not exist until he was dismissed from the Kingsguard by Joffrey Baratheon, the possibility remains that Barristan wants to be reinstated, to serve his purpose as a knight, and to aid Daenerys in revenge for his humiliation. Either way, Barristan's advice is always focused on Daenerys returning to Westeros and being the kind of queen the people will love and he can serve without qualm. To those ends, he advises Daenerys against buying an army of Unsullied, claiming that the people of Westeros will not accept a sovereign who arrives at the head of a slave army.[11] He strongly disagrees with her plan to trade Drogon for the Unsullied, questioning her judgement in front of strangers and earning a rebuke.[12] During the occupation of Meereen, he frequently urges her to quit the city and return to Westeros instead, as staying in Meereen does not advance her ultimate goal to retake the Iron Throne, instead actively harming it as her army slowly bleeds. Yet even Barristan underestimates Daenerys' compassion for her people, and she refuses to abandon all the slaves she has freed and all the Meereenese who accepted her rule.[13]

Although Jorah and Barristan have different methods and different motivations, they both want Daenerys to succeed, to take the Iron Throne and become queen of Westeros. Their advice is well-meant, and their own goals—to return home and regain their honour and prestige—are secondary. However, Daenerys does not always heed their advice; she frequently consolidates their knowledge and arguments and makes her own choices, which seldom pleases both or either of them. For example, she does not tell them about her plan to use the trade agreement with the Astapori to get Drogon into the city to conquer it.[14] Her decision to stay and rule Meereen rather than immediately sailing west to Westeros directly opposes the consistent advice of both Jorah and Barristan, ultimately leading to her disillusionment and loss of self as the Meereenese advisors manipulate her.

"TO RULE MEEREEN, I MUST WIN THE MEEREENESE": THE SELF-SERVING AND DISLOYAL

Courtenay Konshuh argues that the compilers of Æthelred's annals place more blame on the failure of kingship bonds between Æthelred and his *witan* than on Æthelred as a king, and this failure of loyalty can also be seen as a major contributor to Daenerys' failure to govern well in Meereen.[15] One of Daenerys' first acts in Meereen is to dismiss Jorah from her service, leaving only Barristan as a traditional "sworn sword" who serves her out of loyalty and with honest purpose. To expand on Christopher Roman's discussion of Daenerys' struggles between ethics and politics,[16] throughout *A Storm of Swords*, Jorah and Barristan provide complementary advice—Jorah political, Barristan ethical—that helps Daenerys keep a balance between the two. Yet, despite Jorah's consistent pushing towards political expedience, his motivations are to help Daenerys reach her goal of conquering Westeros. When Daenerys reaches Meereen and replaces Jorah with several Meereenese, her council skews towards the political, and her advisors no longer share her goals. No bond of loyalty exists between Daenerys and her Meereenese advisors, and her rule fails as a result.

Two of Daenerys' Meereenese advisors, Reznak mo Reznak and Skahaz mo Kendak, see Daenerys' rule primarily as a means to advance their own positions in Meereenese society. Both ingratiate themselves to Daenerys, endangering their status and even their lives with the Meereenese loyalists, and offer advice that they believe will help her stabilize the city and consolidate her power—and theirs. In the absence of Jorah, Skahaz is the voice for power and conquest, while Reznak argues for a softer touch and following Ghiskari traditions. Skahaz advocates for harsh punishments and torture; he suggests stopping the Sons of the Harpy and their murders by killing a member of each of the families he calls her enemies. Reznak counters this argument by claiming that the Sons are low-born, not of the noble families, and such an act will anger the gods.[17] When Daenerys does agree to take child hostages against the families' good behaviour, she cannot follow through on the implied threat to retaliate against further murders by killing the children, which angers Skahaz.[18] Both men want her to agree to reopen the fighting pits, Reznak because it would bring in tax money and Skahaz because it would earn her the support of the people against the Sons of the Harpy.[19]

While both appear to be assisting Daenerys in ruling Meereen effectively, their own biases and desires—Skahaz to destroy the ruling elite of Meereen and Reznak to stabilize Meereen so he can keep his position—clearly colour their advice. When Daenerys disappears on Drogon, Reznak continues to serve Hizdahr zo Loraq as seneschal, while Skahaz organizes the Brazen Beasts—his answer to the Sons of the Harpy—in resistance against Hizdahr's rule.[20] Their ultimate loyalty to Daenerys is questionable; Reznak appears comfortable serving whoever is in charge, while Skahaz wants to finish Daenerys' overthrow of the previous social and political order, with or without Daenerys.

Finally, Daenerys is advised by several people who put their own goals and priorities before hers, giving her advice that will advance these priorities rather than Daenerys', usually packaged in a way that looks like it helps Daenerys. Xaro Xhoan Daxos in Qarth is the first of these; he offers Daenerys the ships necessary to sail to Westeros and retake the Iron Throne if she will marry him. He does not mention the Qartheen wedding custom that would allow him to request one of her dragons, a request she would not be allowed to refuse; Jorah warns her of this tradition.[21] When Xaro visits her in Meereen, he attempts to convince her that slavery is natural and necessary and once again offers her ships, this time without the price of marriage. In this case, his primary motivation is to remove a disruptive influence from the region so Slavers Bay, Qarth, and Volantis can go back to business as usual.[22]

In Meereen, Galazza Galare and Hizdahr zo Loraq are the primary offenders in this regard. Both want Meereen to go back to the way it was, both encourage actions that would align Daenerys with Ghiskari custom, and either or both may actually be the leader of the resistance, known as "the Harpy." Galazza repeatedly tells Daenerys she should marry a Meereenese man so that the city will more readily accept her rule (Skahaz "volunteers" for this duty).[23] Specifically, Galazza wants Daenerys to marry Hizdahr. When Daenerys finally agrees to the marriage, Galazza pushes her to adhere to all the Ghiskari wedding traditions so the gods and the people of the city will see it as a true union.[24] Galazza also insists that Daenerys wear a *tokar*, the garment of Ghiskari nobility (the connotations of which will be explored below) rather than her Dothraki outfits, in which she is more comfortable. Without a *tokar*, Galazza tells her, she will "forever remain a stranger amongst us, a grotesque outlander, a barbarian conqueror." (Brown Ben Plumm tells her essentially the same thing, but more succinctly: "Man wants to be king o' the rabbits, he'd best wear a pair o' floppy ears."[25]) In order to rule Meereen, Galazza argues, she must be Ghiscari, which includes agreeing to marry a Meereenese man, dressing as a Meereenese noble, and ultimately allowing slavery to return to Slavers Bay.

Hizdahr's motivations have much more to do with his own financial well-being, though he appears to have ties to the Sons of the Harpy. His first appearance is at one of Daenerys' audiences, where he requests for the sixth time that she open the fighting pits, and she turns him down for the sixth time. Daenerys is aware that after the conquest, when she abolished slavery and closed the fighting pits, Hizdahr bought up the nearly worthless property, and reopening could make him a wealthy man.[26] However, all his arguments emphasize Meereenese culture, religion, and tradition and the opportunity for the city to make money. Likewise, Hizdahr agrees to marry Daenerys out of duty to his people and as protection for Daenerys against all those in Slavers Bay she has angered, though his desire for power is transparent.[27]

To further complicate Daenerys' decision-making processes, she also has prophecies from the Undying of Qarth, who warned her about three acts of treason against her: "once for blood and once for gold and once for love."[28] Likewise, Quaithe gives her several warnings and prophecies, just as difficult for Daenerys to parse as the prophecies of the Undying; Quaithe warns her about "Kraken and dark flame, lion and griffin, the sun's son and the mummer's dragon."[29] The reader, having access to more of the story than Daenerys, may recognize Victarion Greyjoy, Moqorro, Tyrion Lannister, Jon Connington, Quentyn Martell, and (possibly) the boy calling himself Aegon Targaryen (more popularly, "Young Griff") in these statements, but Daenerys obviously does not. The prophecies are never far from Daenerys' thoughts, and she is constantly trying to decide which of the treasons has already happened and who might yet betray her. When Jorah's betrayal is revealed, he says "I have loved you," and she thinks, "And there it was. *Three treasons you will know. Once for blood and once for gold and once for love.*"[30] For the rest of *A Dance with Dragons*, she waits for the third treason, having decided Jorah's was the one for love and Mirri Maz Duur's was the one for blood. The prophecies and the conspiracy of the Harpy in Meereen feed into the innate tendency of Targaryens towards madness, a tendency that Daenerys has already shown in her willingness to burn Mirri alive and torture young girls in front of their father.

"Best Wear a Pair o' Floppy Ears": The Effects of Bad Advice

The result of all this advice and the prophecies is Daenerys slowly losing her identity and compromising her principles. Rather than leaving Meereen alone or conquering it and moving on, she occupies it against the advice of both Jorah and Barristan. Once there, she begins wearing the clothing of the Meereenese upper classes, a garment designed specifically to be impractical:

> [A] clumsy thing, a long loose shapeless sheet that had to be wound around her hips and under an arm and over a shoulder, its dangling fringes carefully layered and displayed. Worn too loose, it was like to fall off; wound tight, it would tangle, trip, and bind. Even wound properly, the *tokar* required its wearer to hold it in place with the left hand. Walking in a *tokar* required small, mincing steps and exquisite balance, lest one tread upon those heavy trailing fringes. It was not a garment meant for any man who had to work. The *tokar* was a *master's* garment, a sign of wealth and power.[31]

Daenerys exchanges her more comfortable Dothraki vest, trousers, and boots for this uncomfortable and impractical outfit, her "floppy ears," at Galazza's advice. The *tokar* is a representation of Meereen's slave culture, its purposeful impracticality possible only because the masters have slaves to do every bit of work for them, including dressing them in the *tokar*. Daenerys donning a *tokar* is a very small concession to the slave culture of Meereen, a wedge that opens her to further concessions at Galazza and Hizdahr's urging. This is not the only time that Daenerys dresses to match her surroundings; in Qarth, she wears a traditional Qartheen gown that leaves one breast bare. In both circumstances, she is attempting to blend in to the local nobility to gain acceptance and not be regarded as a barbarian. Notably, both attempts at wearing "floppy ears" to gain the acceptance of the "rabbits" fail.

Daenerys also locks up two of her dragons, giving up part of her power—the dragons are the main reason people fear her—and actively repressing part of her identity; the dragons carry much symbolism, but part of it is the Targaryen heritage. This choice is, of course, for good reason, as the dragons have been wreaking havoc among the farmers, and Drogon kills and eats a small child. While the dragons represent her power, they also represent the Targaryen madness and an unchecked monstrosity. Daenerys does not wish to be a monster, and so she locks up her "children" and, by extension, her own monstrous tendencies, which have shown in her willingness to torture people and forcibly conquer a not-insignificant swath of Essos.[32] However, in suppressing this part of herself, she becomes more open to the influence of her advisors, leaning towards the political rather than the ethical, as Roman frames it.[33] By the time Daenerys marries Hizdahr, she has agreed to everything he and Galazza have demanded, and all she has left is a promise that slavery will not occur within the walls of Meereen, while the rest of Slavers Bay returns to its old ways. She reflects that her peace feels more like defeat and rages that the Yunkish have opened a slave market within sight of the walls of Meereen.[34]

Daenerys reaches her breaking point at the opening of Daznak's Pit, where the choices she has made in listening to Galazza and Hizdahr become viscerally real in the bloodshed and the people's reaction to death. She removes her veils, then unwinds her *tokar*, dispensing of the trappings of Meereenese master culture; when Irri asks what she is doing, Daenerys replies, "Taking off my floppy ears."[35] She repeats the line a moment later, claiming that the people were not cheering for her, but for the image she had presented by wearing the *tokar* and attending the opening of the pit as was expected of a Meereenese noble. Faced with the consequences of her choices, she rejects them, removing the *tokar*, then reuniting with Drogon, her largest and wildest dragon, the one whom she was unable to imprison beneath the pyramid. She rescues him from the Meereenese fighters and flies away on his back, leaving Meereen behind.

In the Dothraki Sea, Daenerys cannot convince Drogon to return her to Meereen, so she begins to walk back. The trip is a misery, a nightmare of delirium and bodily fluids as she makes poor choices in food and drink. Yet the journey allows her to shed the last of what Meereen has made her; she remembers who she was before Meereen and hallucinates Jorah and Quaithe reminding her who she is. She physically purges herself as well, vomiting and defecating, and either experiencing an intense menstrual cycle or possibly miscarrying an early pregnancy. The isolation allows her to consider her actions, the wisdom of listening to the various advisors, and her future plans. Ultimately, she strikes a balance between human and dragon; she does not give in to the full wildness of the dragon by living with Drogon on his mountain, but she does eat charred horsemeat with her bare hands. When Khal Jhaqo's *khalasar* discovers her, she is covered in horse blood, with Drogon standing behind her. Daenerys' ultimate decisions with regard to Meereen will likely be revealed in *The Winds of Winter*.

"I Will Answer Injustice with Justice": Adaptation and Simplification

Unfortunately, *Game of Thrones*, the HBO series based on *A Song of Ice and Fire*, severely reduced the number of advisors Daenerys has at any one time, which caused a loss of political depth. Gone are Galazza Galare, Skahaz mo Kendak, Reznak mo Reznak, Brown Ben Plumm, and Daenerys' *khalasar*. Her council consists of Hizdahr zo Loraq, Barristan, Grey Worm (the commander of her Unsullied forces), Daario Naharis, Mossador (a former slave), (peripherally) Missandei, and (later) Tyrion Lannister. Hizdahr speaks for the entirety of the Meereenese nobility, Mossador for the freedmen of Meereen, Grey Worm for Daenerys' military, Daario for her mercenaries, and Barristan for good rulership and preparation to return to Westeros. As in the books, Jorah is dismissed from Daenerys' service soon after they arrive in Meereen.[36] Throughout Season Five, Daenerys' council is reduced bit by bit: Mossador is executed for murder,[37] Barristan is cut down in the street by the Sons of the Harpy,[38] and Hizdahr is killed in Daznak's Pit by the Sons of the Harpy.[39] Thus, Daenerys' council as she fights the last battle against Volantis, Astapor, and Yunkai consists of only Tyrion (who replaces Barristan), Grey Worm, and Missandei—all people who are personally loyal to her.[40]

Unlike Daenerys' book-advisors, the show-advisors tend to have little internal life or motivations of their own. Thus, it is nearly impossible to sort them into the same categories as their book counterparts. Jorah's motivations have been shifted further towards wanting a romantic relationship with Daenerys, mostly ignoring his desire to return home and regain his birthright. Barristan still wishes Daenerys to be a better ruler than the Lannisters, but his murder removes him from her advisors in the show (he is still very much alive in the books). Mossador essentially replaces Skahaz and Reznak, advocating for harsh treatment of the masters, but out of revenge as a former slave, not out of a desire for his own power or the stability of the city. Hizdahr does argue for the overall stability of the city and Daenerys being accepted as rightful ruler of Meereen, though (as discussed below) his motivation is opaque and his authority in the city lacking in comparison to his book counterpart. Unlike Daenerys' book advisors, most of whom hide their true motivations beneath the surface for the reader to tease out, the show versions are flat and shallow copies.

Removing most of Daenerys' Meereenese advisors has the side effect of reducing the depth of the politics involved in attempting to rule and remake Meereen. Daenerys no longer faces pressure to act more like a Meereenese noble and less like a conquering invader; she never dons a *tokar* in the show, instead opting for gowns with halter necklines that resemble slave collars.[41] This choice visibly aligns her with the slaves she has freed and matches her clear disinterest in integrating with the noble class of Meereen, of whom only Hizdahr appears on screen with any regularity.[42] Without this pressure, Daenerys' choice to marry Hizdahr (without his assurance that he will stop the Sons of the Harpy attacks, as he appears to have no influence over them at all) is nonsensical and irrational, especially as it comes just after she feeds one of the masters to her dragons.[43] In removing the political pressures and those who bring them to bear on Daenerys, yet leaving many of Daenerys' decisions in place, the show reduces Daenerys to an impulsive, irrational, even bloodthirsty queen rather than a young girl doing the best she can with the advice she is given. These impulses cannot even be attributed to the same low-level paranoia she experiences in the books, as the prophecies from the House of the Undying and Quaithe are left out of the show entirely. Rather, she becomes more like her father, Aerys the Mad King: irrational, violent, fire-obsessed, and easily manipulated.

Game of Thrones also has an unfortunate tendency to portray Daenerys requiring the control of a man or men in order to check her violent tendencies. Barristan, Jorah, and Tyrion frequently remind her of her Targaryen heritage and how Aerys treated his subjects to prevent her from unleashing her dragons on cities. Notably, it is just after Barristan's death but before Tyrion reaches her that she executes a Meereenese master by feeding him to Rhaegal and Viserion. Without guidance, Daenerys gives in to anger and a specific brand of Targaryen violence. Late in Season Seven, Tyrion laments that he has failed in stopping her from executing

Randyll and Dickon Tarly via dragonfire, and he and Varys discuss how to control and manipulate her so that she will not become Aerys.[44] Even later, Tyrion tells Cersei that Daenerys will make a better queen than Cersei because she is aware of her own tendencies and impulses and has acquired advisors who will "check" them.[45] (Daenerys herself never says anything that indicates this is why she has named Tyrion her Hand.) Daenerys' ultimate goal is to "break the wheel" of Westeros' political system, though what that means, how she intends to go about it, and what Westeros will look like when she is finished are not explored or explained in any depth.

Season Eight brings this failure in adaptation of Daenerys to its logical conclusion. She is shown refusing to listen to Tyrion anymore, and that is framed as a sign that she is finally succumbing to Targaryen madness rather than recognizing his failure to lead her to victory in Westeros. Her advisors turn against her; Varys plans to replace her with Jon Snow (whose heritage as "Aegon Targaryen," son of Rhaegar Targaryen and Lyanna Stark, has been revealed), for which Daenerys executes him.[46] When Daenerys' army attacks King's Landing, Tyrion tells her over and over that sounding the bells and opening the gates is a sign of surrender and she should stand down, but when it happens, she instead unleashes Drogon on the city. With everyone's worst fears of "Mad Queen Daenerys" realized, Tyrion counsels Jon to save the country by killing Daenerys—which he does.[47]

The oversimplification of politics in *Game of Thrones* radically changes Daenerys' character so that she is not struggling with layers of intrigue and the needs and desires of disparate peoples while attempting to decide who best to trust. The Daenerys of the books is a sympathetic, understandable young woman doing the best she can with her experience and the advice given by those surrounding her, a young woman who believably could make a good queen. Instead of being *unræd*, the Daenerys of the show is a tyrant, ruling through fear and violence, and not an improvement over her father or Cersei Lannister, who sits on the Iron Throne in Season Seven. (Kavita Mudan Finn's chapter in this volume explains why Cersei is also not a good leader in either the books or the show.) However, the (probably unintentional) undertone of her storyline is that a woman's failure to listen to a man's advice, even if that advice is bad, is evidence of madness[48] and said woman must be stopped by any means necessary, then replaced by a man.[49]

"He Held His Kingdom in Much Tribulation and Difficulty": Conclusions

The parallels between Æthelred and Daenerys are interesting and remarkable. Both rulers make poor choices in *witan* and ealdormen, following the advice of those who have ulterior motivations and priorities. Both lose their kingdoms; Æthelred physically loses his to invading forces aided by those inside his court, and Daenerys loses hers more essentially, remaining in charge yet having compromised away everything she hoped for. Yet neither can be fully blamed for the trouble in their kingdoms, as many other people are involved in every issue and failure. In fact, Martin's fiction may well provide insight into how the best intentions of rulers and leaders can go wildly astray when those rulers are not provided with good counsel, and how even well-intentioned leaders can make poor decisions. This is, in fact, one of the themes he mentions frequently, that being a good man does not necessarily mean being a good king, complaining that fantasy often glosses over the details of what being a "good king" looks like.[50] Interestingly, good kingship (and queenship) is a major theme in Anglo-Saxon works such as *Beowulf*, as Kris Swank has discussed elsewhere in this volume. The chroniclers of *The Anglo-Saxon Chronicle* clearly found Æthelred lacking as a king, whereas Martin explores the difference and conflict between intention and outcome.

Of course, the largest difference between Æthelred and Daenerys is the way in which their stories are told. The chronicler of his reign in the *Anglo-Saxon Chronicle* was writing several years after Æthelred's death, with the benefit of hindsight to see how Æthelred's reign went wrong. Simon Keynes points out that the chronicler "telescoped" Æthelred's reign by focusing on one or two incidents per year and "created the impression that the invasions were the only theme worthy of attention and that the country suffered continuously under them."[51] As the centuries progressed, historians and historical commentators such as William of Malmesbury and Henry of Huntingdon added to Æthelred's poor reputation, with "*unræd*" appearing in the early thirteenth century.[52] It is easy to look back at Æthelred and view him as a failed king who lost the country to the Danes—through laziness, or stupidity, or being easily led, or all three—without exploring the immense sociological and political context of the time. However, the difference in styles and purposes between histories and novels gives readers the insight into Daenerys that they cannot get from Æthelred. In this way, Martin might provide an insight into history by presenting a detailed, intimate examination of the difficulties of rule that a reader could then apply to Æthelred. Perhaps instead of viewing Æthelred and Daenerys as "unready," readers can find more depth in their history and come to understand the meaning of "*unræd.*"

NOTES

1. At least by the end of *A Dance with Dragons*, whether she returns to Meereen and manages to retake and rule the city before leaving for Westeros remains to be seen in the forthcoming *The Winds of Winter*.
2. Simon Keynes points out that the nickname is also a play on words, as "Æthelred" means "noble counsel"; "wise counsel, my foot!" is how Keynes interprets "Æthelred Unræd" ("A Tale of Two Kings: Alfred the Great and Æthelred the Unready," *Transactions of the Royal Historical Society* 36 [1986], 195).
3. Charles Insley, "Southumbria," in *A Companion to the Early Middle Ages: Britain and Ireland, c. 500–c.1100 CE*, edited by Pauline Shefford, Malden: Wiley-Blackwell, 2009, 323; N.J. Higham, *The Death of Anglo-Saxon England*, Gloucestershire: Stutton Publishing, 1997, 18.
4. George R.R. Martin, *A Storm of Swords*, New York: Bantam Spectra, 2000; Mass Market Reissue Edition, 2005, 112.
5. For a more thorough exploration of the historical English influences on *A Song of Ice and Fire*, see my essay "Barbarian Colonizers and Post-Colonialism in Westeros and Britain" in *Game of Thrones versus History*, edited by Brian A. Pavlac, New York: John A. Wiley Press, 2017.
6. Martin, *A Game of Thrones*, 37, 111.
7. Martin, *A Storm of Swords*, 303.
8. Ibid., 792.
9. Ibid., 990.
10. Ibid., 791–792.
11. Ibid., 320.
12. Ibid., 370.
13. Martin, *A Dance with Dragons*, New York: Bantam Spectra, 2011; Mass Market Edition, 2013, 236.
14. Martin, *A Storm of Swords*, 380.
15. Courtenay Konshuh, "Anraed in Their Unraed: The Æthelredian Annals (983–1016) and Their Presentation of King and Advisors," *English Studies* 97, no. 2 (2016), 141.
16. Christopher Roman, "The Ethical Movement of Daenerys Targaryen," *Studies in Medievalism* XXIII (2014), 61–68.
17. Martin, *A Dance with Dragons*, 42.

18. Ibid., 322.
19. Ibid., 168.
20. Ibid., 799, 810.
21. Martin, *A Clash of Kings*, New York: Bantam Spectra, 1999; Mass Market Reissue Edition, 2005, 584.
22. Martin, *A Dance with Dragons*, 227–231.
23. Ibid., 46, 323.
24. Ibid., 526.
25. Ibid., 40.
26. Ibid., 45.
27. Ibid., 328.
28. Martin, *A Clash of Kings*, 706.
29. Martin, *A Dance with Dragons*, 166.
30. Martin, *A Storm of Swords*, 990.
31. Martin, *A Dance with Dragons*, 40.
32. It is also significant that Daenerys imprisons the dragons beneath the Great Pyramid in Meereen; literally, the dragons have been buried under one of the most ostentatious representations of power and mastery in the city.
33. Roman, 66–67.
34. Ibid., 723–724.
35. Ibid., 762.
36. "The Mountain and the Viper," *Game of Thrones*, written by David Benioff & D.B. Weiss, directed by Alex Graves (HBO, 2014).
37. "The House of Black and White," *Game of Thrones*, written by David Benioff & D.B. Weiss, directed by Michael Slovis (HBO, 2015).
38. "Sons of the Harpy," *Game of Thrones*, written by Dave Hill, directed by Mark Mylod (HBO, 2015).
39. "The Dance of Dragons," *Game of Thrones*, written by David Benioff & D.B. Weiss, directed by David Nutter (HBO, 2015).
40. "Battle of the Bastards," *Game of Thrones*, written by David Benioff & D.B. Weiss, directed by Miguel Sapochnik (HBO, 2016).
41. See, for example, her white halter gown in "First of His Name," *Game of Thrones*, written by David Benioff & D.B. Weiss, directed by Michelle MacLaren (HBO, 2014).
42. "Great Masters" appear in the early episodes of Season Four as Daenerys takes Meereen and crucifies the 163 masters, but do not appear with any prominence again until Daenerys threatens them and feeds one to her dragons in "Kill the Boy" (*Game of Thrones*, written by Bryan Cogman, directed by Jeremy Podeswa [HBO, 2015]).
43. "Kill the Boy."
44. "Eastwatch," *Game of Thrones*, written by Dave Hill, directed by Matt Shakman (HBO, 2017).

45. "The Dragon and the Wolf," *Game of Thrones*, written by David Benioff & D.B. Weiss, directed by Jeremy Podeswa (HBO, 2017).

46. "The Bells," *Game of Thrones*, written by David Benioff & D.B. Weiss, directed by Miguel Sapochnik (HBO, 2019).

47. "The Iron Throne," *Game of Thrones*, written and directed by David Benioff & D.B. Weiss (HBO, 2019).

48. "Madness" is, of course, never defined in terms of actual mental health, and instead is framed in stereotypical terms: irrationality, violence, and even megalomania.

49. In this case, Bran Stark, who rules the six kingdoms of Westeros at the end of the series.

50. Charlie Jane Anders, "George R.R. Martin: The Complete Unedited Interview," *Observation Deck*, 23 Sept. 2013, http://observationdeck.kinja. com/george-r-r-martin-the-complete-unedited-interview-886117845; "George R.R. Martin on Machiavellian Politics in *Game of Thrones*," *BBC*, 2 Dec. 2013, https://www.youtube.com/watch?v=1mtExw7fbVM

51. Simon Keynes, "The Declining Reputation of Æthelred the Unready," in *Æthelred the Unready: Papers from the Millenary Conference*, edited by David Hill, Oxford: BAR, 1978, 233.

52. Ibid., 238–239.

Bibliography

Anders, Charlie Jane. "George R.R. Martin: The Complete Unedited Interview." *Observation Deck*. 23 Sept. 2013. http://observationdeck.kinja.com/george-r-r-martin-the-complete-unedited-interview-886117845. Accessed 24 Feb. 2016.

"The Bells." *Game of Thrones*. Written by David Benioff & D.B. Weiss. Directed by Miguel Sapochnik. HBO, 2019.

"The Dragon and the Wolf." *Game of Thrones*. Written by David Benioff & D.B. Weiss. Directed by Jeremy Podeswa. HBO, 2017.

"Eastwatch." *Game of Thrones*. Written by Dave Hill. Directed by Matt Shakman. HBO, 2017.

"George R.R. Martin on Machiavellian Plots in *Game of Thrones*." *BBC*, 2 Dec. 2013. https://www.youtube.com/watch?v=1mtExw7fbVM. Accessed 18 Jan. 2018.

Higham, N.J. *The Death of Anglo-Saxon England*. Gloucestershire: Stutton Publishing, 1997.

Insley, Charles. "Southumbria." *A Companion to the Early Middle Ages: Britain and Ireland, c. 500–c. 1100*. Edited by Pauline Stafford. Malden: Wiley-Blackwell, 2009. 322–340.

"The Iron Throne." *Game of Thrones*. Written and directed by David Benioff & D.B. Weiss. HBO, 2019.

Keynes, Simon. "A Tale of Two Kings: Alfred the Great and Æthelred the Unready." *Transactions of the Royal Historical Society* 36 (1986): 195–217.

———. "The Declining Reputation of King Æthelred the Unready." *Ethelred the Unready: Papers from the Millenary Conference*. Ed. David Hill. Oxford: BAR, 1978. 227–253.

"The House of Black and White." *Game of Thrones*. Written by David Benioff & D.B. Weiss. Directed by Michael Slovis. HBO, 2015.

"Kill the Boy." *Game of Thrones*. Written by Bryan Cogman. Directed by Jeremy Podeswa. HBO, 2015.

Konshuh, Courtnay. "Anraed in Their Unraed: The Æthelredian Annals (983–1016) and Their Presentation of King and Advisors." *English Studies* 97.2 (2016): 140–162.

Martin, George R.R. *A Game of Thrones*. New York: Bantam Spectra 1996. Mass Market Reissue Edition, 2005.

———. *A Clash of Kings*. New York: Bantam Spectra, 1999. Mass Market Reissue Edition, 2005.

———. *A Storm of Swords*. New York: Bantam Spectra, 2000. Mass Market Reissue Edition, 2005.

———. *A Dance with Dragons*. New York: Bantam Spectra, 2011. Mass Market Edition, 2013.

"The Mountain and the Viper." *Game of Thrones*. Written by David Benioff & D.B. Weiss. Directed by Alex Graves. HBO, 2014.

Roman, Christopher. "The Ethical Movement of Daenerys Targaryen." *Studies in Medievalism* XXIII (2014): 61–68.

"Sons of the Harpy." *Game of Thrones*. Written by Dave Hill. Directed by Mark Mylod. HBO, 2015.

PART III

The Role of Advice

CHAPTER 9

The Royal Minorities of *Game of Thrones*

Charles E. Beem

In the penultimate episode of Season One of *Games of Thrones* (afterwards *GOT*), King Joffrey Baratheon impetuously ordered the beheading of Eddard "Ned" Stark following a public trial before the people of King's Landing, the capital city of the Iron Throne of Westeros. Prior to this event, Joffrey had seemingly agreed to honour the requests of his mother, Dowager Queen Cersei, and his fiancée, Ned's daughter Sansa Stark, to spare Ned's life after he confessed to treason. The crowds, expecting Joffrey to be merciful, were shocked by the violence of this deed ordered by a teenaged minority king, revealing a streak of cruelty that had hitherto been concealed from his subjects.

Joffrey is reminiscent of several boy kings in history, such as Richard II of England (r. 1377–1399), an intelligent but impetuous youth who became king at the age of ten. As a teenage king who cared little for sage advice and counsel, Richard was thwarted by the more mature members of the nobility, including his own uncles, in a series of violent confrontations during his teenage years, as Joffrey was restrained by both his grandfather Tywin Lannister and his uncle Tyrion.[1] But as Richard matured into his majority reign, he nursed the desire for revenge, culminating in savage

C. E. Beem (✉)
Department of History, University of North Carolina at Pembroke, Pembroke, NC, USA

© The Author(s) 2020
Z. E. Rohr, L. Benz (eds.), *Queenship and the Women of Westeros*, Queenship and Power, https://doi.org/10.1007/978-3-030-25041-6_9

reprisals on those lords who had inhibited his teenage prerogative. For these actions, Richard was later deposed and murdered by his cousin Henry of Bolingbroke, who assumed his throne as the first Lancastrian king, while Joffrey met his own violent end by poisoning through the confederacy of Lady Olenna, matriarch of the Tyrell clan, and Petyr Baelish, a loutish lord perennially looking for his own self-serving opportunities.

Richard II's lack of a direct heir created the dynastic instability that later erupted into the English Wars of the Roses (1455–1485 A.D.) in which the mothers of English boy kings and princes played an authentically historical "game of thrones" on behalf of the rights of their sons.[2] Historian Brian Pavlac has written that George R.R. Martin, the author of *A Song of Fire and Ice* series of novels that spawned *GOT*, was especially drawn to the Wars of the Roses, basing the Lannisters on the Lancastrians, and the Starks on the House of York.[3] Besides the Wars of the Roses, Martin was also entranced by The Hundred Years War between England and France (1437–1453 A.D.), another dynastic conflict fought over who should be the rightful claimant to the French throne.[4] As adapted from the book series, *GOT* is a form of *medievalism*, a literary genre which mines medieval history for content, which is reflected through the lens of the author's own contemporary prejudices and understandings.[5] Martin was influenced by such luminaries in this field as J.R.R. Tolkien, the author of the *Lord of the Rings* trilogy, but he wanted to get away from the usual tropes of medieval fantasy literature, such as damsel in distress love stories, or the black and white dichotomy between good guys and bad guys.

Instead, Martin was interested in creating a more nuanced medieval culture in which the supposed ideals of chivalry, coupled with the reality of endemic violence, misogyny, and dynastic instability, render *GOT* a kind of postmodern form of medieval fantasy in which love and romance usually ends in death while knightly virtues are constantly compromised by the cruel and harsh realities of dynastic struggle in Westeros and Essos.[6] Like the medieval European societies upon which it is based, the kingdoms of Westeros are both patriarchal and male dominant, with the principal female characters, Cersei Lannister, Daenerys Targaryen, and Catelyn and Sansa Stark, all fighting and chafing against the structural boundaries of their female subordination.[7]

In the process of constructing the dynamic elements of the storyline, royal minorities represent an obvious historical model to create the sense of dynastic instability that is at the core of *GOT*. Minority reigns by their very nature represent an inherently unstable form of kingship, an office best served by the authority of a capable and adult king or queen. Nevertheless, minorities are the unavoidable by-products of hereditary systems of succession, in medieval Europe and in *GOT*, making the conduct of a royal minority the acid test of a dynasty's strength and power. A successful minority reign, in fact, represented the triumph of dynastic legitimacy, as kingdoms recognized the hereditary rights of an underage king unable to rule personally rather than electing a capable adult candidate with blood ties to the ruling house. This was not the case during the Early Middle Ages in Europe (c. 500–1000 C.E.), whose societies form the historical model for the various kingdoms of Northern Westeros, in which kingship was usually claimed by a capable adult male of royal lineage.

Nevertheless, by the end of this period, minority reigns began to appear as dynasties became more established and the authority of kings increased in scope and sophistication, allowing consultative bodies such as the Anglo-Saxon Witan to influence royal succession patterns. Anglo-Saxon England, in fact, offered examples that made their way straight into the plotlines of *GOT*, such as the election of 13-year-old Edward the Martyr (962–978), eldest son of Edgar, King of the English, which caused a rift among the Anglo-Saxon aristocracy concerning whether an older but illegitimate son should succeed before a younger but legitimate son. According to one account, Edward was a hard-to-handle teenage monarch, much like Joffrey Baratheon, who offended many persons in his court with his intemperate behaviour and speech.[8] This may have contributed to his murder at Corfe Castle, which allowed the accession of his more mild-mannered younger half-brother Aethelred, whose mother, the Dowager Queen Ælfthryth, may have had a hand in Edward's murder, making her also a likely model for the character of Cersei, who also stops at nothing to achieve her own dynastic objectives.[9]

With the onset of the High Middle Ages (c. 1000–1348 C.E.), primogeniture began to emerge as the dominant mechanism for royal succession in the kingdoms of Western Europe, although conquest and election also remained viable means of gaming a medieval European throne. In Christian Europe, increasing emphasis on the sanctity of marriage as the Middle Ages progressed, as systems of feudal tenure hardened into inheritance law, allowed dynastic legitimacy to become a primary means of perpetuating hereditary successions.[10] But not always; both William the Conqueror, Duke of Normandy and later King of England (1028–1087), and Enrique II of Castile (1334–1379) succeeded as bastards yet established royal houses that relied on dynastic legitimacy.[11] In *GOT*, it was the same with House Baratheon, whose patriarch, Orys Baratheon, was rumoured to have descended from a bastard stock of the Targaryens, the dynasty which held the Iron Throne for centuries prior to the Baratheons.[12] This was the dynastic link which allowed Robert Baratheon to consolidate his hold upon the Iron Throne after the murder of the mad king Aerys II. The Baratheon descent is also reminiscent of the English Tudors, who descended from the Beauforts, the bastard offspring of John of Gaunt (1340–1399), Duke of Lancaster and third son of Edward III, and his mistress Kathryn Swynford, whom he later married.

It is curious that none of the religions of Westeros is as ubiquitous as Christianity was in medieval European and Mediterranean cultures. Nevertheless, the Faith of the Seven, the most widely practised religion in Westeros, evidently imposed rules regarding dynastic legitimacy, as both Jon Snow and Ramsey Bolton were stigmatized as bastard sons of their fathers. When Ned Stark threatened to reveal the secret that Joffrey and his siblings Tommen and Mrycella were not the legitimate offspring of King Robert Baratheon and Queen Cersei but conceived in incest with Cersei's twin brother Jaime, it had the potential to unseat the Baratheon dynasty, and ultimately cost Ned his life. Nevertheless, like the European and Mediterranean polities upon which is was based, there does not seem to be any constitutional or legalistic rules regarding the succession to the Seven kingdoms and the Iron Throne. While there is very little discussion of political theory in *GOT*, its political structures are essentially feudal, in which the bonds between king and subject comprise a personal relationship that appears to supersede any form of common or royally issued laws.

The Royal Minorities of Joffrey and Tommen Baratheon

The minority reigns of Cersei's two sons Joffrey and Tommen replicate the dynastic instabilities endemic in historical royal minorities. In England, there were six between 1216 and 1553, and in France, three between 1224 and 1491. Once a king died and the rights of his minor heir were recognized, mothers, uncles, and other powerful individuals such as high-ranking nobles and churchmen all clamoured for control of the person of the minority king and his government, resulting in two recognizable forms of minority government: sole regencies headed by one person and conciliar regencies which governed collectively.[13] In England when the first post-Norman Conquest royal minority occurred in October 1216, members of the church leadership combined with high-ranking members of the nobility to appoint a sole regent, the aged and highly respected William Marshal, Earl of Pembroke, the same hastily assembled group which had elected nine-year old Henry III as King John's successor a few days earlier.[14]

In later English minorities, in response to overeager royal uncles such as John of Gaunt and Humphrey Duke of Gloucester, conciliar regimes were created for the fourteenth- and fifteenth-century minorities of Richard II (1377–1381) and Henry VI (1422–1437).[15] During Henry VI's minority Humphrey Duke of Gloucester was given the courtesy title Protector of England, but during the minorities of Edward V (1483) and Edward VI (1547–1553), the office of Protector became a powerful form of sole regency.[16] But even sole regencies and protectorates relied on some form of collective support from the nobility and the church to survive; those that did not, failed, such as the Protectorate of Edward Seymour, Duke of Somerset (1547–1549), who served as Protector under his nephew Edward VI of England (r. 1547–1553) and was deposed by his consensus-building rival John Dudley, later Duke of Northumberland, who later facilitated his rival's execution for felony.[17]

Oddly enough, there were no female regencies in medieval England on par with those of Cersei, although Isabella of France (1295–1358) famously helped depose her husband Edward II in 1326 and then derailed the power of the regency council appointed in parliament, operating as a *de facto* regent during her son Edward III's teenage minority, which earned her the epitaph, "the She-Wolf of France."[18] In the late fifteenth century, Elizabeth Woodville, consort of the first Yorkist king Edward IV (r. 1461–1483), attempted to exclude her brother-in-law, Richard Duke of Gloucester, from the minority government of her 12-year-old son, Edward V, with disastrous results for that king and his younger brother, who disappeared inside the Tower of London, never to be seen again, after Gloucester usurped the throne. Martin undoubtedly looked back to these determined and ruthless queens as he constructed Cersei's character.

France also provided models for the creation of Cersei's character. Blanche of Castile (1188–1252) served as regent for her son Louis IX, spending much of her son's minority reign displaying a Cersei-like determination in getting her authority recognized and creating consensus among the fractious French nobility amid sustained English invasions of

France.[19] Anne de Beaujeu (1461–1522), daughter of Louis IX and regent for her younger brother Charles VIII, displayed a similar mettle, keeping aristocratic disturbances at bay while playing the role of Renaissance monarch in the breadth of her learning and the conduct of her foreign policy.[20] Neither queen gained fame as a wicked queen like Cersei, although Isabeau of Bavaria (1370–1435), consort of the mentally deranged Charles VI of France, created a large measure of power and influence for herself in the power vacuum created by her husband's incapacity, protecting the rights of her children and negotiating between rival factions at court.[21] Unfortunately, Isabeau's activities resulted in the besmirching of her character as an adulteress, a particularly heinous crime for a queen in monarchies which particularly valued the purity of royal bloodlines.[22]

Isabeau's entry into the arena of royal power was brought on by her husband's diminished mental state, which also allowed the fifteenth-century English Queen Margaret of Anjou to enjoy a measure of political power. Margaret had married the final Lancastrian King, the timorous and pious Henry VI, in 1445, but failed to conceive a child for the first eight years of her marriage. By 1453, after some Englishmen began to consider the King's cousin Richard Duke of York as heir to the throne, Margaret suddenly conceived, right before Henry VI fell into a catatonic state, later giving birth to her son Edward. While Margaret's successful pregnancy resolved the need for a Lancastrian male heir, it was rumoured that Henry VI was impotent, and the actual father was Edmund Beaufort, Duke of Somerset, a collateral descendant of the House of Lancaster. Margaret was forceful in defending her husband's prerogative and her son's succession rights, and she traditionally has been considered a "wicked" queen for her efforts on behalf of the Lancastrian dynasty, an entirely gendered approach to understanding female power in the Middle Ages.[23] Like Isabella of France, Blanche of Castile, and Elizabeth Woodville, Margaret of Anjou was also influential in creating the character of Cersei Lannister.

The rumours of Margaret's alleged infidelities are reflective of the doubts cast on the dynastic legitimacy of Cersei's children Joffrey, Tonnen, and Myrcella, who, as we have seen, were fathered by Cersei's twin Jaime Lannister. King Robert's first Hand (or first minister), John Arryn, was aware of the secret of the paternity of Cersei's children. Murdered before the start of the series by his own wife, Ned Stark comes to the same conclusion after assuming Arryn's position as Hand, which came to an end after a drunken King Robert is gored by a wild boar while hunting. Before he died, Robert dictated in his will that Ned Stark should be regent and protector during the minority of his eldest son Joffrey. Robert's demise is reminiscent of the sudden death of Edward IV in April 1483, who, in his own will, designated his brother Gloucester as protector of the king and kingdom during his son's minority. While Dowager Queen Elizabeth Woodville made a concerted effort to deprive Gloucester of his Protectorship, she failed miserably, bringing down her son's reign with her.[24] Later, as King Richard III, Edward IV's children with Elizabeth Woodville were bastardized by parliamentary statute.[25]

But in *GOT*, the reverse is true. Joffrey's minority reign was not the triumph of the Baratheon dynasty but a palace coup. There were no precedents to follow; success depended upon acting quickly. Once Robert was dead, Cersei moved quickly to fill the vacuum of power, having 13-year-old Joffrey immediately proclaimed king while assuming the role of queen regent during his minority. This was a common strategy in medieval Europe.[26] Royal women often claimed political power in the name of motherhood, as it is a mother's duty to protect her children and her property.[27] But Cersei was also able to do this because the most powerful man in Westeros, her father, Tywin, head of the House Lannister, Lord of Casterley Rock, and former Hand of Aerys II, was on campaign in the Riverlands when her husband died. When Ned Stark confronted her with Robert's will and the truth of Joffrey's paternity, she rips up the will and warns him that "in the game of thrones, you win or you die." As we have seen, it was Ned who dies, a victim of the essentially feudal politics at work here, in which the rule of law has no chance against brute power.

Despite the success of her palace coup, Cersei's regency faced a host of challenges. Her father Tywin, appointed the King's Hand after Joffrey's accession, has no confidence in Cersei as a political leader, sending his younger son Tyrion, who is a dwarf, in his place as acting Hand, rendering Joffrey's minority a hybrid of a sole regency, as Cersei claims the title of Queen Regent, while the male members of her family dominate the Small Council, normally a body that executes the King's will but, in the case of the minority has assumed regal power. When he returns from campaigning in Season Two, Tywin takes charge of the minority government as the King's Hand, riding his defecating horse into the throne room, and working in an uneasy trio with his daughter and his younger son, who both despise each other.

Cersei was not comfortable having to deal with her father and her brother in this arrangement. Tywin was a textbook misogynist, refusing to acknowledge Cersei as an equal in the minority government. Tyrion, despite his physical challenges and his affinity for wine and whores, was a gifted administrator and tactician, but Cersei despises him and refuses to create a working relationship with him. Indeed, like Elizabeth Woodville, Cersei was not a consensus builder, counselling Joffrey that "anyone who isn't us is the enemy" and reassuring him that "the truth will be whatever you decide it will be."

There were a host of dynastic challengers to the Iron Throne. The brothers of Robert Baratheon, Stannis and Renly, had been made aware of Joffrey's actual paternity, and each were ready to sabotage each other's bid to gain the Iron Throne. Following Ned Stark's execution, his eldest son Robb was declared King of the North, while Balon Greyjoy declared himself King of the Iron Islands, prompting the War of the Five Kings. Tellingly, the war was never a contest between who was more *capable* of ruling. Instead the war was dynastic; the Baratheon brothers based their claim upon dynastic legitimacy, while Stark and Greyjoy both took advantage of the instability of Joffrey's government to assert their regional independence from the Iron Throne. Initially, Joffrey's minority government only controlled the Westerlands and the Crown lands, while the war was brutal on the economy of King's Landing, with the city filled with starving refugees. Although the war was eventually resolved in the Lannisters' favour, with Robb Stark and the Baratheon brothers eventually losing their lives, the infighting within the minority government between Tywin, Cersei, and Tyrion continued to destabilize the Iron Throne. With a bankrupt treasury during and following the War of the Five Kings, the Lannisters were compelled to turn to House Tyrell for financial help, which had previously backed Renly Baratheon in his bid for the Iron Throne before his own untimely demise at the hands of the sorceress Melisandre.

In European history, such alliances were usually accompanied by dynastic marriages to seal the deal in blood. The same is true in *GOT*, as Joffrey's betrothal to Sansa Stark was broken so he could marry Margaery Tyrell, widow of Renly Baratheon, whose brother Loras Tyrell, who had been Renly's lover, was now betrothed to Cersei. Tywin negotiated this arrangement with Olenna Tyrell using Petyr Baelish as an intermediary. For the jilted Sansa, now simply a prisoner and a negotiating pawn, there was her betrothal to Tyrion, who was in love with the prostitute Shae. Tywin presented these arrangements to Cersei and Tyrion as a *fait accompli*. While Cersei chafed under her father's authority, she constantly sought to undermine Tyrion, while doing her best to circumvent Margaery's influence over Joffrey, who operates as a loyal daughter of House Tyrell. Nevertheless, Cersei's determination to maintain her autonomy later reached a boiling point with her father, in which she threatened to expose the real paternity of her sons if he forced her to marry Loras Tyrell.

Of little account in the swirl of power plays surrounding his throne is Joffrey himself. Joffrey has no real attributes or qualities that mark him out for kingship, other than his perceived blood relationship to Robert Baratheon. Of all the characters in *GOT*, it is Joffrey who most slides into caricature. He was, in fact, the worst-case scenario for a teenaged-king: childish, vindictive, violent, and sadistic, while lacking empathy or intellectual interests and military abilities. Joffrey's liabilities are immaterial to his family; he is simply a dynastic prop for the Lannister's, as the decrepit Henry VI was for the Lancastrians. Neither Tywin nor Tyrion Lannister was interested in cultivating Joffrey's goodwill, and both treat the king with undisguised disdain. While still prince and visiting Winterfell with his mother, Tyrion slapped Joffrey repeatedly when he refused to pay his respects to Ned and Catelyn Stark after their son Bran had suffered a crippling fall at the hand of Jaime Lannister. Rather, both their attitudes seem to be that for the foreseeable future, they would be running the Iron Throne while Joffrey was free to torture whomever he wanted. No one is courting Joffrey as a potential ally, except Margaery, and to a certain extent Cersei, who progressively loses what influence she had over her eldest son.

Joffrey's murder was just as dramatic as Ned Stark's execution, occurring during the celebrations following his marriage to Margaery Tyrell. As we have seen, the plot was engineered by Tyrell matriarch Lady Olenna, who could not stomach the thought of her granddaughter married to such a monster. No one appears to mourn Joffrey's death, except for Cersei, Margaery, and Tommen. Instead, it becomes a means to frame Tyrion for Joffrey's poisoning. While Cersei appears to believe Tyrion was guilty of the crime, Tywin knew Tyrion was innocent, but kept him locked up as he consolidated his hold over the succeeding reign of Tommen.

Tommen's minority reign was far different from that of Joffrey. The brothers were in fact polar opposites. Somewhere in his mid-teens upon his accession, Tommen was happy, sweet, and thoughtful; he abhorred physical violence. Tywin considered him king-worthy, which he never did with Joffrey. When Tywin quizzed Tommen on the qualities requisite in a king, he was pleased when he replied that a king should be wise. Tywin in turn replied that wise kings continue to take counsel even when they do not have to, using Joffrey as the model for a bad king, which Tommen acknowledged. Even as a child, Tommen accepted the responsibilities of being as a king, something he shared with his closest historical model, Edward VI of England, who succeeded as King of England at the age of nine in 1547 as the son and heir of Henry VIII. Like Edward, Tommen was earnest in his kingship, visibly desiring to be a good king, which makes him perhaps the most sympathetic of all the kings depicted in *GOT*.[28] At Tommen's coronation, Margaery Tyrell observed to Cersei that "Tommen sits on the throne as if he were born to it." Tommen was portrayed as a king with promise, which made the battle for his heart and mind much more furious, and deadly, than it ever was for Joffrey. Nevertheless, Tommen was easily manipulated. With the King firmly under his control, Tywin swiftly affianced him to Margaery Tyrell, who visited him at night, seeking an opportunity to create an intimate relationship with the King, which Cersei found threatening.

However, the balance of power changed dramatically after Tywin Lannister was murdered by Tyrion at the end of Season Four, who then escaped to join the cause of Daenerys Targaryen, yet another pretender to the Iron Throne. Tywin's death and Tyrion's escape created a power vacuum not just in King's Landing but all over Westeros, which Cersei moved swiftly to fill. Convening the Small Council in Tommen's name, Cersei attempts to step into her father's shoes, naming Mace Tyrell, father of Margaery and Loras, as new Master of the Coin and her loyal henchman Qyburn as Master of Whisperers. Only Cersei's misogynist uncle Kevan Lannister challenges her power play, who declines the position of Master of War until it is confirmed by the king.

By this time Tommen and Margaery are married, which increased Margaery's influence over the king. When Margaery suggested to Tommen that he put his mother out to pasture at the Lannister seat at Casterley Rock, effectively removing her influence over the king, Cersei began to look for new allies to maintain her power as Queen, choosing the Sparrows, who were the followers of an order within the religion of the Faith of the Seven, the Faith Militant, which had been outlawed centuries before. Physically they resembled monastic orders like the Franciscans, dressing in the garb of medieval European mendicants and mutilating their foreheads as a sign of their faith, but psychologically they were much more menacing When the Grand Septon, the High Priest of the Faith of the Seven, was sacked for his immoral behavior, Cersei directed Tommen to replace him with the "High Sparrow," a humble man who fed the poor barefoot who was also the leader of the Sparrows, whose order Tommen makes legal again. It was a risky move, analogous to the election of a peasant as pope in medieval Europe, which of course never happened in history.

But the High Sparrow does have an historical analogue; Girolamo Savonarola, a Dominican friar who, after the fall of the Medici regime in Florence in 1494, sought to ignite a moral renewal and root out luxury and high living, prompting what was known as the "bonfire of the vanities," in which Florentine citizens brought their worldly goods to be burned in the town square.[29] Savonarola had his own Sparrows, the Piagnonim, who enforced his prohibitions against adultery, buggery, and other forms of vice. The first target of the Sparrows was Loras Tyrell, Cersei's former fiancé, who was arrested for homosexuality. Hailed before the High Sparrow, Loras denied the accusation, while Margaery backed up his testimony. The Sparrows then produced Loras' valet Olyvar, who refuted both their testimonies. Loras and Margaery were then arrested by the High Sparrow.

Under these stressful conditions, Tommen does his best to fulfil his responsibilities as king, that is, protecting his queen and his mother. But in his confrontations with the High Sparrow Tommen is unable to secure the release of either Loras or Margaery, but true to his gentle nature, he refuses to countenance any kind of violence to free them. Tommen was unaware that Cersei was behind these arrests in her efforts to curb the influence of Queen Margaery. But Cersei's triumph over the Tyrell's was short-lived, as she also was arrested for incest and her alleged role in the death of Robert Baratheon, and later suffered a humiliating walk of shame through King's Landing to atone for her sins. With Cersei sidelined, the Small Council appointed Tywin's brother Kevan Lannister as both Hand to the King and Protector of the Realm. While Kevan and the other stakeholders in the minority, namely, Olenna Tyrell and Jaime Lannister, now Captain of the King's Guard, attempted to exert their power against the High Sparrow, Tommen himself publicly aligned himself with the Sparrows in a public pronouncement that outlawed trial by combat, which Cersei was counting on for her upcoming trial.

Tommen's conversion to the Sparrow version of the Faith of the Seven was an unexpected development, engineered by Margaery, who had been under strict confinement since her arrest and was eager to avoid the public shaming that Cersei had endured. While Margaery's conversion was hardly sincere, Tommen's was, who increasingly viewed the High Sparrow as a source of wisdom and comfort, much as Edward VI of England was guided by Thomas Cranmer and Bishops Nicholas Ridley and Hugh Latimer, who deployed the King's authority to create England's first Protestant Church.[30]

Yet Cersei refused to remain sidelined. On the day of hers and Loras Tyrell's trial at the Great Sept of Baelor, Cersei failed to show up. As Margaery wailed like Cassandra that they were all in danger, Cersei watched through a window at the Red Keep as the Great Sept exploded in a fireball, killing Margaery, Mace, and Loras Tyrell, Kevan and Lancel Lannister, the High Sparrow, and 700 other people. Having arranged this mass murder with her henchmen Qyburn, which removed all her perceived enemies in one fell swoop, Cersei regained complete control over the minority regime, which swiftly came to a close, as Tommen, who well knew who the culprit was, was so overcome by grief that he committed suicide by falling to his death from another window in the keep. With Tommen's death, and no other viable challengers to the Iron Throne present in King's Landing, Cersei claimed the throne in her own right as first queen of the House of Lannister. At this point, at the end of Season Seven, Cersei appears to have won the game of thrones, successfully threading the needle of her two son's minority reigns, during which all viable challengers to her power and authority in Westeros—Ned Stark, the Baratheon brothers, Robb Stark, Margaery Tyrell, and her father Tywin—had all been eliminated. This left Daenerys Targaryen, the daughter of the Aerys II, and Jon Snow, recently elected King of the North, both of whom were in Essos, as her only challengers.

Cersei's possession of the Iron Throne has few analogues in history, the closest being that of Catherine the Great, who deposed her husband and assumed his place on the Russian imperial throne in 1762, despite having no hereditary claim to the throne. Cersei's performance as queen and mother during the minorities of her sons was complicated, mirroring the experiences of many queen mothers of medieval Western Europe. Despite her lust for power, Cersei appeared to sincerely love her children and mourned their deaths, which, ironically, paved her way to supreme power. She is in fact the one figure who survived the traumatic and fractious minority reigns of her two sons, outliving and overcoming all challengers to her quest for royal power. In the final analysis, Cersei, like her son Joffrey, also slides into caricature, thirsting for power and revenge, the epitome of the wicked queen. But while so many medieval European queens tagged with the wicked label, from Isabella of France to Margaret of Anjou, were often the subjects of misogynistic character assassinations,

Cersei, more than any other male character in *GOT*, epitomizes the savage and remorseless quest for dominance in the game of thrones, played against the background of her two son's minority reigns.

NOTES

1. Gwilym Dodd, "Richard II and the Fiction of Majority Rule," *The Royal Minorities of Medieval and Early Modern Europe*, Charles Beem, ed., New York: Palgrave Macmillan, 2008, 103–160.
2. J.L. Laynesmith, *The Last Medieval Queens: English Queenship 1445–1503*, Oxford: Oxford University Press, 2004, Kavita Mundan Finn, *The Last Plantagenet Consorts: Gender, Genre, and Historiography 1440–1627*, New York: Palgrave Macmillan, 2012.
3. Brian A. Pavlac, "Introduction: The Winter of Our Discontent," Game of Thrones *Versus History*, Brian A. Pavlac, ed., Hoboken N.J.: Wiley Blackwell, 2017, 8–9.
4. Ron Hogan, The Beatrice Interview: George R.R. Martin (2000), *Ron Hogan's Beatrice*. http://www.beatrice.com/interviews/martin/
5. Walter Kudrycz, *The Historical Present: Medievalism and Modernity*, New York: Continuum, 2011, 57–58. Tison Pugh and Angela Jane Weisl, *Medievalisms: Making the Past in the Present*, New York: Routledge, 2013, 1.
6. Shiloh Carroll, *Medievalism in* A Song of Ice and Fire *and* Game of Thrones, Cambridge: D.S. Brewer, 2018, 7–9. Charli Carpenter, "Game of Thrones as Theory," https://www.foreignaffairs.com/articles/2012-03-29/game-thrones-Theory
7. William Clapton and Laura J. Shepherd, "Lessons from Westeros: Gender and Power in Game of Thrones," *Politics*, Vol. 37(1) (2017): 5–18.
8. Frank Stenton, *Anglo-Saxon England*, third edition, Oxford: Oxford University Press, 1971, 372.
9. Christine Fell, *Edward, King and Martyr, Leeds Texts and Monographs*, Leeds: University of Leeds School of English, 1971.
10. Robert Bartlett, *England under the Norman and Plantagenet Kings*, Oxford: Oxford University Press, 2000. Andrew W. Lewis, *Royal Succession in Capetian France: Studies on Familial Order and the State*, Cambridge, Mass.: Harvard University Press, 1981.
11. Jeroen Duindam, *Dynasties: A Global History of Power, 1300–1800*, Cambridge: Cambridge University Press, 2015.
12. *Game of Thrones Wiki*, http://gameofthrones.wikia.com/wiki/House_Baratheon
13. Charles Beem, "Woe to Thee O Land! The Introduction," *The Royal Minorities of Medieval and Early Modern England*, 1–16.

14. Christian Hillen and Frank Wiswall, "The Minority of Henry III in the Context of Europe," in *The Royal Minorities of Medieval and Early Modern England*, 16–66.
15. Appointment of the 'continual council', 1377 (C 65/32, m. 3) National Archives (U.K.) http://www.nationalarchives.gov.uk/education/resources/richard-ii/appointment-of-the-continual-council-1377/. See also Ralph Griffiths, "Henry VI: King of England and France," in *The Royal Minorities of Medieval and Early Modern England*, 161–193.
16. J. S. Roskell, "The Office and Dignity of Protector of England, with Special Reference to its Origins," *English Historical Review*, Vol. 68 (April 1953): 193–233.
17. Charles Beem, "Have Not Wee a Noble Kynge? The Minority of Edward VI," in *The Royal Minorities of Medieval and Early Modern England*, 211–248.
18. J. S. Bothwell, "The More Things Change: Isabella and Mortimer, Edward III, and the Painful Delay of a Royal Minority (1327–1330)," in *The Royal Minorities of Medieval and Early Modern England*, 67–102.
19. Lindy Grant, *Blanche of Castile: Queen of France*, New Haven: Yale University Press, 2016.
20. Sharon L. Jansen, *Anne of France: Lessons for My Daughter*, Cambridge: Boydell and Brewer, 2004.
21. Rachel Gibbons, "Isabeau of Bavaria, Queen of France: Queenship and Political Authority as "Lieutenant Generale" of the Realm," *Queenship, Gender, and Reputation in the Medieval and Early Modern West, 1060–1600*, Zita Eva Rohr and Lisa Benz, eds., New York: Palgrave Macmillan, 2016, 143–160.
22. Tracy Adams, *The Life and Afterlife of Isabeau of Bavaria*, Baltimore: Johns Hopkins University Press, 2010.
23. Helen Mauer, *Margaret of Anjou: Queenship and Power in Late Medieval England*, Woodbridge: Boydell, 2003.
24. Michael Hicks, "A Story of Failure: The Minority of Edward V," in *The Royal Minorities of Medieval and Early Modern England*, 195–210.
25. "Richard III and the Parliament of 1484" *The History of Parliament* https://thehistoryofparliament.wordpress.com/2015/03/26/richard-iii-and-the-parliament-of-1484/
26. *Royal Mothers and Their Ruling Children: Wielding Political Authority*, Carey Fleiner and Elena Woodacre, eds., New York: Palgrave Macmillan, 2016.
27. Jo Ann McNamara and Suzanne Wemple. "The Power of Women Through the Family in Medieval Europe: 500–1100," *Clio's Consciousness Raised: New Perspectives on the History of Women*, Mary S. Hartman and Lois Banner, eds., New York: Harper Colophon, 1974, 103–118.

28. Edward VI kept a political journal for much of his reign, detailing his knowledge of current events and outlining what policies were important to him. The original is British Library Cotton MSS., Nero, C, X.
29. Donald Weinstein, *Savonarola: The Rise and Fall of a Renaissance Prophet*, New Haven: Yale University Press, 2011.
30. Diarmaid Macculloch, *The Boy King: Edward VI and the Protestant Reformation*, Berkeley: University of California Press, 2002.

BIBLIOGRAPHY

Adams, Tracy. *The Life and Afterlife of Isabeau of Bavaria*, Baltimore: Johns Hopkins University Press, 2010.

Bartlett, Robert. *England under the Norman and Plantagenet Kings*, Oxford: Oxford University Press, 2000.

Beem, Charles, ed. *The Royal Minorities of Medieval and Early Modern Europe*, New York: Palgrave Macmillan, 2008.

Carroll, Shiloh. *Medievalism in A Song of Ice and Fire and Game of Thrones*, Cambridge: D.S. Brewer, 2018.

Clapton, William, and Shepherd, Laura J. "Lessons from Westeros: Gender and Power in *Game of Thrones*," *Politics*, 2017, Vol. 37(1) 5–18.

Duindam, Jeroen. *Dynasties: A Global History of Power, 1300–1800*, Cambridge: Cambridge University Press, 2015.

Fell, Christine. *Edward, King and Martyr*, Leeds Texts and Monographs, Leeds: University of Leeds School of English, 1971.

Finn, Kavita Mundan. *The Last Plantagenet Consorts: Gender, Genre, and Historiography 1440–1627*, New York: Palgrave Macmillan, 2012.

Fleiner, Carey and Woodacre, Elena eds. *Royal Mothers and Their Ruling Children: Wielding Political Authority*, New York: Palgrave Macmillan, 2016.

Grant, Lindy. *Blanche of Castile: Queen of* France, New Haven: Yale University Press, 2016.

Jansen, Sharon L. *Anne of France: Lessons for My Daughter*, Cambridge: Boydell and Brewer, 2004.

Kudrycz, Walter. *The Historical Present: Medievalism and Modernity*, New York: Continuum, 2011.

Laynesmith, J.L. *The Last Medieval Queens: English Queenship 1445–1503*, Oxford: Oxford University Press, 2004.

Lewis, Andrew W. *Royal Succession in Capetian France: studies on familial order and the state*, Cambridge, MA: Harvard University Press, 1981.

Macculloch, Diarmaid. *The Boy King: Edward VI and the Protestant* Reformation, Berkeley, CA: University of California Press, 2002.

Mauer, Helen. *Margaret of Anjou: Queenship and Power in Late Medieval England*, Woodbridge: Boydell, 2003.

McNamara, Jo Ann and Wemple, Suzanne. "The Power of Women Through the Family in Medieval Europe: 500–1100," *Clio's Consciousness Raised: New Perspectives on the History of Women*, Mary S. Hartman, Lois Banner, eds., New York: Harper Colophon, 1974, 103–118.

Pavlac, Brian A., ed. Game of Thrones *Versus History* (Hoboken, NJ: Wiley Blackwell, 2017).

Pugh, Tison and Weisl, Angela Jane. *Medievalisms: Making the Past in the Present*, New York: Routledge, 2013.

Rohr, Zita Eva and Benz, Lisa, eds. *Queenship, Gender, and Reputation in the Medieval and Early Modern West, 1060–1600*, New York: Palgrave Macmillan, 2016.

Roskell, J.S. "The Office and Dignity of Protector of England, with Special Reference to its Origins," *English Historical Review* 68 (April 1953): 193–233.

Stenton, Frank. *Anglo-Saxon England*, third edition, Oxford: Oxford University Press, 1971.

Weinstein, Donald. *Savonarola: The Rise and Fall of a Renaissance Prophet*, New Haven: Yale University Press, 2011.

CHAPTER 10

Wicked Women and the Iron Throne: The Twofold Tragedy of Witches as Advisors in *Game of Thrones*

Sheilagh Ilona O'Brien

A Song of Ice and Fire (1996–) and the television series based upon it, *Game of Thrones* (2011–2019), reflect historical concerns over the nature of female power. While more generally providing a wide variety of complex and often flawed female characters across the series, George R.R. Martin's fantasy universe also includes many episodes of gendered violence, and a number of female characters who embody negative stereotypes about women and power.[1] These include several 'witch' characters who possess mystical power and find themselves in positions to influence a ruler, thus reflecting historical and contemporary fears about women's essential nature.

Claimants for the Iron Throne such as Daenerys Targaryen, Cersei Lannister, and Stannis Baratheon accept or disregard the advice of women perceived to be witches in encounters that embody early modern stereotypes of diabolic witchcraft. In each case their interactions with witches reflect preexisting western cultural conceptions of witches and witchcraft,

S. I. O'Brien (✉)
Open Access College, The University of Southern Queensland, Toowoomba, QLD, Australia

© The Author(s) 2020
Z. E. Rohr, L. Benz (eds.), *Queenship and the Women of Westeros*, Queenship and Power, https://doi.org/10.1007/978-3-030-25041-6_10

and each faces tragic consequences for engaging with those who have dark powers. Historically accusations of witchcraft revolved around tragic narratives which involved severe illness or death for the supposed victims, and ordeals including torture and death for many of the accused.[2] Those tragic motifs, particularly those relating to the loss of children, are echoed in the narratives presented in *A Song of Ice and Fire* and *Game of Thrones*. For Daenerys, Stannis, and Cersei, the presence of the witch figure is bound up in personal tragedy, particularly the death of their children.

The world of *A Song of Ice and Fire* does not present a single culture or a single cultural view of women as existing through the world, but the main storylines of the series focus on the Seven Kingdoms of Westeros and the Iron Throne.[3] Westerosi culture therefore dominates most of the storylines, with a very medieval view of female behaviour and propriety that is particularly dominant in the southern region of the Kingdoms. Given the connection Martin himself makes between England's War of the Roses and *A Song of Ice and Fire*, this chapter will draw its comparisons primarily from medieval and early modern England.[4]

This chapter shows that socials concerns over 'female' advice and power and its origins are still pertinent to a modern audience. By examining how these ideas about gender and power are discussed in *A Song of Ice and Fire* and *Game of Thrones*, it will examine the way in which both the books and the TV series position female ambition and power as unnatural, unstable, and evil.[5] These concerns are driven by beliefs that women are themselves volatile, driven by emotion, and ultimately opaque and unknowable—particularly those who use or endorse blood magic.[6]

Women with ambition are therefore positioned as deviant and devious, driven by unhealthy desires rather than seeking to serve others. Attempting to enter the masculine realm of politics and power is portrayed as fundamentally problematic for women. Whether they seek to rule or just to give advice, women in positions of power become targets of gendered criticism in the game of thrones. One of these critical gendered motifs is the tragedies and losses that befall rulers who are influenced by the advice of 'witches'.

The tragedy is almost always twofold, leading to harm for the witch and for those they advise. This chapter will focus on three relationships where a character who is or will be a ruler accepts advice from a 'witch', leading to tragic consequences for the ruler, and, in at least two cases, the witch. It will examine how concerns over evil female/feminine influence and power as portrayed in *A Song of Ice and Fire* and *Game of Thrones* reflect historical reality (and contemporary debates) about female ambition.

These concerns reach their zenith in the figure of the witch, who embodies the dangerous and/or monstrous woman, and is often viewed as sexually rapacious and desirous of power and revenge. Three relationships between rulers and advisors perceived as diabolic will be examined: Daenerys Targaryyen and Mirri Maz Duur, Stannis Baratheon and Melisandre 'The Red Woman', and Cersei Lannister and Maggy the Frog.

HISTORICAL CONTEXTS: THE IMAGE OF THE WITCH

The imagery of witches and witchcraft presented in *A Song of Ice and Fire* and *Game of Thrones* follows many of the concepts presented in early modern Europe and described in historical accounts of the period. Amongst these is the blurry (but nonetheless notable) distinction between those who practised renaissance humanist practices of magic on the one hand and witches on the other—though many demonologists warned that all magic was diabolic.[7] Malcolm Gaskill distilled the image of the witch in 'folk wisdom' into the 'notions that witches made blood pacts, belonged to covens, and congregated at *sabbats*' in seventeenth-century England.[8] Julian Goodare similarly declared that in popular belief, 'there were maleficent, vengeful witches harming their neighbours through secret spells'.[9] These would have been a familiar series of concepts across Europe at the time, and continue as tropes in modern fantasy fiction and supernatural television series. The use of blood, the bodies of dead babies, and other bodily fluids and parts were depicted in images and in the writings of demonologists.[10]

The earliest demonological treatises in Europe portrayed women as being more likely to become witches and not learned practitioners, and claimed they were driven by their sinful nature and a desire for power and revenge. This theme was developed with zeal in the famous test on witches, the *Malleus Maleficarum* (1486).[11] The susceptibility of women to either literal or metaphorical seduction by the Devil had its basis in the story of Eve and the snake in the Garden of Eden.[12] Both works argued that women were, like Eve, susceptible to the influence of the Devil because women were more naturally sinful. Ideas about women being filled with vengeance and hatred, lustful and unstable, drove ideas about women's role in society and the necessity for strong male rule to govern women's weak, susceptible, and emotional natures.

The most notable of the images related to Eve were those of seduction and deceit. This connection allowed the *Malleus Maleficarum* to link dangerous female sexuality with the diabolic power of (female) witchcraft. The *Malleus* claimed that one of the four crimes of witches was that they 'persistently engage in the Devil's filthy deeds through carnal acts with incubus and succubus demons'.[13] Witches were therefore, like Eve, an inversion of God's plan for woman. Witches are therefore everything a good Christian woman and mother was not. Witch-trials in early modern Europe had frequent references to witches who were sexually deviant, engaging in carnal copulation with Devils, sometimes in return for specific acts of magic.[14]

BLOODY HISTORICAL ECHOES

Early modern accounts described incidents involving witches whose imagery would be familiar to readers of *A Song of Ice and Fire* and viewers of *Game of Thrones*. In 1589 a pamphlet was published in London that described how the accused witch Joan Prentice confessed that the Devil had appeared to her in the form of a ferret and demanded first that she give him her soul.[15] When she denied him her soul, he asked her for 'some of thy blood', and she agreed, offering 'him the forefinger of her left hand, the which the Ferrit tooke into his mouth, and setting his former feete vpon that hand, suckt blood ther out, in so much that her finger did smart exceedingye'.[16]

The underlying idea behind Joan's story is that by giving the ferret her blood to suck, she would then be able to do evil acts of magic as she had agreed to give the Devil something of herself.[17] The use of blood or another bodily fluid was described in a number of pamphlets as an explicit or implicit agreement or pact between witch and Devil, a form of payment and exchange that had a deeper meaning. The demonologist Dr. Cornelius Burges argued that there was 'not a Witch that hath the Devil at her beck but she must seale a Covenant to him, sometimes with her blood'.[18] This use of blood has obvious links to the portrayal of witches in Martin's fantasy universe: both Melisandre and Maggy the Frog explicitly use blood for magical ends.[19]

Historically there were connections between concerns over female sexuality, sinfulness, and the Devil's temptation of women into witchcraft. For many demonologists, the supposed weakness of women contributed to the Devil's hold on them. Witches in early modern Europe even described giving birth to the Devil's monstrous offspring. In Suffolk, England in 1645 some witches 'confessed that they have had carnall [sic] copulation with the Devill, one of which said that she had (before her husband dyed) conceived twice by him, but as soone as she was delivered of them they run away in most horrid long and ugly shapes'.[20]

Two stories presented in the second book of the series have women giving birth to monstrous babies. Jon Snow hears a story at Winterfell that 'there were wildlings who would lay with the Others to birth half-human children'.[21] More notably, there is the monstrous shadow of Stannis Baratheon used by Melisandre to assassinate Renly Baratheon.[22] The imagery involved in these incidents is clearly drawn from early modern accounts of monstrous births, and Martin is hardly the first author to mine these tales for fantasy fiction.[23]

But it is the very first encounter with a witch which reveals the extent to which traditional witch tropes are integrated into Martin's universe. Indeed, the first encounter with a witch in Martin's universe also reflects fears over female power, monstrous births, and the influence of an evil elderly woman over a younger woman often encountered in early modern witch narratives.

THE GENTLE PRINCESS AND THE LUSTFUL COUNTESS

At the end of the first book in George R.R. Martin's fantasy series, and the corresponding first season of HBO's *Game of Thrones*, Khal Drogo's *khalesar* is torn apart by a series of decisions made by the young *khaleesi* Daenerys Targaryen, and the actions of the Lhazareen 'godswife' Mirri Maz Duur.[24] These events also lead to the birth of Daenerys' dragons, so it could be seen as an event that has eventual positive consequences for her, but in the short term, the personal and political consequences are dire. The events in Daenerys' storyline in her last four chapters of *A Game of Thrones* and the last three episodes of the first season seem to reflect two traditional fears about the presence of witches: that they destroy or overthrow social order, and that they are motivated by vengeance and hatred.[25] They also play upon the idea that women are driven not by rational calculations, but by chaotic emotions that are damaging in a ruler.

Daenerys by this point has embraced her role as Khaleesi, has been present for the death of her brother, and is bearing her husband Khal Drogo's child. As a result of an attempted assassination of Daenerys, Khal Drogo swears a blood oath that he will lead the Dothraki across the Narrow Sea and claim the Iron Throne for his son, who he believes will be 'The Stallion Who Mounts the World'.[26] In order to pay for the ships to take his khalesar across the sea, he attacks a Lhazareen village in order to take enough slaves to trade, and it is during this attack that Daenerys encounters the Lhazareen 'godswife' Mirri Maz Duur, and decides to claim all the female Lhazareen for herself after she is distressed by seeing young girls and women raped during the attack.[27]

From the outset those around Daenerys attempt to warn her that her decision to save the women of the village will have serious consequences. Jorah Mormont, her knight and closest advisor, warns her that her 'gentle heart' is stopping her from seeing that the rape and destruction of the Lhazareen village is what has always occurred, saying '[t]his is how it has always been. Those men have shed blood for the khal. Now they claim their reward'.[28] In an ominous foreshadowing, Jorah comments that she is her 'brother's sister, in truth'; confused Daenerys believes he is referring to Viserys, but instead he means Rhaegar Targaryen, who in some senses can be seen to have an essentially feminine and romantic nature obsessed with prophecy, which led him into decisions that ultimately destroyed the Targaryen dynasty.[29] This is further reinforced when Daenerys and Mirri Maz Duur later discuss the price needed to save Khal Drogo's life:

> 'Death?' Dany wrapped her arms around herself protectively, rocked back and forth on her heels. 'My death?' She told herself she would die for him, if she must. She was the blood of the dragon, she would not be afraid. Her brother Rhaegar had died for the woman he loved.[30]

In this case however it is her unborn son Rhaego who will die, followed shortly by the catatonic Khal Drogo and Mirri Maz Duur, rather than Daenerys herself.

It is due to the presence of Mirri Maz Duur that we get a blatant discussion of the idea of witchcraft in the first book in *A Song of Ice and Fire*, which presents the 'maegi' as thinly disguised diabolic witches:

> 'Maegi', grunted Haggo, fingering his arakh. His look was dark. Dany remembered the word from a terrifying story that Jhiqui had told her one night by the cookfire. A maegi was a woman who lay with demons and practiced the blackest of sorceries, a vile thing, evil and soulless, who came to men in the dark of night and sucked life and strength from their bodies.[31]

Tales of women who have sex with demons and then, like succubae, come to men in the night and attack them, sucking the 'life and strength from their bodies', seem almost a distillation of the most titillating tales of witches in medieval and early modern Europe.[32] However, in response to the term, Mirri herself states, '[y]ou call me maegi as if it were a curse, but all it means is wise'.[33]

Daenerys' desire to save her husband at any cost is a strikingly romantic and heroic motif, but it also suggests that she is driven primarily by her love of her husband which is presented as having a strong undertone of sexual desire (or, in early modern terminology, lust). The Overbury Affair in the early seventeenth century also featured a noble woman attempting to use magic to achieve her romantic desires. Frances Howard (1590–1632) and her attendant Anne Turner (1576–1615) were accused of causing the impotence of Frances' first husband, Robert Devereux, 3rd Earl of Essex (1591–1646), in order to obtain a divorce for Frances, and murdering the courtier Sir Thomas Overbury (1581–1613) after he objected to Howard's desire for a divorce.

The supposed motive of Frances Howard and her servant Anne Turner was that Frances desired to marry her supposed lover Robert Carr, Earl of Somerset (1587–1645), a great favourite of King James VI of Scotland and King James I of England (1566–1625).[34] Her accusers claimed that Frances won her divorce through witchcraft and murdered Sir Thomas Overbury with witchcraft and poison. Overbury was an important figure at court who had opposed the supposed affair between Carr, his former protégé, and Frances Howard, and had actively sought to prevent her divorce and remarriage.

Alastair Bellany argued that the main theme of the trial of Frances Howard and her maid Anne Turner 'was the link between witchcraft, on the one hand, and the inversion of sexual order on the other – the transgressing of patriarchal norms of female obedience'.[35] The imagery of the women in contemporary publications on the affair was of Frances and Anne as lustful sinners metaphorically seduced by the Devil and obsessed with revenge.[36] These images were based on far older conceptions of women as being tainted by the sins of Eve, and sharing her corruptible nature.

Mirri Maz Duur is driven by revenge in the view of Daenerys, and uses Daenerys' need for her husband to recover from his wound to achieve her objectives in killing Drogo, Rhaego, and scattering the khalasar. Anne Turner was executed—like Mirri Maz Duur—but her aristocratic mistress was eventually pardoned by King James, though this did not mean that Frances Howard was spared suffering for her crime in the eyes of her contemporaries. Like Daenerys, Frances was 'punished' for her use of witchcraft in a way which was directly tied to her ability to conceive and bear children. Following her first and last pregnancy in 1615, when she gave birth while imprisoned for the murder of Thomas Overbury, she had been continuously ill. One of her critics gleefully reported that she had been:

> disabled by the secret punishment of a higher providence from being capable of further copulation; and that thouh[sic] she lived near upon twenty years after it, yet her husband the Earl of Somerset never knew her carnally, but the said infirmity still increased more and more upon her till at last she died of it in very great extremity[.][37]

Unlike Frances Howard however, Daenerys is able to take revenge for herself. Indeed, both *A Game of Thrones* and the series *Game of Thrones* show the context of Daenerys' use of witchcraft rather differently than the circumstances in which Frances Howard and Anne Turner were supposed to have acted.

The details of Mirri Maz Duur's actions and statements are given to us from Daenerys' point of view, and she portrays the events as a tragic betrayal driven by her own attempts to do the right thing, and to protect and heal her husband. But we also get Maz Duur's perspective—though mediated through Daenerys. Mirri accuses Daenerys of not understanding the price paid by ordinary people for Daenerys' ambition and argues that her own actions were moral: 'The stallion who mounts the world will burn no cities now. His khalasar shall trample no nations into dust' she says of Daenerys' stillborn child.[38] Rather than a personal tragedy, Mirri argues that her actions were for the greater good. This is the first in a series of startling inversions of the witch trope that Martin uses in his work to play with audience expectations about the role of these women and their impact on the main characters, though it should be noted Mirri also has a venegful undertone when she scoffs at Danerys claims of having saved her.

Wicked Advisors, Wicked Advice

Concerns over who might be wielding influence, particularly over a ruler, and what their motivations might be appear to have existed as long as societies have been recording the details of political intrigue. In ancient Greece and Rome particular groups or individuals sought and sometimes achieved such political notoriety that they became the subject of oral or written slander, physical violence or assassination, imprisonment or exile. In Ancient Greece, Aspasia of Miletus, the second wife of Pericles the Elder, was accused of being a corrupting influence in Athenian society.[39] The Byzantine Empress Theodora, wife of Justinian, was on the receiving end of attacks on her character and influence over her husband, driven it seems in part by her former career as a dancer, actress, and courtesan.[40] The idea that the queen could become a corrupting influence if her morals were corrupt was an ongoing concern in medieval and early modern Europe.[41]

The *A Song of Ice and Fire* books and the television series based on them repeatedly echo these motifs in its portrayal of female rulers and women who wield power. To comprehend the role of these historic motifs in Martin's creation, and to understand how they are engaged with, it is necessary to discuss several notable historical narratives which are relevant to this discussion. The twofold tragedy unfolds in Martin's universe as a punishment for those who practise magic, and those who use it. As already discussed above it seems that these particular relationships are signified by the destruction not just of the witch, but of those who call upon their services.

Members of the nobility engaging the services of magic users were occasionally a part of broader concern over court favourites, as we have seen in the Overbury Affair, and their potential influence.[42] The most notable court favourites that caused strife and tension were male and sought and received extensive gifts from their royal sponsor; however, many such cases had at least an undertone of improper intimacy between the King or Queen and their favourite. Some of the most famous cases in England included Piers Gaveston (1284–1312), Hugh Despenser (c. 1286–1326), and George Villiers, Duke of Buckingham (1592–1628), male favourites who were rumoured to be more than just friends to their monarch.

In those cases where women were at the heart of concerns about political influence, as in the literary narrative of Daenerys' encounter with Mirri Maz Duur, fears about the gender (including female sexuality and reproduction) of a powerful advisor sometimes intersected with potential diabolism. Women wielding political influence like Jacquetta of Luxembourg and her daughter Queen Elizabeth Woodville, Joan of Arc, or Queen Anne Boleyn at some point faced accusation of witchcraft from their enemies and rivals.[43] As shown above in the case of Frances Howard, concerns over women in positions of power and influence played a role in some court scandals in medieval and early modern Europe. Some court scandals generated or were caused by suggestions of witchcraft intertwined with sexual impropriety. The witch who is used by a woman to gain or continue her relationship with her lover is a recurring theme in several court scandals involving witchcraft in early modern England.

Alice Kytler's story preceded that of Frances Howard by 300 years, yet many of the details were similar: both were accused of using witchcraft to remove inconvenient husbands so that they could marry their lovers. Jacquetta of Luxembourg, Countess Rivers and the mother of Elizabeth Woodville, Edward IV's wife, and Henry VIII's second wife and queen, Anne Boleyn were both accused of using witchcraft to gain the King's attention and to become Queen.

All of these cases led to tragedies of different magnitudes. Both Alice Kytler and Frances Howard's accomplices were executed, and although Frances wasn't executed, she apparently suffered from what her contemporaries thought was divine judgement. Anne Boleyn was executed, and both Jacquetta and her daughter were repeatedly threatened by enemies who sought to use witchcraft accusations to undermine them, or to actually threaten their freedom and life. As with Daenerys, the relationship of these medieval noblewomen with a 'witch' had tragic and even deadly consequences.

Maegi/Witch

It is notable that it is only with Daenerys' encounter with Mirri Maz Duur that the first discussion of 'maegi' in the first book of the series, *A Game of Thrones*, occurs. Prior to this, magic had been treated in the series as something mythical, historical, or foreign. Earlier chapters had referenced Arya naming her direwolf after an 'old witch queen', and the Stark sisters were supposed to travel on the *Wind Witch*, a Braavosi ship.[44] By and large magic is discussed as a thing either to be found in the distant past or far away, and the magic shown in the majority of the first book conforms to Martin's idea of magic being an instinctual process rather than something taught and structured. There is a notable apparent distinction in the books between that natural understanding of magic of 'heroic' characters like Daenerys Targaryen and Bran Stark, who follow their instincts and whose magic is rooted in their relationships with animals, and those who practise magic learned in the East and who seem to conform to more diabolic stereotypes. One can see a contrast being made here between a form of natural magic and unnatural magic.

The location of unnatural magic in the East is particularly notable. There is a hefty dose of Orientalism running through the series, from Varys, the eastern Eunuch, who plays a somewhat sinister role in the unfolding crisis, to the ongoing horrors Daenerys witnesses almost everywhere in Essos, to the dark presence of Asshai by the Shadow in the Far East.[45] The majority of magic-users perceived to be 'evil' in the series are 'eastern', 'learned', and 'diabolic', while those born in Westeros seem to practise 'natural' and more ambiguous or even seemingly good or positive magic.[46] Indeed, both Melisandre and Mirri Maz Duur are explicitly described as having been to Asshai, and claim to have been trained by the shadowbinders.[47]

Overall the impression is that eastern magic is diabolic, but western or 'Westerosi' magic is more natural. The revelation that the Children of the Forest created the White Walkers somewhat belies this; nevertheless, those human magic-users from Westeros, like the Stark children, have a less sinister appearance and narrative in the books published to date. The final episode of the television series also seems to imply that wargs like the Stark children are not a threat to 'the people' like dragon-riders or other 'foreign' (read non-western or 'Westerosi') magic-users.[48]

Those characters practising 'natural' magic also suffer loss and tragedy, but it is not as immediately bound up in their use of magic. For example, Bran does not lose his legs because of his bond with Summer; in fact, it is seemingly the loss of his legs that strengthens this bond. As with early modern accounts, Martin seems to show that there is a price to be paid for associating with a diabolic witch. Short-term gains, such as removing an inconvenient husband, might lead to long-term tragedy. *A Song of Ice and Fire* and *Game of Thrones* both show rulers associating with dark arts as damaging and destructive to them, their families, and their nations. It seems that in Martin's works, there is a particular price to be paid for using blood magic and shadowbinders, which, given their eastern origin, suggests orientalist images of the East are present in the presentation of natural and unnatural (evil) magic in the series. This is in contrast to the presence of evil witches throughout the East and western Europe in the medieval and early modern period. For Martin, evil magic is external to the human inhabitants of Westeros, whereas historically witchcraft was an internal threat coming from within European communities.

WICKED ADVICE?

The most obvious and largest role for a 'witch' in the series has been that of Stannis Baratheon's shadowbinder and red priestess, Melisandre. The first impression of Melisandre, 'the red woman', is provided in *A Clash of Kings* by the ageing master Cressen in the opening prologue of the second book in the series. After Lady Selyse, the wife of Stannis Baratheon, suggests that her husband should kill his brother Renly, Cressen is horrified. Musing to himself on a balcony of Dragonstone he thinks to himself:

> The woman was the heart of it. Not the Lady Selyse, the other one. The red woman [...] Melisandre of Asshai, sorceress, shadowbinder, and priestess to R'hllor, the Lord of Light, the Heart of Fire, the God of Flame and Shadow. Melisandre, whose madness must not be allowed to spread beyond Dragonstone.[49]

As the story continues Melisandre suggests a series of dark and socially unacceptable steps to Stannis, beginning with killing his brother Renly. There are notable parallels between the relationship between Stannis, Melisandre, and Selyse on the one hand and William Shakespeare's Macbeth on the other.

Melisandre with her prophecies seems to echo the offers the witches in *Macbeth* make to the Thane of Cawdor. Like the three witches, Melisandre also leads Stannis to eventual defeat. A notable corollary is that Stannis loses his wife to suicide on the eve of his final battle, which he believes that he cannot lose because of Melisandre's prophecy. The Three Witches also seem to show Macbeth he need have no fear until 'Great Birnam wood to high Dunsinane hill/Shall come against him'; likewise, Melisandre gives Stannis a belief in victory against all odds. Stannis, like Macbeth, is also killed by a character who has lost someone close to them: Macduff's wife and son are killed by Macbeth while he is unable to protect them; similarly, Renly is killed by Stannis' shadow (birthed by Melisandre), leaving Brienne unable to protect him as a Kingsguard should.[50]

The tragedy surrounding Melisandre also reaches out across many of the other major narratives, as it seems her magic may play a role in the death of several major characters. If her curse worked against Stannis' rivals then she may well have been ultimately responsible for the deaths of not only Renly, but Robb Stark, Joffrey Baratheon, and Balon Greyjoy.[51] If her magic is responsible in part for bringing about those deaths, her actions create further chaos, disintegrating stable centres of power across Westeros. Witches in early modern Europe were feared to be the agents of the Devil seeking to invert society, forces in some senses of disruption and chaos.[52]

However, those forces also affect Melisandre. Her apparent failure to correctly identify Azor Ahai, and her actions in support of Stannis, have caused her to lose her own position, and to some extent her own faith is shaken. In killing the Princess Shireen she has lost her most important disciple in Lady Selyse, her new followers, her 'King' and his army, and in the television series this has now seen her return to the East, rather than remaining with Jon Snow, her new candidate for saviour who spurns her after he learns of her actions.

It is important to note through which characters' eyes we see the 'witch' characters. Mirri Maz Duur is seen solely through the eyes of Daenerys; Melisandre is seen primarily through the eyes of Cressen and Davos initially, and later through the eyes of other characters critical of her motives, like Jon Snow. Similarly, Cersei is our primary source for the character Maggy the Frog, though her uncle Kevan does briefly mention her.[53]

Evil Means Make Tragic Ends

The universe of *A Song of Ice and Fire* and *Game of Thrones* portrays women who seek to rule or who believe they should rule as some of the most infamous and destabilising influences on Westeros since Aegon's conquest. Most notable of these have been queens who by their actions cause civil wars, like Rhaenyra Targaryen, a historical figure in the main series, and a main character in the short story *The Princess and the Queen*, and Cersei Lannister.[54] Both of these characters are marked by sexual impropriety, which is then reflected in their unstable and violent reigns. However, impropriety leading to instability is not solely female; indeed, Robert Baratheon is portrayed as a weak ruler, in part, because he is governed by his lusts and desires, rather than governing them. Characters like Ned Stark, Tywin Lannister, and Stannis Baratheon may not have survived, but all three were praised within the books and television series by their contemporaries and feared by their opponents because they exhibited emotional control over themselves, and therefore were able to exert control over their bannermen.[55] As discussed above, Daenerys' actions at the end of the first novel suggest exactly this sort of feminised chaos driven by a lack of emotional control.

Cersei's narrative, however, is about more than just the problematic nature of female rule, and her own concerns about her own gender— Cersei regularly wishes she was male, or had been born male, and despises her own femaleness whilst also using it to her own advantage at times. It also foregrounds the problematic nature of prophecy and particularly the role it plays in the tragic downfall of a main character in the narrative. Not all of the allusions to the past in the book series *A Song of Ice and Fire* can be traced to the medieval and early modern period; indeed, allusions stretch back to the ancient Mediterranean, the Middle East, and Asia. However, the primary source for the allusions discussed in this chapter has been the period of the witch-trials in early modern England. This is in part because the medieval and early modern periods have many allusions made to medieval and early modern England in the series.

Queen Cersei Lannister is one of the characters whose actions have driven the course of events across the books, and her tale is revealed in the fourth book and fourth series of *Game of Thrones* to be a tragedy prophesised by the woods witch Maggy the Frog.[56] According to Cersei, in the tale she tells Qyburn, Maggy 'was mother to a petty lord, a wealthy merchant upjumped by my grandsire'.[57] Cersei further describes how it had been rumoured after she returned with the merchant from the East that she had 'cast a spell on him, though more like the only charm she needed was the one between her thighs'.[58] Her foreignness is further confirmed in Cersei's narrative when she describes Maggy's true name as 'long and eastern and outlandish'.[59] Qyburn suggests that 'Maggy' may be a corruption of the term 'Maegi', and like the other witches noted in this chapter, she came from the 'East'.[60]

THE STAG AND THE LION

Both Stannis Baratheon and Cersei Lannister's interactions with their 'witches' feature concerns over dark magic, dire warnings about the consequences of engaging with such women, suggestions of sexual impropriety and/or of sex magic, and personal tragedy.[61] Tragic narratives featuring prophecy, such as *Macbeth* or *Oedipus Rex*, present characters who, knowing their future, act in response, hastening their own downfall rather than escaping it. Cersei's perspective begins in Book IV, *A Feast for Crows*, after the supposed prophecy (or at least her recollection of it) has begun to come true in the previous book *A Storm of Swords*, beginning with the murder of her son Joffrey. Therefore it is difficult to know whether her assertion that the meeting had played an important role in her thinking over the years was true, or whether it was only more recently that the memory of her encounter with the woods witch had haunted her thoughts.

With Stannis however, the gradual increase in Melisandre's influence is felt by a number of characters. The first intimation of Melisandre appears in *A Game of Thrones*, when Tywin warns his son Tyrion and other allies that Stannis is, in his view, the most dangerous of their opponents, including in the list of dangers 'Stannis bringing a shadowbinder from Asshai'.[62]

Although the truly tragic portion of Stannis story has yet to be completed in the books, it took a decidedly tragic turn in the HBO series with the burning of Princess Shireen in 'The Dance of Dragons'. The final outcome for Stannis in *Game of Thrones* does suggest that Melisandre's prophecies were as problematic as Maester Aemon suggested her proclamation of Stannis as Azor Ahai was.[63] Indeed her prophecies regarding Stannis seem misleading.

The extent of their veracity is not however known by those who hear the prophecies.[64] Both Stannis and Cersei take at least some amount of the prophecies of Melisandre and Maggy the Frog to be true. Though Qyburn tells Cersei she can circumvent the prophecy, the events portrayed on the television series so far have shown that her efforts have actually caused the death of her youngest and last son, Tommen, and also alienated both her younger brothers—one of whom Maggy prophesied would eventually kill Cersei.[65]

Like Oedipus and Macbeth, Cersei has reason to think she has avoided the tragedy of Maggy's prophecy to some extent early in the series, but as she makes moves to prevent the rest of the prophecy after Joffrey's death, she falls further and further into the prophecy and its tragedy. Her attempts to kill her brother lead to the death of Prince Oberyn, and his lover's revenge on her daughter Myrcella.[66] Her later attempts to remove her rival queen, in the form of Margaery, lead to the creation of the faith militant and thus her own imprisonment, her attack on the Great Sept of Balor and the death of Tommen.[67] Seeking to kill Tyrion before he can kill her leads to the death of her father, and her later actions have seemingly driven away her other younger brother, Jaime. It seems that rather than preventing the prophecy, each move she has made has eventually led to its further fulfilment.

Martin has discussed extensively how engaged he has been with feminist thought, particularly during the 1970s and 1980s.[68] This period coincides with the rise of gendered readings of witchcraft outside of academic studies. As Katherine Hodgkin points out, 'the witch' was a 'figure ripe for reclamation' for the feminist movement.[69] To what extent this might have informed Martin's creation of characters like Mirri Maz Duur and Melisandre is unclear. I have argued previously that Martin understands tropes around witches and witchcraft, and in his texts uses and plays with them. Martin draws out the multitude of tragedies that are present in early modern witch trials and beliefs through his witch characters. Melisandre, Mirri Maz Duur, and Maggy the Frog are victims of prejudice and tragedy and, in the eyes of those around them, perpetrators of horrific acts of violence. Mirri Maz Duur seems at first glance a simplistic 'witch' stereotype when viewed through the lens of Daenerys Targaryen's perspective. For Daenerys, Mirri Maz Duur is 'the witch that killed my husband', but as briefly discussed above, seen from the perspective of Mirri, the narrative is very different.[70] Mirri has watched her home and people attacked, killed, raped, and enslaved by the Dothraki. From Mirri's perspective, both Khal Drogo and his unborn son are not beloved family, but warlords who have and/or will bring enormous suffering to thousands of people. Mirri's own explanation is not the revenge-fuelled betrayal that Daenerys perceives, but rather an attempt to forestall further suffering by preventing the birth of '[t]he stallion who mounts the world'.[71] Understood within the conceit of the prophecy of '[t]he stallion who mounts the world', Mirri's actions become more morally complex and nuanced. In killing Khal Drogo, she is avenging her and her people's suffering, and in killing the unborn Rhaego, she believes she is preventing the destruction of others—though arguably she is instead restoring dragons, who may symbolically be the prophesied stallion.[72]

About Maggy we know less, yet in Cersei's description of their encounter, it seems possible that tragedy had also led to her being in a tent rather than in her husband's or son's home. We know that her husband became Lord Spicer, yet she is alone in a tent which in Cersei's memory is neither grand nor wealthy. It is possible that her son, like many others, viewed her as tainted and potentially evil. Her family is also interconnected with another tragedy, as her granddaughter Jayne Westerling becomes Robb Stark's wife, thus breaking his alliance with Lord Walder Frey.[73] Kevan Lannister even cites her as a reason Robb Stark should have avoided Jayne, because her lineage itself is tainted and her mother is, in his view, decidedly untrustworthy.[74]

In conclusion, witches in George R.R. Martin's *A Song of Ice and Fire* books and the television series *Game of Thrones* based upon them reflect medieval and early modern concerns about female instability, the problematic nature of female rule, and the terror and tragedy inherent in the presence and actions of 'witches'. Martin uses the imagery of diabolic witchcraft in the early modern era in creating his 'witch' characters, explicitly in his description of *maegi* in the first book.[75] Though the television series does invert some stereotypes of witchcraft, such as when the 'witch' Melisandre burns the innocent Princess Shireen, it and the books on which it is based more often use the imagery and popular conceptions of witchcraft in early modern Europe in its portrayal of witches and witchcraft.

These are tragic relationships that drive tragic narratives. The relationship between Stannis and Melisandre has echoes of the relationship between Macbeth and the three witches, while Daenerys' relationship with Mirri Maz Duur echoes the themes of court scandals like the Overbury Affair. Cersei Lannister, like Stannis, is on a tragic path of self-destruction. In her case each attempt to evade the fears she has about the witch's prophecy only drives Cersei closer and closer to destruction. Notably no character who has engaged with or benefitted from eastern blood magic was rewarded by the end of the television series, with Stannis, Cersei, and Daenerys all meeting tragic ends—which, in Stannis and Daenerys' case, have direct correlations to their encounter with witches. In the TV series Daenerys' 'child', Drogon, did exactly what Mirri Maz Duur feared Rhaego would do—led a *khalasar* that did indeed burn a city to the ground.[76,77]

Tragedy is a central motif in Martin's fantasy epic fantasy series. This is perhaps best encapsulated in the words of Ramsay (Snow) Bolton: 'If you think this has a happy ending, you haven't been paying attention'. Tragedy is also an integral feature of witchcraft narratives in medieval and early modern Europe, whether literary or historical. These narratives link sin, illness, and death in the person of the witch, usually a woman driven by unnatural desires, unbridled lust, vengeance, or greed. In Martin's universe encounters between the main characters and witches are starting points for tragic and self-destructive arcs. Daenerys, Mirri says, knew the price for saving Drogo, Cersei's increasingly desperate attempts to escape prophecy caused her to make self-destructive decision, and Stannis is first deceived and then abandoned. The twofold tragedy at the heart of these relationships is not an invention of this universe; rather, it is a reflection of early modern narratives of witchcraft.

Notes

1. See, for example, Queen Cersei in the books and TV series on the one hand, and Queen Rhaenys in The Princess in the Queen' on the other hand. See George R.R. Martin, 'The Princess and the Queen' in George R.R. Martin and Gardner Dozios (eds.), *Dangerous Women*, New York: Tor Books, 2013. For more on women and gender in *A Song of Ice and Fire* and *Game of Thrones*, see also Cathleen Cerny, Susan Hatters Friedman, and Delaney Smith, "Television's "Crazy Lady" Trope: Female Psychopathic Traits, Teaching, and Influence of Popular Culture",

Academic Psychiatry 38.2 (2014): 233–241; Clapton, William, and Shephard, Laura J., "Lessons from Westeros: Gender and Power in *Game of Thrones*", *Politics* 37.1 (2016): 5–18; Frankel, Valerie Estelle, *Women in Game of Thrones: Power, Conformity and Resistance*, Jefferson: McFarland & Company, 2014; Gjelsvik, Anne, and Schubart, Rikke (eds.), *Women of Ice and Fire: Gender,* Game of Thrones *and Multiple Media Engagements*, London: I.B. Taurus, 2015.

2. The emphasis on children being harmed has been interpreted differently by modern historians. For example, Deborah Willis argued that concerns over motherhood in the early modern period played an important role in the dynamic of older women being accused by young mothers of harming their children. However, there is also the maternal relationship between the Devil, in the form of an imp, and witches in early modern England. See Deborah Willis, *Malevolent Nurture: Witch-Hunting and Maternal Power in Early Modern England*, Ithaca: Cornell University Press, 1995; on maternal relationship with imps see Sheilagh Ilona O'Brien, "Witches and the Devil in 'a world turn'd upside down': The East Anglian Witch Trials, 1645–1647" PhD diss., The University of Queensland, 2017.

3. In the books, this is explored in relationship to Dorne, and in the TV series, there have been glimpses of this through the Sand Snakes and with freefolk characters like Ygritte and Gilly, though other strong female characters like Val and Arianne Martell have been left out of the HBO adaptation.

4. See Brian A. Palvac, Game of Thrones *versus History: Written in Blood*, Hoboken: John Wiley & Sons, 2017; Carolyne Larrington, *Winter is Coming: The Medieval World of* Game of Thrones, London: I.B. Tauris, 2016; Ishaan Tharoor, "Watch: The real history behind 'Game of Thrones'", *The Washington Post*, May 12, 2015.

5. This is contrasted with women fulfilling more traditional roles. For more on this, see Marta Eidsvag, "Maiden, Mother and Crone: Motherhood in the World of Ice and Fire" in *Women of Ice and Fire: Gender,* Game of Thrones *and Multiple Media Engagements*, London: I.B. Taurus, 2015.

6. See Frankel, *Women in* Game of Thrones*: Power, Conformity and Resistance*. For discussion of women as unknowable objects see Genevieve Lloyd, *The Man of Reason: 'Male' and 'Female' in Western Philosophy*, Minneapolis: University of Minnesota Press, 1993; Hekman, Susan J., *Gender and Knowledge: Elements of a Postmodern Feminism*, Boston: Northeastern University Press; See Mary Ann Doane, *Femmes Fatales: Feminism, Film Theory, Psychoanalysis*, New York: Routledge, 1991.

7. King James VI & I, *Daemonologie in forme of a dialogue, diuided into three books*, Edinburgh, 1597, 7–9.

8. Gaskill, *Witchfinders*, 217.

9. Julian Goodare, *Scottish Witchcraft in its European Context*, in Julian Goodare, Lauren Martin, and Joyce Miller's *Witchcraft and Belief in Early Modern Scotland*, Houndmills, Basingstoke: Palgrave Macmillan, 2008, 42.

10. See Brian P. Levack (ed.), *Gender and Witchcraft: New Perspectives on Witchcraft, Magic, and Demonology, Volume 4: Gender and Witchcraft*, Routledge: London, 2001; Brian P. Levack, *The Witch-Hunt in Early Modern Europe*, 3rd ed., Harlow: Longman/Pearson, 2006.

11. See Edward Peters and Alan Charles Kors (ed.), *Witchcraft in Europe, 400–1700: A Documentary History*, University of Pennsylvania Press, 2001, 155–159; Christopher S. Mackay, The Hammer of Witches: *a complete translation of the Malleus Maleficarum*, Cambridge: Cambridge University Press, 2009, 25–27, 159–172; See also Michael Bailey, "From Sorcery to Witchcraft: Clerical Conceptions of Magic in the Later Middle Ages", *Speculum*, 76.4 (October, 2001): 960–990; See also Hans Peter Broedel, *The* Malleus maleficarum *and the construction of witchcraft: theology and popular belief*, Manchester: Manchester University Press, 2003.

12. Philip Almond, *The Lancashire Witches: A Chronicle of Sorcery and Death on Pendle Hill*, London: Taurus, 2012, 63.

13. Christopher S. Mackay, *The* Hammer of Witches: *a complete translation of the* Malleus maleficarum, Cambridge: Cambridge University Press, 2009, 120.

14. Ewen, *Witch Hunting and Witch Trials*, 52; Notestein, *A History of Witchcraft in England from 1558 to 1718*, 127–129; Macfarlane, *Witchcraft in Tudor and Stuart* England, 139. See also, Thomas, *Religion and the Decline of Magic*; Briggs, *Witches & Neighbours*, 253; Clark, *Thinking with Demons*, 152–153, 473–475; Levack, *The Witch-Hunt in Early Modern Europe*, 14–15, 117–118, 259; Also see Carlo Ginzburg, *The Night Battles*, for an unusual example of the interaction between local superstition and elite demonology.

15. [Anon], *The Apprehension and confession of three notorious Witches, London, 1589, 11.*

16. Ibid.

17. Ibid.

18. Cornelius Burges, *The first sermon, preached to the Honourable House of Commons now assembled in Parliament at their publique fast. Novemb. 17. 1640. By Cornelius Burges Doctor of Divinitie. Published by order of that House*, London, 1641, 64.

19. *Game of Thrones.* "The Dance of Dragons." 5.9. Directed by David Nutter. Written by David Benioff and D.B. Weiss. HBO, June, 2015; See Martin, *A Feast for Crows*, London: HarperCollins, 2012; *Game of Thrones.* "The Wars to Come." 5.1. Directed by Michael Slovis. Written by David Benioff and D.B. Weiss. HBO, April.

20. [Anon] *A true relation of the araignment of eighteene vvitches. that were tried, convicted, and condemned, at a sessions holden at St. Edmunds-bury in Suffolke, and there by the iudge and iustices of the said sessions condemned to die, and so were executed the 27. day of August 1645*, London, 1645.

21. George R.R. Martin, *A Clash of Kings*, London: HarperCollins, 2012, 339.

22. Note, only the birth of Melisandre's second shadow assassin to kill Ser Cortnay Penrose is described in the book. See Martin, *A Clash of Kings*, London: HarperCollins, 2012, 339, 562–563; see also *Game of Thrones*, "Garden of Bones" 2.4. Directed by David Petrarca. Written by Vanessa Taylor, HBO, April, 2012.

23. For an example of a demon birth in fantasy fiction, David Eddings, *Demon Lord of Karanda*, London: Random House, 2010.

24. *Game of Thrones*. "The Pointy End" 1.8. Directed by Daniel Minahan. Written by George R.R. Martin. HBO, June, 2011; *Game of Thrones*. "Baelor" 1.9. Directed by Alan Taylor. Written by David Benioff and D.B. Weiss. HBO, June, 2011; *Game of Thrones*. "Fire and Blood" 1.10. Directed by Alan Taylor. Written by David Benioff and D.B. Weiss. HBO, June, 2011.

25. See Martin, *A Game of Thrones*, London: HarperCollins, 2012, 641–650, 678–691, 726–736, 772–780.

26. Ibid., 573.

27. Ibid., 641–650.

28. Ibid., 644.

29. Ibid.

30. Ibid., 686.

31. Ibid., 647.

32. O'Brien, Sheilagh Ilona, "Witches of Westeros: using and subverting the witch trope in *Game of Thrones*", *The Conversation*, October 29, 2015. Accessed online: http://theconversation.com/witches-of-westeros-using-and-subverting-the-witch-trope-in-game-of-thrones-48735

33. Martin, *A Game of Thrones*, 772.

34. Bellany, *The Politics of Court Scandal*, 148–150.

35. Alastair Bellany, *The Politics of Court Scandal: News Culture and the Overbury Affair, 1603–1660*, Cambridge: Cambridge University Press, 2007, 154.

36. See David Lindley, *The Trials of Frances Howard Fact and Fiction at the Court of King James*, Oxford: Routledge, 1993, 78–79.

37. See Alastair Bellany, 'Book Review: The Trials of Frances Howard: Fact and Fiction at the Court of King James by David Lindley', *Huntington Library Quarterly* 57.4 (1994): 393–399: 393; See also BL, Harley MS. 646, fol. 27r.

38. Martin, *A Game of Thrones*, 734.
39. For an examination of Aspasia and the attacks made on her character by Plutarch and other sources, see Madeline M. Henry, *Prisoner of History: Aspasia of Miletus and Her Biographical Tradition*, Oxford: Oxford University Press, 1995.
40. See David Stone Potter, *Theodora: Actress, Empress, Saint*, Oxford: Oxford University Press, 2015.
41. See Rachel Weil, "Royal Flesh, Gender and the Destruction of Monarchy" in Regina Schulte (ed.), *The Body of the Queen: Gender and Rule in the Courtly World, 1500–2000*, New York, NY: Berghahn Books, 2006; see also Abby Zanger, *Scenes from the Marriage of Louis XIV: Nuptial Fictions and the Making of Absolutist Power*, Stanford: Stanford University Press, 1997.
42. See J.H. Elliott and L.W.B. Brockliss (eds.), *The World of the Favourite*, Yale: Yale University Press, 1999.
43. William R. Jones, "Political Uses of Sorcery in Medieval Europe", 673. See Warnicke, *The Rise and Fall of Anne Boleyn*, 231; See also Ives, *The Life and Death of Anne Boleyn: 'the most happy'*, Malden: Blackwell Publishing, 2004.
44. See Martin, *A Game of Thrones*.
45. For a discussion of the role of Orientalism in the series, see Mat Hardy, "Game of Tropes: The Orientalist Tradition in the Works of G.R.R. Martin", *International Journal of Arts & Sciences* 8.1 (2015): 409–420. Amy Burge, *Representing Difference in the Medieval and Modern Orientalist Romance*, New York: Palgrave Macmillan, 76; James Smalls, "Menace at the Portal: Masculine Desire and the Homoerotics of Orientalism" in Joan DelPlato and Julie Codell (eds.), *Orientalism, Eroticism and Modern Visuality in Global Cultures*, Abingdon: Ashgate, 2016, 38–40.
46. Of course, that is a slight oversimplification. In the series, the 'natural' magic of the White Walkers and the Children of the Forest has been shown to be the cause of the northern threat to Westeros, and potentially a threat to all life. See *Game of Thrones*. "The Door" 6.5. Directed by Jack Bender. Written by David Benioff and D.B. Weiss. HBO, May, 2016.
47. A possible exception to this is the figure of Quaithe, who has not yet been revealed to have either good or evil intentions in the books—although Daenerys does not seem to trust her, perhaps due to her experience with Mirri Maz Duur. In the TV series, Quaithe did not appear after Season 2, while in the books, she seems to be contacting Daenerys in her dreams. See G.R.R. Martin, *A Storm of Swords*, London: HarperCollins, 2012, 113, 375.
48. *Game of Thrones*. "The Climb" 3.6. Directed by Alik Sakharov. Written by David Benioff and D.B. Weiss. HBO, May, 2013.

49. Martin, *A Clash of Kings*, 389–392.
50. Notably this is only in the television series; Stannis has yet to die in the books. Ibid., 454–455. See also William Shakespeare, edited by Barbara A. Mowat and Paul Werstine, *Macbeth*, New York: Simon & Schuster, 2014, 30, 55.
51. Martin, *A Storm of Swords*, 499–502; *Game of Thrones*. "Second Sons".
52. See Stuart Clark, *Thinking with Demons: The Idea of Witchcraft in Early Modern Europe*, Oxford: Oxford University Press, 1997.
53. Martin, *A Storm of Swords*, 271.
54. See Martin, "The Princess and the Queen".
55. This reflects the medieval concern with the king's 'two bodies'. For more on this see Ernst H. Kantorowicz, *The King's Two Bodies: A Study in Medieval Political Theology*, Princeton, N.J.: Princeton University Press, 1997.
56. See Martin, *A Feast for Crows*.
57. Ibid., 614.
58. Ibid.
59. Ibid.
60. Ibid.
61. Ibid.
62. Martin, *A Game of Thrones*, 743.
63. Martin, *A Feast for Crows*, 648; *Game of Thrones*. "The Dance of Dragons".
64. It could be argued that by the time Stannis loses, Melisandre herself no longer believes her own prophecy or perhaps even 'saw' that Stannis would lose in spite of the burning of Shireen. Even with the series, prophecies are regarded as problematic at best, as Marwyn the Mage explains to Samwell Tarly in *A Feast for Crows*. See Martin, *A Feast for Crows*, 774.
65. Ibid., 611.
66. *Game of Thrones*. "The Mountain and the Viper" 4.8. Directed by Alex Graves. Written by David Benioff and D.B. Weiss, HBO, June, 2014; *Game of Thrones*. "Mother's Mercy" 5.8. Directed by David Nutter. Written by David Benioff and D.B. Weiss. HBO, June, 2015.
67. Note this is in the TV series. Much of these storylines has yet to unfold in the final two as yet unpublished books.
68. I am grateful to Dr. Ana Stevenson for her discussion of this in her unpublished paper "Khaleesi Unchained?: George R.R. Martin, Game of Thrones, and the Woman-Slave Analogy". See also Jessica Salter, "Game of Thrones's George RR Martin: 'I'm a feminist at heart'," *Telegraph*, April 1, 2013. Accessed online: http://www.telegraph.co.uk/women/womens-life/9959063/Game-of-Throness-George-RR-Martin-Im-a-feminist.html

69. Katherine Hodgkin, "Gender, Mind and Body: Feminism and Psychoanalysis" in Jonathan Barry and Owen Davies (eds.), *Palgrave Advances in Witchcraft Historiography*, Houndmills: Palgrave Macmillan, 2007, 184–185.
70. Martin, *A Game of Thrones*, 734–735.
71. Ibid., 734.
72. If 'The Stallion who Mounts the World' is Drogon and Daenerys' other dragons, then rather than preventing the prophecy that Daenerys will be the mother of 'The Stallion who Mounts the World', she has instead played an important role in fulfilling the prophecy. This has been a widely discussed theory online, see, for example, Michael Walsh, "History of Thrones: The Dosh Khaleen and the Stallion Who Mounts the World Prophecy", *Nerdist*, (May 12, 2016).
73. Martin, *A Storm of Swords*, 271.
74. Ibid.
75. Melisandre's television portrayal in Season 6 also engages with the idea of the duplicitous hag. See Rebecca-Anne C. Do Rozarion and Deb Waterhouse-Watson, "Beyond Wicked Witches and Fairy Godparents: Ageing and Gender in Children's Fantasy on Screen" in Imelda Whelehan and Joel Gwynne (eds.), *Ageing, Popular Culture and Contemporary Feminism: Harleys and Hormones*, Basingstoke and New York: Palgrave Macmillan, 2014.
76. *Game of Thrones*. "The Irone Thorne" 8.6. Directed by David Benioff and D.B. Weiss. Written by David Benioff and D.B. Weiss. HBO, May, 2019.
77. *Game of Thrones*. "The Climb".

BIBLIOGRAPHY

PRIMARY SOURCES

British Library (BL), Harley MS. 646, fol. 27r.
[Anon], *The Apprehension and confession of three notorious Witches, London, 1589.*
[Anon] *A true relation of the araignment of eighteene vvitches that were tried, convicted, and condemned, at a sessions holden at St. Edmunds-bury in Suffolke, and there by the iudge and iustices of the said sessions condemned to die, and so were executed the 27. day of August 1645*, London, 1645.
Burges, Cornelius, The first sermon, preached to the Honourable House of Commons now assembled in Parliament at their publique fast. Novemb. 17. 1640. By Cornelius Burges Doctor of Divinitie. Published by order of that House, London, 1641.

The Hammer of Witches: a complete translation of the Malleus maleficarum, Mackay, Christopher S., (trans.), Cambridge: Cambridge University Press, 2009.

King James VI & I of Scotland and England, Daemonologie in forme of a dialogue, diuided into three books, Edinburgh, 1597.

Martin, George R. R., "The Princess and the Queen" in George R.R. Martin and Gardner Dozios (eds) Dangerous Women, New York: Tor Books, 2013.

Idem, A Clash of Kings, London: Harper Collins, 2012.

Idem, A Feast for Crows, London: Harper Collins, 2012.

Idem, A Game of Thrones, London: Harper Collins, 2012.

Shakespeare, William, Macbeth, Mowat, Barbara A., and Werstine, Paul, New York: Simon & Schuster, 2014.

SECONDARY SOURCES

Almond, Philip, The Lancashire Witches: A Chronicle of Sorcery and Death on Pendle Hill, London: Taurus, 2012.

Bailey, Michael, "From Sorcery to Witchcraft: Clerical Conceptions of Magic in the Later Middle Ages" Speculum, 76.4 (Oct, 2001), 960–990.

Bellany, Alistair, 'Book Review: The Trials of Frances Howard: Fact and Fiction at the Court of King James by David Lindley', Huntington Library Quarterly, 57, 4 (1994), 393–399.

Idem, The Politics of Court Scandal: News Culture and the Overbury Affair, 1603–1660, Cambridge: Cambridge University Press, 2007.

Briggs, Robin, Witches & Neighbours: The Social and Cultural Context of European Witchcraft, Oxford: Wiley-Blackwell, 2002.

Broedel, Hans Peter, The Malleus maleficarum and the construction of witchcraft: theology and popular belief, Manchester: Manchester University Press, 2003.

Burge, Amy, Representing Difference in the Medieval and Modern Orientalist Romance, New York: Palgrave Macmillan.

Cerny, Cathleen, Friedman, Susan Hatters, and Smith, Delaney, "Television's "Crazy Lady" Trope: Female Psychopathic Traits, Teaching, and Influence of Popular Culture", Academic Psychiatry 38: 2 (2014), 233–241.

Clapton, William, and Shephard, Laura J. "Lessons from Westeros: Gender and power in Game of Thrones", Politics 37: 1 (2016), 5–18.

Clark, Stuart, Thinking with Demons: The Idea of Witchcraft in Early Modern Europe, Oxford: Oxford University Press, 1997.

Do Rozarion, Rebecca-Anne C., and Waterhouse-Watson, Deb, "Beyond Wicked Witches and Fairy Godparents: Ageing and Gender in Children's Fantasy on Screen" in Whelehan, Imelda and Gwynne, Joel, (eds), Ageing, Popular Culture and Contemporary Feminism: Harleys and Hormones, Basingstoke and New York: Palgrave Macmillan, 223–247.

Doane, Mary Ann, *Femmes Fatales: Feminism, Film Theory, Psychoanalysis*, New York: Routledge, 1991.

Eddings, David, *Demon Lord of Karanda*, London: Random House, 2010.

Eidsvag, Marta, "Maiden, Mother and Crone: Motherhood in the World of Ice and Fire" in Gjelsvik, Anne, and Schubart, Rikke (eds), *Women of Ice and Fire: Gender, Game of Thrones and Multiple Media Engagements*, London: I.B. Taurus, 2015.

Elliott, J.H., and Brockliss, L.W.B. (eds), *The World of the Favourite*, Yale: Yale University Press, 1999.

Ewen, C. L'Estrange, *Witch Hunting and Witch Trial: the indictments for witch-craft from the records of 1373 assizes held for the Home Circuit A.D. 1559–1736*, [London: 1929], Abingdon, Oxon and New York: Routledge, 2011.

Frankel, Valerie Estelle, *Women in* Game of Thrones: *Power, Conformity and Resistance*, Jefferson: McFarland & Company, 2014.

Gaskill, Malcolm, *Witchfinders*, London: John Murray (Publishers), 2005.

Ginzburg, Carlo, Tedeschi, John and Anne C. (trans), *The Night Battles: Witchcraft and Agrarian Cults in the Sixteenth and Seventeenth Centuries*, Baltimore, MD: The Johns Hopkins University Press, 2013.

Gjelsvik, Anne, and Schubart, Rikke (eds), *Women of Ice and Fire: Gender*, Game of Thrones *and Multiple Media Engagements*, London: I.B. Taurus, 2015.

Goodare, Julian, "Scottish Witchcraft in its European Context", in Goodare, Julian, Martin, Lauren, and Miller, Joyce (eds), *Witchcraft and Belief in Early Modern Scotland*, Basingstoke: Palgrave Macmillan, 2008, 26–50.

Hardy, Mat, "Game of Tropes: The Orientalist Tradition in the Works of G.R.R. Martin" *International Journal of Arts & Sciences*, 08: 01 (2015), 409–420.

Hekman, Susan J., *Gender and Knowledge: Elements of a Postmodern Feminism*, Boston: Northeastern University Press.

Hodgkin, Katherine "Gender, Mind and Body: Feminism and Psychoanalysis", in *Palgrave Advances in Witchcraft Historiography*, edited by Jonathan Barry and Owen Davies, Houndmills Basingstoke: Palgrave Macmillan, 2007, 217–236.

Ives, Eric, *The Life and Death of Anne Boleyn: 'the most happy'*, Malden: Blackwell Publishing, 2004.

Jones, William R. "Political Uses of Sorcery in Medieval Europe", *The Historian*, 34:4, (Aug. 1972), 670–687.

Kantorowicz, Ernst H., *The King's Two Bodies: A Study in Medieval Political Theology*, Princeton, NJ: Princeton University Press, 1997.

Larrington, Carolyne, *Winter is Coming: The Medieval World of* Game of Thrones, London: I.B. Tauris, 2016.

Levack, Brian P., (ed), *Gender and Witchcraft: New Perspectives on Witchcraft, Magic, and Demonology, Volume 4: Gender and Witchcraft*, Routledge: London, 2001.

Idem, *The Witch-Hunt in Early Modern Europe*, 3rd Ed., Harlow: Longman/ Pearson, 2006.

Lindley, David, *The Trials of Frances Howard Fact and Fiction at the Court of King James*, Oxford, Routledge, 1993.

Lloyd, Genevieve, *The Man of Reason: 'Male' and 'Female' in Western Philosophy*, Minneapolis: University of Minnesota Press, 1993.

Macfarlane, Alan, *Witchcraft in Tudor and Stuart England: A Regional and Comparative Study*, Abingdon Oxon and London: Routledge, 1999.

Notestein, Wallace, *A History of Witchcraft in England from 1558 to 1718*, Baltimore, MD, The Lord Baltimore Press, 1911.

O'Brien, Sheilagh Ilona, "Witches of Westeros: using and subverting the witch trope in *Game of Thrones*", *The Conversation*, October 29, 2015. http://the-conversation.com/witches-of-westeros-using-and-subverting-the-witch-trope-in-game-of-thrones-48735

Idem, "Witches and the Devil in 'a world turn'd upside down': The East Anglian Witch Trials, 1645–1647". PhD diss., The University of Queensland, 2017.

Palvac, Brian A., *Game of Thrones versus History: Written in Blood*, Hoboken, NJ: John Wiley & Sons, 2017.

Peters, Edward, and Kors, Alan Charles, (ed.), *Witchcraft in Europe, 400–1700: A Documentary History*, Philadelphia, PA: University of Pennsylvania Press, 2001.

Potter, David Stone, *Theodora: Actress, Empress, Saint*, Oxford: Oxford University Press, 2015.

Salter, Jessica, "Game of Thrones's George R. R. Martin: 'I'm a feminist at heart'", *Telegraph*, April 1, 2013. http://www.telegraph.co.uk/women/womens-life/9959063/Game-of-Throness-George-RR-Martin-Im-a-feminist.html

Smalls, James, "Menace at the Portal: Masculine Desire and the Homoerotics of Orientalism" in Joan DelPlato and Julie Codell (eds.), *Orientalism, Eroticism and Modern Visuality in Global Cultures*, Abingdon Oxon: Ashgate, 2016, 25–54.

Stevenson, Ana, "Khaleesi Unchained? George R.R. Martin, *Game of Thrones*, and the Woman-Slave Analogy", unpublished paper.

Tharoor, Ishaan, "Watch: The real history behind 'Game of Thrones'", *The Washington Post*, May 12, 2015.

Thomas, Keith, *Religion and the Decline of Magic: Studies in Popular Beliefs in Sixteenth-and Seventeenth Century England*, London: Penguin, 1999.

Walsh, Michael, "History of Thrones: The Dosh Khaleen and the Stallion Who Mounts the World Prophecy", *Nerdist*, (May 12, 2016).

Warnicke, Retha M., *The Rise and Fall of Anne Boleyn: family politics at the court of Henry VIII*, Cambridge and New York: Cambridge University Press, 1989.

Weil, Rachel, "Royal Flesh, Gender and the Destruction of Monarchy" in Regina Schulte (ed.), *The Body of the Queen: Gender and Rule in the Courtly World, 1500–2000*, New York, NY: Berghahn Books, 2006.

Willis, Deborah, *Malevolent Nurture: Witch-hunting and Maternal Power in Early Modern England*, Ithaca, NY: Cornell University Press, 1995.

Zanger, Abby, *Scenes from the Marriage of Louis XIV: Nuptial Fictions and the Making of Absolutist Power*, Stanford: Stanford University Press, 1997.

CHAPTER 11

Afterword: Playing, Winning, and Losing the Game of Thrones—Reflections on Female Succession in George R.R. Martin's *A Song of Ice and Fire* and *Game of Thrones* in Comparison to the Premodern Era

Elena Woodacre

Succession is at the very heart of George R.R Martin's *A Song of Ice and Fire*—it is literally a game of thrones. His game has both male and female contenders, and, as the book and television series progress, it is the latter group which begins to dominate the scene, leading to the point where matriarchs and female claimants, rather than men, fight each other for control of the Iron Throne. Yet, many of these strong female contenders started the series as mere supporters and conduits of their natal dynasties, rather than contestants in their own right. This chapter discusses the trajectory of several key female characters in *A Song of Ice and Fire* and *Game of Thrones* as they progress from mothers, wives, and sisters to formidable queens and leaders. As the contributors to this collection have done, this

E. Woodacre (✉)
The Department of History, University of Winchester,
Winchester, Hampshire, UK

© The Author(s) 2020
Z. E. Rohr, L. Benz (eds.), *Queenship and the Women of Westeros*,
Queenship and Power, https://doi.org/10.1007/978-3-030-25041-6_11

chapter connects the development of these female characters to examples of premodern female rulers who might have inspired Martin, comparing historical succession practices to those of Westeros and Essos.

In this collection, Sheilagh Ilona O'Brien notes that the ambition of female characters is seen as "deviant and devious, driven by unhealthy desires to enter the masculine realm of politics and power".[1] These (would-be) queens are not only dangerous to the androcentric political order of Westeros and Essos, they are also in constant danger from those who would oppose their succession or topple them from power. This mirrors the situation of female claimants and rulers in the premodern era, where women were almost always second-choice successors and in a more vulnerable position than their male counterparts due to their sex. This is not to say that women were unable to claim a throne or rule successfully—history is full of examples of powerful female rulers, including Empress Wu Zeitan of China, Njinga of Angola, Elizabeth I of England, and Catherine II "the Great" of Russia, who will be discussed later in this chapter. However, female claimants were only able to come to the throne where law and custom made it possible and/or when situational factors, such as the lack of direct male heirs, made it necessary.[2] Precedent and a preference for the closest possible blood tie to the previous ruler could smooth the way for an heiress, but she was vulnerable to attacks based on her sex, opposition based on an unpopular husband (particularly if he was foreigner), or the claim of another male relative.[3] Premodern succession practices developed to favour male primogeniture in many areas, and some realms either explicitly or implicitly excluded women or the entire female line.

Indeed, similarities to these androcentric succession practices can be seen in George R.R. Martin's *A Song of Ice and Fire*. Yet, in the early days of Essos's history, Martin writes of the Rhoynar who had rulers of both sexes and whose "women were regarded as the equals of men".[4] These notions of equality came to Westeros via the relationship of the Rhoynish Princess Nymeria who fled with her people to Dorne, marrying Mors Martell and starting an important Westerosi dynasty. That legacy of a favourable attitude to female succession in Dorne can be seen in later eras with the formidable Meria Martell, who ruled during the initial Targaryen invasion of Westeros or Ellaria Sand, who unseated Doran Martell to take power in Season 6 of the television series.

Initially, the Targaryen dynasty seemed similarly egalitarian in that it had a tradition of co-rulership between brother and sister pairs, like the Ptolemaic dynasty of Egypt.[5] Indeed, the dynasty was established in

Westeros by Aegon the Conqueror who ruled alongside two powerful sister-wives, Visenya and Rhaenys, dragon riders who were instrumental in his conquest and rule. However, the accession of Targaryen female rulers in their own right was a different issue entirely. The question was first raised after the unexpected death of Aemon, the heir of Jaehaerys I in 92 AC. Jaehaerys named Aemon's younger brother Baelon "the Brave" heir, over Aemon's daughter, Rhaenys. The narrator of *Fire and Blood*, Archmaester Gyldayn, notes that "the king's decision was in accord with well-established practice" that favoured an agnatic successor over the direct line.[6] This decision upset those who felt that Rhaenys's rights were superior, including Jaehaerys's beloved wife and sister, Good Queen Alysanne. Alysanne angrily stated that "A ruler needs a good head and a true heart ... A cock is not essential. If Your Grace truly believes that women lack the wit to rule, plainly you have no further need of me".[7]

The king's decision was confirmed by the Great Council of 101 AC, which "established an iron precedent on matters of the succession: regardless of seniority, the Iron Throne of Westeros could not pass to a woman, nor through a woman to her male descendants."[8] This is somewhat similar to the so-called Salic Law and the French decision to bar not only women from claiming the throne but their descendants.[9] The French decision to prevent female and female-line claimants was also a response to a succession crisis—the death of Louis X in 1316 without a male heir. Just as in the Targaryen case, the rights of the king's daughter Jeanne were quashed in favour of Louis's brother Philip, who ascended the throne as Philip V.[10] By 1328, both Philip and his younger brother, who had succeeded him as Charles IV, had died with only female issue. To prevent a potential civil war between the princesses (and their powerful husbands) and to keep Edward III of England away from the French throne, it was decided to bar both female claimants and their descendants. Only 30 years later was "Salic Law" retroactively applied in an attempt to justify the exclusion of women from the French succession.[11]

Civil war did eventually erupt in Westeros over the claim of a Targaryen princess, in spite of the ruling of the Great Council on female succession. After the death of his wife and infant son, Viserys I decided to contravene this precedent and name his daughter Rhaenyra as his heir. Just as in the case of the Empress Matilda, who was named as heir to her father Henry I after the death of her brother in the White Ship disaster of 1120, Viserys compelled the lords of Westeros to swear homage to his daughter as his acknowledged heir.[12] However, Viserys married again to Alicent

Hightower, who produced the long-desired sons. This set up the Dance of Dragons, a "savage internecine struggle for Iron Throne of Westeros" between the "Blacks" who supported Rhaenyra's claim versus Queen Alicent and her supporters the "Greens" who fiercely defended her sons' rights.[13] Ultimately, Rhaenyra was never fully able to hold the throne successfully in her own right, but her son eventually came to the throne as Aegon III. Again, as Rohr and Benz point out in their introduction, this mirrors the situation of Empress Matilda, who fought a long and bloody civil war against her cousin Stephen of Blois for the English throne—often referred to as "The Anarchy". Although acknowledged as "Lady of the English", Matilda too was never fully able to hold the English crown in her own right, but her son, Henry II, did eventually gain the throne.[14]

The Dance of Dragons, effectively a battle between women for control of the throne, is a crucial context for *A Song of Ice and Fire* and the *Game of Thrones* series. By the latter stages of the series, it is women: Cersei Lannister, Margaery and Olenna Tyrell, Ellaria Sand and her daughters the "Sand Snakes", Yara Greyjoy, Sansa and Arya Stark, and Daenerys Targaryen, who are the focus of the struggle for power. Yet, while they fight (and kill) one another, they also form alliances. In Season 7, Daenerys holds a war council with Olenna Tyrell, Yara Greyjoy, and Ellaria Sand with the aim of bringing down Cersei.[15] Ultimately, it is Cersei and Daenerys who are effectively battling for control of Westeros in Seasons 7 and 8, with the realm divided once again into factions who support either queen in a Dance of Dragons redux.

Beyond this reprise of the Dance of Dragons, key themes in female succession, including uncles usurping the place of nieces, powerful regents, and the contested place of female successors resonate throughout *A Song of Ice and Fire*. Yara (or Asha) Greyjoy's situation echoes Rhaenys Targayen's when she was displaced in the line of succession by her uncle Baelon "the Brave". It also demonstrates one of the most fundamental issues of female succession—that a female claimant will often struggle against another male claimant in her family, particularly if he is an adult with a record of military success. However, Yara had ample opportunity to demonstrate her own prowess in the field of battle, and her leadership ability was acknowledged and applauded, in contrast to most historical female claimants. Yara was treated as her father's heir, displacing her brother Theon in the succession due to both her abilities and Theon's weaknesses, such as his perceived betrayal of the family and his emasculation by Ramsay Snow. This is similar to the case of Razia Sultan in the thirteenth century who was named heir to the Delhi Sultanate over her brothers because her father "believed that she had better rulership abilities than his sons".[16]

When their father died, after an initial period of tension between the siblings, Theon supported Yara's position as the heir to the Salt Throne. Indeed, Yara was able to win over many supporters at the Kingsmoot held to decide the succession, thanks in part to her brother's impassioned defence of her claim and abilities: "she is your rightful ruler. Those of you that have sailed under her, and there are many of you here, you know what she is! She is a reaver! She is a warrior! She is Ironborn! We will find no better leader! This is our queen!"[17] Yet, she faced a serious challenger in her uncle Euron, who was able to convince the Kingsmoot to crown him as king instead—his gender trumping both her father's nomination and Yara's excellent reputation among the Ironborn. Though Yara and Theon continued to fight Euron for the Salt Throne, Yara was taken prisoner by Euron in Season 7 and the possibility of her ever becoming the Queen of the Iron Islands seemed very remote. Yet Yara ultimately triumphed, thanks to Theon's successful rescue mission at the beginning of Season 8—Euron had been distracted by his overweening ambition to rule not just the Iron Islands but all of Westeros with Cersei Lannister, which not only allowed Yara the opportunity to escape and return to Pyke to seize the Salt Throne but led to Euron's eventual death.

As contributors to this collection point out, Cersei's path to the throne is the least conventional and the most controversial—she had no blood right to the throne whatsoever, but steadily climbed to power first as the consort of Robert Baratheon, then as regent for her sons Joffrey and Tommen, and finally by seizing the throne in her own right following Tommen's suicide at the end of Season 6. Cersei's political career has provoked considerable comparison to various queens of the premodern era. Valerie Frankel suggests similarities with powerful royal mothers Catherine de' Medici, Isabella of France, and Margaret of Anjou—noting how similar the Wars of the Roses is to the War of the Five Kings.[18] Martin himself has acknowledged this historical inspiration, noting that he initially considered writing a novel of the Wars of the Roses before beginning *A Song of Ice and Fire*.[19] Carolyne Larrington also notes connections between Cersei and Margaret of Anjou but argues that Cersei can be "profitably compared with a good number of other troublesome and feisty medieval queens", including Eleanor of Aquitaine and the Merovingian queen Brunhild.[20] Nicole M. Mares also found parallels for Cersei in the sixth century with the controversial Empress Theodora, wife of Justinian, and the Ostrogothic queen regent Amalasuntha.[21]

In this volume, our contributors also make conscious links to the Wars of the Roses. Charles Beem argues that "Martin undoubtedly looked back to these determined and ruthless queens as he constructed Cersei's character".[22] Kavita Mudan Finn posits that, in addition to Margaret of Anjou and Elizabeth Woodville, another legendary queen can also be seen as a possible analogy to Cersei: Guinevere, wife of King Arthur. Finn compares Cersei and Jaime's relationship to Guinevere and Lancelot, arguing that "At the heart of both conflicts, too, is a quintessentially medieval problem: the adulterous queen".[23] She notes that Cersei is portrayed as a highly sexualized character and that her dalliances not only threaten the succession by producing illegitimate heirs, they provide a way to attack the queen. Cersei's promiscuity is used by her enemies as a means to bring her down, particularly the Faith Militant who forces her to perform a humiliating walk of shame through the streets of King's Landing.[24] However, Sylwia Borowska-Szerszun argues that punishing her for her sexual misdeeds is missing the point, noting "The striking point of Martin's narrative is that although Cersei has indeed made grave mistakes as a political leader, she is disciplined as a harlot, not a monarch".[25] Mikayla Hunter concurs that Cersei mismanages her relationship with the Faith Militant and should have imitated her daughter-in-law Margaery's "performative piety", one of the key hallmarks of medieval queenship.[26]

Returning to comparisons between Cersei and premodern queens, Beem suggests another compelling link to the tenth-century queen Ælfthryth. Beem sees a particular connection between the two sons of Cersei and Ælfthryth; both had elder sons who expressed troublesome behaviour as young kings and more malleable second sons. While Cersei did not cause Joffrey's murder, Ælfthryth is reputed to have been involved in her stepson Edward the Martyr's death. Despite this divergence, Beem notes that both queen mothers "stop[ped] at nothing to achieve her own dynastic objectives".[27] James J. Hudson offers another comparison for Cersei in the nineteenth-century Chinese Dowager Empress Cixi. Like Ælfthryth, Hudson asks if Cixi or those close to her were behind the death of her nephew Guangxu, whom she had once raised to the Imperial throne.[28] Hudson argues that like Cixi, Cersei had no qualms about killing those who opposed her or stood in the way of her power.

Hudson offers another Chinese example for comparison with Cersei, the infamous Empress Wu Zetian, who became empress-regent and later empress-regnant in the seventh century. Wu's biographer, Jonathan Clements, describes her with adjectives that could easily apply to Cersei: beautiful, smart, ruthless, strong, and sexually liberated.[29] Wu was also accused of having an incestuous relationship, because she was first a concubine of Emperor Taizong before becoming the empress of his son Gaozong. Like Cersei, Wu ruled on behalf of two sons in turn, deposing her elder son Li Xian when his wife proved too ambitious, in a similar fashion to competition that Cersei faced with the politically savvy Margaery Tyrell. Wu's second son, Li Dan, proved easier to control, but she was forced to quell a revolt against their joint rule to secure the throne. Eventually, in 690, Wu seized the throne herself. Elisabetta Colla notes that, unlike Westeros, there was no edict to prohibit the succession of women, but "there was a silently observed prohibition of a woman becoming emperor".[30]

Another female regent who exploited the lack of a formal barrier to seize power was the Byzantine Empress Irene, Wu's near contemporary, whose succession could also be compared to Cersei's. Irene also began as regent for a young son and fought off those who sought to wrest the throne from them. Later, in a scenario that one could imagine had Joffrey or Tommen lived to adulthood, her son Constantine VI grew tired of coruling with his mother and sought to exile her. Irene's response was to conspire against her son and have him blinded.[31] Irene then made herself emperor—this was not an impossibility as *porphyrogenitas* or princesses "born in the purple" could succeed in their own right as Zoe and her sister Theodora did in the eleventh century.[32] Like Cersei and Wu, Irene seized power not through a royal bloodline, but by manoeuvring her way ever closer to the throne itself as a consort, regent, and then regnant queen. Cersei, Wu, and Irene share a last similarity as all three lost their throne before their death—Wu and Irene were both deposed and forced into retirement, while Cersei was dramatically defeated by her queenly rival, Daenerys Stormborn, in the merciless attack on King's Landing in the penultimate episode of Season 8.

Finally, Curtis Runstedler makes a case for similarities to Elizabeth I of England, even if her path to the throne as an heiress was more traditional than Cersei's: "they are both strong, powerful women within patriarchal societies and trapped by gender norms and societal expectations, both have dominating and controlling fathers (Henry VIII and Tywin Lannister), and they both seek absolute power over their kingdom and often manage to exert it".[33] Ultimately though, Cersei is not precisely like any of these historical analogies—her path to the throne and her situation are both familiar and unique. Nevertheless, we can see similarities with Cersei's situation in the succession of other premodern female rulers who fought ruthlessly to gain and keep power and were able to contravene the norms of accession to take the place of husbands and children on the throne themselves.

Cersei's rival, Daenerys Targaryen, appears to be a more straightforward case with regard to female succession. Daenerys's claim to the Iron Throne came from being the last of House Targaryen, the sole survivor of Robert's Rebellion when her parents and siblings were cruelly murdered, with the exception of her brother Viserys who was spirited away with her to Essos. Like Cersei, at the beginning of *A Song of Ice and Fire*, Daenerys was a bride used by her relatives to secure a valuable alliance by marrying her to Dothraki leader Khal Drogo to gain support for her brother's claim to the Iron Throne. Rather than potentially ruling Westeros as a sibling pair in the Targaryen tradition, Viserys decided that his sister was better deployed to contract an alliance to further his own ambitions. Daenerys was valued for her Targaryen blood but not immediately seen as a contender for the throne of Westeros due to the ruling of the Great Council, which barred female succession. Notwithstanding this, Daenerys did become a female ruler through many different means, developing from a young and naïve bride to a strong queen—or, as Carroll claims in this volume, "a tyrant, ruling through fear and violence", which she ultimately appears to be at the end of Season 8.[34]

Daenerys first came to power through tragedy—the death of her husband, Khal Drogo. This should have reduced her to a powerless, childless dowager—particularly as Daenerys also lost the child she was carrying in a desperate attempt to save her husband with the sorcery of Mirri Maz Duur. However, as O'Brien notes in her chapter, while the actions of Mirri Maz Duur caused personal tragedy in the death of Daenerys's husband and son, they also inadvertently led to political opportunity—she was able to claim her husband's place and became the Khalessi of the Great Grass Sea. Allowing the widow of the previous Khal to lead the khalasar was not typical of Dothraki succession, yet because they chose their leaders based on strength instead of inherited blood right, Daenerys's impressive ability to survive her husband's funeral pyre and hatch three dragon eggs was enough to convince them to make her their new leader.

Succession from husband to wife was unusual, but not unheard of in the premodern era. Eighteenth-century Russia offers two examples in

Catherine I, who became empress-regnant after the death of her husband Peter the Great in 1725, and in Catherine II, who took the throne from her husband, Peter III, in a coup in 1762. Both women were, like Daenerys, foreigners with no blood link to the title whatsoever. Unlike the childless Daenerys, however, both Catherine I and II were mothers. Yet, neither of the empresses were considered to be regents who were merely ruling for an underage male claimant during his minority.[35] Another potential comparison is Safiatuddin Syah who became Sultana of Aceh in 1641 after the death of her husband, Iskandar Thani. However, Safiatuddin was also the daughter of the Sultan Iskandar Muda, and Sher Banu A.L. Khan notes that her accession was made possible by the combination of her marital and natal tie to the throne, with the lack of male heirs created by the elimination of other claimants by her father and husband.[36] Finally, as Hunter notes in this volume, there is strong comparison between the Dothraki and the Mongol khanate. The Mongols also had several strong *khutuns* such as Khutulun in the thirteenth century and Manhuhai (Manduhai/Mandukhai) in the fifteenth century.[37] While Khutulun was a Mongol princess whose blood and formidable skills as a warrior brought her to power, Manhuhai, like Daenerys, rose from being the consort of a Mongol Khan to rule as his widow.

In addition to becoming Khalessi, Daenerys amassed other titles to which she had no blood claim, becoming the Queen of Meereen through her conquest in Slaver's Bay. Elizabeth Beaton claims that Daenerys's tactics in dealing with opposition from the leaders of the vanquished states reflect Machiavelli's analysis of princes who rose to power in foreign lands.[38] Daenerys's campaign is impressive, first adding the Unsullied to her Dothraki horde, and then using this formidable army, along with her three maturing dragons, to sack Astapor and take Yunkai, where the slaves she freed give her new title, that of *mhysa* or "mother". Later she added Meereen to her conquests, but her Westerosi advisors Mormont and Barristan worried this was a distraction from the pursuit of the Iron Throne that was hers by blood right. Daenerys's conquests are different from the ways in which most premodern queens acquired queenly titles. That said, we can point to premodern female rulers who expanded their domains through military means, including Isabel I of Castile who conquered the kingdom of Grenada in 1492, and Catherine II of Russia who annexed the Crimea in 1783 after a long conflict with the Ottoman Empire.

Njinga of Angola offers another example of a queen, who, like Daenerys, raised armies and took lands by conquest. Njinga is also an example of a woman exiled from her own land, adapting herself to become the leader of another people. Njinga married a man from the warlike Imbangala people and took on their practices, including drinking human blood to transform herself "from exiled Mbundu queen to Imbangala captain in her own right"—just as Daenerys ate a raw horse's heart as part of her initiation to the Dothraki.[39] After Njinga was ousted from power in her homeland of Ndongo, she turned to conquest instead, building a formidable army and taking over Matamba, defeating its Queen Muongo. Finally, Njinga "relished" collecting new titles such as "Ngola Njinga Ngombe e Nga" or "Queen Njinga, Master of Arms and Great Warrior", just as Daenerys rejoiced in her designations, "Breaker of Chains" and "Mother of Dragons".[40]

Daenerys is often compared to Elizabeth I, who ruled England alone as a strong regnant queen. Sylwia Borowska-Szerszun, Estelle Paranque, and Valerie Frankel have all made compelling arguments for this association, the latter seeing parallels between Daenerys's military leadership and Elizabeth's famous Tilbury speech wherein she famously claimed to have "the heart and stomach of a king".[41] Yet, Season 7 of the HBO series ends with a potentially seismic shift in Daenerys's situation, which challenges not only the possible comparison with Elizabeth I but her own succession to the Iron Throne. Not only did Daenerys consummate her relationship with Jon Snow, opening up the possibility that she could co-opt him in rule as her consort, it was revealed that he was actually Aegon Targaryen, son of Daenerys's brother Rhaegar and Lyanna Stark. This made Jon her own nephew and, more importantly, since it was revealed that Rhaegar and Lyanna were in fact married prior to his birth, Jon was House Targaryen's legitimate male heir. Indeed, Jon's claim to the throne was superior, as female succession had been barred by the aforementioned ruling of the Great Council. Moreover, as King in the North, Jon was a recognized ruler in Westeros, while Daenerys was still held by many to be an exotic foreigner. Nevertheless, their intimate relationship could have put Daenerys in a stronger position if they claimed the throne together, re-establishing not only House Targaryen, but its long tradition of blood-related spousal co-rulers. As Jon's Targaryen blood gave him the ability to ride dragons and fight alongside Daenerys, as Aegon and his sisters had when they initially conquered Westeros, he would have been the ideal ruling partner—if Daenerys had been willing to change her expectations from being a sole queen regnant to joint ruler.

An historical example of co-rulers, rather than one who was designated as ruler and the other as consort, can be found in William III and Mary II of England. In 1688, during the so-called Glorious Revolution, the couple was invited to England to rule in Mary's father, James II's place.[42] While Daenerys and Jon were not invited to rule Westeros in the same way as William and Mary had been, they had a significant group of supporters who favoured their claim and rulership over Cersei Lannister's. Like Jon, who was recognized as King in the North, William of Orange held the title of Stadholder of the Netherlands. William was not offered the position of king-consort to his wife Mary Stuart, despite the precedent for this in the case of a previous regnant queen of England, Mary Tudor. Her husband, Philip of Spain accepted (albeit somewhat reluctantly) the role of king consort even though he was King of Naples and Sicily in his own right at the time of their marriage.[43] William was given the royal title, rather than the consort's position, in part due to his own legitimate claim to the throne. After Mary and her sister Anne, he was the next legitimate Stuart claimant, via his mother Mary, Princess Royal of England. Accordingly, he was the next male heir—just as Jon was revealed to be at the end of Season 7. As joint sovereigns, William and Mary found a fairly harmonious mode of co-rulership, albeit one which firmly favoured William as the dominant partner.

Isabel I of Castile and her husband Ferdinand II of Aragon are further examples of cousins who were successful co-rulers, reflected in their motto *"Tanto monta, monta tanto-Isabel como Fernando"*.[44] While Ferdinand was not an immediate heir to the Castilian throne, he was a Trastámara cousin and therefore a potential male claimant who could have been a threat to Isabel's sovereignty had she not married him.[45] Their matrimonial agreements confirmed Isabel's position as the regnant queen of Castile and Ferdinand's role as her consort, carefully delineating his power and prerogatives. Ferdinand played a major role in the War of the Castilian Succession, helping Isabel to secure her position against a rival female claimant, her niece Juana. If Daenerys and Jon could have united their joint Targaryen claims to build an effective personal and political partnership as William and Mary, Isabel and Ferdinand, and indeed as their ancestors Jaehaerys I and Alysanne had done, they would have been incredibly powerful pair who could have claimed the Iron Throne together.

Yet Daenerys saw Jon's claim as a threat, rather than an opportunity for co-rulership in the mode of earlier Targaryens. Throughout the final series as Jon's true parentage became known, he repeatedly claimed that he did not want the throne and that Daenerys was his queen. But his avowals meant nothing to Daenerys who told him, "It doesn't matter what you want. You didn't want to be King in the North. What happens when they demand you press your claim and take what is mine?"[46] Ultimately this is exactly what happened as Varys was convinced that Jon was the rightful heir and would make the better king and worked to supplant Daenerys. Varys echoed the words of Good Queen Alysanne in his conclusion that "he's the heir to the throne, yes because he's a man, cocks are important I'm afraid".[47] When Tyrion suggested that they could rule together, Varys replied that it would never work as Daenerys was too strong for him and that "she doesn't like to have her authority questioned".[48] Yet in the final episode, standing before the Iron Throne, Daenerys asked Jon to rule by her side and build a new world together—but Jon, having witnessed her tyranny and madness in the destruction of King's Landing felt impelled to assassinate her, while still asserting: "You are my queen, now and always".[49]

Finally, Sansa Stark is another character who reflects wider issues in female inheritance and succession. At the outset of *A Song of Ice and Fire*, as the betrothed of Prince Joffrey, Sansa is a potential queen consort who was furthering her family's political ambition by buttressing the alliance between the Starks and Baratheons. While ultimately rejected as Joffrey's consort, she was still valued for her Stark blood and continued to be a matrimonial pawn. Kris Swank argues in this volume that Sansa became "the archetypal tragic bride as she is exchanged, manipulated, and abused in the various shifting alliances between the rival Houses of Westeros".[50] Sansa was married off briefly to Joffrey's uncle, Tyrion Lannister, in an attempt to make her a virtual hostage for the Starks' good behaviour. The Boltons later married her to Ramsay Snow as a means of legitimizing their seizure of Winterfell. Petyr Baelish (Littlefinger) desired her both in a perverse continuation of his love for Sansa's mother Catelyn and for her political capital, at one point trying to marry her to another lord in support of his own attempt to take power in the Vale. Danielle Alesi likens Sansa Stark to Elizabeth of York and Margaret Beaufort, two women who were also valued for their royal blood and married off to further dynastic aims and justify conquest.[51]

Over the course of the novels and television series, Sansa's political potential increased as the male members of House Stark are gradually eliminated. Her father Ned was executed in King's Landing; her brother Robb was killed at the Red Wedding; and her two younger brothers, Bran and Rickon, were declared dead by Theon Greyjoy. This series of tragic events makes her apparently the eldest surviving legitimate child of Ned Stark and creates the possibility of putting herself forward as head of House Stark—and potentially Queen in the North. As noted previously, female succession was often the result of tragedy—the deaths of brothers could make a woman the most viable direct heir as in the case of each of the five medieval regnant queens of Navarre.[52] Indeed, Daenerys also appeared to be the only surviving Targaryen, forming the mainstay of her own claim to the Iron Throne.

Jon Snow, who was raised as Ned's illegitimate son and who had a strong military record as an experienced leader as head of the Night Watch, is another surviving Stark. Initially, Jon defers to Sansa's legitimate claim, giving her the lord's chambers as the rightful Lady of Winterfell upon retaking the Stark ancestral home in Season 6. However, when it comes to the lords of the North, Jon's leadership experience and gender ultimately trumps Sansa's legitimacy—Lady Lyanna Mormont declared, "I don't care if he's a bastard, Ned Stark's blood runs through his veins. He's my king, from this day until his last day".[53] Sansa supported Jon's accession as King in the North rather than putting forward her own Stark claim. When her younger brother Bran returns to Winterfell, she defers to him as the rightful Lord of Winterfell, reflecting again the premise of male primogeniture, but he refused to take the position as he was now the Three-Eyed Raven. Others try to stoke Sansa's ambition, encouraging her to push forward her own claims. Some of the Northern lords, who disagreed with Jon's decision to ally with Daenerys, urged Sansa to take his place and rule the North, but she refused to undermine him. Sansa's younger sister Arya accused her of secretly planning to take the throne should Jon fail to return to Winterfell. Conversely, Littlefinger told Sansa that Arya herself dreamed of being Lady of Winterfell. He praised Sansa's ruling ability, encouraging her to turn against her siblings to take power for herself—setting himself up potentially to be her (king) consort or, at the very least, her trusted principal advisor. Ultimately, as Rohr and Benz point out, Sansa, Bran, and Arya turned the tables on Littlefinger, confronting him with his many political crimes and executing him. Swank argues that Sansa's difficult journey from a spoiled, would-be Baratheon consort to the politically savvy Lady of Winterfell can be correlated with several archetypes of Anglo-Saxon literature, rather than specific historical figures of the past: "Sansa has passed from the overly-idealistic peaceweaver, to the tragic bride, and finally into the empowered she-wolf, in command of all her many gifts: passivity and assertiveness, grace and strength, wisdom, mercy and justice".[54]

Sansa then, out of all the queens and female rulers we have seen in *Game of Thrones*, seems to have the most respect for the concept of male primogeniture—repeatedly deferring to her brothers' claims rather than fighting fiercely to defend her birth right as Daenerys and Yara did, or trampling on the conventions of succession as Cersei had in order to take the Iron Throne. In many ways therefore, Sansa's experiences are similar to those of many potential heiresses and princesses in the premodern era— she was a vehicle for matrimonial diplomacy, a representative of her family, and a carrier of Stark blood. While her own claim was never forgotten and repeatedly raised, Sansa appeared to support the patriarchal political framework that deemed her brothers' claims—even when they are younger or supposedly illegitimate—superior to her own. Yet ironically, it is Sansa in the end who became queen, while Daenerys and Cersei were toppled from power. The final scenes of the series show Sansa walking through Winterfell, wearing a dress full of symbolic significance while all bow before her and shouts of "Queen of the North" ring out.[55] As we see Sansa crowned and enthroned, it is clear that the "little bird" is now a regnant, not consort, queen and achieved what her brothers could not—an independent North, free from entanglement in destructive battles for the Iron Throne to the south and free from the threat of White Walkers from beyond the Wall.

In this collection, the contributors have reflected deeply on many aspects of queenship, including succession, underscoring the many challenges that female leaders have faced from rivals, councillors, and the faith. Shiloh Carroll notes that "Westerosi society does not respect a woman's authority", highlighting the difficulties Martin's female characters have in seizing and maintaining power.[56] Daenerys herself comments to Sansa that they both had dealt with the challenge of leading "people who aren't inclined to a woman's rule".[57] Yet, despite the patriarchal frameworks of succession and inheritance that privilege male claimants over women, or even bar them completely, we witness female rulers coming to the fore to dominate the game of thrones—and even though the Iron Throne itself is gone at the end of the series, two queens remain in Westeros in Sansa Stark and Yara Greyjoy. Martin and the series' producers are clearly drawing on historical past as inspiration—we can see this in the connections to female rulers or the premodern era discussed in this chapter, in this collection, and elsewhere. Yet, as Rohr and Benz note in the introduction, this is not a direct reflection of the premodern past but a distorted mirror—we cannot simply and easily equate one to the other. Cersei and Daenerys are like all of the many examples of premodern female regents and monarchs, but their paths to the Iron Throne are not exactly analogous to any of these historical women. Yara Greyjoy's displacement by the claim of an uncle is similar to that of many heiresses, yet not many premodern royal women were swashbuckling military commanders and captains. Sansa's experience reflects that of many premodern princesses who were used as matrimonial pawns and whose rights were trumped by brothers, but her character arc is not like that of any specific royal woman of our past. With regard to succession, however, there are two central elements that ring true in both Martin's fantasy and the reality of the premodern past—that women have always had a challenging path to the throne but that female rulers have also continued to find ways to either leverage accepted rules for succession or subvert them completely to wield power in their own right.

Notes

1. Sheilagh Ilona O'Brien, "Wicked Women and the Iron Throne: The Two-Fold Tragedy of Witches as Advisors in *Game of Thrones*", Chap. 10.
2. See Armin Wolf, "Reigning Queens in Medieval Europe: When, Where and Why", in *Medieval Queenship*, edited by John Carmi Parsons, New York: St Martin's Press, 1998, 169–188.
3. Elena Woodacre, *The Queens Regnant of Navarre: Succession, Politics and Partnership, 1274–1512*, New York: Palgrave Macmillan, 2013, 21–25.
4. George R.R. Martin, Elio Garcia and Linda Antonssen, *The World of Ice & Fire: The Untold History of Westeros and the Game of Thrones*, New York: Random House, 2014, 21.
5. See Sheila L. Ager, "The Power of Excess: Royal Incest and the Ptolemaic Dynasty", *Anthropologica* 48.2 (2006): 165–186.
6. George R.R. Martin, *Fire and Blood: A History of the Targaryen Kings from Aegon the Conqueror to Aegon III*, New York: Harper Voyager, 2018, 341.
7. Martin, *Fire and Blood*, 341.
8. Martin, *Fire and Blood*, 350–351.
9. See Sarah Hanley, "The Politics of Identity and Monarchic Government in France: The Debate over Female Exclusion" in *Women Writers and the Early Modern British Political Tradition*, edited by Hilda L. Smith, Cambridge: Cambridge University Press, 1998, 289–304; Craig Taylor, "Salic Law, French Queenship and the Defence of Women in the Late Middle Ages", *French Historical Studies* 29.4 (2006): 543–564 and

Philippe Contamine, " 'Le royaume de France ne peut tomber en fille'; Fondement, Formulation et implication d'une théorie politique à la fin du Moyen Age", *Perspectives Medievales* 13 (1987): 67–81.

10. Woodacre, *Queens Regnant*, 51–61.

11. See also Derek Whaley, "From a Salic Law to the Salic Law: The Creation and Re-creation of the Royal Succession System of France" in *The Routledge History of Monarchy*, edited by Elena Woodacre, Lucinda H.S. Dean, Russell E. Martin and Zita Eva Rohr, London: Routledge, 2019.

12. See Karl Leyser, "The Anglo-Norman Succession 1120–1125", in *Anglo-Norman Studies XII; The Proceedings of the Battle Conference 1990*, edited by Marjorie Chibnall, Woodbridge: Boydell, 1991, 225–242 and Martin, *Fire and Blood*, 360.

13. George R.R. Martin, "The Princess and the Queen, or The Blacks and the Greens: Being a History of the Causes, Origins, Battles and Betrayals of That Most Tragic Bloodletting Known as the Dance of Dragons, as Set Down by Archmaester Gyldayn", in *Dangerous Women*, edited by George R.R. Martin and Gardner Dozois, New York: Harper Voyager, 2013, 703.

14. See Marjorie Chibnall, *The Empress Matilda: Queen Consort, Queen Mother, and Lady of the English*, Oxford: Blackwell, 1991 and Catherine Hanley, *Matilda: Empress, Queen, Warrior*, New Haven: Yale University Press, 2019.

15. "Stormborn", *Game of Thrones*, Season 7, Episode 2. Dir. Mark Mylod. 2017, HBO.

16. Jyoti Phulera, "Queenship and Female Authority in the Sultanate of Delhi (1206–1526)", in *A Companion to Global Queenship*, edited by Elena Woodacre, Bradford: ARC Humanities Press, 2018, 53–66, 58.

17. "The Door", *Game of Thrones*, Season 6, Episode 5. Dir. Jack Bender. 2016, HBO.

18. Valerie Estelle Frankel, *Women in* Game of Thrones: *Power, Conformity and Resistance*, Jefferson, NC: McFarland, 2014, 96–97.

19. Mikal Gilmore, "George R.R. Martin: The Rolling Stone Interview", *Rolling Stone*, Culture News, April 23, 2014, https://www.rollingstone.com/culture/culture-news/george-r-r-martin-the-rolling-stone-interview-242487/

20. Carolyne Larrington, *Winter Is Coming*, 3.

21. Nicole M. Mares, "Writing the Rules of Their Own Game: Medieval Female Agency", in Game of Thrones *versus History: Written in Blood*, edited by Brian A. Pavlac, Hoboken, NJ: Wiley Blackwell, 2017, 149.

22. Charles Beem, "The Royal Minorities of *Game of Thrones*", Chap. 9.

23. Kavita Mudan Finn, "Queen of Sad Mischance: Medievalism, 'Realism,' and the Case of Cersei Lannister", Chap. 2 in this volume.

24. Larrington, *Winter Is Coming*, 114.

25. Sylwia Borowska-Szerszun, "Westerosi Queens: Medievalist Portrayal of Female Power and Authority in *A Song of Ice and Fire*", Chap. 3 in this volume.

26. Mikalya Hunter, "'All Men Must Die, But We Are Not Men': Eastern Faith and Feminine Power in *A Song of Ice and Fire and HBO's Game of Thrones*", Chap. 7 in this volume.

27. Beem, "Royal Minorities", Chap. 9.

28. James J. Hudson, "*A Game of Thrones* in China: The Case of Cixi, Empress Dowager of the Qing Dynasty (1835–1908)", Chap. 1 in this volume.

29. Jonathan Clements, *Wu: The Chinese Empress Who Schemed, Seduced and Murdered Her Way to Become a Living God*, London: Albert Bridge Books, 2014, 6–7.

30. Elisabetta Colla, "When the Emperor Is a Woman: The Case of Wu Zetian (624–705), The 'Emulator of Heaven' ", in *A Companion to Global Queenship*, edited by Elena Woodacre, Bradford: ARC Humanities Press, 2018, 13–26, 14.

31. Lynda Garland, *Byzantine Empresses: Women and Power in Byzantium 527–1204*, London: Routledge, 1999, 86.

32. See Alexandra Karagianni, "Female Monarchs in the Medieval Byzantine Court: Prejudice, Disbelief and Calumnies", in *Queenship in the Mediterranean: Negotiating the Role of the Queen in the Medieval and Early Modern Eras*, edited by Elena Woodacre, New York: Palgrave Macmillan, 2013, 9–25.

33. Curtis Runstedler, "Cersei Lannister, Regal Commissions, and the Alchemists in *Game of Thrones* and *A Song of Ice and Fire*", Chap. 6 in this volume.

34. Shiloh Carroll, "Daenerys the Unready: Advice and Ruling in Meereen", Chap. 8 in this volume.

35. See Orel Belinson, "Female Rule in Imperial Russia: Is Gender a Useful Category of Historical Analysis?", in *A Companion to Global Queenship*, edited by Elena Woodacre, Bradford: ARC Humanities Press, 2018, 79–93.

36. Sher Banu A.L. Khan, *Sovereign Women in a Muslim Kingdom: The Sultanahs of Aceh, 1641–1699*, Ithaca, NY: Cornell University Press, 2017, 253.

37. See Jack Weatherford, *The Secret History of the Mongol Queens*, New York: Crown Publishers, 2010.

38. Elizabeth Beaton, "Female Machiavellians in Westeros", in *Women of Ice and Fire: Gender,* Game of Thrones *and Multiple Media Engagements*, edited by Anne Gjelsvik and Rikke Schubart, London: Bloomsbury, 2016, 193–218, 204.

39. Linda M. Heywood, *Njinga of Angola: Africa's Warrior Queen*, Cambridge, MA: Harvard University Press, 2017, 119.
40. Heywood, *Njinga*, 124.
41. Frankel, *Women in* Game of Thrones, 159. Estelle Paranque, "Daenerys Targaryen as Elizabeth I of England's Spiritual Daughter", in *Remembering Queens and Kings in Early Modern England and France: Reputation, Reinterpretation, and Reincarnation*, edited by Estelle Paranque, New York: Palgrave Macmillan, 2019.
42. See Jonathan Keates, *William III and Mary II: Partners in Revolution*, London: Penguin, 2015.
43. See Alexander Samson, "Power Sharing: The Co-monarchy of Philip and Mary", in *Tudor Queenship*, edited by Alice Hunt and Anna Whitelock, New York: Palgrave Macmillan, 2010, 159–172.
44. See Theresa Earenfight, "Two Bodies, One Spirit: Isabel and Fernando's Construction of Monarchical Partnership", in *Queen Isabel I of Castile; Power, Personage, Persona*, edited by Barbara F. Weissberger, Woodbridge: Tamesis, 2008, 3–18 and Barbara F. Weissberger, "Tanto Monta: The Catholic Monarch's Nuptial Fiction and the Power of Isabel I of Castile," in *The Rule of Women in Early Modern Europe*, edited by Anne J. Cruz and Mihoko Suzuki, Urbana: University of Illinois Press, 2009, 43–63.
45. Elena Woodacre, "Questionable Authority: Female Sovereigns and Their Consorts in Medieval and Renaissance Chronicles", in *Authority and Gender in Medieval and Renaissance Chronicles*, edited by Juliana Dresvina and Nicholas Sparks, Newcastle upon Tyne: Cambridge Scholars, 2012, 383–384.
46. "The Last of the Starks", *Game of Thrones*, Season 8, Episode 4. Dir. David Nutter. 2019, HBO.
47. "The Last of the Starks".
48. "The Last of the Starks".
49. "The Iron Throne", *Game of Thrones*, Season 8, Episode 6. Dirs. David Benioff and D.B. Weiss. 2019, HBO.
50. Kris Swank, "The Peaceweavers of Winterfell", Chap. 5 in this volume.
51. Danielle Alesi, "The Power of Sansa Stark: Female Agency in Late Medieval England", in in *Game of Thrones versus History: Written in Blood*, edited by Brian A. Pavlac, Hoboken, NJ: Wiley Blackwell, 2017, 161–170.
52. See Woodacre, *Queens Regnant*, passim.
53. "The Winds of Winter", *Game of Thrones*, Series 6, Episode 10. Dir. Miguel Sapochnik. 2016, HBO.
54. Swank, "Peaceweavers", Chap. 5.
55. Rachel Andrews, "Sansa Stark's Final *Game of Thrones* Costume Is Full of Hidden Meanings", *Pretty 52*, http://www.pretty52.com/entertaining/tv-and-film-sansa-starks-final-game-of-thrones-outfit-is-full-of-hidden-meaning-20190521?source=facebook&fbclid=IwAR2I9SDDr_mPwO-

nOo0Zs-APuw0OxSksvzOhuFGCaIL9itc2pPyenaqQx9B8, accessed May 21, 2019.

56. Shiloh Carroll, *Medievalism in* A Song of Ice and Fire *and* Game of Thrones, Woodbridge: D.S. Brewer, 2018, 67.

57. "A Knight of the Seven Kingdoms", *Game of Thrones*, Season 8, Episode 2. Dir. David Nutter. 2019, HBO.

BIBLIOGRAPHY

Ager, Sheila L. "The Power of Excess: Royal Incest and the Ptolemaic Dynasty." *Anthropologica* 48.2 (2006), 165–86.

Alesi, Danielle. "The Power of Sansa Stark: Female Agency in Late Medieval England" in Game of Thrones *versus History: Written in Blood* edited by Brian A. Pavlac, Hoboken, NJ: Wiley Blackwell, 2017, 161–170.

Andrews, Rachel. "Sansa Stark's Final *Game of Thrones* Costume is Full of Hidden Meanings" Pretty 52 http://www.pretty52.com/entertaining/tv-and-film-sansa-starks-final-game-of-thrones-outfit-is-full-of-hidden-meaning-20190521?source=facebook&fbclid=IwAR2l9SDDr_mPwOnOo0Zs-APuw0OxSksvzOhuFGCaIL9itc2pPyenaqQx9B8, accessed May 21, 2019.

Beaton, Elizabeth. "Female Machiavellians in Westeros." In *Women of Ice and Fire: Gender,* Game of Thrones *and Multiple Media Engagements* edited by Anne Gjelsvik and Rikke Schubart, London: Bloomsbury, 2016, 193–218.

Belinson, Orel. "Female Rule in Imperial Russia: Is Gender a Useful Category of Historical Analysis?" In *A Companion to Global Queenship* edited by Elena Woodacre, Bradford: ARC Humanities Press, 2018, 79–93.

Carroll, Shiloh. *Medievalism in* A Song of Ice and Fire *and* Game of Thrones. Woodbridge: D.S. Brewer, 2018.

Chibnall, Marjorie. *The Empress Matilda: Queen Consort, Queen Mother, and Lady of the English*. Oxford: Blackwell, 1991.

Clements, Jonathan. *Wu: The Chinese Empress who Schemed, Seduced and Murdered her way to become a Living God*. London: Albert Bridge Books, 2014.

Colla, Elisabetta. "When the Emperor is a Woman: The Case of Wu Zetian (624–705), The 'Emulator of Heaven'." In *A Companion to Global Queenship* edited by Elena Woodacre, Bradford: ARC Humanities Press, 2018, 13–26.

Contamine, Philippe. "'Le royaume de France ne peut tomber en fille'; Fondement, Formulation et implication d'une théorie politique à la fin du Moyen Age." *Perspectives Médiévales* 13 (1987), 67–81.

Earenfight, Theresa. "Two Bodies, One Spirit: Isabel and Fernando's Construction of Monarchical Partnership." In *Queen Isabel I of Castile; Power, Personage, Persona*, edited by Barbara F. Weissberger, Woodbridge: Tamesis, 2008, 3–18.

Frankel, Valerie Estelle. *Women in* Game of Thrones: *Power, Conformity and Resistance*. Jefferson, NC: McFarland, 2014.

Garland, Lynda. *Byzantine Empresses: Women and Power in Byzantium 527–1204.* London: Routledge, 1999.

Gilmore, Mikal. "George R.R. Martin: The Rolling Stone Interview." *Rolling Stone,* Culture News, April 23, 2014, https://www.rollingstone.com/culture/culture-news/george-r-r-martin-the-rolling-stone-interview-242487/

Hanley, Catherine. *Matilda: Empress, Queen, Warrior.* New Haven: Yale University Press, 2019.

Hanley, Sarah. "The politics of identity and monarchic government in France: the debate over female exclusion." In *Women Writers and the Early Modern British Political Tradition* edited by Hilda L. Smith, Cambridge: Cambridge University Press, 1998, 289–304.

Heywood, Linda M. *Njinga of Angola: Africa's Warrior Queen.* Cambridge, MA: Harvard University Press, 2017.

Karagianni, Alexandra. "Female Monarchs in the Medieval Byzantine Court: Prejudice, Disbelief and Calumnies." In *Queenship in the Mediterranean: Negotiating the Role of the Queen in the Medieval and Early Modern Eras* edited by Elena Woodacre, New York: Palgrave Macmillan, 2013, 9–25.

Keates, Jonathan. *William III and Mary II: Partners in Revolution.* London: Penguin, 2015.

Khan, Sher Banu A.L. *Sovereign Women in a Muslim Kingdom: The Sultanahs of Aceh, 1641–1699.* Ithaca, NY: Cornell University Press, 2017.

Leyser, Karl. "The Anglo-Norman Succession 1120–1125." In *Anglo-Norman Studies XII; The Proceedings of the Battle Conference 1990* edited by Marjorie Chibnall, Woodbridge: Boydell, 1991, 225–242.

Larrington, Carolyne. *Winter is Coming: The Medieval World of* Game of Thrones. London: I.B Tauris, 2016.

Mares, Nicole M. "Writing the Rules of Their Own Game: Medieval Female Agency", in Game of Thrones *versus History: Written in Blood* edited by Brian A. Pavlac, Hoboken, NJ: Wiley Blackwell, 2017, 147–160.

Martin, George R.R. "The Princess and the Queen, or The Blacks and the Greens: Being a History of the Causes, Origins, Battles and Betrayals of that Most Tragic Bloodletting Known as the Dance of Dragons, as set down by Archmaester Gyldayn." In *Dangerous Women* edited by George R.R. Martin and Gardner Dozois, New York: Harper Voyager, 2013, 703–784.

———. *Fire and Blood: A History of the Targaryen Kings from Aegon the Conqueror to Aegon III.* New York: Harper Voyager, 2018.

Martin, George R.R., Elio Garcia and Linda Antonssen. *The World of Ice & Fire: The Untold History of Westeros and the Game of Thrones.* New York: Random House, 2014.

Paranque, Estelle. "Daenerys Targaryen as Elizabeth I of England's Spiritual Daughter", in *Remembering Queens and Kings in Early Modern England and*

France: Reputation, Reinterpretation, and Reincarnation edited by Estelle Paranque. New York: Palgrave Macmillan, 2019, 241–257.

Phulera, Jyoti. "Queenship and Female Authority in the Sultanate of Delhi (1206–1526)." In *A Companion to Global Queenship* edited by Elena Woodacre, Bradford: ARC Humanities Press, 2018, 53–66.

Samson, Alexander. "Power Sharing: The Co-monarchy of Philip and Mary." in *Tudor Queenship* edited by Alice Hunt and Anna Whitelock, New York: Palgrave Macmillan, 2010, 159–172.

Taylor, Craig. "Salic Law, French Queenship and the Defence of Women in the Late Middle Ages." *French Historical Studies* 29.4 (2006), 543–564.

Weatherford, Jack. *The Secret History of the Mongol Queens.* New York: Crown Publishers, 2010.

Weissberger, Barbara F. "Tanto Monta: The Catholic Monarch's Nuptial Fiction and the Power of Isabel I of Castile," in *The Rule of Women in Early Modern Europe* edited by Anne J. Cruz and Mihoko Suzuki, Urbana: University of Illinois Press, 2009, 43–63.

Whaley, Derek. "From a Salic Law to the Salic Law: the creation and re-creation of the royal succession system of France." In *The Routledge History of Monarchy* edited by Elena Woodacre, Lucinda H.S. Dean, Russell E. Martin and Zita Eva Rohr. London: Routledge, 2019, 443–464.

Wolf, Armin. "Reigning Queens in Medieval Europe: When, Where and Why." In *Medieval Queenship* edited by John Carmi Parsons, New York: St Martin's Press, 1998, 169–188.

Woodacre, Elena. *The Queens Regnant of Navarre: Succession, Politics and Partnership, 1274–1512.* New York: Palgrave Macmillan, 2013.

Woodacre, Elena. "Questionable Authority: Female Sovereigns and their Consorts in Medieval and Renaissance Chronicles" in *Authority and Gender in Medieval and Renaissance Chronicles* edited by Juliana Dresvina and Nicholas Sparks, Newcastle upon Tyne: Cambridge Scholars, 2012, 376–406.

Index[1]

---

[1] Note: Page numbers followed by 'n' refer to notes.

© The Author(s) 2020

Z. E. Rohr, L. Benz (eds.), *Queenship and the Women of Westeros*, Queenship and Power, https://doi.org/10.1007/978-3-030-25041-6